MOONCHILD RISING

Shadows of the Sun
Book One

By

Mina Ambrose

Full Quiver Publishing
Pakenham, Ontario

Moonchild Rising
Shadows of the Sun #1
Copyright 2020 Mina Ambrose

Published by
Full Quiver Publishing
PO Box 244
Pakenham, Ontario K0A 2X0
www.fullquiverpublishing.com

ISBN 978-1-987970-15-9
Printed and bound in the USA
Cover design: James Hrkach
Cover photo: Zeferli iStock

NATIONAL LIBRARY OF CANADA
CATALOGUING IN PUBLICATION

Published by FQ Publishing

A Division of Innate Productions

'*Diamonds are shadows of the sun;*
They drink his rays and show a spark:
My soul some gleams of thy great shine hath won
And round me slays the dark.'

George MacDonald

THE PROPHECY

We, who once were men but men no more
Will rule the earth when blood-red star
And darkened sun doth signify
A virgin's blood shall satisfy.
The sacred spear shall lead the way
To pierce the power of Sun's bright ray
Victory to him who wears the ring
To sacrifice the blood of a king.
But hold! The era's end shall thus portend
That sting of death for us, not men
The moon twice blue shall be the sign
Of light to foil our scheme malign.
Upon her brow the twelve-starr'd crown
She who rules has mark'd her own
Above the blade a key of gold
Her shield of virtue he shall hold.
Beware that spawn of night and day
Whose deeds his own kin shall betray
Beware ye, who prey on men of earth
A radiant moon reveals his birth.

The Huntress

California. March 1998

Her first warning was that unnatural chill in the night. Mara Dawn Amarantides froze, listened. Caught the slight whisper of a cloak and a flapping sound, as of bat's wings. And that choking smell of death, faint but unmistakable. Vampire!

She twisted around, her long, golden braid swinging across her back and glinting in the circle of white cast from the streetlights. Where...? That alley across the way? No, no, further... She ran down the sidewalk, dodging the occasional pedestrian, frightening them perhaps, but—no time to apologize, this was urgent. A matter of life and death. She peered down side streets and alleyways, eagle eyes missing nothing as she flew past. Nothing...there was nothing out of the ordinary. *Where is it? Have to find it before...*

There—a rhythmic squeaking sound was moving away from her down an alley and out onto another street. She squinted into the distance; the light wasn't good in that concrete-and-brick canyon. Just at the far end was the faint glow of a streetlight. Ah, there—a boy on an old bike, not in any hurry, it seemed, apparently oblivious to the horror hot on his trail. She felt that telltale chill again, stronger now, wrinkled her nose at the unpleasant smell, and looked around, eyes piercing the shadows. Nothing but the usual reeking garbage and clutter tossed carelessly about or jammed against the wall.

A cat yowled, dashing between her feet; she leaped aside, heart pounding. Good grief, what next! She'd no more than restored her calm and resumed her dash down the alley, when movement caught her eye, up ahead and off to the right a bit. Her heart jerked into overdrive again; stake in hand, she was ready for business. Just a rat, this time; it slithered behind a garbage can and was gone. She exhaled slowly.

Then she saw it. Even to her, the vampire looked like nothing more than a black blur, so fast did it move. Most mortals wouldn't have seen that much; would, in fact, have had no warning at all.

She caught a glimpse of the boy on the bike again, just as he was about to turn the corner from the alley onto a quiet street. It looked as though he sensed something, then; maybe he felt that chill cloud of gloom bearing down on him, for he glanced back and stared. His eyes went wide with terror, and he surged into action, pedaling at a furious rate, his bike squeaking madly.

He might as well have been standing still; he'd never outrun the thing, Mara knew. It would be on him before he reached the end of the block.

She swept the surrounding area with a swift glance, missing nothing. Only one this time? Vampires were loners, true, but perpetually hungry, and more often than not several would emerge to hunt at any given time, to scatter in every direction, no doubt to foil her attempts to catch them all. An exercise in futility; she tracked them down quite quickly, as a rule.

No time to think about that now. This one was the immediate danger, all that mattered at the moment. Shadowy arms reached out toward its prey, long gleaming claws reflecting the meager light. Too close. Fast as she was, she'd never catch up in time to stake it.

She slipped a hand inside her jacket, exchanged the stake for her small crossbow. With narrowed eyes locked on that shadow-blur, she loosed an arrow. And another, right behind it, in one swift motion. Two bolts! Overkill, maybe—she'd never failed to hit her target dead-on, but—no, she couldn't have that thing take the boy down just because she got overconfident. She was good at this, but vampires were fast and could kill in a heartbeat.

Her bolts flew true; one-two, straight to the middle of that shadow-shape. It shrieked, a long, pitiful wail, and fell writhing to the pavement. Then it disintegrated.

The boy glanced around, eyes huge, but he never slowed; sped up, if anything. That spine-chilling cry must have scared him half to death, but Mara doubted he'd seen anything, except maybe a cloud of dust if he was very sharp. He likely hadn't seen her either. Her black attire blended her into the shadows; she wasn't easy to see even when you knew she was there, and most people didn't.

As soon as the boy was away, down the street and around the next corner, she went to retrieve her arrows. Her soft boots made no sound on the pavement.

The evening breeze had picked up, wafting away the last bits of vampire dust. The air smelled fresh and clean again. All clear now. Stars were out, sparkling overhead. It was a nice night, after all. Even so, she did not relax her vigilance. That could be fatal in her line of work. For others, if not herself.

She was about to be on her way when she heard a fluttering sound. A paper loosely tacked to the nearby wooden pole of a streetlight had torn loose at one corner and was flapping in the breeze. On it was a grainy photograph and bold black letters proclaiming: MISSING. Her heart sank. Not another one! She walked nearer and reached up to smooth the poster. A new one, obviously, so clean and white next to those other notices faded and tattered at the edges. Again some vampire had slipped past, it seemed, despite her watchfulness, to prey on the humans she was bound to protect.

How did they manage to elude her? Was there another gate to the Underworld that she didn't know about, where they sneaked out a back door while she stood guard here at the main gate? Father Mike had assured her that this insignificant little town of Archangel was the gate; the only one, at this time. And he should know.

Deep in thought, she made her way to the public library, open late tonight, where she had arranged to meet her friends to study. Despite her calling, she still had to get through college.

Out of the Depths

The Prince weaved his way through dark tunnels, down and down, deep underground, through a maze of winding passages and caverns that lay well beneath the surface. Some of these passages narrowed to mere crevices and were therefore inaccessible to the average cave explorer, even had they discovered the entrance and braved the eerie, pervasive, unnatural chill it exuded. But none of this impeded the regular residents of the caverns. Not the thousands of bats, which had inhabited these particular caves long before the Prince and his kind had moved in over a century ago. Nor was it a difficulty for the Prince or any other vampire to flow through spaces impossible to a mortal creature of that size.

As he glided along the passage, flowing amongst stalactites and stalagmites without slackening his pace, his dead black eyes unhindered by the total darkness, the Prince made his way to the Great Hall, the throne room where Charon, master vampire, awaited him.

Of the myriad chambers in that extensive maze, the Great Hall was the vastest and most splendid, as befitted the abode of the king of the Underworld, yet for all its grandeur bleak and desolate as a palace ruin blasted by war and plundered of its beauty and light. Rock formations like gigantic fangs hung from high vaulted ceilings and lined the walls; eerily like a great hungry beast lying in wait, mouth open, for its unsuspecting prey. These held no horror for the Prince. He knew they merely led to yet more narrow winding corridors, either upward toward the world of men, or downward to crypts and the depths.

The Prince paused at the entrance of the Great Hall. All was dark as Hades there, except for the faint light of the spitting flames of pitch-burning torches fastened high up on the walls. Acrid smoke spiraled upward to vanish into darkness. Black rivulets of melted pitch streamed down, almost as though the Earth itself was bleeding.

At the far end of the Hall stood the only object of beauty in that bleak, quake-blasted ruin, the only thing remaining to suggest the perhaps once-upon-a-time richness of a palace — an ornate throne, tall and imposing, of fiery alabaster, ivory and jade, inlaid with gold set with rubies and other precious stones that sparkled with unnatural brilliance in the dim light. Two delicately carved spiral columns thrust upward from the back of the throne to support a crown of spikes high above. On these spikes were affixed human heads, a gruesome display when not obscured by drifting smoke.

There Charon, master vampire, sat alone, slouched on the elaborate throne, darkly brooding over the recent turn of events. All his careful planning had gone awry. His Adversary had raised up another huntress from the mass of mortal men. A holy terror, this one was. In just a score of years, she had wreaked havoc amongst the Brotherhood, harrowing his domain with methodical precision, without even once setting foot in the Underworld.

The Prince knew this was why he was being summoned. He would be commanded to stop the Huntress. He was the most able, the strongest, and most cunning. Charon would have taken care of her himself, but he could not leave the underground. He dared not expose himself to any light reflected from the sun, nor even the least glimmer of starlight. Aside from that, he had much else to do of great importance, and time was running out. He would have much preferred to be at the worktable in his study chamber, poring over ancient texts and plotting his destiny. Charts, maps, and diagrams were piled high on the table and elsewhere about the room, on shelves or tacked to walls, right at his fingertips for instant reference. Now, after many centuries of study, planning, and failed experiments, his search for the missing all-important key to world domination was almost at an end. He was sure of it. And here was this pesky huntress, interfering with his precious work.

Charon raised his brooding eyes as the Prince entered.

"You know what task I now set before you. Another huntress must be destroyed. At once. I have full confidence that you shall be victorious. You have slain that huntress of the north, after all, and she was not your first."

Taking out a huntress was never easy, and this one was certain to be especially difficult. Within the short span of her career, she had torn through their kind like wildfire, depleting their numbers with shocking rapidity. That was all they knew about her for certain, aside from the fact that she lived at the very Gate of the Underworld in the town of Archangel, California. There she prowled the night, slaying any vampire that she caught daring to venture into the Upperworld.

Charon was a harsh master, ruling with an iron hand. Though his heart was as of stone, the Prince knew he was like a son to him, the one he was grooming for a high position in his New Kingdom, that realm of his dreams in which the creatures of the night might walk in daylight with no fear of the sun. Mortals would be put in their proper place, then. After all, what were they but a source of food for the Great Ones, the undead, superior immortal beings? It was time they realized.

The Prince took as his due the fact that he was recognized as having no equal in the Underworld. Cold and deadly, he was a dark angel of wonderful grace and captivating beauty. His face, oddly symmetrical, was a study in perfection, his silken skin flawless white, his eyes empty black, his smile cruel. He was the envy of the Vampire Brotherhood; his strength and speed commanded their respect, his charisma, their loyalty, but never their love, for they loved no one. And as the master's favorite, his position was one of uncontested privilege.

Charon narrowed his eyes at him. "The Huntress must be destroyed at once. How to do this?" He cast his gaze to the heads displayed above, settling for a moment on the one head that refused to decay. He frowned. "My first thought was to send a legion with you, but I fear that wily huntress would sense numbers and take precautions. A small task force might prevail, I then thought, but no; that strategy is as old as sin. So, I've settled on a new, totally unexpected tactic. You shall act as a solitary assassin. Catch her off guard. Once the battle has begun, she will discover too late that she is outmatched.

The Prince had brought home more than one huntress's head over the centuries to adorn Charon's throne. However, he had never accomplished the feat alone. Was it even possible?

"Your reward," continued Charon, "will be the honor of ruling at my right hand for all eternity, in power and glory. Indeed, to be a god."

Though couched as a request, the Prince knew it to be an order. A lesser being would have quailed. Not he. In his arrogance, he believed himself invincible. He had heard many a tale of this nightmare of a huntress and laughed. Granted, her total kill-quotient exceeded that of any other huntress for the few short years of her career, to his knowledge. But she had not met him yet. And he, having tasted of such blood in the past, knew its worth. His powers had been enhanced immeasurably each time. For that reason alone would he take the risk. And to bring to her knees this mortal who dared to so defy them would be a triumph indeed.

"Your wish is my command, Master. Consider it done. Send me, and rest assured she shall trouble you no more."

"Yes, taste her blood. Drink deep, if you wish." Charon smiled coldly. "Just bring me her head."

Her head. The Prince looked up at the heads ornamenting the canopy high above his master's throne. One of Charon's prized collections. Trophies of past victories or merely mementos of blood feasts. Most were skulls, barebone by now;

some had wisps of hair or bits of rotting flesh attached. Several were comparatively recent, streaked with black and worm-ridden, surrounded by their expected miasma. Those did not concern the Prince.

His eyes fixed instead upon that particular head, still incorrupt after nearly a hundred and twenty-nine years, its face peaceful in death, its raven-black hair long and shining in the torchlight. He raised his fist in salute, and his lip curled in scorn. "Fear not, Huntress! I will bring you a companion soon."

This was not the first occasion upon which he had found himself taunting the head that defied nature; the head of that huntress of the north, who had defied him. He never admitted, even to himself, how she had disturbed him by her words and by her blood. Even in defeat, she haunted him still. He had thought to please Charon by presenting her head to him and to witness her disgrace as it rotted away, stinking. But unlike other heads, hers had not decayed. Instead, it seemed to emit a sweet odor of wildflowers and remained a perpetual reminder of his shame. Of what she had said, of what he had seen. Marie. That young Indian woman, huntress of the far northern regions, who, for the sake of her people, had, at the cost of her own life, banished his kind from her land.

He snarled faintly. That the name of a mere mortal should stick in his memory like a burr rankled. Her head, after all, was only one among many that adorned the master's throne.

The Prince turned his back on the anomaly and his thoughts to a topic more agreeable, such as how he longed to turn a huntress just because it was said to be impossible. But there was time enough for experimentation in the future. For now, Charon's wishes were paramount.

Though he anticipated the satisfaction of a task well done and the thrill of demonstrating his awesome power, these meant less to the Prince than Charon's approval. Or of pleasing Nyx, whom he thought of as his mother.

He looked across the cavern to where he knew she was watching, ever at Charon's right hand. Dear Nyx had made him into this wonderful immortal creature centuries ago. He knew it was she who had urged Charon to send him, her favorite child, to kill the Huntress Mara, and by so doing had put the world at his feet.

As if drawn by his eyes upon her, Nyx moved closer.

Charon called him back to the business at hand. "You, Prince, shall bring me this new huntress's head."

With that, Charon presented a jewel-handled dagger to the Prince. Its blade had been forged in the depths of the Earth, of metal hard and indestructible; a metal which, it was said, could cut anything. A fine weapon, and a glorious thing it was, indeed. Every color of the rainbow flashed about the Great Hall from the precious stones around the tiger's eye adorning the hilt, and from the silvery curve of the blade, as well, which was known as the Dragon's Tooth. A worthy weapon with which to behead a huntress.

The Prince accepted the knife, honored beyond words. Charon did not part with his treasures lightly, especially those acquired in the depths.

Steel hissed against leather as the Prince with due reverence slid the knife into its sheath and attached it to his belt.

Nyx stepped forward to adjust the knife at his waist to a more dashing angle. Her black eyes glowed with pride as she stepped back to admire her handiwork. "Yes, you will do, my Prince." Her teeth gleamed in a smile. "Bring back her head, by all means. But first, do one small thing for me. Crush her spirit! Take her innocence. Oh, how I love the ruin of virtue!"

As the Prince well knew. But now the Prince's cold smile mirrored hers. "As you wish," he said, with a glance up at his master for approval.

"Do whatever you like," Charon said indifferently. "Just bring her head to me."

At sunset, Nyx bade the Prince farewell, reminding him once again of the importance of his quest. "Charon loves you above all others. Take down this proud huntress, bring back your trophy, and you shall rule the world beside him forever." Her kiss was sweet and her commendation music to his ears.

The Prince, who liked to think of himself as Samael, the Angel of Death, made his way upward through the labyrinthine ways. As he approached the surface, he shifted to a form somewhat resembling a shadowy black mist and oozed from the Underground through a jagged crack gaping like a wound in the park at the center of the town of Archangel. He slithered along the ground until he sensed that the coast was clear, then drifted upward and caught the night wind in a cloudless sky. To track the Huntress was a simple matter for one of his talents, though even he could not escape detection by her for long. She was no ordinary mortal. This would be no silent, instantaneous coup de grâce in the darkness. He smiled. Indeed, what would be the fun in that? After an exhilarating battle, victory, and the taste of her blood, would be the sweeter.

His arrival in town caused no ripples. To ordinary mortals, he was only another shadow in the dark moonless night. He drifted downward, flowing among buildings and trees. Hidden by cloak and speed, it was only when he chose to reveal himself that he could be seen. Generally, that was a prelude to death, and few lived to tell of it.

Something Wicked This Way Comes

Mara was at once aware of his presence, and of what he was. She shivered. All her life, she had battled vampires and vanquished them with ease. Ordinarily, it was she who hunted them; this was something else. This rogue had to be a cut above any vampire she had ever encountered, for he was stalking her. She touched the small silver crucifix at her throat, breathed a quick prayer, and proceeded, every muscle tensed. She scanned the ill-lit street and the line of motley buildings at its edge and unzipped her dark jacket for easier access to her weapons.

She listened to the sounds of night. There seemed to be nothing out of the ordinary. Tinny dance music and whooping and singing came from Norbie's Tavern down the street. An occasional footstep echoed from nearby buildings. A car rumbled by, and the faint smell of exhaust competed momentarily with the effluvia of trash down the alley. Neon lights gleamed at storefronts, and a flickering Coca-Cola sign hummed and snapped in the window of Bud's all-night café.

Mara glanced around, on the alert for any movement of shadow within shadow as she moved on past the café and the tall, narrow antique shop locked and barred for the night. Between the shop and a stucco apartment building next to it was a narrow space, dark; the glow of the streetlight did not reach into it. The enemy often lurked in such places, Mara knew. She approached cautiously and peered in. Nothing there.

She felt a chill and glanced upward. Again she saw nothing. But she felt something. The back of her neck prickled; she shivered and moved on. It wasn't until she neared the imposing gray stone, neo-Gothic façade of St. Michael's Church that she finally caught a familiar whiff of death.

Choking, unmistakable.

Vampire.

Mara halted. Keen though her hearing was, she felt rather than heard her silent stalker. She scanned the shadows, searching the tall narrow buildings across the street from top to bottom. There was nothing there. But that feeling, that smell, never lied. She sensed a cold presence, very near, though she could neither see nor hear it. Nerves taut, eyes narrowed, she had just turned to scan her surroundings once more when a sibilant sound came out of the night, breaking the taut silence. A whisper? It sounded like words, but... no, maybe not words. Vampires didn't ordinarily talk to her. They fled from her as fast as they could.

Footsteps suddenly scuffed on the walk behind her. She whipped around, ready for action, but it was only a man staggering down the sidewalk, a bit worse for wear after patronizing Norbie's. She noted that his shirt buttons were done up wrong, and exhaled in relief as he lurched past, an alcoholic vapor trailing in his wake. With scarcely veiled impatience, she watched as he turned the corner and vanished from sight. He had no idea of his peril, of course.

She returned to the matter at hand, her eyes darting about for some sign of the enemy, her senses aquiver once more. Almost at once, she heard the eerie sound again. This time, she had no doubt. It was a whisper. And words.

The sound echoed off the walls around her; she couldn't tell from which direction it came. Nor could she quite make out the words. Now a scrabbling came from high above and behind her; something clattered onto the street. A broken bit of tile? She spun around into a defensive stance and looked up, her eyes narrowed to pierce the gloom. Nothing, except the familiar skyline.

She froze, listening. A slight breeze carried dry leaves and bits of paper rattling along the pavement. A car drove past. Music from the bar down the street rose and fell dimly in the background. Otherwise, nothing. That set her internal alarm bells ringing. She waited, every muscle tensed.

The whisper came again, closer now. "Come to me."

It sounded like the hissing of a snake. She had no fear of vampires. But this?! What did it mean?

Something scrabbled in the darkness. She caught a glimpse of movement from the corner of her eye and glanced up toward the apartment roof just as a shadow slithered around the corner of the building. At last!

She whipped out a stake and turned to face the general direction of her elusive opponent, ever watchful for its reappearance, from anywhere. "Okay, why don't you just get over here, and let's finish this!"

Silence. She held her breath, listening, all senses alert. Nothing happened. Seconds crept by. Attack already! Still nothing. She inhaled deeply, meaning to shout out a challenge again, to ease the tension one way or another. Though it was not her usual practice, conversing with vampires.

An unpleasant laugh broke the silence, like something dry and dead rasping in the wind. Not human. The sound made her flesh creep. She exhaled slowly, poised for action.

A sudden rush of wind was her only warning. The stake flew out of her hand, though the vampire did not physically touch her. She had seen him, though only as a blur, and felt the wind of his passing.

As the vampire whipped around, his cloak snapped open, and she caught sight of a momentary flash of light at his midsection. She had no time to think what that might mean, for he flowed in fast to the attack again. His face loomed in front of her, his teeth white and sharp, his cold black eyes promising death.

She reacted automatically. Her foot connected, perhaps with his jaw. He crashed to the pavement. She stared, shaken. Her first impression was right; this was no ordinary vampire.

Just as she scooped up her stake without taking her eyes off her foe, he rippled to his feet and paused, his crimson crescent smile revealing sharp white teeth again. His eyes were empty black, dead as the white of his face. Then he spoke in a voice like the crushing of dead leaves. "Come, be my bride."

She gave him a cold, hard stare so he wouldn't see how he rattled her. Holy! Like some cheesy line from a cheap comic book! What next? Looked like she'd have to be prepared for anything. So when he opened his jaws wide, with a terrible display of teeth, and hissed, she didn't back off in fright, as he no doubt expected. Instead, she attacked.

With a quick, fluid move, he easily avoided her stake, then lifted a hand, and without touching her, threw her against the wall. Her stake took flight, but she landed on her feet like a cat, poised for action. His surprise tactic shook her, but she let none of this show in her expression or her stance. She did not back off when he flowed in to finish it, but instead stepped forward and punched him in the throat. He rocked back but recovered at once, and with a deep inhuman growl, came at her again. Another stake appeared in her hand as if by magic. Only his lightning-fast reflexes enabled him to avoid the sharp point. He scrambled into the shadowed corner where wall and sidewalk met. Eyes hard, Mara followed with a relentless stride.

Just then, the church door opened. A woman emerged and stopped short, a startled look on her face at the sight of Mara coming at her, stake in hand, and the vampire hidden in shadow, Mara hoped.

The woman's hand flew to her mouth to stifle a scream.

"Run!" Mara shouted as she dived for her foe.

He seemed to melt away, out of her reach, a dark blur flowing toward the portal arch, into the woman's path. At all costs, Mara remained determined to protect the innocent; she leaped forward to intercept him. Between one moment and the next, the woman was gone. Had she heeded Mara's warning? It all happened so fast that perhaps the woman wouldn't understand what she had seen. Thank God. (It was so much easier not to have to explain things.)

The vampire flung himself through the open doorway to

avoid Mara's deadly rush. Once across the threshold, he sprang to his feet and visibly shuddered as a wave of dread rolled over him. Mara knew that if she had not been blocking the doorway, he would have fled. He was at a distinct disadvantage and knew it. This was her Master's turf.

Though Mara was not so irreverent as to choose the church for her battlefield, she had no qualms. This was not about honor; it was about extermination. A vampire had no power here; he was as good as finished the moment he entered that door. He would not escape her now. She followed him into the vestibule as the heavy oaken door slowly closed. Saw him cast a quick glance of misgiving through the open inner doors to the nave.

Mara leaped forward, stake in hand. But the vampire was quick; he scrambled up the stone wall and melted into the shadows high above. Tensely she gripped her stake and cautiously edged around the pillar, peering upward, straining to see. The faint red flicker of the distant sanctuary lamp and the yellow glow of a few lit votive candles before Our Lady's statue gave little illumination. Instead, they rather deepened the shadow.

She heard claws scrabble against stone and glimpsed a slight movement above. Ah, there it was, hard to see, that black against black, with only a faint blur of white hands clinging to a corbel and above them a pale inverted triangular shape. Her eyes adjusted. It looked like a white mask with two black holes where the eyes should be. They seemed to be looking down at her.

How odd that they should flare like that. Then they glowed red, like demon eyes in a movie. At once she saw the danger. She dropped to the floor just as twin beams of fire shot from those eyes. And missed! *Dear God, what is this thing?* She scrambled to her feet and stood panting. A tendril of smoke curled up from her scorched jacket sleeve. Too close! She glanced up and saw a gleam of teeth. She felt a chill. *Courage, Mara.*

She steeled herself, squared her shoulders, and called out a challenge: "Come down from there and fight me, if you dare!"

Nothing, for a moment, then out of the darkness above came a terrible piercing shriek that set her teeth on edge; she had to resist the impulse to cover her ears. As the sound diminished to a deep growl, the vampire sprang out of the gloom, sideways and down, and clung to the pillar, hissing, his teeth bared. A terrifying sight.

It's just a bluff, she told herself. *He can't last long in here.*

She rushed to meet him, stake in one hand and knife in the other. In a blur of movement, he sprang up, fast, to pause just out of reach, his eyes fixed on her. This time she was wary of their glow. She did what she thought he would least expect, and took a great leap upward, ran along the wall toward the pillar in a gravity-defying stunt, and flung herself at him, stake-point first. That quick, he scrambled up the wall to melt into shadow once more. Unable to follow him to the top, she slid down the wall and landed lightly on her feet.

"Oh, come on, you're finished, and you know it." She stood with the stake hanging loosely from her fingers in pretended nonchalance; no sound came from above. She tried again. "We're in a church, in case you haven't noticed. Let's get this over with."

At that, a string of blasphemies so foul issued from above that even she (who thought she had heard everything) was startled. And grieved, quickly making an interior act of reparation for the insult to her dear Lord. But the battle must go on. She would not be intimidated.

"So, that hurt a little, did it?"

At this taunt, the vampire dropped from the ceiling, cloak flapping, teeth and claws foremost, and eyes aglow. She did not retreat in confusion as he may have expected or hoped, but instead lunged forward to meet his attack with a powerful upward thrust of the stake. To avoid impalement, he twisted in midair and threw himself through the doorway into the nave. She followed. He whipped to his feet and crouched to face her with a snarl, like a cornered beast. As well he might, with the sanctuary at his back.

Light on her feet, she danced around him. "Is that all you've got? Bring it on!"

With a stake ready in her right hand, she beckoned with her left, assured of victory now. They were in a church, after all.

There was a sudden blur of black and a quick flash of claws. That was all she saw, and something seemed very wrong, somehow. For the first time in her life, her lightning-swift reflexes failed her. She couldn't seem to move, even to lift her arms. For some unknown reason, her whole body seemed frozen, and her brain was numb. When at length some life began creeping back into it, she vaguely recalled that just after she had issued her challenge, a sharp clap of thunder had echoed through the church… then nothing.

She shook her head in an attempt to clear it. Sensation began to return, and sense. Her breath caught at the choking smell of vampire. *Jesus, help me!* She felt something touching her, something dry and smooth and slippery, and hard and cold as death. *Oh, horror.* She fought panic, managed to breathe again, and tried to think. Her mind sprang to full consciousness and terror. For she knew then that what held her immobile — pressing her against the marble pillar with his body was her foe.

Mommy! was her first, little-girl-in-a-nightmare, reaction. This was her first time ever in a vampire's embrace.

Stop. Think. She steeled herself to lift her gaze to his death-pale face, though quailing inside. His death-black eyes were devoid of pity. His cruel red mouth curved into a smile, showing razor-sharp teeth.

"Oh, how swiftly do our fortunes change," the vampire said, his voice unexpectedly soft. "Even in… this place. Behold, I am the way, the way to immortality. Truly I say unto you, this day you will be with me in paradise." He laughed, delighting in his blasphemous mockery; his writhing red lips a horrible contrast to his dead eyes — and those teeth! He pressed his cold, hard body against her; the silken fabric of his cloak felt to her like a billowing shroud. He lowered his voice to a whisper. "Give yourself to me, sweet. I will show you heaven. Let us rule the world together."

"That'll be the day!" *Creep*! She struggled but lost her breath as he tightened his grip with unnatural ease and pressed her hard against the pillar.

His arms and legs, his whole body, felt like iron, immovable, no matter what she did. Wherever he touched her, she felt cold leaching into her, like death. His terrible eyes would not release hers. His smile was horrifying, his touch paralyzing. Was he mesmerizing her? No, impossible; she was immune to that sort of thing (wasn't she?). With a superhuman effort, she willed her head to clear, and her gaze to break from his.

Like a steel vise, his long fingers caught at her hand, brutally twisting until she cried out in pain, and her eyes filled with tears. The stake (she did not recall holding) clattered to the floor. The vampire smiled as he touched her cheek and slowly drew his claws upward into her hair. She shuddered and turned her face away. He grabbed her braid and pulled her head back. Flat black eyes looked down into her face; his tongue flicked out between his pointed teeth, long and snaky. She tried to shrink away.

He laughed. "Oh, never fear. I am not going to bite you. Yet. Maybe you would like me to kiss you instead, hmm?"

"In your dreams!" she spat. "I'd rather die!"

His eyes narrowed. "So be it. Come to hell with me, then." With that, he bared his fangs, and swift as a viper, struck at her throat, but immediately jerked back with a hiss from the small silver crucifix nestled there.

In his instant of paralysis, she twisted free and kneed him in the groin.

"Kiss that, creep!"

Then he was down on his knees on the cold stone floor, his proud head bowed before her. This was not the first vampire to have underestimated her. More than one had found this revelation a prelude to oblivion.

Yet Mara knew her foe was only momentarily rendered harmless and would quickly get up to kill her, if she let him. She was not about to wait around for him to carry out his threat. Could he steal her virtue? That was not the vampire way, in her experience. But they were creatures of darkness, so why not? They had no compunction. They were predators; humans were their prey. That was all. Ordinarily, they were only ever out for blood, to her knowledge. Other people's, usually, since she, as Huntress, posed too great a threat. Odd that this one should hunt her with other motives.

Kiss me? Never!

She scooped up the stake that had dropped at her feet, whipped it up high and brought it downward with a powerful stroke aimed at the vampire's heart. She had staked many a vampire and knew what she was about. This time the stake unexplainably glanced off and flew out of her hand to clatter into the shadows. She stared after it in shock for a moment. Weird.

From the corner of her eye, she saw the vampire begin to rise. She snatched up her bow even as she dashed around the tall marble angel holding a shell full of holy water, putting the font between them. His dead black eyes fixed on her. She lifted her bow, but for a moment, it snagged in her clothing. *What the heck?*

The vampire levitated and flew at her.

No time to think. She dropped the bow, dipped both hands into the font, and flung a great scoop of holy water at him. A cloud of sizzling steam rose from his face and chest. He came to a dead stop in mid-flight, roared with pain and rage, and fell back against a pillar, writhing and cursing.

She retrieved her crossbow, whipped it up and took aim. Enough already. *I should have done this sooner.* He wouldn't get close to her again. She would finish this now. She let fly a quarrel. It ricocheted off the pillar and lodged in the wooden door beyond. Thunk. She stared in horror for a moment, then glanced down at the offending bow and frowned.

The vampire had by that time wiped the holy water from his face. Though still in pain, he fixed his eyes on her once more. His smile was gone; his cold gaze glowed with rekindled fury.

"Mortal woman, you dare to defy me?" he rasped. "I am Samael, the Angel of Death. Taste and see!" With that, he turned the power of his eyes on her.

She dived. The fiery beam missed her by a hair. Sparks flew from the holy water font. She rolled to her feet, brought up her bow, and aimed. A slight movement of the vampire's hand threw her back just as she pulled the trigger, and her arrow went wide. The bow flew from her hand and skittered across the floor. She rebounded and stood panting, blood trickling from her nose.

The vampire hissed. His tongue whipped out, snake-like; his eyes glowed. *Uh-oh. Blood.* She dashed it away with the back of her hand (as if that would help!). Those eyes again! She sprang forward, and with a spinning kick smashed him in the jaw.

He slammed against a pew and whipped around. There was that dazzle of light again, within the swirling dark of his cloak, like a bolt of lightning in a thundercloud. Curious. He levitated and in a blur of movement came at her again. She met him with an uppercut that snapped his head back. He looked dazed for a split second (at least something fazed him!). *St. Michael, help me!* she prayed, as she drew out another stake and leaped forward.

The vampire had swiftly recovered, though; he whirled and caught her with a backhand, slamming her against a marble column. She managed to keep her feet and stood gasping for breath, watching his every move. Then he sprang. She lashed out in sheer desperation, sent him flying with a roundhouse kick to the kidneys. "Die, you ugly thing!" she panted, fighting a growing fear as she felt herself beginning to tire. This was taking too long.

He whirled and flowed to his feet, hell glowing in his eyes as he faced her again. Wary now, but still arrogant, he beckoned with his long, white fingers. "Come here. Come to me now."

She felt a twinge of panic. *Does he know I've about had it?* Her battles never lasted this long. With sharp, experienced eyes, she assessed his condition. He didn't appear to have suffered any real damage. A rare occurrence for her any time or place, but in a church? She narrowed her eyes. "Never! You come to me, creep! And die!" With that, she attacked with one of her never-fail one-two combination moves.

The vampire dodged her flying kick with unexpected ease and grabbed her wrist in mid-swing. His sharp, brutal twist was intended to render her helpless on the floor, but she went with it, flipped, and with a flying foot, caught him in the temple and sent him crashing against the pews again.

He rose with a shake of his head and glanced a little anxiously toward the tabernacle where the red vigil lamp flickered, then turned to her again. She had very nearly given up on any assistance from that quarter; it was almost as though he had some sort of immunity. *Odd.* In her experience, the Holy Presence should have put him out of commission long since. Of course, this wasn't an ordinary vampire. Had she only imagined that fleeting look of dread?

He levitated and rushed at her once more. She kicked him in the chin. He staggered back, hissing and snarling. Her hopes rose; he seemed to be retreating. A last stand? She hoped so; she was feeling the strain. Was afraid her blood-smeared face and sweat-dampened strands escaping her flying braid must give away the true state of affairs that she meant to conceal.

With renewed resolve, she snatched up another stake and charged. The point was at his chest when she saw his foot come up. The air blasted from her lungs as he went down, propelling her over his head. No! Caught by the oldest trick in the book! She twisted in midair to save herself, to recover her edge. With a whirl of his ebony cape, the vampire was up and facing her – somewhat desperately, it appeared. Ah. She had him now.

But the pillar was nearer than she'd thought. Her

momentum slammed her against the marble column; her head hit with a loud crack. A huntress could take such punishment without mortal injury, but the force of the collision half-stunned her for an instant.

That was all it took.

Road to Damascus

The Prince well knew of her resilience; she might in an instant return to full fighting form. In a blur of speed almost careless in its desperation, he flung out his hand and struck with all the force at his command. The blow knocked her flying. The stake slipped from her fingers as she hit the floor.

Wary, lest she awaken, he swiftly knelt beside her, unbuckled her belt and threw it, with its dagger and quiver of bolts, into the shadows. He picked up the stake, shielded his eyes with one hand as he slid the point under the chain around her neck, and gave a sharp pull. The links parted, and the small crucifix went flying. The stake quickly followed.

Exultant in his victory, he grasped her shoulders with long fingers and drew her to himself as he flowed to his feet. He stood for a moment, enchanted by the warmth, by the feel of a living heartbeat against his chest. Its thrumming set him on fire and roused the savage hunger in him. With a shiver of excitement, he pressed her close. Too soon he felt the approach of the point of no return. With an effort, he relaxed his grip, let her head fall back and gazed at the pulse in her throat, savoring the moment.

"No, Huntress, now you die. The master shall have your head, but first, I drink your blood. All your power shall be mine. All of it." Belatedly he remembered Nyx's request. He looked down. Traced the lithe form with his eyes. Lovely, and yet... it was blood that enticed him, that held the stronger fascination. But he must please Nyx.

A taste first, to weaken her. For some unaccountable reason, he felt admiration for this dauntless little huntress; a foreign feeling that had afflicted him several times during the battle.

Puzzled by this anomaly, he quickly brushed the recollection aside. *When she awakes, I shall crush her proud spirit. Nyx will have her prize after I first taste.* He bent his head to the white throat.

A beam of light caught him suddenly. He stood transfixed, unable to move. The light came from above; though compelled to look, he could see nothing but that blinding white light.

"Stop!" commanded a voice of great authority. "You would harm the favored one of Our Lady?"

Who dares to question me? "Who—who are you?" The Prince stammered and hated the quaver in his own voice.

"I am Michael, her protector," said the voice.

The Prince recovered quickly from his initial disorientation and replied with his customary arrogance. "And I am Samael, the Angel of Death, Prince of the Underworld. I have no need to explain to you, but I will tell you this. As you see, I have defeated the Huntress. First, I shall drink her blood. Then I shall possess her entirely, body and soul. After that, I will cut off her head and take it to my master, as he has commanded."

"Down on your knees to your Lord, proud creature!" the voice thundered. "Speak not of defiling the innocent in this sanctuary!"

The Prince was instantly slammed to his knees as though struck down by a bolt of lightning. Stunned at first, he quickly recovered and attempted to rise, but in vain. He found his voice. "I have taken her in battle," he said imperiously. "I hold her, defeated, in my arms."

"Do you think you defeated her on your own? Know this. You are but a creature and may only do that which the Lord God allows," the voice said sternly.

Outraged, the Prince responded, "I beat her fair and square. I, myself." But what was this? Something unfamiliar was happening within him. He looked down at the girl in his arms and felt that stirring of admiration for her again. "It was not easy, though, I admit that," he conceded. Heretofore, the

Prince had only felt respect for the master and very few others of his own kind; never for mortals. He hardened his heart at once, his lip curled with contempt. She was, after all, nothing but a helpless mortal, at his mercy like any other.

"Who deflected the stake meant for your heart while you were down on your knees before her?" the voice boomed.

"What?" the Prince choked. Someone saw *that*?

"Who turned away the bolt she sent toward you while you were blinded and in pain from holy water? She would not have missed."

The Prince bared his teeth to snarl but paused as a sudden thought hit him. *Is there a God who sees all? Did I know that once, long ago?*

"Yes. Choose your master," commanded the voice.

I have a choice?

"Our Lord Jesus Christ died for your sins," said the voice, suddenly gentle. "He gives you this one more chance. He shed his blood for you, too, child, and He wants you for His own."

The Prince was confused, his mind a mad tumult of unbidden memories, chaotic, impossible to sort out. *Hail Mary, full of grace. Where did that come from?*

"Your mother. Remember her?"

My mother? Nyx?

"Not Nyx. She is accursed and brought you death. No, your real mother, she who gave you life, held you on her knee, taught you to pray and to love the Lord your God. Have you forgotten?"

Memories came unbidden to his mind from deep in the past. Images appeared in rapid succession: of white clouds drifting high above in an azure sky as brilliant sunlight warmed the earth; the tall spire of the village church visible above trees stirring in the summer breeze; vineyards covering the rolling slopes; a garden heavy with fragrances of rose and honeysuckle; children laughing at play and a dog barking; comforting arms and a sweet, gentle voice praying, "Ave Maria, rose without thorns, you were born to comfort me. A queen of high birth, help me that I shall not be lost." *Mama? What's happening to me?*

"She awaits you, with your heavenly Mother."

"But why me? How can I deserve — I killed her! I killed them all!" The Prince choked on the words, on the horror of it. *I was proud of myself, of what I did.* He saw the carnage, the spilled blood of his father, mother, his whole family; and through all of it, Nyx's smile of satisfaction. She had done this, and he, he was but her puppet. Now he saw his evil deeds as though through newly opened eyes. As though the beam of light shone on his past and revealed its stark ugliness. *No, how can this be?* "Nyx made me into this beautiful immortal being that I am," he protested weakly.

"Nyx made you into a shell of the beautiful creature that God intended for you to become. She made you a vessel of corruption and decay, a creature puffed up with pride that brings suffering and cruel death to mortals before their time, a parasite that sucks the lifeblood from the living, endlessly seeking to satisfy an unquenchable thirst."

Now many eyes reproached him, of innocents lying broken, bleeding, dead. All the atrocities he had committed through the centuries passed before his eyes, an endless panoply of vignettes flipping by in quick succession. The verdict was clear and unavoidable. Guilty. Guilty. Guilty. And for what? A child here, a man there, dead before their time just to feed his craving — which was never satisfied, ever. He only became emptier and more voracious. And brought woe and desolation upon them, and himself, as well. That was the truth. Truth?

"Yes, you deserve hell for what you have done," the voice went on, implacably. "Give thanks to God for your mother and father, brothers, sisters; all of them. All, all those beloved by Him and holy in His sight. It is due to their prayers; it is for their sake, and that of others, that the Lord grants you this time of grace. Come to Jesus. He will quench your thirst with the Water of Life and make of you a necessary instrument in His plan to save mankind from the storm of evil looming on the horizon.

Is it possible? He looked at the girl in his arms and choked back a sob, strangely. *Huntress? Who are you? What are you? What have you done to me?* A face came into view in his mind's eye: dark, golden, beautiful; black eyes calm; long black hair flying, fanning out, intriguing somehow, even as she defied him, meant to kill him. Another huntress. Marie? With utter disdain, he had put her on the ground, stood over her, ruined her beauty and drunk her blood. Even as she lay dying, she had defied him still. Her words were darts more damaging, more painful, more disturbing to his cold heart than her stake could have been.

What is this? Memories? No, not that. But they came in a rush, and would not be denied: a sweet nightingale voice, pleading, calling his name (he who had no mercy), silenced forever. A child's red hair pressed against his face, a boy, crying. *My own brother, dying slowly, painfully.* He groaned.

"Give up evil, child of light."

No one could forgive the things I have done. His throat constricted so that he could not speak the words aloud, but that did not seem to matter.

"He can. He died for you and forgives all if you but repent."

"I would have killed Him myself," the Prince said in profound self-reproach, his resistance falling away like dead scales. "Can He forgive that?"

"His mercy is infinite. Remember the one known as the Good Thief. It is not too late for you, yet. Choose now." The voice rolled out with awesome power. This Being and the hope offered attracted him. It was something he would never have thought possible. Or thought about at all.

The Prince felt his world being torn from him and was overwhelmed by the realization of light's great power to dispel darkness. *I have a choice?* The thought intrigued him. He felt a hunger within him, but not the usual kind. A thirst, for what? True, the thirst for blood was never slaked. What had seemed so pleasurable was in this light revealed as nothing more than a diabolical craving. A terrible need, offering temporary pleasure, or no, not even that, but only a glut that now disgusted him, followed by a greater thirst than before. Disappointment. And sometimes it palled. Yes, boredom drowned in blood.

He felt an irresistible attraction to the light. Desired it with all the strength of his being. But when he would have grasped it, he was unable to move. His limbs seemed heavy like stone, which was not his nature. A frightening thing. Should he not be light enough to drift on the wind currents? *What is happening to me?*

"Those are your sins. Evils weigh you down. Is that what you want, forever? Choose light and life."

Is it possible? But I am unworthy of this favor, Lord.

At that, an excruciating pain tore through his chest. Another voice, deep and resonant, yet of inexpressible sweetness, spoke, "I will break your heart of stone and give you a heart of flesh."

He opened his mouth to scream, but no sound came out. A great clamor arose in his mind, as every part of him, his very nature as a vampire, resisted with a roaring and shrieking of pain and rage, as of hideous creatures of nightmare. Of hell itself. Overwhelmed by a terror such as he had never known, he cried out, *Help me!*

Unsure whether aloud or within himself, or to whom he pleaded. But God knew.

Warmth flowed through him. He could not know that it was an infusion of grace and the restoration of his lost human soul; his soul that had long been trapped between the living and the dead. Only now, because of his humble admission and plea for help had it been released, and reunited to his body.

At first, the sensation was not unpleasant, but soon a sense of awareness struck him. All the evil deeds he had committed and their dire effects crashed down on him, in a cavalcade of images, crystal clear in every minute detail, with nothing omitted, nothing to excuse him. He saw all the sorrows he had wrought through the centuries, the cruel deaths. Memories came at him relentlessly, beating him down to the ground with a full and heavy sense of guilt. Entirely justified, he knew now.

That vision of the Huntress Marie returned, her sweet face, which by his hand had changed from warm and golden to cold and gray, appearing for but a fleeting moment. For the first time, he clearly beheld the significance of the reproach in those dark eyes and the prophecy she had made. A sob caught in his throat as he remembered all, all.

Just when he had sated himself with the power of her blood, as he was standing on top of the world and thinking he was equal with God, that unwanted memory had blasted him. And then came her warning. He had never forgotten her words: *You will come to regret this day.* So this was what she had meant!

And he had laughed.

Killing her had not erased the memory. Presenting her head to Charon had not. Neither had adorning the master's throne with it. The most disturbing thing was that the head had not changed. Over a hundred years had gone by, and yet there was no apparent decay, the long dark hair still held its lifelike sheen; the face was set as though in sweet repose, though spiked high above the throne in the Great Hall. He had tried to make himself think it meant nothing. It was the dry cold of the underground preventing natural decomposition, he told himself. Never mind that none of the other ornamental heads had remained incorrupt. In time, all were reduced to mere skulls. All except hers.

Determined not to let one mortal woman disturb him, he had thereafter proceeded to fill his mind with other things, worse things, and had convinced himself that none of it mattered. She was mistaken if she thought her words bothered him. He was above all that. He could do as he pleased, with impunity. He was a god.

Now the full impact of those wrongs he had done hit him with a sledgehammer blow. He saw his loving family lying scattered and dead while he laughed and gloried in his own supposed omnipotence, with no remorse or thought that he might someday be called to account. And through the centuries, more innocents, all beloved by God. Rivers — indeed, an ocean — of blood accused him.

O my God, what have I done? He shuddered at the thought of how he had so offended his Lord and Creator. Saw clearly the tremendous difference between Creator and creature, and trembled at his own presumption in thinking he was God's equal. He, a mere creature. He saw the tragic effects manifested in the sufferings and death of Jesus on the cross and recognized his own part in it. Accepted, for the first time in five centuries, his guilt. A devastating sense of grief and regret overwhelmed him.

Interiorly, he abased himself at last.

"What have I done? What have I done?" he wailed aloud. He bowed his head and wept bitterly.

After a time, he realized that the beam of light had gone. He looked down at the girl in his arms. He truly saw and appreciated beauty for the first time, and in that moment, he fell in love. He had never in his entire existence done anything halfway, and this was no different. His surrender was total.

He saw the reflection of God's own perfection in the curve of those long lashes resting on rose-petal cheeks, in the roses in her lips, in the gold of her hair. A long-forgotten emotion stirred within him. He felt a strong desire to kiss her sweet face, as that most powerful of human instincts reawakened. For centuries, his primary attraction to human beings had been due to a cruel impulse, that demonic craving to feed on their blood. Now he hesitated, confused and disturbed by the unfamiliar and conflicting emotions.

His conscience, long dead, had also awakened. He loathed himself for his recent actions, struck now by the realization that the body of this beautiful human being was a temple of the Holy Spirit, not to be desecrated — as all human beings were meant to be. For the first time in centuries, he knew and cared. He saw now that he had been blinded by evil. At once overwhelmed by guilt, he shed bitter tears as he recollected his own loss of innocence so long ago.

Unnoticed by him, some of those impossible vampire tears splashed down onto the fair maiden's breast. True as Cupid's golden arrows, they pierced her to the heart.

He would never again be the same, but the thirst for blood was an integral part of his vampire nature, and that had not changed. The difference lay in his awareness of its evil, in accepting it as a weakness to be resisted and, if possible, conquered. He looked down at the warm and living human being in his arms and feared that weakness. No longer was he able to act on his impulses with no consequences and no regrets. Centuries of seizing what he wanted with no remorse had taken its toll. He suddenly realized how the sensation of holding her close drew him, stirred him, tempted him. There was nothing for it but to put some distance between himself and her.

He lowered the girl to the floor. Gently, not only because he cared, but also because he was afraid she would awaken and hate him. She knew what he was.

He found a cloth on a small table nearby, rolled it into a bundle and put the makeshift pillow under her head. When he looked down into her face and saw the damage he had inflicted there, his heart was torn by regret. With long, graceful fingers, he touched that beautiful face, unable to resist one lingering caress, even at the risk of awakening her.

Then he reluctantly turned and glided away down the aisle, lost in this new and unfamiliar state of being. Although he felt uneasy within the peaceful atmosphere of the church, outside seemed yet uninviting. He felt different, as though riven by light, pierced to the very core of his being. Not so much as though he was bereft of anything, but rather that he now was possessed of something that changed him, or completed him. The answer came: his soul, long forgotten, was now restored to him.

As of yet, his consciousness could not absorb all that had transpired, but he knew that he no longer belonged to the cold, dark world from whence he had so recently come. There was no question of returning to the Brotherhood. He had no illusions. He was a traitor. He had chosen the camp of the enemy; he *was* the enemy. There was no going back, even if he so wished. But how could he want that? What did he have in common with them now?

The Huntress was still in grave danger. He himself had been the single most dangerous threat, but there were others. The master had decreed her death and would not stop until the deed was accomplished. She stood in the way of his New Kingdom.

Caught in a limbo of sorts, the Prince scanned the darkened church with eyes no longer flat and dead, but bright with the reflection of his newfound soul. Yet even now, he must shield them from the crucifix standing out so vividly at the main altar. *I am still a vampire,* he thought with profound sorrow. He felt so changed, he had hoped…

He had to avert his eyes from that which he could not look upon, so he cast them down to the glimmering marble of the floor. Even there, he found no escape. Its mottled design seemed to shift; and before his eyes appeared the image of that exquisite creature lying wounded by his own accursed hand. Sickened, he pressed his hand to his middle, where it inadvertently touched the jeweled hilt of the knife with which he had meant to behead her. His hand recoiled as though it had been burned. *O God, forgive me,* he cried out in his soul. His grief increased tenfold as he recalled his vile intentions toward her. How could he have presumed?

He turned his eyes away from her image, but others seemed to materialize, of his many victims, wasted upon the ground, gray-faced, lifeless eyes accusing. *Oh, what have I done?* Struck to the heart, for the first time, he thought of his keen night vision as a curse. A deep groan escaped him; his face convulsed with sorrow as he clutched at his heart. Was there to be no escape from this torment? He lifted his eyes to the arches and frescoes, the statues and stained glass windows, and was compelled to admire their color and harmony. Higher, on the vaulted ceiling, was a vision of beauty impossible to mortal eyes in this lack of light. With his vampire eyes, he beheld it in awe, this promise of heaven represented by paintings of the Trinity, the Blessed Virgin, angels and saints in rainbow hues, with halos emblazoned in gold.

As he gazed, the paintings faded, and other images came alive. Other faces formed before his eyes. More angels? No. What, then? Gradually they became clear and were now visibly familiar. Mama, Papa? Kristina… Georg? My family? He blinked in an attempt to dispel the illusion. The faces did not vanish but instead drew nearer. Katherine and her family, Gerda and her new husband Walter; Rudi, Willi, all of them. Karlchen, Werner, Rainer, Ursi. Serene, happy, and at peace. And there, baby Luisa, and Theo. And Grandfather?

He turned away his gaze in shame. They were together now. Only *he* remained behind in this vale of tears.

He felt compelled to lift his eyes again. Now he could almost reach out and touch them, they were that close. Yet he dared not. He was a little frightened. Would they now exact their revenge? *But no, what's this*? They looked upon him with such… Was that love in those eyes? How was that possible, after what he had done? He closed his eyes for a fraction of a second. *Forgive me, Mama, and all of you. Thank you for your prayers, which I do not deserve.* When he looked again, one small figure had detached itself from the group and was drawing nearer. Large beatific eyes bent upon him a look so sweet; red hair like flame above that serene childish face, the body slender and perfectly angelic, clad in light. Willi!

The Prince's anguished interior cry seemed to be lifted up on wings toward heaven. *Oh, what have I done*? How unworthy he was to look upon these poor innocents whom he had untimely sent to their deaths. He threw himself down, face to the floor.

My Jesus, mercy!

Gentle hands lifted him up. "Stand, my brother, and accept this gift from our Redeemer."

He was on his feet once more, eyes cast down. Even so, he saw, felt that red hair, soft against his cheek, heard the fearful cries, tasted the innocent blood of his own brother. And was sick with self-loathing.

Willi reached out to trace a cross upon his forehead. Oh, how it burned with a heavenly fire, with an ecstasy he had never remotely imagined, consuming in the heat and light and pain that sordid parody he had once taken for the sweetest of rapture (and had so wickedly pursued at the cost of innocent blood). Tears flowed down his cheeks, as for the second time, he wept.

Then came the words, unspoken, but clear. *Do not despair, dear brother Niki. You are forgiven all.*

At that, the light flared up so brightly that he had to close his eyes. When next he opened them, the light had vanished, and the vision was gone. The ceiling was as before. The figures of God and the angels and saints looked down on him with detached equanimity.

He gazed around in bewilderment. What was to become of him? Was he forgiven? It was unbelievable; undeserved. His parents—all of his family—were at peace, happy, and loved him still, it seemed. But he was less than the dust on their shoes. No, this heavenly peace was not for him. The wings upon which his soul had for a moment soared and caught a glimpse of hope now plummeted down, down, into the dark abyss of despair. If only the floor would open up and swallow him. He wanted to die, but he himself had long ago rendered that impossible.

"Oh, God," he groaned. "Help me." There was no reply.

He turned his eyes in despair from the unattainable heights and from the dreaded sanctuary. He spotted an ornamented archway and felt drawn to it. He glided over to find that it was a chapel; in front of its altar was a bank of unlit votive candles. Above them hung a painting so lovely he could not take his eyes off it. *Like heaven*, he thought, as he entered the chapel without realizing he was going to. With his vampire eyes, he could see even in the gloom the image of a woman of unsurpassed beauty and grace standing beneath scalloped arches of golden lacework. Her delicate features expressed a love so sweet and gentle that he wished to gaze upon them forever. Her dress was crimson and gold, the raiment of a queen; her outstretched arms spread a green velvet mantle over a group of petitioners. Bishops, priests, monks, lords and ladies, and even peasants; all had flocked to the protection of their sovereign Lady.

A sharp longing pierced the Prince's heart. How he wanted that. He opened his mouth to voice a prayer, but could not speak, so choked was he by emotion at the realization of his own unworthiness. All at once, unplanned by him and completely unexpected, words poured unimpeded from his heart. *O beautiful Lady, I humbly beg of you, if it please you, let me shelter under your mantle too.*

The answer came at once, clear and sweet. *It does so please me.*

He fell to his knees and wept for the third time, head bowed. After the storm of tears had passed, he raised his head. He lifted his gaze to that sweet face regarding him still, and wondered at those gentle eyes so filled with love. There was no condemnation or reproach.

Another prayer poured forth from the depths of his soul. *Forgive me, dear Mother, for even looking upon thy pure sweet face. Please approach thy Son for me, He Whom I am not able to so much as cast my eyes upon, nor even to draw near of my own accord. I beseech thee most humbly, to ask His pardon for all that I have done. I am not worthy to approach thee, but I implore thee, please, be my mother too. Help me. O teach me to pray.* Within his soul sprang up a terrible awareness of his cold vampire heart's incapacity to accept or express love.

She nodded assent and smiled tenderly. *Jesus has already marked you for His own. Now he sends you His love, my son.*

Son? He felt a rush of gratitude that she should so acknowledge him. Before he could protest his unworthiness of such an honor, his gaze was drawn toward a familiar face amidst those beneath the shelter of the Lady's mantle.

The woman had not been there when he had first looked. Her long black hair shimmered as she turned dark eyes upon him, her mouth set in a determined line. She raised a golden bow and aimed directly at his heart. That graceful figure in the blue dress and high moccasins; how could he ever forget her? She had a glow about her now, shining from within. Hers was the face from atop the throne, the face he had tried to ignore for over a hundred years.

Marie, huntress of the north.

With rising dread, he regarded her in helpless fascination. *I killed you! Must you pursue me through all eternity?* Yet he stood resigned, unable to move, knowing he deserved all that and more, that nothing she could do was punishment enough, even if for all eternity.

You will come to regret this day, she had told him.

She released the string; the golden arrow flew toward him. He could not move; could not avoid it even as he saw it come. He could only watch dispassionately as it pierced his chest. He felt a searing pain, then ineffable sweetness filled his heart, and he knew no more.

Golden Arrow

Mara opened her eyes and saw the Gothic arches soaring into the shadows of the vaulted ceiling high above. It took a second or two to register where she was and what had happened.

Horrors, what the — ?

She scrambled to her feet, automatically reached for her weapons, and found none. Quickly she scanned the church's interior for some sign of her adversary. Nothing.

She reeled. *Ow.* Cautiously she reached up, felt a tender bump on the back of her head. Closed her eyes until the dizziness passed. Tried to think what had happened. There had been a battle. How had she come to be lying on the floor? Not dead. Or undead.

Then she felt it, faintly at first. Her enemy's presence. The vampire was still here; it hadn't fled. *But, what's this?* Something had changed. He had changed, or seemed different somehow. *No, that just isn't possible!* She tried to sort this out in her mind, all the while with every sense alert. There was no sound or other indication of his presence; only that feeling.

She glanced down, wondering at the cloth lying on the floor as though someone had placed it under her head to make her more comfortable. But whom? Suspicious, she looked around. Nothing was stirring. The church appeared to be empty. But it was not. She knew that, beyond all doubt.

It was dark. Not even a moonbeam found its way through the clerestory windows. The only light was the red glow of the vigil lamp and the faint yellowish glimmer of votive candles, as before. Odd that the smell of burning beeswax was as strong as ever, but the stench of vampire had faded. Was he still here? Yes, he was! Then why — ? Mara genuflected hastily, whispering a short prayer as she cast a wary glance around.

One thought jolted her: *why am I still alive*? Had someone come to her rescue—but whom? Father Mike would try, but even he… and anyway, he wouldn't leave her lying there. No, that made no sense. Mortals were at a disadvantage against even ordinary vampires; this one was anything but ordinary. Who could stand up to him if she couldn't? She shuddered even now, remembering. The things he'd said, and the way he'd looked at her. He'd touched her. She felt sick at the thought. A quick investigation revealed that her clothing was intact, and she breathed a sigh of relief. Still, she felt dirtied.

She shook off the feeling and took stock. Her weapons were gone, belt and all. She looked around and finally spotted her bow lying on the floor. As she went to retrieve it, her memory jogged. *I missed his heart*? *I never miss*! She picked up the scattered quarrels, but the one stuck in the door resisted her every attempt to dislodge it. She glanced nervously over her shoulder, then decided to abandon it. Quickly she reloaded and spanned her bow. Then she espied her belt, the dagger still in its sheath and the remaining bolts in the quiver, lying on the floor as though carelessly tossed. She buckled it on.

Bow at the ready, she edged down the side aisle, listening, searching the shadows. She said a prayer under her breath and reached up out of habit to touch the crucifix at her throat; it was gone! She felt a stab of panic; her glance swept the darkened nave once more, but there was no sign of the crucifix. Later. No time now.

She advanced, all senses alert. A faint smell of death lingered; an unnatural chill lifted the hair on the back of her neck. She fully expected one of those terrible lightning attacks at any moment. Nothing happened. All was silent. Unnaturally so. *Where are you? I know you're here.* Her every muscle was taut, ready to spring into action. Her eyes raked every dark corner, high and low. She couldn't get his enigmatic words out of her mind. Creep. Her finger tensed on the trigger. *Come out, come out, wherever you are. I won't miss this time.*

She thought she had seen it all, after hunting vampires for much of her young life. Her routine was to track down the enemy, engage it in battle. One final blow and the job was done. Simple. Not so tonight.

Silent stalking was as natural to her as to a cat. She seemed almost to flow from one shadow to the next. If not as unnaturally as her quarry, more gracefully and smoothly than other humans. And with her cat-like night vision and other enhanced senses, the darkness was no impediment.

As she passed down the aisle, her glance swept each side chapel. At St. Jude's shrine, she paused to breathe a silent prayer to that patron of impossible cases. How she needed his guidance through this jungle of confusion! She had no idea what to expect. That worried her.

When she came to the Mother of Mercy chapel, she halted, nerves tingling. Something was different about it. This, her favorite refuge, was ordinarily a haven of peace and consolation. But now, now she felt a waft of chill air. Not from the outside; she took a quick look to be sure, but no, the outer door had not opened. It came from here, within the chapel, and she knew what it signified. Vampire.

She paused, listening intently, but could hear nothing in the absolute stillness of the church. Even that smell of death was not as strong as it ought to be. She scanned the shadows, moving only her eyes. It felt as though she was standing on a threshold; that behind this curtain of shadow lay mysterious consequences that would change her life forever. Dare she step across and draw aside the veil? Did she have a choice?

She felt a stirring, caught a whiff of death again, too faint, but... *There! He is there!* She was certain of it now. Nerves taut, her soft-soled boots silent on the marble floor, she stepped into the chapel. At first, she didn't notice the dark form lying on the stone floor, face down and arms flung out in the shape of a cross. Then, suddenly, it dawned on her.

There, in the shadow at her feet, was her adversary. She sprang back, heart pounding, her bow aimed at his heart. She couldn't have said why she didn't pull the trigger at once. Her usual practice was to get the unpleasantness over with a minimum of fuss. But there was something odd about this. Why would the thing just lie there? She narrowed her eyes.

The supine figure didn't move. Was he dead? No, that would be too easy. But she had never seen a vampire intentionally lay itself open like this. A vampire with a death wish? Hah! Bait for a trap? Whatever that would be. Odd.

She recalled his words, the sensation of his cold body against hers, and was sickened anew. Her mind traveled at light speed, her eyes darted around suspiciously, as she wondered from which quarter would come a surprise attack. Is there really nothing else here? She listened. Nothing. Incomprehensible that he would just lie there, apparently at her mercy. Mercy?

She looked up at the picture. Mother of Mercy. Her bow hand was steady as she stepped nearer. She turned her cold gaze downward and aimed at the vampire's heart. Let him leap to the attack; that would be his last move. But he didn't.

Oh well. Sayonara, creep. Her finger curled on the trigger. Just as she was about to let the arrow fly, a voice spoke. A voice of infinite sweetness, interiorly or aloud, she could not have said. One word.

Stop.

It was a command. She knew the voice and relaxed her trigger finger at once, but her aim didn't waver. She looked down at the thing on the floor, and her stomach twisted with nausea as she recalled how those horrid spidery fingers had felt. And his words, his presumption in daring to suggest... No! She must not think of that now. She returned her attention to the voice.

I can't just stand here doing nothing. I must kill him, or I fail in my duty.

No. He belongs to my Son.

She lowered the bow but kept a wary eye on the thing lying at her feet. After what he said to me? After what he said about

Jesus, and all that's holy?

No answer.

She backed up a few paces. "Get up, beast!" she barked, her bow ready. He didn't move, just lay there, unnaturally, vampire still. Then she sensed something. A spark? Something almost like… life (or not, this was the undead!). Maybe a will to move, not visible to the eye; an inner trembling, sensed rather than seen. She tensed, waiting.

After several heart-pounding moments, the dark form rippled and slowly began to rise, with that unnatural, fluid movement of the vampire. Her finger tightened on the trigger, her bow aimed. There was that order not to shoot, of course, but it was impossible for her to let down her guard. Due to her life's training, she could do naught else; if he attacked, a moment's inattention on her part would be fatal. Anyway, she really wanted to kill him. *Oh, yes. Just give me a reason.*

His black cloak whispered faintly as he turned to face her. One pale hand clutched his chest; an expression of pain flickered across his face and was gone.

Suffer, creep! She thought coldly.

But then she looked into his eyes. They were different than she remembered. Are these the same eyes? There were now great depths in them; they were no longer empty and flat and dead. An unexpected thing, and therefore frightening. She couldn't look away, not because she was hypnotized (never that); rather, she was entranced by the strange and unexpected expression of… She couldn't place it and was intrigued by its mystery.

But he's a demon! she remonstrated herself. The recollection of what he had done and said was still vivid in her mind. Bile rose in her throat. Wait a minute. What had Our Lady said? 'He belongs to my Son.' How is that possible? She did not doubt Our Lady, only her own sanity. *Did I hear what I thought I heard? I did get quite a bump on the head. Maybe this isn't real.*

But there was something different about those eyes. She met the vampire's gaze. Something passed between them, and she knew then that she could no longer think of him as just a thing. She didn't know how much time passed as she searched those eyes. The white face was composed, beautiful in a tragic way, yet she was scarcely conscious of anything but those eyes. Or even that she had thought such a thing.

"I love you," he said. At once, his eyes widened as though the words shocked him as much as they did her. He dropped his gaze at once, then raised it slowly, the expression unreadable.

She certainly had not expected that to come out of his mouth. Not only the words, for which she could not account at all, but also the sound of his voice was different. Not like before. No longer harsh and rasping, but beautiful. No. She was immune to vampires' hypnotic powers. This was disturbing. She took a step back and narrowed her eyes.

"Whatever. Vampires can't love!"

"I know that. And yet, it appears I can." His eyes seemed to pierce her through. Gone was the cold, unfeeling look that tainted everything it touched. In its place was something so compelling that she had to look away.

Was it feeling? *No, impossible!* Were those eyes now windows to… no, this can't be happening! Vampires have no souls. But what, then?

"How is that?" Her voice was the harsh one now.

"I—I don't know what happened. I—" he sounded lost, dazed. Gone were the arrogance and the cold, cruel smile.

"What about 'Come, be my bride'?" She nearly choked on the words but forced herself to continue. "'You are mine now,' you said. That was you, wasn't it?" She frowned, unsure, now.

A shadow crossed his face. He looked away. "Yes. Sorry. That was unforgivable."

He was ashamed? She stared in disbelief. And yet, somehow she knew that this was no lie. For the first time, she doubted her judgment and stood resolutely facing him.

Something glittered on his cheek. Tears? *Now I've seen everything! Vampires can't cry, either. They don't have tears. Okay, what's going on?* She blinked, but the illusion didn't go away. "So. I'm a little confused. Um—" She made a slight movement with her bow. "I'm sworn to kill you, you know."

His gaze lifted to meet hers. "Do so, then. I deserve no mercy. I have given none. Ever."

She bit her lip and frowned. Every word that came out of his mouth was wrong. Or, not wrong. That was the odd thing. It was like she had been warped into an alternate dimension where everything was the opposite of what it should be. Maybe she had stepped through the Looking Glass. This was certainly a very peculiar conversation. She thought of Alice and the caterpillar and shook a little. *Okay, what kind of a smokescreen here… vampire, demon, liar?*

She felt a bit dizzy again, swayed, but caught her balance. His white brow furrowed with concern; he reached out as though to assist. She recoiled and steadied her bow.

A shadow passed behind his eyes. The pale hand vanished within the folds of his cloak. "I am sorry I hurt you."

"You're sorry? Why? I was trying to kill you. And you were trying to kill me, too, or worse."

He looked away. "I understand you not forgiving me that. Still, for what it is worth, I am sorry." His voice was so low she could scarcely hear him.

She deliberated. Her whole world had just been turned upside down. She was the Huntress, and the creatures of the night were the enemy. To her, black had always been black, and white, white. She never carried on conversations with her quarries, never dialogued with them; she just killed them, and her job was done. A flurry of questions flitted through her conscious thought. She took her eyes off his and looked up at the picture.

"Yes," said the vampire, his gaze following the direction of hers. "It was she who saved me from myself, from despair." With a graceful hand, he indicated the Lady in the picture. "And gave me that gift from her Son."

He does seem different. No, what am I thinking? This is a vampire!

Why would I trust anything he says? I saw death in those eyes only a little while ago. And yet, there was no fury or arrogance now, or even that empty, dead look. She dared not relax her guard, however. She had had a taste of his lightning swiftness, his power, and knew well the deviousness of the vampire. Never mind what she felt. *Oh, what is this strange breathlessness I feel?*

"Listen to your heart," he said. "It speaks true."

Her eyes narrowed. *He can't read my mind, surely.*

He turned away to look at the picture, unconsciously presenting to her his profile, pale and fine against the shadow. So perfect and almost luminous, as though cut from alabaster. How striking that noble brow and deep-set eyes, the slightly curved nose, the delicately chiseled mouth. His cloak was fastened at the throat by a sparkling jeweled clasp, from which it fell in long, black folds to his feet. It blended him into the shadows, but could not conceal his power and grace.

He's beautiful, like an angel, or a fairy-tale prince! Good grief, what am I thinking? This is a vampire, a demon. The enemy! But she could not look away. *Isn't this the beast that I fought tonight? My sworn enemy? Why, then do those mysterious dark eyes melt my heart? Love? No. Where did that come from? This is so not happening to me. A Huntress kills vampires. But those eyes, those eyes… God, help me.*

He turned and saw her looking at him. She reddened and quickly dropped her gaze. Her eyes filled with tears. Unable to contain her conflicting thoughts and emotions any longer, she turned and ran down the aisle. The heavy wooden door opened at her touch, and she slipped outside, into the night. The door whispered shut behind her.

She looked up at the starry sky. *Where are You when I need you?* She reached up to wipe away the tears and found that she was still holding her bow. Tears flooded her eyes again. *Why didn't you let me kill him? Now what am I to do?*

She began to run. The rush of wind cooled her tear-tracked cheeks but did nothing for her tortured heart. Finally, out of breath, she paused and looked around. She was in the park.

The wind sighed through the trees, echoing her woe as she stumbled down the trail.

What now? I can't go home. How could I face Mom and Dad, or explain? I've never run from an opponent or a battle. Never! I've betrayed my calling. Oh, what's happened to me?

She sat down beneath a tree and leaned against it. Tears streamed down her cheeks. She pulled her jacket close around her against the chill of the night and sobbed as though her heart would break. In a way, it had. After this, nothing could be the same; everything was changed forever. The impossible had happened, though she did not understand it yet. She felt as though set adrift in an alien sea.

Finally, exhausted from weeping, she sank into a dreamless sleep, unaware of the dark figure not far away, standing guard until dawn's waxing light forced him to seek shelter from the approach of the sun's rays.

The World Turned Upside Down

In the days following, Mara tried to get on with her life, but it seemed to her that nothing would be the same again, ever. She attended her college classes as usual but found it difficult to concentrate or to take halfway decent notes on the lectures. Nothing else seemed to go right, either; even her martial arts practice suffered. This, in particular, was worrying. For her, a minor slip-up could mean death, or worse. Her instructor tried to rouse her enthusiasm by showing her some new moves but without success. She was too preoccupied with trying to sort out the how and why of her first-ever loss in a fight with a vampire. Defeated and yet still alive! And that other…

Her parents were concerned but did not press her. Nor did Father Mike, though that little wrinkle on his brow whenever they met told her he suspected something was up. But how was she to confide something she herself didn't understand?

Even her friends couldn't draw her out, though not for lack of trying, until one day while they sat in the cafeteria having lunch. Amidst all the usual social chatter, Sabrina was giving Mara looks of such concern, she didn't have the heart to just brush her off. Again. Instead, she tried making a joke about it, which fell flat. No one but Mara laughed, and her laugh sounded hollow, even to herself.

"Okay. Something's up, we all know that," Maggie said, exasperated. "Just spill it! You can't go on like this."

Mara frowned and pushed carrot medallions around her plate with her fork.

"Come on, we're your friends, for heaven's sake," Sabrina said.

"Hey," Josh interrupted, "If you're not going to eat that perfectly good chicken cordon bleu, I will."

"Fine, have it." Mara pushed her plate toward him. Eagerly he reached for it.

"Josh, stop," Maggie remonstrated. "She hasn't eaten a bite of it. I don't believe she's eaten anything for days. Look at her. She's fading away!"

"What's up, Mara?" George put in. "This is just wrong. I don't get it. You love food more than any other girl I know."

"Hey, that better be a compliment, pal," she tried to joke, but again without success. She heaved a long sigh. "No, you're right. I haven't felt like eating lately."

"Aha! I get it!" Sabrina chirped. "You're in love! So who's the lucky guy?"

"No, it can't be that," said Mara, then turned red.

"Whoa. Mara's taken a hit. She's down for the count," announced Josh.

She didn't laugh at his attempted levity but instead appeared more downcast. The boys looked away, at their plates, anywhere but at her.

"It's okay, Mara, we're all friends here," Maggie said kindly. "I mean, it's not the end of the world, right?"

Mara shrugged, but made no answer, afraid she might burst into tears. If only they knew. But how could she ever tell them? A vampire?!

"It's okay, don't mind us; we just want to help, if we can," said Sabrina, her irrepressible sense of humor dampened. She would never intentionally hurt anyone.

"Sorry, guys." Mara blinked back tears. "It's just not something I can talk about right now."

Maggie and Sabrina exchanged concerned glances. The boys shifted their feet. Mara? Tears?

"It must be serious. You didn't mind talking about that star quarterback in high school who had a crush on you a couple of years ago, if I recall," Maggie pointed out. "Or last year, that pre-med student you thought was pretty cute."

"Hey, that was just puppy love, and she was over them in no time," Josh interjected. "Happens to everyone. Just give it time and maybe—"

"But Josh, she's not talking now. And she's crying. That worries me," said Maggie.

"Maybe the difference is, she's the one fallen in love," Sabrina remarked. "Or maybe it's actually Mr. Right this time."

"Hey, guys, I'm sitting right here, okay?"

There was a silence for a moment, and sheepish looks, then apologies and a prolonged silence.

"Why not go see Father Mike about it?" George blurted out, finally. Everyone stared. This, from George? He looked around self-consciously. "What? You always say he has all the answers."

"You're right, I suppose." Mara dabbed at her eyes with a napkin. "But I'm not sure how he'll take, um, something like this."

Relieved that she had at least admitted that there was a problem, though they had no idea why it should be a problem, the others, in a chorus of concern, added their pleas to George's.

"Go," said Maggie. "He's always helped you before."

"He's your mentor. How can you not tell him?" put in Josh, trying to make amends. "He'll know how to sort things out."

"You think?" Mara asked hopefully.

Sabrina's twinkle returned. "Go on, see Father about it. Then you can tell us, too, about him."

"It's not like that. I mean, not what you think. Really. Oh, fine, then. I'll go." Her wan smile was like the sun trying to shine through an overcast sky.

"Thank God," said Josh. "We're getting damn tired of your moping around. You know? Now. About your chicken?" He caught Maggie's frown. "Or not."

"Sure, Josh. I just can't eat right now, Maggie. Thanks, guys, I know I haven't been good company lately."

Their quick protests warmed her heart. What would she do without her four faithful friends? They were always there for each other, through thick and thin. In truth, Mara was grateful for this final little push she needed to at last confront the problem.

Once again, she found herself in her confessor's parlor.

"Have an oatmeal chocolate chip cookie," said Father Michael O'Donovan, pushing the tray closer to Mara. "Smell that; mmm, wonderful. Mrs. O'Hara baked them just this morning."

Father Mike was the one person who truly understood the strange double life Mara led. Throughout her young life, he had listened patiently to her troubles and triumphs on a regular basis, according each his undivided attention. Mara had come to think of him as the wisest person ever, and mostly accepted his direction without question.

A bright rectangular patch lay on the carpet as the setting sun cast its rosy glow through the window beneath a half-drawn shade, but the room was cool, a relief from the heat of the late afternoon. Books lined up on shelves and worn upholstered chairs gave the parlor a comfortable, homey air. A tray of cookies and two tall glasses of iced tea stood on the coffee table. No visitor left Father Mike's house without refreshment. His housekeeper fussed over him like a mother hen. She provided plain but nutritious meals three times a day, as well as abundant home baking; more than enough to share with visitors.

Mara managed a smile. It was difficult not to, in Father Mike's company. Her stomach seemed to be tied in knots; she doubted she could eat anything but accepted one cookie to please him. Ice cubes rattled as she sipped her drink, giving away the trembling of her hand. She quickly set the glass down, hoping he hadn't noticed.

Father Mike didn't miss much but kindly refrained from comment and began with small talk to ease her into the subject at hand. After all attempts failed, he finally said outright, "So. Let's get to the real reason why you're here."

The dam burst; a flood of tears first, then, "I have a problem, Father, that you're not going to believe."

"Try me. I've already heard things most people wouldn't believe. From yourself, too, if I recall."

"Right." She sniffled and dashed the tears from her cheeks. He handed her a box of Kleenex. "I—oh, I hardly know how to begin. It's never happened before. I mean, I never would have thought—" She took a Kleenex and blew her nose. When finally she glanced up, his steady gaze was upon her with kindly expectancy.

"You've fallen in love."

She blushed. "Oh, how did you—? No, it can't be that. Oh, dear, do you think so? My friends, too…"

"It was bound to happen, sooner or later, I suppose." He sighed but seemed unaware that he had done so.

"Father, er, maybe I should go. This is, um—" His look was so kind that she settled back into her chair after all. "I, er, I think it's not quite what you expect."

He raised an eyebrow. "Let's hear it, then."

She took a deep breath and forced herself to relax, her hands resting on the carved wooden arms of the chair. "Okay, I'll start at the very beginning. I'm warning you right now, I'll probably make a short story long, because, well, I'm trying to understand it myself. Anyway, I was out patrolling one night…"

She told her tale, pouring out her fears and feelings to her mentor as she always had. "Yeah, I know, right? He didn't run away screaming at the sight of me, like an ordinary vampire. I should have staked and beheaded him, but—I don't know. Maybe he's some kind of super vampire. He could like, throw lightning bolts and hit without actual physical contact. And shoot fire from his eyes. I know, crazy, right? I wouldn't believe it myself if I hadn't seen it. And most vampires go to pieces in a church. Not this one. Not so you'd notice.

"Though my crucifix stopped him from biting me, and holy water burned him, so he *was* a vampire, and not some new and totally different sort of thing. He wasn't invincible; he felt the pain I dished out. But I—my arrow, my stake—I can't believe I missed! I was starting to get tired, and a bit scared, even, until I got my second wind. Kind of. But just when I thought I had him in the bag, he, um, well, he whipped me but good." She reddened, unused to admitting defeat. "The oddest thing was, when I came to, I was still alive! And he was still in the church! Now that was scary! Then I realized he'd changed… I know, impossible, right? But I felt it, saw it, looked into his face, into those eyes. Something about those eyes; I don't know. I—"

"Not mesmerization?" Father Mike frowned.

"No, not that. And he spoke, in the sweetest tone. Oh, my goodness, did I really just say that?" She blushed, then hurried on, "He said, er, he said he, um—loved me." She paused, forced her hands to remain still in her lap, and waited for a reaction. It came.

"What?! What vampire says that? You didn't fall for it, I hope! Why, it's a line as old as the hills! Scoundrels of the worst type use it! And a vampire, of all things! It doesn't mean a thing!"

Tears filled her eyes, and Father Mike nudged the box of tissues toward her.

"I'm sorry I—" he said in a softer tone. "I just didn't expect—"

"I told you." She dabbed at her eyes with a tissue. "Good grief. This is so silly, but I can't help it."

"No, no. Cry, if you must. We have more than enough tissues. Take your time. When you're ready, child, finish your story."

"It gets worse." She halted at his sudden stricken expression and looked away, swallowing hard. Finally, she lifted her gaze. "I ran away, Father. I didn't go home to my own bed, where I'd be safe. No. I cried myself to sleep under a tree."

She dashed her hand across her eyes. "Out in the open, where they could have killed me."

"Oh, thank God!" he burst out in a tone of relief. At her puzzled glance, he quickly amended, "I thought you were going to say—er, I mean, please continue."

"Do you suppose I'm losing it?" she said anxiously.

"No, you're not losing it. But a vampire? Love? That's—um, a little difficult to swallow."

"What did I tell you?"

"Fine. Er, have you seen this vampire since then?"

"No, but at night I can sense that he's out there."

"He hasn't tried to interfere or make contact?"

A tear escaped again. She quickly brushed it away. "No, but that's not what worries me. It's how I feel about him. I don't understand. Can vampires love?" She searched her mentor's face. "Gosh, and here I am, killing them."

"Hold on. What is a vampire, as we understand it?"

"Easy. It's a corpse that leaves its grave to suck the blood of mortals. Animated, some say, by a demon. It possesses preternatural powers, but can't tolerate sunlight and is essentially evil, in thrall to the powers of darkness." She rattled it off from memory, like reciting her catechism.

"Right. So, can darkness tolerate light? No more can evil love."

"Yes, but what about, you know, when he told me that Mary had taught him how to love? And unbelievable as it sounds, it was her voice telling me not to kill him." She felt suddenly uncomfortable under Father Mike's steady gray gaze and looked down. "Hey, I know that voice."

"Light and darkness cannot coexist."

"You said yourself that darkness is extinguished when confronted by light."

"Oh, so you do listen!" he said with a laugh, then grew serious again. "And the other side to the coin?"

"Darkness, if we give in to it, may snuff out the light. Yeah, I know, but what I'm saying is, at first contact, I got this sense of evil, as usual with vampires, right? Later it felt totally different. You know? Oh, how can I explain?"

Father Mike sat in silence, elbows on knees and chin resting on the steeple of his fingers, while she waited anxiously for him to respond. Finally, he sighed. "The decisions we make in life, all, all entail sacrifice. Often it is very difficult, but we must never base decisions solely on fickle feelings. If you—"

"Just a minute, Father," Mara broke in, "I didn't want this." Her eyes brimmed with tears again. "If it's just a feeling, tell me how to make it go away."

His gaze softened. "I only wish I could. I will say this: pray unceasingly. God's purpose is often not evident at first. We are part of His plan. We can't see the big picture, so we must trust in Him and serve Him always. You've been blessed, though I know it sometimes feels like a curse, and you're doing a fine job. If I may suggest something?" His calm somewhat allayed her anxiety, and she nodded. "If you see this vampire again, find out what he wants. I know, I know," he added hastily at her quick protest. "It's a risk. But this may be a test. Keep your wits about you and your heavenly guardians at your side, always. Your virtue is your shield and your buckler, as the saying goes. Evil is ever foiled by innocence."

"But," she said, her voice barely audible, "What if he gets inside your heart? Um, mine, that is."

The priest closed his eyes. She waited, anxious, afraid, yet hoping for the magic words that would make all this go away.

After a long moment, he lifted his gaze and spoke quietly. "Remember, you are set apart. Will Our Lord be pleased if you give yourself to a demon?"

"Our Lady said—"

"But was it she? The devil can appear in the most beautiful of forms and is the consummate mimic. You see, when he finds your weakness, by that door he will enter. Just don't plunge headlong into anything. Find out its purpose if you can, but be alert for treachery. From your own feelings, as well."

"My feelings?" The thought troubled her.

"Pray; always pray. The test of time will reveal the truth."

"I see," she said, blushing unaccountably.

"And if you have a problem, tell him to see me. I'll give him the third degree. Trust me. Finished that cookie yet? Drink your tea. Never let it be said that Father Michael sent you away hungry. Chin up!"

She had to smile. To please him, she managed to finish the cookie and iced tea. Then she rose from the chair. "Thanks, Father. I'd better scram, or I'll be late for supper. Anyway, I should let you go; it's almost time for evening Mass."

"Heavens, I didn't realize!" He glanced at his watch as he saw her to the door. "Is there anything else?"

"No, Father. That's it for now. Thanks. Or, wait a minute. My silver crucifix went missing that night at the church. If someone comes across it, well, I'd appreciate… "

"Actually, someone found an arrow stuck in the door; but your crucifix? You might need that. Wait right here," he said, his brow furrowed with concern. "I'll get you another. It'll only take a minute." He reached into his pocket for his keys.

"Oh, no, don't worry about it. My old one'll turn up." She grinned. "You wouldn't want those little old ladies starting Mass without you."

"Right. It's nearly five already. If you're sure?"

"I'll be fine," she assured him. "'Bye, I've got to run."

Mara had arranged to meet her friends that evening at Cup o' Java, the coffee shop where Sabrina worked. She hadn't been much fun lately, she was sure. Maggie, Josh, George, and Sabrina had been her friends ever since the days of sandboxes and mud pies. Even after they started school and made other friends, their original core group remained intact and more closely bonded than ever, even while others moved on.

She arrived early and stood in line to order. "I'll just have a cinnamon latte, Sabrina. We need to talk. No, don't ask."

"Sure. I'll be off in ten." Sabrina managed a smile. "The others'll be here after Maggie gets out of music practice."

"Okay, I'll grab a table outside."

Mara went out to the patio. Now that the sun was down, a cool breeze wafted off the mountains, refreshing after the heat of the day. She sat at one of the little round tables to sip the cinnamon-sprinkled froth of her drink. Though she had resolved to leave her problems at the door, it seemed that they had followed her. With a sigh, she leaned back and looked up. The Milky Way cut a glittering swath across the darkening blue velvet of the sky, visible to her keen eyes despite the glare of the town's lights. To take her mind off her troubles, trying not to think of him, she began picking out familiar celestial bodies and constellations. It didn't work. She glanced over her shoulder, furtively, and shivered at a sudden chill, her senses at once on high alert. This was not that mountain breeze. Automatically she reached for a hidden weapon, but then her heart skipped a beat, and her hand stopped. *Oh, dear. Not him again!*

The stars were forgotten, the darkness ominous as it pressed in on her. All conversation and clatter from the café faded as fainter sounds took center stage: most notably the whispering of the trees outside the pool of light and the sense of something unnatural lurking there. That chilled her.

She sipped her latte, trying in vain to focus her attention on its sweet coffee flavor and the just-as-sweet memory that it conjured up: of her dad whipping up a cappuccino Sunday morning after Mass on her thirteenth birthday, introducing her to the then-exotic beverage, that she'd thought was a taste of heaven (dear Dad!). But to no avail; the memory vanished, and she could sense the vampire's presence as surely as if he stood before her in broad daylight. *Leave me alone!* Outside the glow of patio lanterns was a wall of shadow, but she knew he was there.

"If you're going to hang around, show yourself!" she said a little sharply as she tried in vain to retrieve her cool.

She drew a quick breath as he materialized from the shadow at once.

She dared not look up; just the feel of his intense gaze on her was disturbing. To meet those eyes would be— She swirled her drink. "Okay, what do you want? I hate pests," she muttered, slapping a mosquito.

"You are in great peril, and I have come to protect you."

His voice was not unpleasant. That very fact annoyed her for some reason. She lifted her eyes to meet his. "You protect me? Hah! From what?" Though she felt a twinge of guilt for her bad manners, she was not about to let him see that.

"From vampires," he said quietly.

Vampires? He's one himself. Or, could he be ashamed? No, impossible! She pushed the thought down out of sight. "So. I need protection, now, do I? In case you haven't noticed, I'm always in great peril, and I kill vampires, regularly!" She was a bit disconcerted by how sneering that sounded, but, well, it was the truth. A shadow seemed to pass behind his eyes. *Suffer, creep! I haven't forgotten what you said, and did, and meant to do!* With self-righteous indignation, she tried to justify herself.

He spoke softly. "But now the master wants your head."

"Well, I'm sorry to disappoint him, but—no, actually, I'm not! Anyway, he's not going to get it. I've never had any trouble with vampires before, thank you very much. Nothing I couldn't handle, at least. Until you came along, that is," she amended. *Why did I just say that?* She gave him a long look with narrowed eyes. "Hey, they've always been out to get me, right from day one. And they haven't succeeded yet, have they?"

"No, not yet. And mostly, you've been out to get them," he contradicted. "Us, that is. Indeed, you have been much too efficient. So I was sent to get you. There is a difference, you see."

"And? You didn't get me, did you? For your bride, or otherwise. And if you're not careful, I'll have you down on your knees again."

He flinched as though she had struck him.

Ashamed, she lowered her eyes to her latte. *Hey, he deserved that.*

"Beware. They grow in strength," he said evenly.

Belatedly she recalled that she had meant to ask him to explain himself. She opened her mouth to speak, but he had vanished. She felt a sudden emptiness inside. An aching sense of loss and longing, as though she had stepped on a butterfly and crushed it beneath her foot, thoughtlessly destroying a thing of beauty.

The ache turned to self-deprecation. *Idiot! What if he knows something?* Father Mike said to talk to him, not insult him. *Oh, why is he doing this to me?* Tears sprang to her eyes.

Sabrina slid in beside her. "Holy! Who was that?"

Mara started as Sabrina's cheery voice broke into her gloom. She quickly dashed away her tears. "Oh, just some guy."

Sabrina plunked a sandwich and coffee on the table. "Nice! And you brushed him off?" She unwrapped her sandwich and took a big bite. "So. Is *he* the one? How come you didn't introduce him? Tell me. Quick, the other guys'll be showing up any minute."

Mara debated. Sabrina was kindhearted and pretty good at keeping secrets. It would be a relief to confide in someone her own age. "All right, but don't tell anyone."

"Cross my heart and hope to die."

Cold claws gripped Mara's insides. She shook herself; it's just a saying! "Um, it's not what you think. Really."

"You *have* fallen in love!" Sabrina's grin outshone her freckles in the glare of lights. "That's so cool. I'd so be on cloud nine!"

"Hold on. It's not like that. Really." Mara sighed. "It's a long story."

"I'm listening." Sandwich forgotten, Sabrina leaned her chin on her hand with an expectant air.

Mara lowered her voice. She sensed his presence yet, not

near, but still in the vicinity, and vampires had very keen senses. That was all she needed, to have him overhear her confession. "Well, Sabrina," she said softly, "You recall me mentioning that I go out at night and um, kill vampires."

"Yeah, but..." She gave Mara a long look. "Oh, dear, I don't know how to say this. It's just so far out and scary I decided that maybe you didn't mean it literally. It's, er, kind of off the wall, isn't it?"

"Totally. That's why I don't talk about it much—I mean, well, people kind of give me that look, like I belong in the psych ward."

"I get that, totally," Sabrina said sympathetically, though with a little crease of worry between her brows. "A question. So how come I've never seen a vampire? If they're real, that is."

"Believe me, they're real." You've just seen one, Mara almost said, but couldn't quite get the words out. "Hey, I'm not making this up."

"Oh, Mara, I know you wouldn't lie." Sabrina gave her a troubled glance. "Not that I want to see one—gosh, no. I even hate vampire movies." She shuddered. "So gory and gross. Ugh."

"You have no idea," Mara said under her breath.

Sabrina went on. "My little brother tells me all I never wanted to know about them. Timmy's read every vampire comic book he can get his hands on." She giggled, but when Mara didn't join in, her grin faded. "Would you just get to the good part? I mean about you falling in love. Anyway, what does that have to do with vampires?"

"Hush. He'll hear you."

Sabrina looked around. "What?" she whispered. "Oh, that guy?"

Mara took a deep breath and lowered her voice even more. "You've just seen him."

"Gosh! Really? That handsome guy is your..."

"Hold on. I'm not finished." She took the plunge. "You've

seen a vampire. He's a vampire."

Sabrina stared. "No! You mean…?"

"Yes. He keeps following me around, to protect me, he says. I don't know why. I've managed fine up until now. And he said he loves me, but hey — he's the enemy! Or was. Anyway, vampires can't love. So you see what a fine mess I'm in." Mara heaved a long sigh and leaned her head on her hands, pressing her temples.

"You love him?"

"No, of course not. Or, I don't know, maybe that's what this is all about. How am I supposed to know? It's never happened to me before. It's a little scary, under the circumstances."

"No, it's kind of cool, actually." She lowered her voice. "He, er, he looks human to me. And gorgeous! I thought vampires were ugly, creepy-looking things. Of course, I only caught a glimpse. You're sure he's a vampire?"

"Yes, he is. Believe me, he wasn't gorgeous when I first saw him, but something happened, I don't know what, and — " Mara sighed. "I knew it. You don't believe me."

"I'm sorry, Mara, I want to believe you. He's not just wearing a costume?"

Mara shook her head in exasperation. Leaning close, she whispered, "No, Sabrina, he's not. I ought to know. We fought; he tried to bite me. He has totally sharp teeth and sucks blood. He levitates, and can burn you just by looking at you, or hit you with an invisible force — "

"Gosh!" Sabrina said, agog. "Vampires can really do that?"

"Shh, keep it down, would you? They have very good hearing," Mara whispered. "To answer your question, yes, apparently they can. Or some of them, anyway. He can. Believe me, I saw it, felt it; I guess I ought to know."

"Okay," Sabrina said slowly, her brow creasing again. "Does he love you because you, um, taste good, or — sorry. Erase that. I didn't mean to make a joke of it. It's just that, well, you know."

"Right. I'm so unlovable. It's not funny. Sabrina, I don't

know what to do. It just happened. We didn't plan it. One minute we were trying to kill each other, and the next, well—"

"You fell in love?"

"Oh dear. I said I don't know." Mara was beginning to regret having told her, but it was so lonely keeping things to herself.

"That's so romantic," cried Sabrina. "I think. Are you going to introduce him? Er, he won't bite us, will he?"

A commotion announced the arrival of Maggie, George, and Josh. Mara gave Sabrina the keep mum signal. She meant to confide in them soon, but not yet.

Josh pulled up a chair and sat down at the table. "Who's biting?" Tall and dark-haired, he was something of an artistic jack-of-all-trades, particularly adept at metalwork. He had attended martial arts classes with Mara since he was ten and liked to imagine himself another Jackie Chan.

"This espresso has a real bite to it," George said as he pushed his thick, black-framed glasses back into place. He was the computer nerd of their group. "I wonder what they put in it." He took a sip. "Ow! It's hot!"

"Tabasco sauce?" Josh joked. "What are you drinking, Mara? Oh, a latte. Not spiked; your long face says it all. Come on, life's not so bad when you consider the alternative."

The boys' clowning around and stale jokes were just a ploy to cheer her up, Mara knew, and felt a rush of warmth. To please them, she attempted a laugh.

Maggie apologized for being late as she tied her long dark hair back with a red band. "You know how it is. The opera's in two weeks; I can't miss even one practice." She played the cello in the college orchestra, which accompanied the performances of the drama class.

Mara made an effort to join in the banter, to hide her inner turmoil. Peals of laughter rang out in the night. Some were hers.

The Prince watched longingly from the shadows. Her rebuff

cut deep, and he only just managed not to stagger as he retreated to the shelter of the grove. Only with great effort did he quell those ancient monsters of fury and frustration and despair rising up to engulf him. While his interior battle raged, the roaring in his ears drowned out Mara's conversation with Sabrina. By the time he finally regained his usual calm, he heard her laughter, and it seemed to him as though she had not a care in the world. None for him, at least. And he felt as though his heart had been shredded.

The Underworld Stirs

Mara said goodnight to her friends as they parted company, dismissing their offer to walk her home. She was fine, she told them; it was she who must walk them home, when necessary. They laughed as usual; this had always been a standing joke, and they were used to her odd sense of humor. Yet, for some reason, this time, their laughter rang a bit hollow. Were they starting to realize that it was all true, after all?

Whenever she had on occasion mentioned to them about her dealings with vampires, they nodded and smiled, and oohed and aahed, or sometimes got a bit scared, but it only seemed like when as children they'd tell ghost stories around a bonfire at night. Not real, whatever she said, not even when she lectured on the wonders of garlic or hinted that after sundown, she became a walking arsenal, a sort of lone vigilante. Even when she unzipped her jacket and showed them. She was their friend; they accepted her, quirks and all. Even now, after all, she had told Sabrina (and she had even caught a glimpse of him), she could tell that even Sabrina didn't get it.

Before Mara reached the hedge of pink azaleas along the street near her home, she sensed the presence of vampires. She continued walking as though nothing was out of the ordinary. It wasn't, except for the fact that she was accustomed to encountering vampires singly—two or three at most—not large groups of them. These were the common garden variety, too; nothing like the fell beast she'd battled in the church. But these didn't cut and run, as vampires usually did when they realized who she was. (She often had to chase them down.) As she felt the chill warning of imminent attack, weapons sprang into her hands almost of their own accord. The vampires' charge was blundering, inept; they were no match for her, and they should have known that. Eleven she staked in a matter of minutes; the rest fled, and within seconds had vanished.

Fifteen! She frowned. *Something strange is afoot.*

The four survivors reported to the master that the Huntress was alive and well. There was no sign of the Prince. The cavern shook as Charon roared in fury and frustration. What had happened to his favorite? The four slunk away, trembling and relieved to have escaped with their hides intact.

Charon fell silent and sat for a long time, brooding. Impossible that the Huntress should defeat the Prince. Likely he was biding his time for reasons known only to himself. But Charon recalled his feeling of unease, and this was his favorite. More importantly, he had no time for riddles and games. His New Kingdom was at hand. If something critical had altered, he needed to know now.

He chose Nyx to lead the next expedition into enemy territory, seeking the Prince or definite information about him. A little band of the elite would accompany her. Ten of the best set forth under a new and darkened moon, a time when their keen night vision gave them the edge. The Huntress was not to be taken lightly, even so, but they were confident that she would find them much more of a challenge than the initial scouting party.

A week later, Mara was leaving the downtown Starlight Theater with her friends just before midnight when she sensed his presence at once. Still, she wasn't about to admit that she might have missed him.

She looked around furtively, on edge. There was no moon, and a thin, dark veil of mist crept upward, gradually obscuring the stars. She knew that the enemy favored the darkest nights when she couldn't see them in the shadows. Her other senses compensated, however. She could still smell them, hear them, and feel the chill of their presence. She could also distinguish somewhat between individual vampires. No doubt about which one this was—would he never stop haunting her? She continued on with her friends, making an effort to join in the laughter and discussion of the movie, despite being keenly aware of him.

Josh pumped his fists into the air and did a bit of shadowboxing. "That last fight scene was totally rad!"

"Yeah, Jackie Chan has some neat moves, all right," agreed Mara, trying to look attentive, though her mind was elsewhere.

"Whoa, man, that tall guy could totally do the splits," Josh raved. "If I could do that, I—"

"Hmhmm," she said absently, even as she concentrated on the faint sounds hidden behind traffic noises and the chatter of groups of moviegoers leaving the theater. Something wasn't right.

"Are you still with us, Mara?" said Maggie. "I have to admit, it was actually a pretty entertaining movie, though I'm not usually keen on the martial arts stuff."

"Timmy loves Jackie Chan movies," Sabrina put in, referring to her twelve-year-old brother. "I, myself, on the other hand..."

"They're funny, too," said George, adjusting his glasses. "I love it when he wrecks cars. I wonder if it's real, or—how do they do that?" He stared off into the distance. He was experimenting with games and software programming, and Mara figured he was working out the graphics in his head for some new scenario.

"If you've seen one, you've seen them all," Sabrina yawned. "They wreck cars in every movie."

"Hey. Not all of them," protested George. "Like—"

"The old Chinese ones are really cool." Josh threw a few punches just short of George's head. "Even without cars."

George ducked, as a matter of course, but was still off in la-la land. "Hey! I could use that! You know how they—"

"What's Humpty-Dumpty doing out this late at night?"

Maggie interrupted, pointing toward the neighborhood ice cream truck parked at an odd angle against the curb, just up the street. Humpty-Dumpty was the name they had privately assigned to the pudgy driver.

"Maybe he fell off the wall—I mean the wagon," Josh snickered. "And all the king's horses and, well, you know."

This time his joking didn't bring a smile to Mara's face. She broke into a run, her heart pounding. She caught a faint sound, almost like a whisper. A warning? Or was it only the breeze sighing through the trees?

"What the heck's with her now?" Josh muttered.

She neared the truck, saw the set gray face of the driver slumped over the wheel, the twin puncture wounds at his throat. Too late. He was dead.

"Call nine-one-one," she ordered when Josh came up behind her, panting after his sprint up the street.

Sabrina's mouth fell open. "Oh, poor Humpty-Dumpty!"

Mara turned away, leaped to the sidewalk and paused, scanning for signs. There! She ran like a deer around the corner and into a vacant lot. The body of a man lay in the weeds, his ashen face turned to the sky and eyes dulled by death. A broken bottle lay beside him. Wine stained his shirt and the ground. On his throat were the marks of fangs.

As she paused in the alley to reconnoiter, Mara thought she heard that whisper again, so faint that she had to stop panting to listen. It could have been the wind through the trees, but in her heart, she knew.

Wait, not now. They are many, and you…

Leave me alone. This is my life. I know what I'm doing.

She ran down the alley, following signs invisible to ordinary mortals. From above came the sound of fluttering wings, at first faintly and then louder, until she wanted to duck her head. She quickly scanned the sky; it was empty. From up ahead came a scrabbling of claws on brick. She hastened toward the sound.

A chill crept over her like a blast of cold air in the warm

night. They were here. She couldn't see them, but she could sense them. Her ears picked up faint sounds—the rustling of cloaks and the rush of air currents in the wake of movement—echoing all around. Now, with every sense aquiver, she felt their presence. *St. Michael, help me.* As she paused to warily scan her surroundings, her hands automatically went for her stakes.

These weren't ordinary vampires, easily done away with; and not just one, but seven, eight, no—ten of them?! That gave her pause, but for only a moment. She had faced more, and worse (though only one, *that* time). But she had survived, hadn't she? For the first time, she felt a qualm. No, no time for that. She breathed a quick prayer, trusting in the aid of her celestial protectors more than any strength or device of her own.

The crunch of her feet on the gravel was loud in the night. Noises echoed all around her, scrabbling, slithering, as shadow melted into shadow. High above, wings flapped, or at least it sounded like wings.

The Prince was never very far away. He followed her, wanting to help, but refraining. By her reputation as well as personal experience, he was aware of her capabilities. She knew what she was about when it came to killing vampires. He told himself that he need not be anxious on her account. Still, everything had changed now. He would gladly fight every battle for her to preserve her from the slightest hurt. Unfortunately, his one attempt to impose his protection upon her had shown him the sharp edge of her tongue, a keen awareness of her mixed feelings about him, and even more definite ones about her independence.

So, she thought she didn't need him. She did need him. A mere girl standing alone against the legions of the Underworld as they manifested themselves in her physical world. How could she not see? He was offering to help; how had she dared refuse him? His first impulse was to throw up his hands and leave her to her fate, to rend and tear in a fury all that should oppose his will. But no, that was the old Prince, who had cared for nothing and no one but himself, who had valued power and blood above all. Everything was different now. No. *He* was different.

He had tried to warn her; she threw his kind offer back into his teeth. Flames of fury engulfed his heart in an instant at the thought; but no, he dared not let anger possess him. She didn't understand; didn't know she needed him. She didn't trust him and so dared not accept the help of her former foe. Or, perhaps she didn't need him, but he needed her. How unworthy he was, he realized. She knew that, of course. A terrifying thought. If she should reject him, he was lost. She was his lifeline, a gossamer thread only, but his sole link to any hope of redemption, and the one thing that kept him from falling into despair.

He watched from the shadows, following her every move. Because of him, Mara was in greater danger than ever, and there was nothing he could do to change that.

Nyx's presence meant the master was concerned about the Prince's failure to return, perhaps thinking he needed their help—or was beyond it. No matter his whereabouts, elimination of the Huntress was still the prime directive. Once they discovered he wasn't going back, the order of his own demise would be running a close second. He had no illusions. The master was not forgiving of transgressions.

No matter. He had no concern for that. First of all, he did not believe they could defeat him. He feared more that the full power of the master's diabolical inventiveness would be ranged against one mere girl, huntress though she was. He recalled other huntresses; those with whom he himself had dealt. It had not been easy, but was worth the risk; even now he could taste the power of their blood! And shuddered with the effort not to remember, to not sink into despair at the evil of all that he had done. Or, heaven forbid, be tempted once more. He could not afford that now. Not if she needed his help.

Her soft footfalls whispered from the alley, and his spirit was drawn from the abyss once more. Just knowing she was there, alive, beautiful, and good, his heart overflowed, and he wanted to burst into song. He sensed her determination, recalled her repudiation of his help. If only she would not let the tangle of emotions distract her. Paradoxically, his cold heart rejoiced that he should be the cause of her disturbance, though anxious lest that very thing increase her peril.

As the vampires moved in to surround her, they didn't notice him at all, strangely. But dealing with a huntress was apt to take all one's concentration, he knew.

The Prince drifted nearer, a blur of black flowing from one shadow to melt into the next. The alley was lined with buildings defaced by graffiti, some of wood with peeling paint, others of old brick or crumbling adobe. A chain-link fence, hung with litter, bordered a vacant lot.

He heard the clattering of a pebble dislodged somewhere down the alley, a scrabbling on the roof, and something slithering down the side of a building. These were the faint sounds of her foes' stealthy approach. Stronger was his perception of each one of them, so familiar, these his former comrades.

Nyx was leading (the master would send her!), but that was no reason to despair. She did not have him by her side, and a huntress was no easy mark at the best of times. Now she flowed into the narrow opening between a brick building and the wooden one next to it.

He could see the Sandman creeping over the eaves and down the brick wall. Silently, until his claws slipped with a faint scrabbling sound.

At that, Mara paused. As if on cue, all sound died. The Sandman was invisible to mortal eyes as he clung to the wall in deathlike stillness. Across the way, the pale glimmer of moon-bright locks on the shop roof betrayed Styx's position. Sweet William had folded his tall, slender form in the shadow of a garbage can. As soon as Mara moved on, the Rocket scuttled across the next roof and the others crept closer. Though hidden from their quarry, they were plain to the watcher. He saw Reed waft in from the far end of the alley. Sirocco was following in the wake of the Huntress. Bellatrix flitted down out of the sky with her two boys at her elbows.

The Prince watched as Mara listened and scanned the area. Once more, the whole world seemed to stand still. Then she tensely resumed her pace down the alley, past a row of garbage cans beside a faded green door, until at last, she came alongside the brick building.

Mara anticipated their descent. They were there in a sudden rush of wind, dropping out of the sky, swooping down on her from the roofs and out of narrow spaces between buildings. They came, several at once, and then one after another, yet keeping just out of reach of her flying hands and feet.

As she whirled to fend them off, a cloak brushed her cheek. She sidestepped and her fists landed solidly, spinning her attacker off balance. From the corner of her eye, she caught sight of another coming back at her, fast; his gaping mouth loomed over her shoulder. She whipped up an elbow to smash his face and knocked him to the ground. He shook his head, dazed. Now a stake to the heart. But suddenly, she was too busy, fending off two more coming at her from opposite directions. And more. She lost count. Too many.

She did a flip out of their reach, her golden braid flying, and landed in a crouch, whipped out a stake and turned slowly to face them all. They stood around her in a semi-circle, barely visible in their cloaks that blended them into the shadows. Nine of them (*oh, where is the tenth?*) crouching, snarling, hissing. Teeth glinted in the dark; all those eyes were flat and dead. None were glowing to shoot fire, thank God.

Upon the heels of that thought came the missing tenth one. She seemed to materialize from their midst, her purposeful gaze upon Mara. Mara's stake automatically pointed toward this new threat as unerringly as a compass points to true north. For some reason, this one seemed strangely unconcerned, standing out from the rest as perhaps a more powerful foe. The leader, maybe, though smallest of all. Her black cloak was gorgeous, studded with stars; her wild black hair framed a delicate, heart-shaped face. At first glance, she seemed just a pretty girl in stylish harem pants and black leather boots—until she smiled. Those teeth were not pretty. Nor was the horrible, long tongue that whipped out to lick blood from her lips.

Mara had seen the same many times before, but now she felt sickened. Angered and aggrieved at the thought of Humpty-Dumpty and the man in the vacant lot. It was their blood. She took it as a personal affront. She should have prevented those deaths. Instead, she was gallivanting with her friends at the theater when she should have been out patrolling, keeping the streets safe (from the immortal foe, at least).

With an effort, she locked these distracting emotions into a corner of her consciousness, concentrating with cold detachment on the task before her. She focused on the star-cloaked one. "Come and get it, you—" she halted as those eyes began to glow.

Mara had learned her lesson during her battle with the beast in the church. Her long knife appeared like magic. She flipped her hand so that the beam that shot out toward her from those terrible eyes ricocheted from the flat of her blade and flashed back at her attackers. They shrieked and scattered. She had no time to breathe a sigh of relief; the little leader rushed to the attack. Mara leaped forward to meet her with stake foremost and blade swinging, but the vampire threw herself aside. At the same moment, Mara sensed movement behind and spun around to plunge the stake into another vampire heart, sending the tall, skinny, colorless vampire writhing and screeching to the ground, clawing at his chest until he exploded into dust.

Mara whirled back, but had not quite recovered her balance when something slammed into her and knocked her to the ground. Her knife went skittering across the alley. The attacking vampire spun around and rushed to take advantage. Mara rolled and came up in a crouch to face him, stake in hand. He halted, growling. Another appeared beside him. And another. So many black cloaks and black eyes all fixed on her, tongues flicking out.

"Come on, suckers, what are you waiting for?" She muttered, her eyes darting from one to the next.

As if on a signal, the blonde with blood on her mouth moved in on her right; the sandy-haired one in the trench coat eased in on her left. From the corner of her eye, Mara caught a glimpse of long red hair as a wiry one slunk in behind her, but when she turned to keep them all in view, he melted into the shadows. The others backed away from her glare, for her bold stance intimidated them. It was now mostly bluff, but they didn't know that. Mara wasn't one to quail, no matter the odds, but this time…*He warned me. If only I had my crossbow. He knew, somehow. I should have listened. Lord, forgive me my pride. Okay, St. Michael, don't let me down. Eyes hard, she faced her foe. This is my job. I will do it.*

When in doubt, attack. A swift forward thrust kick caught the bloody chin of the blonde with a snap that sent her back against the fence. The sandy-haired one levitated and rushed at Mara. She spun in midair and kicked him in the head, sending him flying against a brick wall. The redhead materialized before her. A fist to the throat knocked him back. A fourth moved in, a distraction as a fifth sprang. She hadn't seen him coming, that lively Arab-looking one, but quick reflexes and desperation saved her. The stake struck dead on, but she hit the ground hard with him on top, the breath slammed out of her. Trapped! A high-pitched shriek at her ear jolted her to her senses. She scrambled to extricate herself as the staked vampire writhed for a moment, but he disintegrated, taking the tangle of cloak with him as the dust of his remains settled around her. She rolled away.

Too late. Shadows sprang from all sides and descended from

above, crushing her beneath them. She was pinned fast to the ground as surely as a butterfly to a board. Billowing cloaks settled down around her, their fetid odor suffocating, her cheek pressed into the gravel.

She prayed, *Jesus, help me!*

In that moment of deepest urgency, she remembered that she wasn't wearing her crucifix. *No!* To be caught without that most necessary defense!

She arched her back, laboring to breathe, to throw them off, but their weight pressed her to the ground. A thought struck her: how can such light, flying creatures be so heavy?

The Prince drifted upward, unnoticed, to get a clearer view. He was hopeful now (yet not entirely certain) that Mara would emerge from this altercation unscathed. Presently he descended to the roof of a bleak warehouse and crouched in the lee of a chimney to observe, unseen.

Back and forth the battle went, from one side of the alley to the other, a whirlwind of vampires spun through with one valiant little huntress. The Prince was awed at the ease with which she dealt with his kind while minimizing the danger to herself (his previous such encounters were seen from quite a different perspective). He leaned forward intently. Each huntress had her own style. Even they were not invincible, however; he was a little on edge, but he reminded himself that in the battle with him, she had held her own.

Though against ten of the elite... How quickly she dispatched Reed and Sirocco! He could not help smiling a little proudly; both were veterans of many a battle, long before he himself had come on the scene. It had always seemed that they would be around forever. Just as he was expecting her to send the rest of them fleeing in disarray (or to annihilate them all), she went down and did not get up. She disappeared beneath the black as before, but this time she did not reappear.

He waited, but no graceful, golden-haired heroine parted that tangle of shadow to rise again in full battle mode. He leaned forward. Coldness grew inside as he sensed vampire triumph, and life force slowly diminishing. He felt a pang of fear within his heart. No, deeper — in his very soul.

Frozen, disbelieving, he stared down at the terrible black vortex that had swallowed her. He sensed her horror and dismay, her silent plea. Where were her protectors? His eyes tried to pierce the billowing cloaks that had settled down around her, drowning her in shadow. Nothing. No bright golden gleam of hair, no flashing blade or leaping stake, no white avenging arm rising above the dark.

And then he was down, off the roof and in the alley, scattering them. She revived at once. Leaped to her feet and breathed deeply of air and freedom. He exulted at the sight. He felt her warmth, heard her heartbeat even at a distance, for he had swooped in, and in the next instant was far removed from the scene, unwilling to intrude. His relief that she was not dead was almost more than he could bear.

She assumed her defensive stance at once, her eyes darting here and there, scanning for the enemy. He felt her confusion and unaccustomed disorientation. As though uncertain of how she had been freed, or what dark force had scattered the enemy. Perhaps disbelieving what her senses told her, or rejecting it, and him?

He held back, concealed in shadow, heavy of heart. *Must let her be.* It took all the strength of his resolve to fade further into shadow, to steel himself not to impose. He turned away with an effort, only wanting to die. If she turned on him in fury, if he lost her, everything else was dust and ash.

A mad scramble of flying gravel and sounds as of wings flapping reached a swift crescendo, and he knew that her attackers had swarmed upon her again, instantaneously. He sensed that strange disorientation that still had her in its grip, and turned back. She had been caught off guard. Though she tried bravely to defend herself, they all converged upon her at once. She should not have let them... Something was wrong. They had her pinned again.

Odd that they did not notice what he had done; they did not appear to sense his presence at all. Mystified, he looked on as they crowded around the Huntress, gripping her arms, her throat, her hair, and pressed her to the wall. Their swirling cloaks all but hid her as they snarled in her face.

How had they managed, when he himself had not? was his fleeting thought.

Restrained as she was, they were still afraid of her. Her struggles to escape were of no avail, but she looked into the very face of death, her indomitable spirit undimmed.

And he stood admiring. He felt detached in some strange way, as though in some no-man's-land; at a crossroads, perhaps, caught between worlds. Newly aligned with the Huntress by love and honor-bound to protect her from his kind, yet he could not find it in himself to coldly dismiss five hundred years of loyalty to the Brotherhood. Not without some consideration, some action of the will, some conscious deliberation and the making of a decision. Not when that very sense of honor, which, warped though it may have been, was his only redeeming quality for five centuries.

He looked upon them now—comrades, though with no possibility of love between them, they had been as brothers-in-arms. That, even to the evil, commanded some loyalty.

Constrained by the vestiges of his erstwhile feelings for them, he saw them now: the proud and scornful Nyx; the elegant and sulky Rocket; sweet-faced Styx. He knew them all. On the far side were the slinky Sweet William and the tousle-haired Sandman (though minus his usual boyish grin and scanning the skies as though he sensed danger). Creeping up warily was that shameless wench Bellatrix in her flashy dress, with her two boy-shadows, the sneaky little redheaded back-stabber Rojo and pretty-boy poet China Boy.

Their exultant victory, their condescension toward the captured Huntress, their intention of drinking her blood and assuming her power came at him in waves, in sensations that were overwhelming. They had not killed her yet? He stood dazed, looking. No, of course not. But they were so close, too close.

He would not allow… and yet, how could he help but empathize with them? The feeling, powerful, compelling, all in all to a vampire, the heat of mortal blood flowing through the veins. He leaned forward without thought, afire with anticipation, stark hunger rising.

He felt again the red-haired angel's fiery touch upon his brow and shook himself. *What am I doing? My love…* With a snarl, he was upon them. He threw Styx aside and turned as the Sandman rushed him. He caught him by the throat in a vise-like grip and pinned him against the wall, his jaws wide and threatening.

"Prince!" the Sandman cried out in the shock of sudden recognition. "Brother! It is I, the Sandman. You wouldn't kill me, would you?" he added with some misgiving.

Am I different somehow, that he did not know me? The Prince, somewhat disconcerted, relaxed his grip, and as the Sandman darted out of reach, realized his mistake. They had not known! Now there was nothing for it but to brazen it out, to try to recover the chance he had so madly thrown away. He turned to face Nyx. Her knowing gaze caught his; her lips curved into a smile.

"So you are still with us, are you, Prince?" she said softly. A warning, he realized, with her razor-sharp claws at Mara's throat. He dared not make the wrong move.

He could not think. How had he let Mara get into their clutches? *My fault.* His eyes flicked toward the sulky-faced Rocket holding Mara's other arm. A look of apprehension crossed the Rocket's face under the Prince's glance, but his lip curled, and he tightened his grip.

How to answer? Her question seemed loaded with meaning. Did she guess? Maybe it was best to pretend everything was as it should be and going according to plan.

"We've caught your Huntress," said Bella at his elbow. "Thanks to your flushing her out for us. Neat trick." Rojo and

China Boy had assumed strategic positions at Bella's elbows.

The Prince turned his head to meet those sultry black eyes. Thanks to you... neat trick. The words echoed through his mind: Neat trick... neat trick. No, it is not true. I... "This is my huntress," he growled. "What are you doing here?" The red glow of his eyes reflected in Bella's, and suddenly she was no longer at his elbow. From a safer distance, she and her two boy-shadows fixed apprehensive gazes upon him.

Styx seemed perplexed and distressed by his mad action.

The Sandman watched with unblinking eyes. "Sorry, Prince," he said in a careful tone. "We thought—"

The Rocket shifted nervously, his eyes flicking from Nyx to the Prince and back as he realized that he was in the unenviable position of perhaps being caught in a crossfire. Sweet William slunk in from behind and halted just short of the danger zone.

"You thought—you thought what?" the Prince said in his more natural tone, soft, dangerous. Bent upon reassuring them that he was his usual self, but suspecting that he had already blown it.

"The master was worried," Nyx replied, her tone at once conciliatory. "When you did not return... and, well, the Huntress was still up to her usual tricks..."

Of course. The master trusted no one. Not even his favorite. "As you can see, I am here." He tried to steady his voice. "This is my mission alone. I will do this my own way. Leave it to me. Now."

Nyx looked him in the eyes. She knew. He blinked and shook his head. Did those beautiful black eyes still have the power to mesmerize him just as they had so long ago? None of that, now. It would be of no use to tempt fate.

"Be careful, Prince," Nyx said, "She's lively yet. Let's—"

"I'll deal with it!" he snarled.

They all flinched, even Nyx, but she recovered at once. "We only ask that you share, after we caught her for you."

Maybe he had not fooled her or any of them. If only he could think straight. He felt the heat of the mortal body from where he was standing; heard the racing of the heart, felt the anxiety that the Huntress so valiantly tried to conceal.

"After you, of course," Nyx hastened to add, still unsure of him, maybe. "And I demand my satisfaction." Her voice lowered to a growl. "You promised."

He *had* promised. But that was before. Now he could not stop staring at that sweet, perfect face. He knew all eyes were on him, but could not seem to help himself. That hair of shining gold, disheveled after her fight and the rough handling by her captors, was still beautiful; and her eyes, blue as the summer sky.

"If you can't do this," Bella ventured, "my Rojo will."

At that, he whipped around, eyes blazing; they all shrank back, Rojo absolutely cringing at being singled out. Satisfied that they showed the fear to which he was accustomed, the Prince turned to confront Nyx once more. She was not afraid, surely.

She fixed him with narrowed eyes. He managed, with an effort, to reclaim his calm, somewhat. It would take a clear head to deal with her.

Despite his resolve, the Prince looked at Mara again. A pain like an arrow pierced his heart.

"Are you well?" Nyx said from somewhere far away. "Say something, Prince. Prince!" He knew his eyes were glowing, but couldn't seem to stop them. "Prince, no! Don't. We—"

The Rocket hissed.

"The master, he waits," said Bella, her hungry look on him now. "Bring in her head tonight and ¡ay de mi! Your reward will be beyond your most loveliest dream, I heard him say."

"You will rule at his right hand forever." Nyx spoke softly, but her eyes flared red.

With effort, he subdued his own glow.

"So," she resumed, seemingly covering her relief with a patina of concern, "What is going on here? Has something happened?"

"Yes." That got their attention. "She is mine. You have done your part. I will take her now."

At that, they exchanged uneasy glances.

"Styx!" rasped the Sandman.

At once, Styx had her arms around his waist, her blonde head pressed against his chest, just like old times, but not; he found he could no longer coldheartedly push her away.

"What's wrong, my sweet Prince?" Those big blue eyes tugged at his heart. They were blue, like Mara's, yet not like them in any other way. "Come back to us," she whined. "What's happened to you? You're different."

He tried to extricate himself; she clung to him so tenaciously, and he found himself reluctant to hurt her. Oh, how could Styx, or any of them, affect him so? He felt blindsided just as he had begun to piece together all the recent events. First Mara, now this? Could it be that his newfound capacity for love and decency applied to these too? He looked upon them now with grieving, compassionate eyes.

"Take your prize to the master, my Prince," Nyx pleaded. "Now, tonight, and the world will be at your feet. Think of it!"

Had she guessed that he did not mean to? Did they know?

"Whatever will I do? You made me for yourself," Styx wailed, as though in answer to his unspoken thoughts.

He turned his face away; felt torn apart inside by this reminder of what he had been, and done. He tried to escape those clinging hands. If only he could think clearly.

"Whatever has happened, you are one of us," Nyx said softly. "Nothing can change that." She still had the power to manipulate his feelings, it seemed, even when he was not looking into her eyes.

And Styx. Her touch, her voice, and ah, such sweet memories. He found himself fighting a terrible interior battle for clarity in the midst of confusion, for his very soul.

"The master need never know," the Sandman said. "We'll never tell."

The Rocket turned his face aside, but could not hide his sneer.

Never know? Never tell? What did they guess? The Prince tried to think. One corner of his mind noted that Mara had renewed her struggle against her captors. She had seen the effect they were having on him. Was it so obvious, his turmoil? He felt shamed, and yet he had to sort through the tangle. Somehow.

"Samael, my Angel of Death." Nyx well knew the persuasive power of his chosen name. "You belong to me. You are mine. I made you." She touched his cheek; her tone grew tender. "How drawn you look, Prince. You haven't neglected to feed, have you?"

He bared his teeth in an involuntary grimace of disgust. And yet, he felt that insidious stirring within.

Styx slid her arms around his neck. "Yes, you must feed, dear. Here, let me help." And she kissed him on the mouth.

At the taste of blood, the hunger hit him like a bolt of lightning. The others smiled and exchanged knowing glances. Mara knew, too, what had happened; he felt her fear, the sudden racing of her pulse, from where he stood. And the inevitable response inside himself. The monster had awakened.

"That's it," said Styx softly. "Feel that heartbeat. Blood is what you want. Need. Come, have a bite. I will help you."

"Get me my prize," hissed Nyx, eyes aglow. "Now."

The Prince slowly turned, and his eyes fixed on Mara. He felt her heartbeat take hold of him. Only the Rocket held her now; he was stronger than he looked and had her pinned to the wall so she couldn't move, couldn't escape. His tongue flicked against her cheek. She turned her face away in disgust.

The Rocket laughed. "Better hurry if you want the first bite, Prince," he dared to say. "I'm ravenous!"

The Prince was silent, caught up in an interior struggle against the dark forces threatening to pull him under: Styx's siren song; Nyx's explicit reminders of the euphoria of times past. Other victims, other huntresses. The blood, the power, the ecstasy. The fire. Ah, to feel that again. The drumming grew louder; it seemed to pulse in his own veins. The mortal was nearer to him now. The warmth of that living human body, and its precious heartbeat, drew him. Against his will, images crowded his mind, overwhelming, irresistible. Here was the blood of a huntress right at his fingertips; powerful, sweet, there was nothing like it, he knew well. It was to feel alive, or the nearest thing to it, at least. *Ah, one small taste couldn't hurt.* Oh, how he needed this!

"Come on, Prince. You get the first bite, then we'll join in the feasting. Just like old times." The Sandman's voice, intense and hungry, jarred him.

"Oh, yes!" The Rocket pressed close.

With a languid hand, the Prince reached out to touch Mara's hair, to grasp it as he had once before. A lifetime ago? She lifted her gaze to his face. His heart was stabbed to the quick as he thought of what she must see there. What a sight he must be, with blood on his lips and his tongue flicking out to taste! And yet... He couldn't distinguish the meaning rising from the gaze of her eyes. Not reproach, fear, loathing, nor the bitterness of betrayal.

Could it be love and forgiveness? Surely not.

The temptation was overwhelming. Confusion, hunger, sorrow, all threatened to drown him in the terrible morass of his craving. His gaze dropped to the pulse at her throat. He bent his head. There was no crucifix this time to fend him off. He felt her quick panting breaths at his ear, the quiver of warm, perfect flesh as she shrank from his touch, from his teeth.

"St. Michael, Blessed Mother, help him," she breathed.

His head snapped back as her words jolted him into the real world, the fog in his mind cleared away in an instant. Struck to the heart by that reminder of the transformation done in him, by whom, and where. *Ah, Mother of Mercy, what have I done? So soon after...*

He looked down at that sweet face so entirely at his mercy — he had been about to hurt, to kill, his one true love. And with it his own soul and hope of redemption. How near he had come to returning to the mire from whence he had so recently been drawn! He dropped his gaze in shame. His first major temptation, and he had nearly blown it. In sorrow and despair, in absolute self-disgust, he turned his face away. He wanted to weep, to die.

But neither was possible. Not for a vampire.

Was there to be no deliverance from this terrible curse? *Forgive me, my God! Why did you choose me for this honor, unworthy vessel that I am? How can she ever love such as I?*

A thought struck him: she had prayed not for herself, but for him. She hadn't pleaded for her life, though maybe she should have, for all the good it would do if… Yes, she did need him. But that seemed irrelevant now. *I love her; that is all that need be said.* He slowly lifted his gaze to hers. His hand slid from its terrible grasp of her hair, downward to caress her cheek. Oblivious to his audience, he gazed, enraptured, into that face, those eyes. And revealed his heart to them all.

A hiss brought him back to the stark reality of danger. With a flash of fangs, the Rocket went for Mara's throat. The Prince was faster; he slammed the Rocket against the wall. Other hands grasped at the Prince. He turned to shrug them off, and in that split second of inattention, the Rocket flung himself out of reach. He turned with a defiant sneer, looked into the Prince's blazing eyes, but dared no more than a petulant glare as he fled.

The Sandman scrambled away in haste on seeing that the Huntress was loose once more. He joined the others as they hovered, watching, perplexed by this turn of events.

"Prince, my love," Styx whined. "What is this? You would choose a mortal over us? That's impossible! Has she bewitched you?"

"You'd leave us for her?" cried Nyx, her tone shrill, frantic, disbelieving.

The Prince knew, within his very soul, that Mara was his only possible choice. But Nyx had for so long been his. This self-revelation shocked him. Oh, how her stricken face did tear at his heart that was no longer stone. "I must," he said sadly.

"But, Prince," she pleaded, tragic, as of love betrayed. "It was I who made you what you are. It was I who gave you power and beauty and perpetual youth. And you choose her over me?"

Just as the Prince was certain that his heart would be torn asunder, he read triumph in her eyes. And recalled the centuries of what he knew now to be a shameless manipulating of him to her own ends. With sudden clarity, he saw her for what she was.

"You lied to me, Nyx. You said I would live forever. Instead you stole my innocence and brought me unending death. You made me a horror to God and man."

"Do not grieve me," said she, persisting to the last in her charade (he had to keep reminding himself). "Oh, where is my Samael, my Angel of Death?"

He gave her a long look. "I am Samael no more, the Angel of Death no more. It is over. Leave me now."

Nyx stood dumbfounded, searching his eyes. Saw that he meant it, this rejection of his own chosen name and of her, after five centuries. She had thought he was hers forever. Her eyes blazed.

"You turncoat!" she shrieked in fury. "You betray your master, and you betray me! We are your kind, not she! You are one of us and always will be. Forever! For all eternity!" She spat the words like venom. "I did not force you. You chose this! I only wanted you," she added softly, then barked an unpleasant laugh. "You wanted me too. I gave you your wish, and I kept my promise. I never touched your family, not even one of them! You killed them! You killed them all! Is she going to love you now?"

The Prince flinched as her accusations hit him like blows. All that she said was true. He could not deny it; dared not look at Mara. Filled with shame, he cast his eyes to the ground.

But Nyx was not finished. "The master made you his own,

and you spurn him now? He would put the world at your feet, and you throw it away for this — this mortal? You are not her kind. You are one of us, and you must feed. You must hunt and kill mortals, and so she will kill you. That is what she does!"

He lifted his gaze to meet hers at last. "All is changed now. I have changed," he said in a tone quiet but resolute. "I serve a different master now. Our Lord Jesus Christ."

At the sound of that dreaded Holy Name, all vampires hissed and shrank back. They stood gaping, astounded that the Prince could speak it without flinching.

Nyx recovered first, saw that he meant what he said, and her eyes blazed. "The master will hear of this!" she snarled.

"Don't leave me!" Styx wailed. The Sandman caught her in time to prevent her throwing herself at the Prince's feet.

The Prince held out his hand. "Come, join me."

But they were struck with terror at the sight of his vampire eyes with the soul in them, and fled into the night.

Night Kisses Day

The night was suddenly still. The mad whirlwind of chaos had departed. Small sounds seemed oddly loud. A pebble clattered to the pavement as a stray cat jumped onto a ledge. A cricket chirped near the corner of the building. Sounds of late-night partying drifted near and then faded. A telephone rang, discordant in the night. Streetlights dimmed beneath the star-filled sky.

All seemed as before, and yet nothing was the same. A deep and abiding love had burst into existence like wildfire fanned into flame by a summer wind; a love as unlikely as the union of night and day. The Prince stood unmoving, gazing wistfully into the night.

"Sorry about that," Mara said. "Your friends, I mean."

He turned, his face a pale blur in the darkness, his eyes in deep shadow. "They made their choice."

***

He glided nearer, slowly, to avoid any appearance of aggression, for his own sake as well as hers. He meant her no harm, but held no illusions as to her ability to defend herself, and meant not to antagonize her, either.

***

This is a vampire, she told herself sternly. But when she looked up into his face, she was unable to think of anything except her rude words outside the coffee shop. And now this—this immolation of his former self, for her sake.

"And, I'm sorry for, um, the other night," she said with an effort. "I—it was so totally rude. Can you ever forgive me?"

He stared. "But there is nothing to forgive. It is I who should be asking your forgiveness." He closed his eyes as anguish flashed across his face. "I nearly killed you." At that, he went down on one knee in the gravel, head bowed. "You are right. I should be on my knees before you, begging your pardon."

She looked down at his bowed head and thought what a change had taken place in this proud creature. To see her former foe bend his knee to her, willingly! The full meaning suddenly crashed in on her. Before she knew she was about to, she reached out and stroked his dark, silky hair. She had never touched a vampire before, except with fists and feet... oh dear, why had she done that? What was she thinking? What would he think? She hastily drew her hand back.

"Get up, please. Um, you don't have to kneel to me."

"I will be yours forever. Then, perhaps... " He captured her hand and kissed it, then lifted his eyes to her face. "Oh, how your goodness and beauty do vanquish my heart."

He's a poet! And—and he kissed my hand! To her surprise, she rather liked it. She looked into those eyes, saw the desolation there, and realized something that had not occurred to her before: for her sake, he was caught between two worlds, belonging to neither, with all the pain of loss and loneliness, with nothing and no one, except her.

"Get up, please, love." *Did I just say that? Good grief! I've never called anyone that.*

He flowed to his feet and bowed slightly. "As you wish, my lady." She caught his somber look before he dropped his eyes. When he lifted them again, he said, "Did you just call me love?"

She met his gaze squarely. "Um, I guess I did."

In troubled silence, they looked into each other's eyes.

"This is not possible," he said finally, turning away. "I will not do this thing to you."

"Wait," she said.

He turned back, his mouth set in a stern line.

In his eyes, she saw great sorrow before a dark veil hid it once more. "You're too late. It's already done."

***

He shook his head and with great effort tore his gaze away and cast it down, disconsolately. "No. It cannot be." He tried to appear arrogantly uncaring but failed.

***

"So. You, er, you say you love me, then you dump me without even a 'let's just be friends?' Forget that, Mister." Mara softened her tone. "Hey, I totally meant what I said. Forever. Didn't you?" *Gosh, what am I saying? Isn't this the enemy?*

Heartbreak filled his eyes. "Yes, of course. But how can I, in all honor, do this? I will be your slave, and no more."

"Honor? I thought you said—so you don't honor your word? Hey, if it's love, being my slave isn't enough. It's too late to change what's already been said, and done."

He shook his head with downcast eyes, obviously distraught. "No. How could one such as I presume?" Pale hands appeared from within the folds of blackness to trace in the air a graceful gesture of utter futility. Hands so plainly vampiric as to produce a shock effect, as though meant to bring her to her senses.

She stared, a little dazed. Here was a vampire, so recently the enemy; changed somehow, but still a vampire. And it seemed she loved him with all her heart, without a clue as to how that had come about. He said he loved her; proved it by saving her life and ditching his former brothers for her sake. Unbelievable, yet true. "It's not your doing, nor mine, I'm afraid," she ventured. "I don't get what happened at the church that night; all I know is something did." He looked up at her with eyes so alive; no longer empty. *How beautiful he is. Gosh, who'd have thought I'd say that of a vampire?* she said to herself a little anxiously.

"My heart shivers," he said softly. "You do not understand how utterly devastated I am by your very presence." He did not move, only looked at her.

"Hey, this is new to me, too." She felt disconcerted by his

unexpected words and his steady regard. "I've never—I mean, I never expected or planned to—er, find anyone. Especially not you. Oh. I'm sorry about how that must sound."

"How could you ever—how could it be otherwise? Wait, listen to me. You must not forget what I am. I wanted to bite you."

"But, you didn't."

"No, but you have no idea how close… the possibility lurks within me still. You cannot just forget it happened."

She somehow felt as though she was fighting for her very life. "I said I'd forgive you, not that I'd forget it." Then she added lightly, "Just don't let it happen again."

"No, never!" he said vehemently. "Kill me if I do. Do not hesitate for an instant. I mean that."

She burst out laughing at his seriousness. "It's a joke, okay? Where have you been?" Her smile quickly faded as she realized what she had just said. "Oops. Um, I, uh, sorry."

"Pardon my ignorance, but I have been on the outskirts of your world for a few centuries."

He sounded so serious; she was relieved to see a glint of amusement in his eyes. "I see we really need to get to know each other better," she went on. "Um, I mean—" *Did I really just say that, to a vampire?*

The curtain seemed to veil his eyes again as though his thoughts ran along the same lines. "Perhaps not. I am not worthy to kiss your feet, Huntress."

"I should hope not!" she blurted out, then, "What I meant to say was—" She began again. "It's not my feet I'd want you to kiss—" She stopped, truly mortified now.

At once, he caught up her hand and brought it to his lips, with genteel discretion, as though unaware of her confusion. "As you wish, my lady."

His gallantry was touching, but the smooth, cold touch of his hand, and that of his lips, like marble covered in silk, was rather disquieting. Yet there was heat in the black eyes that surveyed her above the hand. That set her heart aflutter in a strange and unexpected way. She hastily retrieved her hand, suddenly at a loss for words, just when she needed them most.

He backed off gracefully. "A thousand pardons, Huntress. I should not have presumed. I meant no disrespect."

"No—no, of course not. None taken. I just… "

He bowed, but his eyes never left her face. "I understand. As you say, we must get to know each other. Please forgive my ignorance of your time and place. It is to me as though I only just now have awakened in a different world."

"Yeah, um, I kind of get that."

"Please do not mistake my ardent gaze. I love you, just as I said, with all my heart. But the most earthshaking fact is that I can love at all." He shook his head. "It is difficult now for me to believe that for five hundred years, I thought I was the most wonderful creature to walk the face of the Earth. And now, to have my eyes opened. It is quite—shattering. Then I saw you. That was when I realized what heaven was. And I wanted it."

She found herself enraptured by his words, and also because the sweetness of his voice was like music. His face seemed like that of an angel. "I remind you of heaven?" she murmured. "What are you, then, to me?"

He turned his head, and the streetlight briefly outlined the planes of his face in pale alabaster set against the velvet darkness of night. She caught her breath, captivated.

"I thought I was a god," he went on. "But was I satisfied with that? No. I longed to be like the master." His brow furrowed. "The master! His power, his malice; none can equal him. I tried. He named me his crown prince and was proud of what I became, as though he had created me. And, yes, I was his, body and—well, without the soul. That is why he so confidently sent me to get you. Yes, let us not forget. He meant you harm then and does still."

"Right. I have noticed some odd things lately, like vampires with a death wish. Is there a connection? I don't mean to brag, but they're no match for me, and they know it. Still, they don't run away—they actually dare to attack me! What's with that?"

"That should tell you something of how much they fear Charon. They prefer to face you and your mercy than the master and his lack thereof. He wants your head and means to get it. See this knife?" He whipped open his cloak to reveal the jeweled haft at his belt. "One of his treasures, given to me for that very purpose. To cut off your head."

She saw that this was the source of that mysterious sparkle she had seen at his waist during the battle in the church. "Oh, really. May I see it, please?"

"Certainly, my lady." The blade sang as he drew it from its sheath, its jewels flashing in the night. He presented it to her.

"Holy!" she murmured, admiring. The hilt was a dazzling mass of rainbow colors, the blade a slender, shining curve a good foot long. "Old Spanish steel, I daresay, or something similar, and razor-sharp. These gems are real, right?"

"Nothing but the best for the master, for his favorite, or for you. It is a showpiece, but useful too. It will cut anything, I am told, even adamant."

"Adamant? What's that?"

"A legendary metal delved from the depths of the earth, shining and hard as diamond, with which one may fashion a chain that will bind anything, even a vampire as powerful as the master himself. You did not know? I thought you knew all about us."

"Hey, I only kill vampires. I never learned how to keep them prisoner." She managed a rueful laugh.

His eyes softened. "There is no need, perhaps. You have already taken my heart prisoner—without adamantine chains."

She tore her gaze from his, a little flustered. "Um, yeah, this is one cool knife, all right. A bit long for my taste, though," she added lightly, and murmured, "How would I hide it?"

"Its name in the ancient tongue means 'Dragon's Tooth,'" he went on, as though he hadn't noticed.

"Good grief! All this, for me?" She couldn't help smiling a

little proudly at the thought.

"Hah! You are the ultimate thorn in the master's side. Do you realize the damage you have caused? You stand in the way of his grand plan for world domination. Thus he would be rid of you at all costs. The reward is out of this world for anyone who kills you, or discovers your Achilles' heel."

"What is this 'grand plan'?"

"I will gladly tell you all I know of it, though he keeps some secrets for his very own. The general idea is that when certain signs in the heavens occur, he must perform a precise ritual involving the sacrifice of innocent blood. Lo and behold, his New Kingdom is born!"

Mara couldn't help a skeptical look. "Vampires are usually all about sucking blood. So what's new about this ritual?"

"This is a sacrifice on an actual altar, of an innocent victim. I have seen it, even assisted him; he has not been successful yet, however. He requires a solar eclipse, as well as a number of other requirements, which must coincide exactly. Apparently, they have not yet."

"Sacrifice? An altar? Vampires do stuff like that?" She gave him a sidelong glance. Surely, he wouldn't joke about something like this. "Um… sounds like some weird fantasy comic."

He looked amused. "Remember, we have been around for a long time. Sacrifice is still valid and necessary to honor our God, though I realize many humans in these times prefer to think otherwise. Charon's god is Satan, or something of that ilk that glorifies itself, to its own detriment."

She shook her head, trying to take it all in. This promised to be more of a life-changing event than she had thought. "Well. Looks like I've got my work cut out for me," was all she could think of to say.

"Yes, you must prevent him establishing his New Kingdom. That would signify the end of life on Earth as you know it. Vampires walking in daylight and the master ruling all; not a pleasant thought. But here I am to do what I can to help."

"And you would have been his crown prince in this New Kingdom. Kind of an important position, I'd imagine," she said slowly. "So tell me, how did it happen that his most trusted one has turned against him?" She gave him a long steady look.

"True, I could have had anything I wanted, ruling by his side. Except you." At that, his gaze was filled with such longing that she had to look away. He dropped his eyes at once. "It happened in the church; I do not know how. Only that I was struck by a light and then... I did not know what love was, nor was I capable of it. But the moment I looked upon you with newly opened eyes, my heart was changed: I loved." Almost as though unaware of what he was doing, he reached out to caress her cheek, tenderly.

She put her hand on his. So cold it was, though strangely no longer repugnant. Yet it reminded her that this was not a man but a vampire. Troubled, she said a quick prayer under her breath. Then took another cautious look at his eyes and was reassured. Without a doubt, he did have a soul.

A cricket chirped nearby, and the spell that held her mute and immobile was broken. With a quick blur of movement, the Prince was holding out his hands toward her, cupped together. He parted them just a little. At first, she was puzzled, then she heard the chirp of a cricket from within his hands. She smiled, and in return, his gaze upon her face so suddenly filled with such tenderness that she felt certain he meant to kiss her.

Instead, he looked away and only said, "See this?"

"The cricket?"

"Yes, is it not amazing? It is so alive!" The cricket's eyes and body reflected the streetlight. It chirped.

She couldn't help but laugh at his delight. "Yeah, and—?"

He opened his hands to set the cricket free. "So wonderful. I did not appreciate living creatures before. Never noticed beauty; not once I tasted blood. After that, blood was everything to me. All else was nothing; whatever did not exist for my pleasure, to feed my craving, was of no account. How to explain? Now I am free. I feel alive, almost." He smiled.

Her heart did another of those strange flutters. "That's cool. I guess I'm so used to—" She turned at the sound of running footsteps coming down the alley.

"Hey, are you okay?" called Maggie breathlessly.

Sabrina, George, and Josh were right at her heels, all talking at once.

"You'll never guess what happened!"

"The ambulance and cops showed up, and—"

"There's another body in the vacant lot—but you probably knew that."

"Are you okay, Mara?"

"Uh, sure, I had lots of help. This is—" Mara turned to introduce the Prince, but he had vanished.

In a way, she was relieved. She was not quite ready to explain things to her friends. And yet, his absence left her feeling a little lost and alone, as though something essential was missing that she had not noticed before he came into her life. Already it seemed that he belonged there. She furtively scanned the shadows, but there was no sign of him.

Getting to Know You

From then on, the moment she embarked upon her patrolling of the streets after dark, she sensed his presence. He did not intrude (she had never required assistance in her battles), but it now warmed her heart to know he was there.

After one evening's encounter, which proved fatal for three vampires that dared much, she dusted off her hands and jogged down the path to the park. Her weapons once more out of sight, she might have been an ordinary girl out for a run, had it been daylight.

The park was always a pretty scene, even in the dark, especially when the moon was full, spilling its light over everything, outlining grass and trees and flowering shrubs. Their fragrance was a fine thing too, after the stink of vampires.

She jogged over to a park bench and threw herself down to catch her breath. Crickets stopped chirping momentarily but soon resumed their chorus. She could sense that the Prince was nearby and very much wanted to call out to him to come and talk, but her mother would say that wasn't proper. Then he did show, of his own accord. Though she tried for an air of calm, her heart thumped so hard she was sure it must give her away.

"May I sit?" he said pleasantly, as though he had not noticed.

Of course, he had. He was a vampire; it was impossible for him not to hear heartbeats. But it was difficult now to think of him as she did other vampires.

"If you like."

He discreetly sat at the far end of the bench. His face was a pale blur, but she could see the sparkle of moonlight in his eyes. "Resting after a hard night's work?" he said presently, in a conversational tone meant to set her at ease.

She felt suddenly shy as she realized he was interested in her as a person, not just for her looks, as most men seemed to be, nor for her blood, as a vampire would be. Those she could deal with, no problem. "Um, not hard, really," she managed. "I often come here to veg out after a battle. The roses smell so nice." She sighed before she knew she was going to, or why.

"Do not be sad. I will never stop loving you." Unnoticed by either of them, he had moved closer.

She wondered if he was reading her thoughts again. His eyes were shadows in the paleness of his face, though that glint of moonlight gave them away. What once would have been a macabre apparition to her now had an entirely different aspect. Her natural reserve melted away. "I know. What are we to do?"

He reached over and put his hand on hers. She did not shudder this time at its deathlike coldness. She looked into his eyes and let herself be lost in them.

"May I call you Mara?" he said suddenly, breaking the spell.

"Er, sure, why not? That's my name."

"Mara, my sweet," he said, experimentally it seemed.

"Actually, it means bitterness," she said with a self-conscious laugh.

"Mara," he murmured, not smiling, only gazing as though entranced. "Beautiful." He kissed her lightly on the cheek. "Sorry." He hastily drew back. "I did not mean to… Yes, you have every right to reproach me with those eyes."

"I didn't. I mean, it's okay," she said, touching his cold cheek for the first time.

He reached up and put his hand on hers. "No, it is not. That I should presume…you are so innocent, and I, with my bloodstained lips, dare to…" He looked desolate. "Forgive me." To her dismay, he fell to his knees before her, head bowed.

"Get up, would you please?" She was suddenly overcome by an irrational fear that he would kiss her foot next. "Er, it's not the custom nowadays? Please get up."

"If you wish." He rose to his feet in an unnatural fluid motion. "But it was you who suggested that I should be on my knees." At her stricken expression, he hastily added, "But it is true, and nothing will ever change that."

"I feel awful. Oh, how could I have said such a thing? It was so rude. I'm sorry. Can you forgive me?"

"If I may?" He took her hand and kissed it. "I would indeed forgive you, were any offense taken. I must confess that at the time, my heart was wounded, but a vampire heals quickly."

"Sure, um, if you say so. I mean, thanks. Er, just sit down, okay? Unless you'd rather walk."

He tugged at her hand. "Let us walk."

It felt so right that the Prince should walk beside her. The hand holding hers was strong, but gentle and secure. For the first time in her life, she felt she did not need to rely solely upon herself. *Nice. I could get used to this.*

She glanced over at him, admiring. *Who are you? What is the meaning of all this? And—oh, dear, what will Father Mike say?*

The Prince's eyes met hers, and he smiled.

***

The Prince was impressed by the fact that the Huntress walked by his side. She had once been his sworn enemy, and now… He glanced over at her wonderingly, recalling how at one time, he had arrogantly assumed that he possessed the higher status. Never mind that she had somehow been elevated to huntress, to him she was just another mortal, food for the undead, the immortals. After his transformation, his eyes were opened, and it became clear to him that things were not quite as he had supposed, but nearly the opposite. She was, as were all humans, created in the image and likeness of God, whereas he and his kind, once of that high estate, had fallen lower than the beasts. In her innocence, she retained an original beauty of spirit, while he was corrupted, defiled by evil. It was clear to him now that he was unworthy of her; that only through God's infinite mercy had he been granted a reprieve. Sorrow and despair threatened to overwhelm him at the thought. And he knew: she who had been his direst foe was now his joy and hope.

He was able to see Mara clearly because of his keen night vision. He was fascinated by her innocence and her beauty, with that long golden braid, fair skin like sunlight, and eyes blue as the daytime sky. *That is as close to daylight as I'll ever get.*

Is it? The insidious words came into his mind. *In the New Kingdom, we will walk in daylight. We shall rule the world! Then you may walk beside her under the summer sun. Think of it.*

He shook off the thought. Impossible!

The master wants you back, even now; you can have it all, all you ever wanted.

But he wants her head. He will not give that up. No, I cannot; the price is too high.

But to walk in daylight?

He crushed the longing within him. Without her, it would be as dust and ashes in his mouth. Without her, there would be no love, no beauty, no happiness—ever.

Turn her. She trusts you now. You wanted to turn a Huntress.

True... He felt himself wavering.

Give her the gift Nyx gave you.

Gift? With that, the full horror of what he was considering struck him. *Never!*

Then you will be alone. The master demands her death. In any event, she is mortal; sooner or later, one day she will die.

The reminder hit him with stunning force. Die! Of course she would die. And that would be sooner rather than later, if the master had his way. Charon had sent him forth for that very purpose. Though his favorite had flown, he would find others to do his bidding. At that, the Prince felt a bit of panic. It was up to him to protect Mara now. Did she understand? He turned to her with furrowed brow, unsure how to impress upon her the urgency of the situation. She seemed so self-assured, even intimidating.

***

She glanced over at him, her quick smile fading as she caught his look of concern. "What?"

"My dear, again I warn you. Be careful. Never forget it for even a moment. The master has decreed your death, and there are others who will risk much to bring him your head."

At this interruption of her pleasant thoughts, she frowned. "I don't get it. If he's so smart, why send common ordinary vampires against me? Hey, I could whip them all, blindfolded and with my hands tied behind my back! He should know that."

"He sent me, and then the others I took you from. He is not finished yet. Do not underestimate him. He has been around for a long time; at least five thousand years. We may have foiled his plan for the moment, but he is not stupid. I am afraid for you."

"I should just go get him. Face him down. Rid the world of this cockroach for good." With a faint smile, she awaited the reaction she knew would be forthcoming.

His long fingers caught her arms like a steel trap. "Stay away from him!" he said vehemently. "Promise me!"

Adrenaline rush. Flashback to that night in the church. She sprang into defense mode, her eyes narrowed, mouth in a grim line; every inch of her set to attack.

He quickly stepped back. "Sorry, I..."

She exhaled and took a deep breath as panic subsided. "Um, it's, er, it's okay. I just, you know. You took me by surprise there for a second. I've kind of got this hair-trigger... " His look reassured her after a moment of collecting herself. Would she ever get used to this? He stood there, looking serious. "All right, I admit it's kind of nice to have someone protect me for a change. But hey, I'm perfectly capable of defending myself."

"I see that. But promise you'll not go after him alone?"

"Fine. I promise. What you said." She rubbed her arms. "Ow, that's quite the grip you have."

"Sorry." He reached out, then caught himself.

"Really, I'm okay. I know better than to stick my head into the lion's mouth. I was kidding. Really. You're so serious, you just invite teasing."

"Yes. Well. To me this is serious, especially since it is your head the master wants."

"And you want it for yourself, do you?" she teased.

He finally gave in and smiled a little. "Yes, I do. But I prefer it attached to your body."

She thought for a moment, then blushed. Subject change. "So… where is this great, all-powerful master? I've often wondered why he doesn't come out and try to kill me himself."

"If the master were not confined underground, you would have encountered him long ago, to your detriment, perhaps. It is said that many centuries past, an ancient enemy cast a spell upon him so that he is unable to withstand any celestial light; not only that of the sun, but of the moon and stars as well. That is why he rarely appears above ground. Only on the darkest of nights, under cover." The Prince's expressive eyes searched her face (they were nothing like the dead vampire eyes to which she was accustomed). "To go underground to meet him would be, I am certain, to court death. Do not smile. I am serious. You would do well to take heed of what I say! As for where his lair is, well. By the time you, my dear, rose up to combat us here at the very Gate of the Underworld, we had dwelt here undisturbed for over a hundred years. Imagine the master's frustration. Here we were, quite comfortably settled in and steadily increasing our numbers after the terrible huntress of the north so sorely depleted them, when another huntress arises, even more deadly. Ignoring you did not make you go away. It only allowed you to reduce our ranks once again."

"You must know where he is. Didn't you come from there?"

"Yes, I did. But my advice to you, even knowing what you are, is, stay out of his lair. No mortal can withstand him, not face-to-face and alone. Not even you."

She stood, hands on hips, and raised an eyebrow. "Hey, this is my job, right?"

"You are good, I know that. You would have defeated me but for divine intervention. Still, I love you now, and that makes all the difference. To underestimate Charon would be fatal."

She relented. "I won't. Don't mind me. You're just fun to bug."

The look he gave her was a mix of uneasiness and solicitude; serious, as usual. "The master is something even you, perhaps, cannot imagine. Anyway, he is sure to relocate again when he hears of my defection. Probably already has."

"I suppose you're right. But sometimes a little humor keeps the spirits up. This job gets really heavy at times."

"Too much for one little girl," he murmured, then hastened to add, "Even if you are the terror of the Underworld. Every vampire cringes at the mention of your name and flees Charon's wrath each time you cut another swath through the ranks. But times are changing, I am afraid. His frustration at his ever-tightening fetters grows, along with his increasing power, which somehow seems to feed on the evil that men do, especially the killing of innocents. Time is running out, the ancient prophecy is about to be realized, and he means to be ready. He swore you would not ruin it for him, as happened in the north." His expression grew thoughtful. "Maybe it is for your sake that I was plucked from the very jaws of hell. I do not know. But I pledge myself to your service. If you want me, that is, I am yours."

She tried to smile, but tears kept getting in the way. "There you go, making me cry again. Gosh, I'm such a baby." Impulsively she embraced him.

Taken by surprise. He stiffened and held her somewhat gingerly. She put that down to his natural reserve and her unexpected display of affection. She had surprised herself, too, but her heart was so suddenly full of irrepressible feeling that she had to share it. She sighed and leaned her head against his chest. At last, his arms went around her, and his cheek pressed against her hair. It felt so right, as though she had come home.

The shrilling of a siren pierced the night; she started, suddenly self-conscious. "Oh, I'd better get back. I have, um, homework. A big assignment due. See you around." She extricated herself with a speed that left him staring, and turned to go.

He clung to her hand. "Wait."

She looked at him rather breathlessly, afraid to linger, disturbed by the ambush of thoughts and emotions.

He reached within his cloak and pulled out a cloth twisted into a small bundle, which he held rather gingerly. "Here. I believe this is yours. You might need it."

With a puzzled little frown, she opened the cloth and emptied its contents into her hand. Heard his involuntary hiss at the sight of the small silver crucifix she had lost at the church. She lifted her eyes to meet his.

"I am sorry, I meant to return it sooner, but my heart failed when you were… so unapproachable. Then I, er, forgot."

She reddened. "Uh, thanks. It could mean the difference between life and death, as I found out the other night. Gosh, I guess I nearly got my just desserts, didn't I? Lucky for me you don't hold a grudge."

"No, no. My fault entirely."

At that, she felt such a rush of tenderness that she stood on tiptoe and kissed his cheek before she knew she was going to. Then, reddening at her audacity, she hurried away down the path, leaving him standing in stunned silence.

Emerald Ring

Vampire attacks had ceased for over a month – an ominous sign. To Mara, it did not seem that the master would give up so easily after he had vowed to put her out of the picture; certainly, he would not tolerate the insubordination of one of his own. This had to be the calm before the storm. But she was glad of the lull; her schoolwork had suffered of late, and now there were finals to think about. And other things…

It was during her late afternoon class that she had started thinking of the gardens at the zoo; it felt as though the Prince was calling to her. So much so that she had trouble attending to the lecture. Of course, he wouldn't be out in the daytime, she told herself; they couldn't meet until after sunset, anyway.

She went upstairs after supper to study, as usual, but her eyes kept straying from her books to her bedroom window. The sun had never seemed so near to standing still. Even when her cat jumped onto her lap, purring loudly, she was too distracted to notice. Only when he began sliding off her lap and meowed in protest did she finally take heed. She gave him a hug, pressing her cheek against his fur.

"Poor Smoky, have I been neglecting you?" True, she had had a lot on her mind lately. He purred loudly and settled in. She petted him and doggedly went back to working on her essay.

After what seemed an eternity, the sun vanished from sight, though rays of red and gold still shone on the scattering of clouds, treetops, and windows of neighboring houses. When at last they winked out, she tossed the startled cat onto her bed, snatched up her weapons and tucked them into their accustomed hiding places about her person, donned her jacket and was out the door.

The wind rushed past her ears as she ran to the park. At the rose garden, the Prince appeared beside her and took her hand. She wasn't startled; she knew he was there. They walked in silence for a while, delighting in each other's presence. Some things could never be expressed in words alone. But words did come, and the discovery of shared interests. Finally, when silence surrounded them once more, the Prince sprung his surprise.

"I brought you something." He drew a small gold box from within his cloak and pressed it into her hand.

"Cool. What's this?"

"Open it. It is for you, if you so choose. But consider your decision carefully, for I come with it." A tinge of anxiety crept into his light tone.

The box itself was embossed with glyphs, a lovely work of art. Delighted, she traced the design, then pressed the catch. The lid sprang open and a flame leapt up, flaring green in the moonlight. It was an emerald ring.

Mara gasped. "Oh, my goodness, it's gorgeous!"

"A little beauty I picked up in the Cave of Gems."

"The Cave of Gems?"

"One of Charon's many treasure troves. Precious stones gathered from his mines are placed there."

"Mines? Treasure? But vampires don't care about such things."

"Ah, but they do. The master, at least. He has many interests. Mines are but one of them. Precious metals, gems, you name it, popular vampire lore notwithstanding. I know what they say. The general run may care for nothing but the next blood feast, but vampires do vary in this state of existence, just as in the former."

"Um, you'd know, I guess," Mara murmured, nonplussed. "Learn something new every day. I thought I knew vampires. Most people know even less. Thanks. I do need you, don't I?"

"Of course." He looked pleased.

For some reason, she blushed at this and, to cover her confusion, blurted out, "How could I say no to such a treasure as this?" And could have kicked herself for sounding so mercenary.

But he only gave her a fond glance as he went on. "According to medieval legend, emeralds come from the depths of hell. Some say from Lucifer's crown. For this reason, they were often used to combat demonic forces. Think of this as from Charon's crown, and that it likewise may shield you as you battle vampires."

"That's so cool. From Charon's crown; or his crown prince, at any rate." She turned the ring over in her hand and saw the inscription etched inside the band. *Yours for eternity.* She lifted her gaze to his face and was disconcerted by his intense look of longing. Her heart raced, and the blood rushed to her cheeks. She scrambled to think of something to say. "So. Vampires work in mines?" She had never thought of them doing anything besides hunting humans for blood. Now she pictured them marching off to work like the seven dwarfs, Hi-ho, hi-ho. She just managed not to burst out laughing.

"Not vampires, no," the Prince went on as though he hadn't noticed (caught up as he was in repressing his instincts at that sweet rush of blood). "Minions do most of the labor. Even the master must rely on the assistance of mortals. I need not tell you that it vexes him to no end. They are well rewarded, indeed, but he is a predator, after all. You can guess the rest. Once bitten, they are hooked. If things get out of hand, they die, or become one of us. But those are the hazards of making deals with the devil."

"Oh," she said, disturbed by his apparently complacent attitude toward the fate of those humans. "But that's why I'm here. My job is to make sure the likes of Charon never take advantage of the weak or innocent ever again."

"You are right, of course," the Prince said in a chastened tone. "I am sorry if I seem not to care. After five hundred years of mortals throwing themselves at us, literally begging for our attentions, it rather deadens the capacity for sympathy, even now. Still, I thank you for calling it to my attention. You see? I would be lost without you as my guiding light."

"Thank you for reminding me that I have my work cut out for me." Her mind was still on the poor lost mortals caught up in the web of a terrible master who was able to ensnare them despite his confinement underground. She frowned. "So how does he lay his hands on these minions, anyway? And he's got to feed, so how—I mean, you say he's stuck underground? I don't get it."

He looked away. "Um, we brought them. Those of us that managed to slip past you, that is." His voice trembled a bit, then steadied as he went on. "No mortal can find the Great Hall on its own, but by invitation only, with a vampire escort. The master welcomes mortals to his parties and feasts with great eagerness, for that is the only way he may satisfy his voracious appetite for blood. Those who survive are in due time escorted back to the Upperworld, though they are only too eager to return, bringing others with them."

"That's just wrong! I must kill him, you know. Charon. Will you help me find him?"

"My darling, be cautious."

"Cautious." She looked him straight in the eye. "While he lays waste to the world, never mind that he can't appear above ground even at night? There must be a way to deal with him once and for all. It's up to me to find it."

"I will do what I can, except help you rush headlong to destruction. What good is the Huntress dead? Or undead? Venture into Charon's realm and believe me..."

"Hey. I have a job to do. Lately, it seems I've been thinking a whole lot of myself, my feelings, what I want. No more. That's not what being the Huntress is all about."

"I thought you would say that." He reached for the ring. "May I? That is what this is all about." He took her hand and slipped the ring onto her finger. "With this ring I pledge myself to you for all eternity. I will be by your side always. You kill vampires; I will be there to aid and protect you. You need me. Here I am. But let us stay out of Charon's lair, for now."

"Okay, I get it," she said, a little squelched by his warning, but warmed by his promise. What if she couldn't defeat the master without the Prince's help? That was a thought that had not occurred to her before. Always had she fought alone and won. Immersed in her thoughts, she belatedly realized that the Prince was talking.

"—the emerald, associated with purity and innocence." He seemed unaware that her mind had wandered from this topic most dear to him. "I even found a jeweler who was able to place it in a setting worthy of my beloved."

"My beloved," he said. Her heart lurched, her thoughts suddenly in turmoil. *Of course. A ring means… no, this isn't a diamond—and he's a vampire, for goodness sake!* Suddenly she realized that he was awaiting her answer. Not that she had any doubt as to what she must say. There was a reason he had come into her life, and this was only his way of pledging his loyalty and assistance—wasn't it? Or, could it mean something more? Anyway, life without him now would be desolate; she could hardly refuse him now. She turned her hand to admire the ring. The moonlight struck sparks of green from the emerald and traced the intertwined vines and leaves of its setting with white lines.

"I accept." She lifted her gaze to meet his.

His eyes flared up like hot embers. "Sorry," he said, at her quick indrawn breath, and the glow subsided to deep-water black.

"It's okay," she murmured, though her heart was still in her throat. "I know you wouldn't… "

"No, I would never harm you. This power of the eyes, it is in your service, always. And I am yours forever, as the inscription says. If you wish it so, that is."

Sorry that she had seemed to mistrust him, she let herself fall into the depths of his eyes. As though from a great distance, she heard herself say, "I do wish it. I'll wear this ring always."

She came to herself when she felt the soft fabric of his cloak pressed against her cheek and his strong arms around her. She felt how cold he was, but it was different now; the effect reversed so that the heat of her body seemed to warm his. Almost as though he were alive, though his lack of breath and heartbeat were disconcerting. Could one grow accustomed to such as that?

He held her gently, as something fragile and precious; he kissed her golden hair. "I will love you forever."

Overwhelmed, she could not speak. How she grieved for his unnatural state of being. He was at once a strange and beautiful creature, and a sad and pathetic monstrosity. And she loved him with all her heart.

She wanted to enjoy the bliss of his embrace forever, but the real world was out there, waiting.

A day or two later, she was in the kitchen helping her mother clean up after supper. The sunshine yellow curtains above the sink stirred slightly as a breeze wafted in through the open window.

Mara turned on the tap. "I'll wash if you dry, Mom." At that, she got a surprised look. "I know, right? Hey, my nails could use a good soak after playing in the dirt all day," she joked.

Her mother laughed. "And here I thought you outgrew that long ago, but I won't say no. We hardly see each other anymore, it seems." She set up the dish rack. "Speaking of dirt, I was weeding flower beds today. Those dandelions are impossible!"

"Dad won't appreciate it if you get rid of them all," grinned Mara. "He'll want a crop for his wine."

Her mother shook her head, smiling. Mara was absently watching the suds foam up, when her mother exclaimed, "What a pretty ring! I don't believe I've seen that one before."

"Oh, uh—" Mara glanced self-consciously at her left hand;

her mother was looking at her expectantly. Well, the ring was impossible to miss. Ever since the Prince had given it to her, she had longed to confide in her mother, but it was sometimes hard to find the right words. "You're right. I guess we haven't seen each other much lately. But I only just got it. Um—"

She was relieved when her mother didn't press for an explanation, but only said kindly, "May I see it?"

"Of course. Anyway, I guess I should take it off while I wash dishes." Mara reluctantly took it off and handed it over.

"Yes, you wouldn't want to lose it down the drain. That happens, you know. My goodness, it looks like a real antique, not just cheap costume jewelry." Flashes of green danced around the room as her mother turned the ring to admire the emerald. She read the inscription etched inside the band with a quick glance of inquiry, then set the ring on the windowsill amidst a collection of decorative salt-and-pepper shakers and picked up a towel. "You didn't buy this—someone gave it to you?" She attempted to sound casual.

Mara took a deep breath. "Well, Mom, I guess you have a right to know. I've met this guy. He's, um, well, different, but you'll like him." *I think.*

"Different, in what way?" To the point, as usual.

"Um, well, he's a few years older than my other friends," she hedged. *Five hundred years!* "Not old, though," she hastened to add, with a mental reservation: he just stayed the same age longer than most people. "What can I say? He's hard to describe."

Mara never had trouble with descriptions.

"Ah. Have you known him long?"

"Not long. I guess you could almost say it was love at first sight."

"Time isn't everything, it's true. Still, it's good to give it a while, to make sure it's the real thing. You can't really love someone unless you know him. If you're thinking of marriage, sometimes it's good to be friends, first."

"Marriage?" Mara reddened. "Mom. Just because I like a

guy, it doesn't mean... Er, it's not even a diamond," she quickly added. Her mom had a knack for hitting the nail on the head and just putting it right out there.

"Well, you said—I was just looking ahead, and other stones can be used for—"

"But Mom!" Mara burst out. "I mean, uh, don't jump to conclusions." (Of course, she had no idea he was a vampire.) "Just hold on. I mean, it's just that—well, he hasn't exactly mentioned marriage."

"Well, you say 'love at first sight,' and he gives you a ring with that inscription? Dear child, I wasn't born yesterday."

"Let's take this one step at a time, okay?" Mara retreated into a distressed silence.

Her mother gave her a concerned glance; this loss for words was uncharacteristic of Mara. "Is something wrong? Do you want to talk about it?"

"No... no. I can deal with it." *I hope.*

"As Grandma told me when I was your age," her mother went on, "'you may lose your heart, but don't lose your head.' And remember, your situation is different from that of most girls. What with your calling, well, you know what I mean. Not just any man could deal with that."

"Yes, Mom, I know that. He, er, he... understands. Anyway, we're still just getting to know each other. Give us time. We'll work it out somehow."

Her mother glanced at her sharply, but Mara couldn't bring herself to explain further at the moment. Believing in vampires was one thing; accepting the idea of her daughter marrying one was certain to be an entirely different matter. In fact, Mara needed to study up on it herself.

After an extended silence interrupted only by the clatter of dishes, her mother once again related the story of how she and Mara's father had met. Now that she was able to relate, Mara was touched by the romance of it. But they were both mortal; that made a huge difference, no doubt about it. Her own situation wasn't natural, really; the morality of it was questionable, as Father Mike had intimated. How easy it was to fall in love without thinking of consequences; of the right or wrong of it.

"Is he married?"

"No, of course not."

"Well, that's a relief. I thought for a minute that… "

"No, no. Nothing like that."

"Well, if he gives you a ring of that value, he must be pretty serious. Isn't it time we met him?"

"Uh, sure, I guess."

"How about supper one evening? You pick the day."

"Er—"

"Come on, it'll be fine. We can have something easy, like fried chicken and potato salad."

"I don't think… let's not, er—"

Though not quite sure how it happened, Mara ended by agreeing to invite the Prince over for supper. When she had time to reflect, it was too late to back out.

I'm inviting a vampire to meet my parents? And for supper! Good grief, what have I got myself into?

Of course, it wasn't as though he were just any vampire. And her parents had never actually seen a vampire. With any luck, she could maybe pull it off without them guessing. She wanted to tell them the truth, but how?

Mom, Dad, he's a vampire. No, too blunt.

Mom, about supper? I'm sure he'd love the fried chicken, but just so you know, he's on a special diet. You might have to rob the blood bank. No, that was just silly.

Mom, Dad, don't freak out, but like I said, he's a bit older. Only about five hundred years…but hey, what's a few centuries one way or the other between friends?

Uh-uh. That won't do at all. I'll tell them later. When the time comes, I'll know. The right words will come to me. I hope.

But marriage? *Oh, what am I going to do? What is the Prince thinking? He never said anything about that. Not once did he breathe a hint of it. Oh, that's right, he doesn't breathe.* A giggle escaped her, but ended in a sob. The confusion of thoughts rattled around in her head and gave her no peace. She had no idea how the Prince would react to the invitation.

Happily, her mother turned the conversation to other subjects, more ordinary and common everyday topics, like the happenings at the local library, where she worked part-time. Also the latest concerning the annual bazaar and other fundraising events hosted by the ladies' church group at St. Michael's. "You could think about helping out this year. It's always a lot of fun."

"I don't know, Mom. As you know, I'm pretty busy, what with college and, well, you know—my nights are all taken, and I need to sleep sometime. But sure, I'll think about it."

Distracted by their animated conversation, neither Mara nor her mother noticed the shadow at the window or the pale, slender hand that reached in and snatched the ring from the sill. The presence of a vampire should have alerted the Huntress, but Mara had just at that moment turned her back on the window as she helped put dishes away, or she'd never have missed seeing that flash of movement, however quick it was.

Then, just as she was hanging the towels to dry, her friends phoned to invite her to a movie—hurry, it's starting in ten minutes! Meet you at the theater! With a "See you later, Mom," she dashed away, without the ring.

She had planned to see the Prince again that evening. Now she ran to meet her friends, having all but decided to go to the movie instead, just to avoid the subject of the dinner invitation. But she missed the Prince, after not seeing him all day. At the thought of him, she absently felt for the ring.

Her finger was bare! *Oh dear, I must have left it on the window sill! What's he going to think? Oh, how could I have forgotten it?* She hesitated for a moment, debating whether to go back for it.

But there, in front of the theater, her friends were anxiously waiting for her. She glanced up at the marquee. "John Carpenter's *Vampires*! Why didn't you tell me? I think I'll pass. I've seen this one already. I don't like the way they diss my Church, and it's overly gory and violent even for a vampire movie." She sighed distractedly. "Anyway, I prefer the real thing."

It was only when they all laughed that she realized what she had said. To her relief, they thought she was joking. Except for Sabrina, who caught her eye and winked.

"Aw?" said George, disappointed. "I have this idea for a vampire game, and I need to gather all the info I can get. Watching movies helps a lot, but only if you pick them apart for me. I need you!"

"Okay, I just did that. Watch a different one."

"I second that!" cried Sabrina. "I hate horror movies."

"Aren't there scads of vampire games out already?" Maggie scolded George.

"Yeah," Josh cried enthusiastically. "Some pretty good, too, like *Legacy of Kain, Soulreaver, Van Helsing…* "

"But I'll have the jump on even the best of them," George said, a little defensively. "Because I know someone who deals with vampires in real life. Right, Mara? Come on, it'll be really cool."

"Sorry, I can't tonight." She was pleased that he valued her input, but felt bad that he was so disappointed. "It'll be a great game, George, I'm sure; another time, but not that movie. There must be something else playing."

The four friends went into the theater somewhat chastened, while she returned home. Since she was about to go on patrol, she had to arm herself anyway, and then she could retrieve the ring, as well. How could she meet the Prince without it, when she'd promised to wear it always?

It was not on the windowsill. Had her mom put it away somewhere safe? She called, but only Smoky answered. Her parents must have gone out. She couldn't find the ring, couldn't guess where her mother might have put it. It all seemed a bit odd. A little anxiously she left the house to begin her nightly patrol. What would the Prince say?

She glanced around, expecting him to join her, now that she was alone. He always seemed to shy away from crowds. She'd often sensed his presence while she was with her friends, but never did he show himself. Maybe he found mortals in warm breathing packs irresistible. She contemplated this for a moment. *Oh dear, what am I doing? This is a vampire! Was he thinking of marriage?*

She wandered into the rose garden, but was too preoccupied this time to notice the beauty around her, and how every flower and leaf and blade of grass was edged in silver wherever the moonlight fell, until a blast of arctic breath jolted her from her daydreaming. It wasn't the Prince. *Yikes! If I don't look sharp, the master will get my head yet.* She scanned the shadows, all senses alert, but the chill had receded at once, like a wave on the beach. Gone! She breathed again, now that the danger was past. Still, she should have killed it. *Wake up, Mara!*

That reminded her of George and one of the problems he claimed to address in his project he was working on for the computer programming class. He considered it her destiny to save not just her own hometown from vampires, but the rest of the world, as well. She was pretty sure that to him, it was a fantasy, all part of his game. Still, his heart was in the right place; he meant to find a solution. Might it actually work in real life? All she had ever been able to do was wait in ambush here at the Gate of the Underworld. Vampires were pretty fast and sometimes got loose; she couldn't hope to track them all, everywhere, by herself. Yet she did not put too much stock in George's plan. Computers and games were not high in her esteem. The development that seemed most promising to her was the Prince. He knew vampires and was her backup on patrol.

Without warning, he appeared beside her and took her hand, and they proceeded down the flagstone walk. She smiled up at him, and he responded with a squeeze of the hand that made her heart beat a little faster. She noticed that he glanced at her fingers.

"Um, yeah, sorry I'm not wearing the ring," she stammered, quickly explaining what had happened.

"It's fine, I understand," he said, but she couldn't help wondering if he was disappointed. She had made a promise, after all. "It's okay," he insisted, drawing her closer as they went down the path, and she was somewhat comforted.

She felt happy in his company. For the first time in her life, there was someone she could talk to without reserve, someone who would not snicker or look at her oddly if she mentioned vampires or her nightlife. But to marry him? Was that possible?

After a time of walking in silence, and of talking of other things, she finally gathered enough courage to bring up the more immediate troubling subject. "Would you like to meet my parents?" she began and rushed on without waiting for a reply. "Because, my mom, uh, well, she asked me to invite you to supper."

"Supper?" For a minute, she had the horrible feeling that he would laugh, but he only said, "And the main course would be...?"

"Um, chicken." How silly that must sound. She felt like crying. "I don't know why I agreed. Just say no if you don't want to." *Please say no.*

The look he gave her was completely unexpected. Compassion, understanding and... delight? "I am honored that your mother invites me. Please thank her for me and tell her I accept."

She blinked back tears, her heart full to bursting at his sweetness, his Old World courtesy. *How can I ever deserve him?* She suddenly realized his eyes were on her; he expected a response. "Oh. Yes. Yes, I'll tell her. Thank you, of course."

"Good. That is settled then."

He seemed so confident. How did he expect to pull this off,

with supper and… "Er, my parents have no idea you're a vampire. If you don't mind, I'd like to keep it that way for now." His expression was unreadable; she hastened to explain, "It's just that my parents worry about me a lot. They know vampires are real and that I kill them, but I'm afraid they wouldn't understand about us. I'll tell them—have to tell them—but I'm not ready yet."

"I understand. It is true that I am no longer a man, but a monster, and only natural that they will find this difficult to accept. But never mind that now. Let them get to know me first."

"Yes. Well," she said uncertainly, wondering if he wasn't a little offended. She had essentially denied him. Conversation flagged. She turned to continue down the path. *This is so hard. Gosh! Romeo and Juliet thought they had it tough.*

They came out of the grove of trees into an area flooded by bright lights. There stood a long, low concrete building from which large cages of steel and concrete radiated outward. The rank odor of confined animals hung heavy in the air.

"The zoo," said Mara with forced lightness, as though he couldn't read the sign emblazoned across the entrance. "You'll like the tiger. He's so cool."

She led the way down the promenade, past a row of cages. A black bear pacing behind strong steel bars sniffed the air, then bolted through the door of the building and disappeared inside. Claws clicked on concrete floors, and hoofs pattered across the ground as other animals stirred, growling and snorting. Fear was almost palpable in the night. The noises spread along the compound. *Odd. No, maybe not.* The animals were afraid of the Prince!

She paused, about to remark upon this, but the Prince had looked away and moved on. Almost as though—was he ashamed? And then she realized. A vampire that would not attack humans must take whatever it could get. Had the Prince drunk their blood? She crushed the rising revulsion. Sucking blood was, after all, an identifying feature of the vampire, and she knew what he was. Still.

"These animals are wild, meant to be free," he said then, as though to change the subject (had he read her thought?). "Is it cruel to confine them?"

She played along. "But if not for zoos, some of us would never get to see a real live bear or tiger." She tugged at his hand. "Come, you have to see the tiger. He'll be outside now. Last time I was here, he stayed inside and wouldn't come out." She remembered the glare of sunlight; there was no shade in the tiger's cage during the day. Now the great animal was pacing its cage. Its sleek red-gold hide rippled in the moonlight, revealing the grace and power of the muscles beneath. "What we fighters wouldn't do to be like that tiger," she said a little enviously, with a glance at the Prince. *Okay, he was.* He turned and caught her staring. Flustered, she looked away.

"What's supposed to be in here, beside the tiger?" he said, as though he hadn't noticed. The gate to the next cage stood ajar.

"Wow, that's a pretty heavy-duty cage. Maybe they're getting another tiger, or some other exotic beast like—" she laughed, thinking of Jurassic Park, "—a raptor?"

The night of the supper arrived. Mara had spent most of the afternoon helping her mother clean floors and wash windows. Time seemed to drag, but at last, redness crept across the sky as the fiery ball of the sun went down. Quite suddenly, it was as though a great purple curtain was drawn. Darkness settled over the town.

Mara gave the mirror near the front door a last swipe with the duster and went out to the kitchen to see if her mother needed any last-minute help with the meal. Her stomach was tied in knots. How could she have let her mother go through all the work of preparing a meal when the Prince could eat none of it? Maybe he won't be able to come, or…

"It's nearly time." Her mother's voice broke into her thoughts. "Everything's ready."

Mara felt a pang of guilt. But once her parents got to know him, they would surely love him. Time enough to spring the truth on them then.

Good Night, Sweet Prince

After dark, the Prince ventured out, his heart singing. He averted his eyes from the limp bundle of fur under the bushes; nothing must ruin his mood on this night of nights. Would he never shake the stigma of shame he felt at having to feed off the blood of animals? Yet his newly formed conscience left him no other option. There was no pleasure to be had by taking blood from animals, no rush of memories, knowledge or emotion. Only the warm living blood of a human pulsing through his veins could fly him to the heights of ecstasy and set him on fire with that incomparable feeling resembling life. The occasional blood of an animal sustained him; took the edge off his hunger. That was all.

This time a dog wandering outside alone in the evening had the misfortune to cross his path. It was small and died before he could stop. Guilt plagued him now; he had heard the old woman calling in vain for her pet. Next time he would settle for a rat, though they were the dregs. Still, even that was better than to have the monster within arise at an inopportune moment. He dared not trust himself near humans when famished, as he was so often now.

He was looking forward to meeting Mara's parents. He longed for a loving family, desperately. Loneliness had ever been his lot, it seemed; since his recent transformation, it had gained a bitter edge. Now he was the ultimate outcast, belonging to neither the Brotherhood of Vampires nor the world of men. No more could he drown his miseries in a sea of blood, lose himself in a savage, scorching storm of ecstasy and forgetfulness — *no! Stop!*

This dinner invitation (even if he could eat nothing they offered) was his dream about to come true; a family of his own once again, and a society. He had to remember that – had to be aware that his weakness could ruin all in a heartbeat. At all costs, he must circumvent the obstacles and gain acceptance by these people. Her people. His people now, if all went well.

He straightened his cloak, polished his jeweled clasp to a brilliant shine, wiped all traces of blood from his mouth with a worn linen handkerchief and flicked the dust from his boots. Everything must be perfect for the occasion. In his heart, he was walking on air as he followed the street map in his mind toward the home of his beloved.

Little gusts of warm summer air stirred the trees and shrubs, wafting flowery fragrances. Though he could not breathe, he could bask in them with all his senses. Tall palm trees whispered against the gem-studded deep blue of the sky. He exulted in the wonder of creation, its loveliness and power to inspire poetry in his heart. Even man-made constructions of brick, wood and adobe, pavement, concrete sidewalks, streetlights and buildings, filled him with delight. This was her world.

A sudden chill in the air brought him to a halt. He fell off cloud nine and crashed in the real world, his every sense alert. There, the scent of fresh human blood, so tantalizing… no! With an effort, he fought down the rising hunger. "Nyx, show yourself!"

She materialized before him, her mouth bright with blood. The lovely heart-shaped face tugged at his heartstrings even now, though her lip curled unpleasantly at his reaction to the scent of human blood. "Come with me, Prince. You know you want to."

He frowned. "Leave me alone, Nyx."

"Why pretend? You are one of us, always and ever. Supper! Hah! Are you going to eat with them, or are you going to eat them? I doubt your new fling would take kindly to that." She laughed. "A fine pickle you've got yourself into!"

"It is over, Nyx. Leave me be." He feigned indifference but

was shaken to the core. How easily she had exposed his deepest fear. Her petty insults did not concern him, but… she knew of his dinner invitation. What else did she know?

"You've been feeding off animals," she went on, "I can smell it from here, you poor excuse for a vampire! What you need is a good feed, my dear. Of fresh human blood. Come with me."

"Leave me!" he snarled as his craving clawed at his insides; he feared that a half-second more would vanquish him.

"Leave you to the Huntress? Not a chance. You are mine." When he didn't respond, her tone turned bitter. "After I transformed you into a proud prince, you let a huntress make a pet of you? What a feather in her cap to enslave the master's favorite. No doubt she makes mock of you with her friends."

"She is not like that. But you would not understand. What do you know of love?"

"Hah! How do you think I seduced you in the first place? It's déjà vu. She knows all the tricks, believe me. Foolish boy! When will you learn?"

He felt a stab of doubt, even knowing that she was manipulating him heartlessly as she always had. "You lie! She will never betray me."

"Hah. Face it. To her, you are nothing."

"Alas, it is so."

For a moment, she stared, at a loss for words. Then her tone softened, and her eyes grew sad. "What has happened to you? The Prince I know would bend his proud head to no one. After what we had, and you throw it all away? Five centuries. How could you?"

He felt himself weakening, but quickly caught himself and shook off her hypnotic stare. He shivered at the close call. The thought of Mara sustained him. "I have made my choice, Nyx."

She gave him a long look. "I did not want to do this, but you force my hand." Her eyes hardened; her mouth, her tone. "Come with me now, or you'll never see her again."

He looked into her cold obsidian eyes and felt a tearing

inside. "What have you done?"

"Just a little persuasion. Insurance, if you will."

For a moment he was at a loss for words. Then, "You lie, Nyx! She is safe at home." Waiting for me. Surely.

"Safe with the Sandman, yes." Her smile was cruel. "Fine, don't believe me. I am sure he will take good care of her." She held out her hand. On her pale palm the emerald ring flared green in the moonlight. "See this?"

He reached out, stunned for a moment. He couldn't think. Had Mara found the ring, after all? "How did you—"

She snatched her hand back out of reach. "Come, dear. Hell is near. Follow me." With a musical little laugh she was gone.

He rushed after her with a roar of outrage. She was swift, but not difficult to follow. Then he realized; she was heading for the zoo, one of Mara's haunts. Had Mara come out to meet him? Did they catch her, and that's how Nyx got the ring? All thoughts of the sky, flowers, trees and the beauty of the night fled from his mind. It seemed that all of creation raged against him now. Fear tore at his vitals; in his mind's eye he saw Mara in the arms of the smiling Sandman.

He entered the brightly lit wild animal compound. Saw Nyx by the tiger's cage, beckoning. He sensed other vampires, too. Where was Mara? As he drew near, he wondered at the fear in Nyx's eyes. Nyx afraid, of him? She turned her head to look into the empty cage next to the tiger. Something was not right.

The scent of fresh human blood hit him, like a blow to the solar plexus. He felt a surge of fire and fought his craving. He looked through the bars. A huddled female figure knelt on the concrete in the middle of the cage, head bowed, her long golden hair in disarray. Blood stained her white shirtfront, clear and red. A faint moan escaped her.

Mara! It was as though all light and life were struck from him in an instant. A sob escaped him. In one swift move, he was through the gate and at her side. She lifted her head slowly. He was looking into the face of a stranger. It wasn't Mara.

He whirled, snarling, just as the gate clanged shut. The bolt rattled, caught and locked. Nyx's laugh was shrill with triumph. Dark forms with glowing eyes emerged from the shadows. In a blur of movement, the Prince was at the gate. His heart plunged into an abyss of despair when he saw the gleam of the adamantine chain and lock. With terrible strength born of desperation, he shook the gate, but the lock held fast.

"Where is she?" he hissed.

"Fool." Nyx smiled. "We do not have her… yet. But we have you."

Realization struck like a bolt of lightning. It was a trap!

The narrow, petulant face of the Rocket sneered through the bars. "Now you die, Prince High-and-Mighty."

"You have a few hours to think before the dawn comes," said Nyx. "I think you may yet come to regret your choice."

"Never!" he snarled, to hide his fear. But they knew. Facing the dawn was their own worst nightmare.

The Sandman smiled as he leaned toward the bars. "I brought you a proper last meal, so you don't disgrace us by your plebian tastes. Sorry, I took the first bite this time." He looked anything but sorry.

Styx joined the little group as they stood in a half-circle reveling in the Prince's misfortune. "You could get down on your knees and beg. Maybe then we will open the gate." Her tone was so sweetly sad that even now, he felt a tug at his heart.

"Styx," said the Sandman, not liking the look of this. "Go keep an eye on the security guard." He fixed his eyes on the Prince. "You see how it is. No one can help you now. Styx will take care of the guard, sweetly. You taught her well."

They knew how to twist the knife. The Prince turned his back on them and glided over to inspect the door into the building. It was solid, of heavy wood reinforced with metal and barred from the inside. He managed to fight free of his initial panic and regain a modicum of self-possession. A circuit of the cage and a bit of testing of the steel bars assured him that they would restrain even such as he. But the door — it was of wood! He returned to it and struck it a powerful blow. The door shivered, the sound reverberating through the compound, but that was all.

He whipped back to the gate. The vampires backed off in haste and hovered, watching, poised to flee. For the moment, he ignored them; he extended his hands and willed fiercely that the gate open. With a raucous creak, it bowed out, straining the lock.

"Accept your fate, traitor!" shrilled Nyx, to break his concentration. She flitted around as though she was the one looking for escape. She knew him well and was afraid.

The lock on the gate was, of course, no ordinary lock; his captors had brought their own for the sole purpose of holding him, that was clear. They had planned well. Even as he reached through the bars with nimble fingers, he knew it was hopeless. Still, he had to try. He ignored the hostile eyes anxiously watching his every move and wracked his brain for possible alternatives. Pick the lock. A tool? *Ah, the dagger.* Swiftly he slid it from its sheath, reached through the bars and poked the point of the blade into the keyhole with a delicate touch. He sensed his captors' alarm, but concentrated on the task, listening for the telltale click. Just about there …

The Rocket whipped in, knocked the dagger to the ground and kicked it out of reach. Then he rejoined the Sandman and turned to gloat. In a fury, the Prince struck the gate with his fist. The Rocket and the Sandman scrambled for cover, from which they watched in trepidation. To their relief, the gate remained firm, and the lock held. Against adamant even the Prince could not prevail. He turned to his tormentors. Flame shot from his eyes. They fled, cloaks smoking.

The jeweled hilt of his blade winked at him from the grass outside the fence, and a thought struck him: the Dragon's Tooth could cut anything. Too late! There it lay, just out of reach. Lost, his one chance! Somewhat daunted, he began to prowl the cage, searching for any weakness. So this was why the tiger paced endlessly; useless, and yet it seemed to make his captors uneasy. They had always feared his superior intelligence and power, his ability to see through the cleverest of their plans. Even now.

The night air stirred, and he became intensely aware of the girl again as she huddled, dazed and bleeding, on the concrete. Her blood would renew his strength. He shook off the thought; despised himself for it. And was surprised that he felt pity, stronger than the desire for blood. For the moment, at least. The thought comforted him, and he found the courage to go to her. He tore a piece from the tail of her shirt, wadded it up and pressed it against the oozing fang marks at her throat. Against his will, the scent of blood stirred the fires within, and he dared not trust himself near her. He placed her hand on the cloth. "Here, hold this." She turned her lethargic gaze upon him. But he saw that she understood, and glided away.

"How far you've fallen, proud Prince," the Rocket sneered. "Always lording it over the rest of us. What would the master say if he saw you now? Serving a mortal!"

"Come on, drink her blood," said the Sandman. "Who knows? It might give you the strength to escape the dawn."

Afraid the suggestion might weaken his resolve, the Prince occupied himself by making the rounds of the cage again. He tested the bars across the top; they were solid, with a strong component of iron. Next, he examined the door in the archway. Its frame and hinges were well made, set into a wall of thick concrete. With a burst of energy, he attacked the door again. His claws scored the surface; nothing more. He paid no heed to the gibes from outside the fence as he prowled the cage for the nth time, taking stock of his prison. The entire floor consisted of concrete, with iron bars sunk deep. If there had been bare earth, he could have dug his way out, or at least a grave for protection from the dawn. But there was none. He bowed his head in despair.

The tiger began pacing again. The Prince recalled the visit to the zoo with Mara, and the restiveness of the animals. He considered riling them again, but that would be useless, as the Sandman had said, while Styx kept the guard company. He felt a deep sadness at his lost dreams; sorrow overwhelmed him. The sun would burn him to ash; he would never see Mara again. Would she think he had betrayed her? And she would no longer have his protection… although, in retrospect, that did not seem to be worth much.

He heard the girl shivering. Moved to pity, he removed his cloak and covered her with it. The scent of fresh blood hit him again. Almost overcome, it was all he could do to move away. He went to sit in the shallow recess of the doorway. The vampires finally tired of heckling him when he did not respond, though they continued to lurk about the compound like uneasy shadows. Then Styx reappeared, her mouth stained crimson.

The Sandman frowned. "Hey, you didn't kill that guard, did you? We can't have someone nosing around just yet."

"I only had a taste," she whined. "I got hungry, and—" At the Sandman's impatient gesture, she shut her mouth and stood forlornly gazing through the fence at the Prince.

The Sandman turned to the cage with his unpleasant half-smile. "We'll get that little huntress, you'll see. It won't take long, now that you're out of the way."

The Prince's face tightened with menace. "See you do not underestimate her, lest you follow me into oblivion. And I am not done yet. Touch her, and you answer to me." The Sandman backed away in undignified haste from the glow of his eyes.

The Rocket edged toward the fence. "You have lost, Prince," he sneered. "Now we will kiss her for you."

The Prince directed his fiery gaze toward the perpetrator of this fresh gibe. The Rocket flung himself to the side, into the bushes—in something of a panic—the Prince noted, with an unpleasant smile. For he knew that the Rocket's preferred method of escape was to fly straight up, but that was out of the question with the dawn so near; instead, he had to scuttle into the underbrush, lucky to escape with nothing worse than a smoking cloak and an injured ego. From there he shrieked invective.

The Prince ignored the noise, turning to face Nyx as she approached the fence and stood looking. "The great Prince," she scoffed. "Samael, Angel of Death. Ruined, ruined. So easy to catch. What kind of vampire falls in love? And with his dinner? Hah!"

He did not dignify her insult with a response. "Where did you get the ring? You do not have her."

"You will die wondering!" she hissed, in a paroxysm of fury. "Know this: I will have her soon. You failed to bring her to the Master. I will not!" With that, she threw the ring.

As it bounced off the wall with a clang, the Prince reached out and caught it. It seemed to him that her fury was quite out of proportion to the provocation. Maybe they were not so certain of victory after all. A consoling thought.

"You are a fool, Prince. That huntress is just using you. She does not love you," Nyx sneered. "How could she, knowing what you are?" When there was no response, her face grew ugly with malice, "Know this, Prince. She was not wearing your ring when I took it. Think about that when the dawn comes."

And then they were gone.

Of course, Mara wasn't wearing the ring. She had explained that, and apologized. Still, it hurt. Mara had said she would wear it always, and despite himself, he felt cut to the heart. He bowed his head. Would the coming of the dawn be his release?

Mara glanced at the clock again. Suppertime, and still no Prince. Mara and her parents waited an hour and more before starting without him. From time to time, Mara glanced out the window. She had been so certain he would come. A breeze stirred the shrubbery outside. Distant points of light winked through the moving foliage, but still there was no familiar silhouette coming up the walk.

Her mother observed kindly that there must be a good reason for him to be late. Her father retired to the living room, tight-lipped and red-faced with the effort to refrain from comment.

Mara was alternately angry, worried, relieved, and disappointed as time marched on, and the Prince didn't show. By the time the dishes were put away and the kitchen tidied, it was nearly midnight. She fought back tears as she took one last glance toward the kitchen window. Still no sign of the Prince.

"I think we'll have to assume he's not coming, Mara," said her mother, interrupting her thoughts. "Maybe you ought to go to bed, unless of course, you have to go out again tonight. Why don't you take a break for once?"

Something in her tone gave Mara a jolt. How tired her mother sounded. She thought of her deceit and sighed. "Oh, Mom, you went through all that work tonight for nothing… "

"I don't mind. I just hope nothing's wrong."

"I can't think what." Mara blinked back tears. "He was so looking forward to coming over." She went into the living room. Her dad's chair was vacant now.

"I'm sure he'll have a perfectly good explanation," her mother said from the doorway. "But it's late. If you don't mind, I'll go to bed now."

"Sure. Good night, Mom. I should go out on patrol, anyway." Maybe I'll run into the Prince somewhere. She thought of the ring again; her mom hadn't taken it after all. So what had happened to it? How to explain to the Prince that she'd lost his precious gift? The thought depressed her; she didn't have the heart to go out just yet. Anyway, what if he showed up? Unable to stem her tears any longer, Mara sank into her favorite overstuffed chair, leaned her head against its arm and cried herself to sleep. And dreamed.

A tiger, rippling white and silken, flows through the tall grass, like a study in moonlight and shadow, powerful and deadly, its eyes gleaming like emerald. Then man-shaped shadows appear, creeping through the night, toward the tiger. It leaps up and bounds away, into the jungle. There, in a clearing, stands a cage. It's a trap! Mara tries to shout a warning, but as is the way of dreams, she can make no sound. The trap springs shut, and the tiger is caught. The trees shiver as it roars, under the waning moon. She watches in helpless horror as the men draw nearer. They raise their bows, and fiery arrows fly to their mark. Feathered shafts sprout from the tiger; it sinks to the ground, its eyes glazing to a dull black.

Dawn Comes Stalking

A slight whispering of sound announced Styx's presence at the gate. "I cannot stay, Prince," she said, with great sorrowful eyes. "When dawn comes, you'll make a fine flash; I'd love to see it, but alas…" With one last longing look at him over her shoulder, she vanished among the trees.

Her parting shot brought home to the Prince the inevitability of his doom. He glanced apprehensively at the sky, at the faint lightening in the east heralding the coming dawn and his immolation. Fire, a daunting prospect. *Yes, Styx, savor your revenge. Even this death by fire is too good for me. I am no better than Nyx. Just as she seduced me, so did I deceive you. I took your innocent life and made of you an immortal horror, caught in a web of fierce desire for all eternity. God, forgive me – I took Your own bride! How can I ever atone?*

His crime loomed large in his memory, like a giant, ever accusing; there was no blotting it out. She had left him alone, and gone, now. He was about to die and could never make it right. Overcome by remorse, he called out, his voice breaking, "Styx! Styx! Do not leave me like this!"

To his astonishment, she appeared at the fence at once. "You called, Prince?" Her voice stabbed him to the heart, so sweet, so sad.

"I am sorry, Styx. Forgive me."

"I do not understand."

"If only I could go back and change it all, I would. But alas, I am not a god, after all." Silence. "I know it is too little, too late. But I thought you should know." She did not respond, and he pressed on, "It was not your fault, but mine, entirely. Can you ever forgive me?"

"How can I?" she said slowly. "You took everything from me. I cannot forgive, you know that." Her tone suddenly became brittle. "Anyway, I do not want to go back. I like what I am."

"Oh, Styx." He bowed his head in shame and sorrow. "I ruined your life, your soul. You were good and beautiful and innocent, and I took it all away from you."

She laughed bitterly. "Good? How little you know! Innocence is nothing but ignorance. Why would I want that? I would be dead now, rotting in my grave, if not for you. You made me immortal. I am beautiful and young forever. You gave me a taste for blood, and you gave me ecstasy. I wanted it, do you hear? What else is there?"

"Styx—"

"But you," she interrupted, "You made me to love only you. You were my delight. Even when you spurned me, I was grateful for a touch, a look. But now—" Her voice lowered to a deep demonic growl. "Now you toss me aside for this mortal, another innocent. Why do you not drink her blood? Destroy her virtue!" Then, whining, she said, "Kill her. Or turn her. I will share. Prince, come back. How lost I am without you."

"Yes, lost, alas. You have cause to hate me. But if you ever loved me, please open the cage."

She stood silent and unmoved. He regretted the impulse to appeal to her nonexistent sympathy. His pride lashed him for having begged. He dropped his gaze and turned away.

"No, no," she relented, sounding a little desperate now. "Say you will come back. We will let you out, I promise."

He lifted his gaze to meet hers. It took an effort to resist those soft blue, pleading eyes, but he managed to choke out, "I can never go back."

At once, her eyes glittered black with hatred. "You think I would save you for her? Never! I hate you! I hope you suffer! Die! You—you—oh, how I wish I could watch you burn!" She took one quick look at the fading of the night sky and fled.

After she had gone, he felt deserted. With sinking heart, he stood looking toward the grove of trees into which she had vanished. If only… but no. It was poetic justice, after all.

He scanned the area and listened. The security guard's irregular breathing was faintly audible; there would be no help from that quarter. The animals were still restive, but gradually calming down. No one was about in the pre-dawn chill.

He began pacing the cage, searching yet again for escape, but as that seemed hopeless, the effort was more to distract himself from the girl huddled on the concrete. Despite the imminence of sunrise and his own destruction, his hunger had reawakened. The Sandman's suggestion that drinking blood may aid him to escape wormed its way into his mind. Should he? He was able to drink blood and yet stop short of killing. Though at the moment, he could not be certain of that.

Anyway, that was beside the point. Humans were beloved in the sight of God, not to be demeaned by feeding off them. When he thought of what Mara would think of him, he had his answer. That was the real test. Yes, better to keep his distance. The dog he had fed upon earlier had not been very satisfying. The presence of the more intoxicating elixir trapped in the cage with him could well be his undoing.

He drifted toward the tiger's cage. The animal reacted with a low growl, its ears laid back. It began to pace its enclosure again, making the circuit, growling each time it passed him. He floated, motionless, near the overhead bars in ominous silence, watching it. All at once, without warning, he rushed at the tiger with a shriek that echoed through the compound. Brought up short by the barrier between them, he gnashed his teeth against the bars and subsided to a deep demonic growl. The tiger spat and hissed, all dignity lost as it scrambled to the far side of its cage. The entire compound came alive with stamping feet and cries of alarm, bellowing and hissing and barking; animals of every kind joined in the cacophony.

The Prince listened for the sound of running feet; human feet. Nothing. With a glance of desperation at the fading sky, he sprang once more to the door of the barn and tore madly at it. Obviously, the door had been constructed for wild beasts. Its wood was like iron. Even his hard, sharp nails could not prevail – not in such a short time.

The light was brighter now, though the sun had not yet appeared above the horizon, and he began to feel its effects. Apprehensively he glanced toward the east. He glided over to the girl and retrieved his cloak.

"I need this now," he said apologetically as he donned it. "The sun will soon warm you." Or was she dead? He leaned down. Saw the sparkle of red at her throat and was nearly undone. Quickly he averted his eyes. She stirred, and the soft slow sound of her heartbeat sent tremors through him. His tongue flicked out before he thought; he felt his hunger flare into life. He reached out slowly, then tore himself away and leaped to attack the door again. He was soon spent, though he had barely scratched the surface. No time. Now the thrumming of that heartbeat filled the air, the world around him, and pierced him through. He forced himself not to look, to think of something else… anything else.

He turned his gaze to the sky and saw the reddening in the east. Too bright. It burned his eyes; he turned them away. Flattened himself against the door, trying to keep within the archway, the only shade, his only safety. Even that would give him but a very short time of grace, after which the increasing heat and reflective sunlight would finally become too much for even his night-black cloak. Then would come the direct sunlight and he would burn.

He wedged himself in the archway, pressing his back against the door, which seemed almost to possess a will of its own, as though it would push him out into the path of the sun. Panic. Destroy! No, he was the perversion, the unnatural being. It was only right that all of nature should oppose him. Soon the sun's rays would reach out to creep inexorably across the compound, through the cage, to finally touch him and set him on fire. Already the brightening sky hurt his eyes. He pulled the cloak over his head, withdrew inside himself, and let his mind drift into that narrow space between waking and sleep.

Once he thought he saw Mara as in a swirling mist, her sapphire eyes and her long single braid of fine-spun gold aglow in the pale morning light. *Her sweet face and bright smile…like the sun, the death of me.*

He reached out to her and was jolted awake when a flash of fire seared his hand. With an involuntary whimper of pain, he snatched it back from the ray of sunlight. Brightness surrounded him now; it weighed him down. He pressed his face into the corner, into the darkness of his cloak; he felt himself sinking down, down, melting as wax. Felt a weakness such as he had never known. Must the great Prince come to such an ignominious end?

Nyx was right. I am a creature of the night. Have I, like Icarus, flown too close to the sun?

He would have wept, but had no tears. Deep sorrow rolled over him in waves, dragging him down and down, into an abyss of despair. All is lost, all is lost. A deep groan wrenched from somewhere inside him. A prayer. *Mother of Mercy, help me.* And peace came over him. *Mother? Ave Maria, rose without thorns, help me that I shall not be lost.* Loving arms opened to receive him. He let himself fall, willing to rest in them forever.

With a cry, Mara jarred herself awake. She looked around, trying to think where she was. Her cheek lay on the tear-wet arm of the chair. Home. She was at home. What was she doing asleep when she ought to be out on patrol? She sat up. *Oh, yeah, my Prince never came.*

That dream! It was so vivid, so real, she could not shake it off. There was a tiger, a white one. Trapped in a cage? Into her mind flashed an image of the zoo and the Prince on the night of their visit there. And now this dream; she closed her eyes tight and held her head in anguish. What could it mean? The tiger, swift, graceful, powerful, like the Prince. Like the Prince… "What's this cage for?" she remembered him asking.

"Maybe some exotic beast," she had replied.

Now a great roaring filled her ears. Images cascaded through her mind. The cage, the tiger, the Prince. A trap, fiery arrows and the senseless destruction of a beautiful creature. Those fathomless dark eyes, and that look in them…was it a plea for help? She recalled that other tiger, in the zoo, and no shade once the sun was up.

The twittering of birds, those small heralds of morning, broke into her thoughts. Dawn! Mara sprang out of the chair; her intuitive mind was quick to recognize a need for immediate action, although not sure why, yet. One glance at the window revealed the lightness of the sky that signaled the approach of sunrise. She wasted no time grabbing her weapons. No need, with the breaking of dawn. All vampires would have vanished.

She felt the chill of early morning as she ran toward the park, and wished she had grabbed her jacket, but there was no time to go back for it. Somehow, she knew that. Her breath came in ragged gasps as she leaped fences, dodged among hedges and took shortcuts through backyards. Stars were fading as she entered the compound and ran toward the tiger's cage. The great orange beast crouched in the center, its ears back. Something flashed at her feet. The Prince's dagger! She stifled a sob, picked up the knife and tucked it into her belt. *He is here!*

She saw at once that the gate next to the tiger's cage was closed; the one that they had last seen standing open. And the cage was no longer empty. A pathetic figure huddled on the concrete, a girl with long blonde hair and a bloodstained shirt. Mara caught her breath. The victim of a vampire! And here she would find the Prince. No, not the Prince! Her eyes flooded with tears; she dashed them away. No time for that now.

She looked through the bars, toward the building. A dark form crouched in the doorway, almost hidden in shadow, the only shade in the cage; a very narrow strip of shade. Under the inexorable brightening of the sky, the stars were nearly all washed out. Mara flew to the gate and tried the latch.

"Prince! Prince, are you okay?"

The dark form moved; a pale hand appeared, drawing back the cloak to reveal his face. Gray-blue shadows smudged his eyes and the hollows of his cheeks, emphasizing the deathly white of his complexion. Gone was that beauty so striking in the night. The dawn's rays revealed the true state of his being. Even his eyes seemed dull in the growing light.

"Mara." His voice was faint, resigned.

No, he couldn't die now! Not the Prince! "Wait! I'll get someone."

"Too late," he said, or was it just a sigh?

No, silly, vampires don't sigh. Even from a distance, she could see that the light had weakened him; he was fighting to stay conscious. Soon the sun's rays would strike him down; would burn him to ash. She had seen that before, a few times. Not pretty, but very effective.

But those were just… vampires! This was the Prince.

He was wedged in the narrow doorway in an attempt to stave off the inevitable, but that reprieve would soon be ended. She saw death in those eyes before he covered his face again with his cloak, his only protection against the light.

"Don't leave me," she cried, tears falling unheeded. "I need you. Hang on, someone has to have a key."

She ran. The security guard was sitting glassy-eyed in his office with a large mug in one hand. He did not seem aware that he was drinking his coffee cold.

"Quick!" she shouted. "Open that empty cage out there; the one next to the tiger. Someone's locked inside." He slowly raised his head and looked at her, uncomprehending. "Come on!" She tugged on his arm, but got no reaction. Then she saw the twin puncture wounds at his throat. "The keys!" she yelled. "Give me the keys! I'll do it myself."

Only when she had managed to get the ring of keys off his belt did she finally meet with feeble resistance. With a hasty apology, she darted away, madly sorting through the collection of keys as she ran back to the gate. *Which one, oh, which one is it? Please help me, God.* With trembling fingers, she jammed a likely looking key into the lock. No luck. She tried another, and another, fumbling and almost dropping them in the process. They were all wrong. The lock was wrong, somehow. She could not think why; it just was. She wept with frustration; wanted to throw the keys. A hundred, and none of them fit. Useless. Of course, this wasn't a standard lock. Its key would be altogether different than these. It was not on the ring. *Please, Mother of Mercy, save the Prince. You had a plan for him. I know you did. Please don't let him be lost to me now.*

The sun peeped through the trees, sending out feelers of fiery light. The jeweled haft at her waist glittered in the morning sun. The knife with the Dragon's Tooth blade. He had said it would cut anything. With a surge of rising hope, she whipped it out of her belt and hacked at the links holding the lock.

The chain fell free with a clinking rattle and slithered to the ground; the lock followed. In a heartbeat, Mara was at the Prince's side, standing over him to block out the sun. She glanced toward the east. The deadly rays were creeping across the ground, toward the Prince. Soon they would destroy him.

"Hurry, it's time to go! Hurry!" she cried.

He stirred. "Too late. Sorry, I… "

Her heart sank as she saw that several streams of light had lengthened and were now stretched across the cage. The Prince would have to pass through them to reach the gate. A thought came to her: the inside door.

"No, we're not done yet, Prince. Hold on."

Again she ran. Around the cages, down the cement walkway to the entrance of the building. That door was locked, too. One of the keys had to fit. Had to. She fumbled with the ring once more, chose a key and stabbed it into the lock. It did not work. *Don't panic, just try another. St. Michael, help me.* This has to work. *St. Jude, please.* Her hands shook; she tried another. No luck. Then the next key. And the next. To her surprise and relief, that one slid in, and the lock clicked open.

She hurried inside. Into the dim passageway she ran, her footsteps pattering on the concrete floor. It was taking too long, this solving of the riddle of a maze while racing against time. The sun, always an ally in its dispelling of the creatures of the night, was now a deadly enemy. *Hurry.*

Finally, after what seemed an eternity of searching, she felt as if guided by an unseen hand; and there before her was the tiger's inside enclosure. Next to that had to be the one she was looking for. *Number seventeen*, it said. She breathed a prayer of thanks, adding, *Don't let me be too late.* A simple bolt slid easily aside to unlatch the door. She slipped into the inside pen, flung back the bar securing the outside door and pulled the handle. The heavy wooden door opened inward.

She caught the Prince in her arms as he fell through the doorway onto his knees. Smoke rose from his cloak where the sun's rays had touched it. His eyes were half-closed; he seemed quite out of it and leaned heavily against her. She kissed his forehead, her eyes brimming. She held him tightly against her breast and stroked his dark hair.

"I thought I'd lost you," she wept.

"And I, you," he said faintly. "It was a trap."

She saw that he was exhausted from his ordeal. "Don't talk now. Just rest." She eased him toward a heap of fresh straw in the corner of the enclosure.

His eyelids drooped, but with an effort, he roused himself and spoke again. "Please stand guard while I sleep?"

"Always."

"Don't let anyone in here, for my sake or theirs." He reached up and touched her cheek.

"Your hand!" she cried. A darkened, blistered area marred the smooth white skin.

"Sun," he whispered.

Her throat constricted as she thought of how near she had come to losing him. His eyes closed and he slept. She lowered him to the floor. One pale hand lay on his chest. Her troubled gaze lingered a moment before she turned away.

She opened the door to the outside a crack and slipped through. As she made sure it was closed securely, she noticed deep furrows marring its surface. Fresh scratches, clearly evidence of a beast's frantic efforts to escape. What would people think? With sinking heart, she turned to face the early morning beams of sunlight now illuminating the entire cage. And winced at the sight of the bent gate. *Ouch! Not something I can fix on the spur of the moment. That'll stir things up, for sure. Just what we need. Gosh, I can't leave him alone for a minute without everything crashing down around our heads.*

She shook her head and went to the girl, who had sunk down and was lying on the concrete now. Mara checked for a pulse. The heartbeat was strong; the girl would live. That was the good news. The bloodied shirt and fang marks at the throat told another tale. One that she would rather not face right now. It doesn't mean the Prince... It could have been one of the others. But he was a vampire, trapped with his natural prey. She blinked back tears. Had he been tempted beyond his strength? She fingered the haft of the knife and wanted to kill those who had done this.

She took a deep breath and turned to the girl. "Come on. Upsy." She helped her to her feet.

The girl was shivering from cold, shock, and loss of blood, and leaned heavily against her. Mara helped her through the gate, toward the guardhouse. She glanced often over her shoulder, concerned that someone might enter the enclosure in which the Prince slept. To disturb a sleeping vampire was to flirt with death, but her main anxiety was for the Prince's sake. A vampire was vulnerable while it slept.

She soon had the girl safely ensconced in a chair in the security office. The guard was still dazed, so she called nine-one-one. The key to the big door of the barn she put into her pocket, leaving him the remainder, then hurried back to the enclosure where the Prince slept. She bolted the outer door so that it could not be opened from the outside, then secured the inner door, hoping that there were no immediate plans for moving an animal into number seventeen cage today. That would bring someone snooping, for certain. If only they held off at least until tomorrow. By then the Prince would be long gone. She was a bit on edge about that damage; someone was sure to notice.

The Prince lay fast asleep in a dark corner. Wrapped in his cloak, he was invisible in the dark interior but for the faint pale blurs of hands and face. Mara gazed upon him, torn. Her heart belonged to him and yet…marriage? Good grief! What was she to do now?

A slight frown creased her brow as she considered the impact of that on Father Mike. Yet very little surprised him. She was not certain how the Prince would react if she suggested he meet with her mentor, but she was reluctant to proceed without Father Mike's approval. She had learned long ago to trust his judgment; experience had taught her that the natural consequences of ignoring his kindly advice were often swift and harsh. She heaved a deep sigh.

Faint sounds of increased activity due to the arrival of ambulance and police, as well as the zoo attendants and groundskeepers beginning their work, reached her even here, in the depths of the concrete building. No light penetrated the windowless enclosure. The Prince slept in the safety of darkness, so Mara felt she could leave him temporarily to investigate matters on the outside. Anyway, she needed her morning coffee.

She bolted the door and exited the building. The ambulance had taken the security guard and the girl to the hospital. The police were questioning the newly arrived workers. Mara tried to look as though she belonged and managed to avoid complications. She joined the cluster of people at the concession when it opened, bought a cup of coffee and sat down with it at a picnic table, where she could keep an eye on things.

Death Awakens

It would be a long wait, Mara could see, as she sipped her coffee. As usual, the police had no idea what to make of the signs of vampire activity, but would strive to find a natural explanation. Finally they drove away, leaving the workers to their usual routine. Mara breathed a sigh of relief. It seemed no one had yet noticed the damage, but it was sure to happen sooner or later. In that event, they would investigate, and she had no idea how to prevent disaster, yet she had to be ready to do what she could.

Cup of coffee in hand, Mara drifted toward the giraffes' pen, where she feigned interest in the animals while scanning the grounds for a good vantage point from which to observe the main door and the cage as well. While the Prince slept there was danger; only she knew how dangerous. *Do I really want this for the rest of my life?*

She trudged up a grassy rise toward a wooded area where the walking trails began, and sat on a bench in the shade to finish her coffee. She leaned back with a sigh. From there, she had a clear view of the door. As the morning wore on, the air grew warmer, and her eyelids began to droop. She had not slept well last night. A faint breeze whispered among the trees. The hiss of spraying water and the drone of a lawnmower faded. She dreamed.

She is walking in a meadow, her face turned up to the sun, her eyes half-closed. Her hands trail through the tall grass; feathery seed heads brush her fingertips. Bees hum in the sweet clover, whose fragrance hangs heavy in the summer air. A flock of birds explode out of a nearby aspen grove and fan out across the field. Something has frightened them—a white tiger! It lifts its head from the grass and growls. Its eyes glow red and fix on her as it rises to its feet. It springs at her.

She awoke with a cry, heart pounding. The sun was beating down on her. There was no tiger. She looked around in confusion. That sudden gabble of voices... what... where...? She smelled animals and recalled she was at the zoo. The white tiger... No, that was a dream. She must have fallen asleep. Scary, but it was only a dream. She stretched, looked down the hill toward the compound and saw...the barn door was ajar!

That jolted her into full awareness. She leaped to her feet and ran down the slope. At the door she paused; there were a million reasons why someone might enter the building. Yet she could not shake the feeling of disquietude. Not after that dream; another dream of the white tiger! She slipped through the door and waited for her eyes to adjust to the darkness of the interior. It was cool after the heat of the sun outside. She moved down the passage in her soft-soled boots, occasionally stopping to listen.

Silence. Wait! Was that someone talking? She paused in mid-stride, heard a faint murmur of voices. Her heart in her throat, she surged forward on silent cat feet. The sound was coming from the direction of the Prince's temporary sleeping quarters. *Oh, dear Jesus, help!* Her heart hammered. She took a deep breath and told herself it was unlikely anyone would have reason to enter that vacant enclosure.

She turned the corner, every nerve tense. The gate to number seventeen was not quite latched! Her breath caught. At that moment, she heard a shout and a low unearthly growl.

At noon, Chuck and Trevor paused in front of the monkeys' cage, their T-shirts clinging to their backs — Chuck's muscular one and Trevor's very skinny one — after a strenuous morning's work. They'd been friends since high school and were inseparable. Cleaning cages and feeding animals at the zoo was their part-time job during the school year and full-time job during the summer, so they knew the routine.

"Man, I'm beat!" Chuck said, wiping beads of sweat from his

brow. "That's hot work. I need a joint."

"Hey, cage seventeen's still empty. I bet no one will be going in there," Trevor said. "That'd be the perfect place."

After storing their tools in the shed, they slipped unobserved into the building. The barn was dim after the bright sunshine, but they soon found number seventeen and noiselessly slid back the bolt. The door opened with a faint creak. They eased through, and Trevor pushed it almost closed.

"Shoot! I can't see nothing!" Chuck cursed as he fumbled in the dark.

"Here, man, I've got a lighter." Trevor brushed his flop of hair out of his narrow brown eyes and peered into the dark, then pulled a Bic from his pocket and flicked it. The tiny flame cast giant shadows around the stall as he shone it on the weed. His friend rolled a joint and lit up with trembling hands. Each inhaled deeply. "Man, that's wicked," rasped Trevor.

"It's the good stuff. From my brother-in-law. You know Todd."

"Yeah, man. Like, gimme some more of that."

Chuck handed the joint back to Trevor and reached for the lighter. It went out. "Whoa! Where's that light?" He chuckled as he flicked it on again and moved further into the enclosure. "Hey, this is cool. We should party in here sometime." He held the light up higher and looked around. "Think anybody'd notice?"

"Yeah. Maybe invite some girls," Trevor agreed, grinning. "Be fun to bring a six-pack or two and—"

"Holy—!" Chuck's muted exclamation interrupted Trevor's rambling. "Some dude's sleeping in here! Or maybe he's dead?"

Trevor turned just as Chuck leaned down to shine the feeble light of the Bic further into the shadowy corner. Sure enough, a dark form lay on its back on the straw-strewn floor, its face a white blur in the blackness. It was still as a wax figure, with eyes closed and deeply shadowed. Odd how red the lips were. One pale hand lay on its chest, with nails long and shining.

Chuck thrust the lighter nearer the face. "Why, if it ain't Dracula!" He smirked over his shoulder.

As Trevor strained to see, the eyes sprang open, empty and black. He jerked back. Chuck saw the look on his face and spun back around. The red mouth opened, and sharp white teeth gleamed in the faint light. The hiss that issued from that mouth was the most terrifying sound Trevor had ever heard in his life.

"What the hell?" Chuck staggered back and crashed into Trevor. He dropped the lighter and the flame went out, leaving them in utter blackness. "The light! Damn!"

They fell to the floor in a confusion of limbs and curses, searching frantically. Trevor whimpered in terror as he scrabbled about, feeling for the lighter. At last. He fumbled it and nearly panicked at the sound of a faint rustling in the straw, but heard Chuck's panting beside him and breathed again. Chuck would deal with it; he always welcomed a chance to flex his muscles and prove how tough he was.

Finally, Trevor managed to flick the light on. The tiny flame threw shadows on the wall as he lifted the Bic with a shaking hand. And nearly fainted as a dark form rose with a fluid motion to tower above them. It looked human, and yet not. But—but—vampires weren't real! Then its eyes blazed like red-hot coals.

Trevor wanted to scream, but all his breath was gone. He could only watch in horror as white hands snaked out from the black shadow and caught up Chuck as easily as if he were a rag doll. Big, tough Chuck, who let no one push him around.

"Mommy!" squeaked Trevor, gibbering. "Chuck, do something!"

But Chuck was looking into those eyes, slack-jawed. The vampire growled, pulled him into its embrace, opened its mouth and leaned in to bite.

"Chuck! No-oo-ooo!" Without a thought for his own hide, Trevor lunged. He snagged a handful of Chuck's T-shirt and tried to run, but his knees had turned to jelly.

Feeble though it was, the effort was enough. The vampire paused to brush him off. Trevor hit the wall with such force he was stunned for a moment. He blinked as the door flew open and a girl leaped in with a shout, her golden braid flying. She landed between the vampire and its intended victim. The small crucifix at her throat swung toward it and knocked it reeling against the wall.

Chuck, suddenly released, collapsed to the floor. "Ho—lee—! Wicked stuff, man!" he said, smiling and starry-eyed as he lay there. He made no attempt to regain his feet.

Trevor stared at Chuck, then at the girl and the vampire. It *was* a vampire!

"Get out of here," the girl barked. "Take your friend and get out. Now!"

Trevor wilted under her glare. He quickly shook the smiling Chuck by the shoulder. "Come on, man. Party's over. Let's go."

The vampire was cringing near the wall. Trevor wondered at the girl daring to stand with her back to it. How he got Chuck to his feet, he never knew, but he soon had him hustled out the door. With a sob of relief, he cast a quick, apprehensive glance back.

The girl was watching them with hard blue eyes. Then the door closed and hid her from sight. He heard a clank as the bolt slid home. By now the fuzz was gone from his brain; he hurried Chuck to the bright sunshine and safety. Then Trevor collapsed onto a bench, shaking.

Mara secured the gate, though she was pretty certain the boys would not be back. But what if they told someone? No, they had no business being there, and dared not talk if they valued their jobs; not with that little pot-smoking venture during work hours. Even if they did, *nobody believed in vampires*, she told herself. Still, she felt uneasy. *This is going to be a long day.*

She sighed and turned to the Prince. He crouched against the wall, the picture of misery. She reached out to touch his shoulder in a gesture of consolation.

"I'm so sorry," she murmured. "I, um, fell asleep."

"Why didn't you let me die?" His voice broke.

His terrible grief tore at her heart. All doubt melted away like wax before a flame, just as quickly as had his fearsome vampire persona. She pressed him close.

"Don't say that. I can't lose you now. What would I do without my heart?"

"Your heart. Ah, how can you love me? I'm a monster. If you hadn't come in just then, I'd have killed that boy. Doesn't that bother you?"

Tears stung her eyes. "Of course it does. But I can't seem to help myself. What did you do to me that night in the church?"

"I don't know. I don't know that I did anything. I'm afraid you may come to regret that you didn't kill me." He held her close, touched her hair. "I regret it already."

"Don't. I wouldn't trade you for anything in the world. I didn't expect this and wouldn't have chosen it—not in a million years—but it happened. We're pledged to each other forever, now, and… " She went cold as she remembered the ring. The ring he had given her. Already it was lost, and "forever" had hardly begun.

As if he had read her thought, he reached inside his cloak and drew out a flash of green. Speechless with dismay, she could only stare at the ring lying accusingly on his palm. He said nothing but only looked at her. She could not read in his face what was going through his mind and imagined the worst. When finally he spoke, it was nothing like she expected.

"I release you from your pledge, if you so wish. After what happened tonight, I cannot hold you to it. Someday I may kill someone. I may kill you. My life is a torment. You have no idea of the hunger, the thirst; I don't know how long I can…oh my dear, you must see that I am not worthy of you. If you wish to be free, I understand. You do not need me to drag you down."

She burst into tears. "I'm so sorry. I can't believe I lost the ring. I don't understand how—it just disappeared." She dashed the tears away. "Anyway, you totally can't release me from my pledge. Only God can, and He won't, because I meant what I said. If you don't want me—tough! You've got me." She dried her eyes on her sleeve. He was silent, so she went on, "Or why don't you just kill me now? You're tearing my heart out anyway, with all this talk of—of—" At that her voice failed her, but with an effort she managed to compose herself. "I'll have that ring back now, if you don't mind."

He closed his eyes and was still for so long that she began to feel anxious, until his eyes opened, finally. He spoke softly, in a tone of awe. "You still want me?"

Tears welled up in her eyes again; she dared not speak. All her doubts and fears fled. He took her hand almost reverently and slipped the ring onto her finger.

The rest of the day passed without incident. A minor flurry of excitement surrounded the discovery that a key was missing, but no one was able to account for its disappearance. Chuck and Trevor dared not come forward during the investigation. By then, they were wondering if they'd been hallucinating and tacitly agreed not to talk about their experience. This pact lasted until the scare wore off. By the time the next party rolled around, they let slip a hint or two, then allowed themselves to be cajoled into telling the story, with certain embellishments, to a rapt audience. The girls were impressed, and even some of the boys. Probably no one believed them, but the entertainment value was worth a mint.

Mara and the Prince spent the rest of the day in the darkness of the enclosure, waiting for the sun to set. Now that the Prince was awake, Mara was a bit more at ease; they would not be taken by surprise again.

The hours passed quickly as they talked. The Prince asked about her life. Mara told of how, as a small child, she had nearly driven her parents to distraction with what they thought was either an overactive imagination or nightmares. Though she claimed it was real, those faces at her upstairs window, tapping on the glass and begging her to let them in, and such-like. Her parents were troubled at her detailed description of vampires; how could she know of such things? They did not own a television set and were vigilant about what she watched elsewhere. Was it demonic?

They confided in Father Mike. He at once recognized Mara as the Huntress, pointing out the mark on her forehead, put there by an angel of the Lord. Her parents glanced at one another uneasily; neither of them could see it. Then her mother recalled one night, when Mara was not yet a year old, how she had noticed a glow around the crib in the baby's darkened bedroom. She had halted at the doorway, struck with awe by the shining figure of a young man (an angel?) bending over the sleeping child. With one finger he had traced a cross on her brow, then vanished. She had afterward persuaded herself that this was only a dream, for though the glowing cross had remained for a time, it had then faded. Apparently, Father Mike could see it even then, several years afterward. How, he could not say.

He did try to explain the significance of Mara's dreams and experiences. That their child should hold the fate of the world in her hands filled them with both terror and delight. It was difficult to believe at first, but they were relieved and grateful for Father Mike. Him they could trust; he seemed to know something of what this was about, and did not doubt their sanity. At their request, he had agreed to guide her as she grew. It seemed to them that God had already chosen him, since only he had seen the mark. He advised them not to let this startling revelation disrupt their normal family life. Mara needed a stable home, the same as any other child.

At first, Mara thought everyone was like her, with all six senses highly developed. Only gradually did she learn that her gifts were unique, and why, as Father Mike prepared her for her mission in life. Her teenage years went relatively smoothly, with only the occasional (mild) rebellion against serious commitment. He saw to her spiritual training, teaching her that virtue was her shield. For her physical training, he mentored her in martial arts and the development of her naturally acute senses. She loved to read, and from books, she learned everything known to man of her primary enemy, the vampire. The eventual harsh lessons of experience taught her the rest.

She became adept at steeling herself to the task, to plunge a stake into the heart of a vampire or to cut off its head without hesitation. Disordered sympathy could mean her death or other unwanted consequences. The truly merciful act was to release the undead body into the sleep of real death, and the trapped soul into the Hands of its Maker. Her cold efficiency in dispatching vampires did not in any way dampen her warmth and compassion toward mortals.

Now, in the dimness of the enclosure, she contemplated the Prince as vampire and wondered: Had she failed in her duty? Should she have killed him too? But that was no longer possible, it appeared. Anyway, now he had a soul.

The opportunity arose for her to broach the topic of consulting Father Mike. Here the Prince had serious reservations. She sensed a sudden withdrawal into himself. So he still feared the sacred, she realized, like any other vampire. Her heart sank. What could it mean? The harder she tried to solve these riddles, the more they seemed to multiply.

"It's the only way," she said finally. "I never make a serious decision without running it past Father Mike."

The Prince was silent for a long time. She could see that he got her meaning; this was an ultimatum, a necessary condition, if he wanted her for his own. She waited, on edge, feeling that her whole life hung in the balance.

"I will see him," he said reluctantly, "if you wish."

She exhaled then, unaware until that moment that she had been holding her breath. "It'll be okay." She took his hand and pressed it to her cheek. "You'll like him. He's a real father."

He looked away. "I never again want to let you out of my sight. You cannot imagine the devastation of my heart when I thought the Sandman had you." His hold on her hand tightened, though he did not seem aware of it.

"Ouch! Watch that grip, will you? I'm only a poor helpless girl, you know."

"Sorry." He let go of her hand, then realized she was joking. "Helpless? Not so. But you still need me. The master is still out there with the power of darkness at his command, and he wants you, dead or undead."

"I'm not afraid. Bring it on, I say. I've prepared for this my whole life. To face him. It's what I was born for."

"And yet, God bent His law to put me on your side; there has to be a reason for that. Not for me; I did nothing to deserve it. It is for your sake only. I think because He knows you will need an ally in the coming battle."

She looked thoughtful for a moment. "It makes sense," she conceded, "considering all that's happened."

"And I promise you this: if I can't bite you, no one else is going to, either," he said, his face expressionless.

"Uh, er...." she began, at a loss for words for a moment. Then she realized he was joking. She laughed.

And he thought, *That is a sound I could listen to forever. For her I will even see the priest she holds in such high esteem.* That man (something he could never again be, and jealousy, like a poisoned dart, pierced him through). That priest (the thought of facing a priest made his very soul lurch with dread). But for her, he would do anything, he told himself.

The Prince knew when the sun set, without the benefit of a watch or any other mechanical device. The knowledge came from within, along with a gnawing hunger to awaken him and his eternal hunting instinct.

She was too warm and too close. "It is time," he said. With that, he flung open the gate and was gone.

Mara stared after him for a moment, then ran to the door and looked around outside. There was no sign of him. No sense of him at all. *Well, so much for that.* She left the zoo and headed for home. *And he didn't want to let me out of his sight?* She shrugged. *What can I say? He's a vampire. Will I ever get used to this?* A big yawn ambushed her. *Gosh, I'm tired, and hungry, too. I guess I haven't eaten since last night. Hmm, those leftovers would taste pretty good about now. A chicken sandwich, with lettuce and tomato....* A thought struck her: Of course, that was why... the Prince was hungry too! So maybe he hadn't bitten that girl, back there in the cage.

After she had walked awhile, he suddenly appeared beside her. She jumped, heart pounding, shakily breathed again, and thanked God that this was not some other vampire taking her unawares. He took her hand in his. Cold. Vampire. She dared not look at him, afraid she would see a smear of blood, maybe, and she did not want to think about that right now.

"This is your home?"

She looked up and there it was. The familiar pale Spanish-style two-story house with arches and a red-tiled roof, right in front of her. Home. He knew.

"Why, um, so it is." She lifted her gaze to his at last. There was no sign of blood on that face so white it almost seemed to have a glow of its own in the darkness, like the moon. So perfect, so apparently pristine. The exquisite face that had so awed her that night in the church. Not the death mask of this morning. Had he changed because it was night, or because he had fed? A disturbing thought.

"Where were you?" she blurted without thinking, then flushed. "Oh dear, I shouldn't have said...."

"I—" he faltered and dropped his eyes, then lifted them to hers, dark and intense. "I was hungry."

"Of course. I—I just...I missed you and...I'm sorry, it slipped out."

"It was an animal. And I did not bite that girl, if you are wondering."

She felt a rush of relief. And was embarrassed that he had

read her thoughts again, or that she had exposed his shame. With an effort, she managed to quell the image of him feeding, and her revulsion. She would not think about it now. "I, uh, I didn't mean to accuse...."

"You have every reason to doubt me. I am a vampire. But just so you know, the very thought of it is a horror to me now, though my craving remains. To do the things I've done and to care; you have no idea." He closed his eyes as though in pain. "I will regret my deeds forever. Forever."

Moved by pity, she put her arms around him and leaned her head against his chest. His arms tightened around her for a moment, then he released her and stepped back.

She turned to put a hand to the latch. He stood there looking, as though he would devour her with his eyes. The really disturbing part was how much she wanted to fly to him. With an effort, she tried to compose herself, to think of something ordinary to say. "Er, since you're here, would you like to meet my parents? Just for a minute."

"If you wish." He almost sounded uncertain.

Her gaze swept over him in quick appraisal, anxious now. How would her parents see him? Would they guess? Of course, how could they not? *Oh, dear. Am I ready for this? Is he? Are they?* "What if, you, um, took off the cloak? I wouldn't want them to be too shocked." She flushed. "Not that I—I mean, er...." She felt a rush of relief at his look of amusement.

"Your wish is my command." He whipped off the cloak, and it seemed to vanish into thin air. She realized only in retrospect that he had folded it to handkerchief-size and tucked it into a pocket with vampire deftness, too fast for the mortal eye to follow. He struck a pose. "Am I now suitably attired?"

Um, okay, he means to be funny. Yes, he looked very handsome in black; the dated style rather suited him. "It'll do." She managed a smile. And for the first time in her life, she invited a vampire into her home.

In Vino Veritas

Mara's parents were sitting on the couch holding hands, heads together over maps and brochures spread across the coffee table. Each had a glass of wine. At the sound of the door closing, her mother glanced up.

"Oh, Mara, you're home. I saved your supper. It might still be warm. Oh! I didn't realize..." Flustered at the sight of a stranger, she retrieved her hand and it fluttered in an automatic attempt to tidy her hair as she rose from the chair and hastened over to them. "Hello, um..."

"Er, Mom, I was telling you about..." Mara began.

Her mother extended her hand, smiling, though a bit tentatively. "Oh, yes. I don't recall if you mentioned a name..."

"I, um, this is, er, I mean, I guess I..." His name!

The Prince stepped forward to clasp her mother's hand. "Niklaus Sperling," he said easily. "Just call me Niki. My pleasure, Madam. I have been looking forward to meeting you."

Her mother's smile wavered, and she snatched her hand from his as though burned, or so it seemed to Mara. Or, cold? *Uh-oh. Busted already!*

"Why, thank you, er, Niki. We were anxious to meet you, too. I'm Annie. Mara's dad is Joe, there."

"I apologize. We did not mean to interrupt... "

"Oh, no, that's fine. We have plenty of time to plan our vacation. Come over here, Joe. Be civil, at least."

Mara's father was gathering the maps and papers into a neat stack.

"Dad," said Mara.

"This is wonderful," her mother said, covering for his lack of

152

courtesy. "We get to meet you at last."

The Prince caught her meaning. "Forgive me for failing to show last night. I was unavoidably detained."

Mara suppressed the urge to laugh hysterically. Nerves. *Chill, Mara.*

"These things happen," said her mother. She tore her gaze from the Prince's. "But if we'd known you were coming, I'd have prepared…"

"Mom, it's okay. I thought since he walked me home, you could meet him while I grab a bite to eat and…"

"And I've already eaten, thanks," the Prince said.

Mara's father finally came over to shake hands with the visitor. She noted that he seemed to approve of the firm grip, but the cold hand, the distinctive pallor, and the dated attire had to be a dead giveaway. He knew vampires were real.

"So, you finally show up," Joe said in a chilly tone. Annie gave him a warning look; he thawed a little. "Somewhat late, but… since you're here, you may as well come in so we can have a look at you."

"Thank you, sir," the Prince said. "You are very kind."

Mara cringed at the look on her dad's face; he meant to find a chink in that cool exterior. "What exactly are your intentions toward my daughter?" he said then.

"Dad." Distressed, Mara glanced at the Prince uncertainly. His hand unobtrusively caught hers and gave it a squeeze.

"They are honorable, I assure you. And despite our inauspicious beginning, I promise to prove more punctual in the future."

Joe gave him a cool glance. "That's a bit presumptuous, isn't it?" He caught Mara's look, and without waiting for a reply, he went on. "So, Mr. Sperling, what line of work are you in?"

"Please, just call me Niki. Um… at the moment, I'm assisting Mara. In, er, an advisory capacity and as bodyguard."

"Since when does Mara need a bodyguard?" Joe muttered. To the Prince, he said bluntly, "So you're out of a job, are you?" He emptied his wineglass. "Vampires?" he said under his breath as he turned away, "Ought to fit right in. He even looks like one."

Mara's mother gave him a grim look and turned to the guest. "Won't you come into the living room? Have a chair and make yourself comfortable."

"I really can't stay," said the Prince (his keen ears having picked up Joe's every word).

"No, no, please. Come in for a few minutes. I'll put on the teakettle." She led the way as though never doubting that he would follow.

Mara clung to the Prince's hand, a little on edge. "Would you like a cup of tea?" she asked him, unsure if he drank tea.

"Never mind tea," said her father, his jaw set grimly. "Let him try some of my wine. He must be of age. Right?" Without waiting for an answer, he left the room.

"They like you already," Mara whispered anxiously.

"Certainly. What's not to like?" the Prince said softly, and she had to smile.

She led him to the couch, her confidence returning once more as she looked into his eyes. He was so self-assured and sweet. How could she have doubted? Her parents would soon love him too.

The sound of her father clearing his throat snapped her back to the real world. He had set a bottle of wine and two more long-stemmed glasses on the coffee table. "We'll try the Concord first. It's my best this year." He feigned not to notice their confusion, though he chuckled, a little maliciously, perhaps, as he splashed amethyst-red wine into the two goblets and handed one to each of them, then refilled his own. He raised his glass to his lips, watching the Prince with narrowed eyes.

"Careful," Mara warned under her breath. "It may be stronger than you think." This was not the first time her father had had occasion to ply young men with his wine, meaning to expose the face beneath the mask. She was not sure of the effects of alcohol on a vampire. Would the Prince give himself away? What would his true face look like to her parents? How would they take it?

Her father began discussing wines; he soon discovered that his guest was not ignorant of the subject (perhaps somewhat oddly well informed for one so young). Still, Mara was relieved that the Prince seemed immune to provocation and unlikely to be goaded to anger or intemperance. It seemed she could safely leave them to it. She excused herself and went to the kitchen, where her mother was arranging cookies on a serving plate.

"I happened to have these on hand. But cheese and crackers go better with wine. Maybe I should run to the store and—"

"Mom, he already ate, and Dad likes cookies. I'll just eat my supper." Her plate was still warm. "Gosh, Mom, this looks so good." She heard a meow and scratching at the back door and went to open it. Smoky slipped through like a shadow into the kitchen and did a figure eight around her ankles; she picked him up.

"Where is this young man from?" said her mother in a low voice. "He does seem a bit, er, foreign."

"I, um, I didn't think to ask," Mara managed, as she cuddled the cat. *How to answer that? Hell? The Underworld?*

Her mother took the hint and shelved the question for the moment. "Okay, this is ready. It's not quite what... I feel so bad that he missed supper last night."

"Down you go, Smoky." The cat made a beeline into the living room, toward its favorite chair.

Mara reached for her plate, while her mother picked up the cookie tray. At that moment they heard a screech from the living room, and hissing and spitting. Mara exchanged a quick glance with her mother and ran to look. The cat stood as though petrified in the center of the room, fur standing on end and ears laid back, its eyes fixed on the Prince.

On the Prince's face was a look of slight surprise.

"What the hell?" said Mara's father.

Her mother stared over her shoulder.

What next? "Come here, Smoky." Mara managed a soothing tone, picked up the trembling cat and hurried out of the room. Smoky clawed his way out of her arms and dashed upstairs. "Ow." Mara brushed cat hair from her shirt, glad she was wearing long sleeves. Her nerves were almost as frazzled as Smoky's when she returned to the living room with her plate of food in hand. Her mother cast a doubtful glance at the Prince as she set the tray of cookies on the coffee table.

"That isn't like him," Joe was saying.

"Um, he's—he's not used to strangers?" Mara managed.

Her mother gave her a sharp look. "My goodness! Cats are so temperamental. Would anyone like some cookies?"

The Prince politely declined, but Mara's father helped himself. "Smoky's never like that. Maybe you hate cats, and he senses it?" he suggested, as he refilled their glasses.

The Prince shrugged. "I had a dog once. Maybe he knew."

Mara's father looked at the Prince with sudden interest. "Where did you say you were from?"

"I have not said. But I was born in, uh, Germany—in a village called Engelsburg, in the Mosel region. It was very small. You will not find it on a map."

"Ah, that's it then," Joe said with a speculative look. "Your accent is so slight, I couldn't quite place it."

Mara cast an anxious glance toward her dad. One of his hobbies was languages, and he was pretty sharp. The Prince's accent was rather ambiguous. That in itself might give him away.

The Prince raised an eyebrow but did not comment.

"That would be the heart of wine country, right?" said Joe, renewing the previous discussion.

And Mara thought, *Gosh, Dad learns more about the Prince in one short visit than I found out in… but I guess that's because I never asked.* Now her dad seemed quite taken by the Prince, which was odd, so sudden after the initial unpleasantness. She tried not to think of why. Was it ethical for the Prince to so employ his vampire powers? Or maybe he had captivated her dad by his quick wit and surprising knowledge. That could be it. Funny, she had thought him overly serious; this sense of humor surprised her. He was more like her father than she had supposed.

Yet in looks they were nothing alike. Her father was of average height and build, his hair and skin as golden as the California sun, with thoughtful blue eyes that betrayed a keen intelligence and an easy smile that had a youthful charm belying his apparent seriousness. He never wore black, because, he stated firmly, he was neither a priest nor an undertaker.

The Prince, on the other hand, was tall and spare, and he always wore black. His dark hair and eyes were a stark contrast to his skin pale as moonlight. Though usually somber, he had a ready wit, and his black eyes betrayed profound depths of thought. Tonight he even smiled; so lovely, those fine teeth gleaming and white. And there was that subtle grace and power even in repose.

Tiger. He's so handsome, and he's mine. She sighed.

Her father brought out the chessboard and challenged the Prince. Several games later, Mara finally suggested that it was time to break it up if they were to patrol the town before dawn.

"Hey, I have to beat him once, at least," her father chuckled. "And he hasn't tried the dandelion yet. Anyway, it's not even midnight. And this boy's not Cinderella."

A coach transforming into a pumpkin isn't quite what I... "Next time, Dad? I promise I'll bring him back."

"Fine. I'll hold you to it."

As they walked the streets of town, talking, Mara wondered. Had she been unwise to invite the Prince into their home? When he said he enjoyed the visit and that he liked her dad, what exactly did that mean to a vampire, and where would it lead? The ease with which he had pulled off the dreaded meeting with her parents was a little disturbing, actually.

"You, you wouldn't bite him, would you?" Somehow, that

came out all wrong. She gave the Prince a quick glance, but he did not appear to be insulted.

With a look of amusement, he only replied, "Not unless he bites me first."

"So where did Niklaus Sperling come from?" she said more sharply than she had intended, uncertain of this comic mood. "And Niki?" How did alcohol affect a vampire?

"Ah. The name. It was the one I had long ago. I decided to try it on for size once again."

Of course, he must have had a name, once, she reminded herself; like any mortal. *Now he's a vampire*. The thought turned her cold inside.

Savage Garden

Mara's bedroom was bright with sunshine when Smoky's loud purring next to her ear awakened her. She squinted at the clock and groggily sat up. "Good grief, look at the time! I'll be late for class." The big gray cat settled in next to her pillow. She gave him an affectionate shove. "Don't get too comfortable, crazy cat. After last night? I ought to disown you." She headed for the shower.

She had returned home just before dawn. Only then, when she saw her reflection in the mirror just inside the front door, did the thought strike her. The mirror! Had her mother seen that the Prince had no reflection? She had looked at him rather strangely. *Oh, dear. Did they guess?*

When she went downstairs to the kitchen, the house was empty; she would have to wait until later for answers. Fine. She wasn't ready to face the music yet. The coffee was still hot, so she filled a travel mug and set out for school.

After class, she met Maggie and Sabrina at the mall for an afternoon of shopping. Maggie found a black gown to wear to the opera. Sabrina couldn't resist a green dress that matched her eyes. Mara approved their choices and tried on a few outfits to join in the fun, but her mind was elsewhere. By the time they took a break, heat waves were shimmering above the pavement. They walked to the Cup o' Java and found a table in the shade on the patio. There they sat, fanning themselves and sipping iced cappuccinos as they chattered.

Mara fell to talking of the Prince; her eloquence could not begin to do him justice, she admitted. "I guess you'll just have to see him for yourself."

"I love this!" Sabrina sighed. "It's so romantic."

"I'm so totally curious it isn't funny," said Maggie. "At least point him out so we can see what he looks like."

Mara was just scrounging up the courage to tell Maggie he was a vampire when Josh and George arrived, and the moment was lost. There were greetings all around as the boys pulled up chairs and joined them.

"Hey, did you hear what happened over at the park?" Josh blared as he bit into a roast beef sandwich. "Cops, ambulance… it was a regular zoo around there!" He laughed heartily at his own joke.

"Seriously? An accident at the zoo?" Sabrina said.

"Yeah, or something. A couple of people got hauled to the hospital. One was the night watchman. And you should see that cage! You know, the empty one? Bogus, dude!" Josh took another bite of his sandwich.

"It was wicked!" George squeaked in his excitement. "We had a look. The gate was bashed out of shape, and the lock cut clean off! Inside the cage, the door of the building was scratched all to hell. By razor-sharp claws, it looked like."

"Demon claws," Josh said in a shivery voice, curving his fingers into claws, dramatically. "Like something was trying to escape… but there was nothing in the cage!" He started humming the theme song from *The Twilight Zone*.

"Cool," Sabrina said, though she looked worried.

"Nobody saw anything?" Mara asked.

"Yeah, actually," Josh said with a wink.

"Hey, you're asking us?" George grinned. "Rumor has it that you were there."

"Was I?" Mara tried for nonchalance. "Fine, I'll bite. What is it… the rumor, I mean? I can see you're dying to tell."

"Aw, come on, Mara," said Josh. "You claim to prowl around at all hours of the night fighting monsters. What was it this time?"

"We're your friends," George coaxed, smiling. "Come on, tell us. Was it you?"

"You first," Mara said.

George adjusted his glasses. "Well. This guy Trevor in my computer class tells me that a weird thing happened to him and his buddy while they were working at the zoo. They were in that building there when they saw this vampire, or something. He was going to call Ghostbusters, but just then this little Xena charges in and saves the day. When he mentioned her long blonde braid, I thought, *That's gotta be Mara!* Was it you?"

Mara glanced away. "And what were they smoking?"

He looked a little deflated. "Yeah, I know. They were on their break, toking up in that empty stall where they thought no one would see them. Still, where there's smoke, there's fire. And I don't mean pot smoke." He gave her a knowing look.

"So who was this guy spreading rumors about me?" Mara said.

George was intent on unwrapping his brownie. "Trevor. Yeah, he's a pothead. It was probably nothing," he added, disappointed that his story had fallen flat.

"Sorry, George," Mara relented. "What else did he say? Really. Maybe he knows who I am and.... Don't worry, I won't beat him up. Who's going to believe him, anyway, right?"

"Yeah." George reddened. "His story was a bit mixed up, something about it being pitch dark in there. And just as they lit up, Dracula jumped out at them. They nearly ate their shorts. Never even had time to think about Ghostbusters. He was joking about that. But he swears the rest of it really happened. Says it was the scariest thing he ever saw in his life; he nearly swore off dope for good. His buddy still has the marks where he got bit. That's what he said, anyway. I didn't see them myself."

"That must have been some harsh weed," Mara managed. *Dracula? This is my Prince they're talking about.* She frowned. *And he did not bite the guy!*

"Does your mother know what kind of people you hang out with, George?" Maggie said, raising an eyebrow.

"Game freaks," sniffed Sabrina. "Okay, subject change. Something more exciting. And not just a rumor. Mara has a boyfriend."

With a grateful glance at Sabrina, Mara took a deep breath. "Right. I suppose it's time I introduced him to you guys." Dracula? She wanted to cry.

"Mara has a boyfriend?" George was agog.

Josh swore under his breath.

"Josh thought you loved him," laughed Maggie unkindly.

"I'm sure she does; just not like that," Sabrina said.

Josh scowled, his face red.

"Okay, okay. Give it up, will you?" Mara said. "I love you all, okay? But this is something else, you know?"

"He's a real prince," sighed Sabrina.

George stared. "What? He's a prince?"

"His name's Niki Sperling," Maggie put in. "But he's called the Prince. Neat, huh?"

"He's as handsome as a prince in a fairy tale," said Mara wistfully, before she thought.

"Who is this guy?" Josh said.

"Yeah, how come we haven't heard of Prince Charming before now?" said George with an edge to his tone.

"You have to be careful of strangers," Josh advised.

"Chill, Josh. You're not her dad," said Maggie.

"Actually, my dad was charmed," Mara said. Charmed? She rushed on, "You should have seen them. Dad brought out the wine, and they played chess until all hours. You know my dad. But the Pr—er, Niki held his own. My dad was so impressed."

"Niki," Josh sneered. "Sounds girly."

"That's rude," Maggie scolded. "It can be a guy's name, too, Josh."

He looked chastened. "Sorry, Mara. It must be serious if you took him home to meet your mom and dad. Before us, even." Despite himself, he sounded a bit hurt.

Mara gave him a sympathetic glance, but couldn't help

holding up her hand proudly. The emerald sparkled.

"Ooh, I love this!" said Sabrina, and hugged Mara.

Mara blushed, grateful for Sabrina's total acceptance. *But Dracula? Oh, what would they think of him?*

"Nice rock!" Maggie joked. "He must be loaded."

"Hmm, bogus," said George, though he sounded uncertain.

Josh glanced darkly at the ring. "Is it real?"

"Josh," Maggie warned.

"I didn't mean it," he mumbled. "Nice ring."

"Gosh, think of it," Sabrina said. "Someone interesting enough to suit you!"

Mara sighed. "Oh, he's interesting, all right."

"So. When are you going to bring this Prince of yours around to meet us?" Josh said, adding sotto voce, "So I can arrange to be elsewhere."

Maggie jabbed him with her elbow.

"Come on down, Mara," George teased. "Come on down off cloud nine. You've kept him under wraps long enough."

"Okay." Mara blushed. "Whenever."

"Hey, call him right now," Maggie said. "He can meet us here for coffee."

"Er, uh—" Mara was at a loss for a moment. *In daylight? Of course, how could they know?*

"It's probably kind of short notice," Sabrina said, coming to her rescue with a surreptitious wink.

"That's right," said Mara hastily. "Er, what if I bring him around one evening. When and where?"

"Well, I for one want to meet this elusive prince, like yesterday, you know?" said Maggie. "It's been long enough, I'd say. We are your best friends, after all."

"I concur," George intoned. "If he meets with our approval—well, then."

Mara wadded up the brownie wrapper and winged it at him. It hit him on the head and bounced off.

"Ow, my eye!" he howled, one hand over his face. "You put out my eye!"

"Give it a rest, goof," said Maggie. "She's not going to kiss it better."

George ceased his dramatics at once and looked his usual serious self. "We could meet here later."

"Good idea," said Sabrina. "Let's say nine o'clock."

"And you guys better show up," said Maggie with a pointed look at Josh.

"Gotcha," he said reluctantly.

After the sun had set, Mara went for a jog in the park. She breathed deeply of the warm evening air, trying to psych herself up for the occasion. She couldn't recall the last time she had felt so nervous. Okay, that play in eighth grade, major stage fright. But that was years ago.

The sky darkened to a deep blue-black, and points of light appeared with stark suddenness. A faint breeze sighed through the trees, carrying with it the fragrance of roses and far-off traffic noises. Her footsteps crunched softly on the gravel of the pathway. She looked at her watch. *Where are you, Prince?* He usually found her along the way, just after sunset.

A sudden chill swept over her. Red alert. This was not the Prince, but the enemy. She proceeded warily, eyes narrowed, hand slipped inside her jacket to grip a stake. Every muscle tensed, ready to spring to the attack. Then the chill receded and vanished as quickly as it had come. The hair stood up on the back of her neck. She did not relax just yet, but remained ready for action. The Prince had warned her. They were still after her.

A few moments later, she sensed the Prince, and then he was beside her. With a sigh of relief, she took his hand and smiled up at him. He looked into her eyes; no words were necessary to convey their feelings. They walked a little way, making small talk before she could say what was on her mind.

"I'd like you to meet my friends. If you don't mind, that is." She was not sure; he had disappeared so quickly after the fight in the alley. "They can't be as scary as my parents."

"If you say so. But I survived that; I guess I am ready for anything, now." Despite the words, his smile was tight.

"You'll be fine." She laughed a little nervously. "Er, they're meeting us at Cup o' Java. You know, where—"

"Yes, my love, I have not forgotten. That was where you ripped my heart to shreds when it was at its most tender."

"I'm so sorry! Must you—" she glanced up and saw his look of amusement. "Okay, I deserved that."

"No, it's fine. I understand now, and I—I am sorry, that was cruel. I apologize most humbly for twisting the knife."

"Yes, okay. Here we are. Already." She took a few deep breaths. She couldn't tell them what he was. Not yet. She trembled at the thought. *No, better that they get to know him first. And love him. Oh, what would they think*?

"Okay, the cloak," he murmured, with an anxious little frown. His cloak vanished.

The lighting was dim at the Cup o' Java, except for the stage lights illuminating the live local band playing a tribute to Savage Garden. The bar was open; the college crowd filled the little shop to bursting.

"Oh, dear, it's so crowded. I forgot, Thursday's always packed," said Mara. "But we're meeting my friends out on the patio. It should be nice outside. Not so crowded, anyway."

"Not so quiet as last time," the Prince remarked.

Mara ordered virgin Irish coffees (she was not yet twenty) and asked that they be brought out to the patio. She took the Prince's hand and led the way through the crowd, out the side door. Most of the outside tables were as yet unoccupied. The lights were low, but they could see Sabrina sitting alone on the far side. Two glasses stood on the table in front of her.

"Hey, it's not good to drink alone. Two-handed, especially," Mara teased. "Mind if we join you?"

"It's only pop, and they're not both mine," Sabrina protested, smiling. "Maggie just went to powder her nose. Have a chair." Her gaze lit on the Prince's face, and her jaw dropped. She stared in frank admiration for a moment, then managed to collect herself as Mara introduced them. She stammered a greeting and shook his hand. "Everyone's here already. Somewhere. The boys are over there ordering something. Please, won't you sit down?" She clapped a hand over her mouth to stop her babbling.

"Okay, boys, give him a chance, for Mara," Maggie said softly to Josh and George as she passed them on her way back to the table.

The boys were standing at the till paying for their soft drinks and nachos. They started in on the chips and watched with hard eyes as Mara introduced the Prince to Maggie. He bowed slightly and spoke; they couldn't hear the words due to the loud music.

"Look at the girls, all starry-eyed. I hate him already," said Josh, with an uncomplimentary epithet.

"But Mara likes him," George said doubtfully.

"Look at him, bowing and—whatever he's saying. Holy! Looked like he was going to kiss her hand. What a priss! And they're lapping it up!" Josh choked. "I don't believe it!"

"Well, she called him the Prince. Maybe he really is one. They have to learn all those fine manners. Where did she say he was from?"

"She didn't, now that you mention it."

They watched in silence, except for their munching of chips, reluctant to join the girls, for once. Sabrina was talking animatedly. It seemed she couldn't take her eyes off the Prince's face. He said something and then they were laughing. Even Maggie.

"Would you look at that!" exclaimed George. "Maggie's usually so standoffish at first."

"That's what I just said," scowled Josh. "Has he hypnotized the lot of them? Dude, that's just wrong!"

George eyed them dubiously. "I'm not sure I want to meet him, now. What if you're right?"

"I was kidding, George. Nobody can do that. You play too many games."

"Okay," said George meekly. "Mara looks so happy. Maybe—"

"What the hell movie did this guy just step out of?" Josh blurted with a curl of his lip. "Ooh, so prim and proper, like he's got a—man, I don't believe this!"

George blinked. "Shh. Dude, I think he heard you."

"Not likely, with the music blasting."

"He looked over here when you said that."

"Hell if I care."

"Mara might."

Josh had the grace to look sheepish. "Okay, you're right." He heaved a great sigh. "Fine. Let's get this over with."

George eyed the Prince somewhat dubiously as he walked over to the table.

"Hi, I'm George," he said hesitantly, extending a hand.

"Put her there, man," said the Prince, slapping his palm. "High five, George. This is real swell, meeting Mara's chums."

Mara blinked, looking a bit stunned.

"Okay, moving right along," said George, retrieving his hand and unconsciously giving it a shake. *Ow. Cold.*

"And, er, this is Josh," Mara managed, a little red in the face. "The Prince. Niki Sperling."

Josh went forward with a smile not too pleasant. They shook hands. "So. Do we call you Niki or the Prince?"

"Yo dude, whatever turns your crank," responded the Prince. "It's all wicked, or bogus. I'm cool with it."

Mara gave the Prince a look and said something that they did not catch.

***

What a goof! Josh thought scornfully, and forgot his intent to avoid meeting the Prince's eyes. For some reason, he had been wary of looking directly at that enchanting face. And all of a sudden, he realized George was right. This guy had heard his every word. He felt cold inside.

Those eyes seemed to glow for a fraction of a second as they locked on his and held them fast. When they released him, he

167

felt a curious wonder. No, those eyes weren't glowing. But he couldn't remember the last time he had met someone so fascinating.

***

Mara was relieved when the Prince meekly took her hint and dropped the jargon. Well, it was more than just a hint. She had surreptitiously jabbed him with her elbow, given him a look, and muttered through gritted teeth, "Enough with the slang, dear. Good grief, it's all wrong. Please be yourself, for heaven's sake."

At that, he reverted to his usual Old World courtliness with obvious relief and shook each proffered hand with his usual grace and charm. And she breathed again. Okay, he was just trying to fit in, with disastrous results, of course. Maybe if he had not mixed… All went smoothly from then on, though Mara was pretty certain her friends had surrendered much too easily to his charm. Yet she couldn't find it in her to be sorry, however shamelessly the Prince employed his powers of mesmerization. He was discreet; he didn't annihilate wills. There was no harm in it, surely. She did so want him to make a good impression; wanted them to accept him. Before they found out what he was, and all was lost.

And here he was, playing the fool! *Okay, all's good.* At least, everything seemed to settle into normalcy after that. Josh and George sat at the next table. Appetizers arrived and drinks. Soon everyone was munching except the Prince. Mara noted the line of puzzlement on Sabrina's brow, though the others seemed blithely unaware. *I told her, and she even…*

"Come on, Niki," Sabrina urged. "Have some appies. I ordered plenty, just for you. I mean, uh, for the occasion." She blushed.

Mara hoped no one else heard the Prince hiss at the sudden rush of blood. She cast an anxious glance at him. At least his eyes weren't glowing. He took her hand and squeezed it. To reassure her, or to steady himself, maybe.

"Thanks, but, no, I shouldn't," he said to Sabrina. "I ate

before I came. I did not expect… no, really, I will just have the drink, if you don't mind."

"Ah, Irish coffee, I see." Sabrina smiled. "Cool. You like Irish, too. I'm Irish, you know," she teased.

The Prince gave a little bow. "Yes, what is not to love about the Irish?" he said with an amused look. "But for now, their coffee will have to do."

Sabrina's laugh was a little puzzled. She flagged down the waitress and ordered another round. Mara wondered if she would make it through the evening. Still, she couldn't complain. The Prince had won over the girls easily enough. As for the boys…

He must have read her mind, because as soon as the drinks came, he thanked Sabrina politely and with some comment about round two, got up with his drink to move to the boys' table, which was next to theirs, but might have been across the room for all that they could carry on a conversation over the loud music.

George was holding forth on his favorite topic, a new computer game just out. The conversation flagged when the Prince moved to their table. The boys shifted in their chairs. True, they had accepted him, but couldn't think why at the moment, or why the initial hostility. Something seemed not right about this.

The Prince seemed unaware of their discomfort. "Nice knife," he said, indicating the one Josh wore in a sheath at his belt. "You made it?"

"Yeah." After a furtive glance around, Josh unsheathed it and handed it to the Prince. "It's not legal, the blade's ten inches, so I don't usually flash it around. But I like wearing it sometimes. Mara told you I make knives?"

"Yes, and the like." The Prince tested its shining curved edge with his thumb. "You've got a gift, Josh. Do you make Mara's weapons, too?"

"I'd like to, but she doesn't think I'm ready for that yet. She's pretty serious about this secret ninja life of hers and needs special blades and such for killing vampires. Er, I don't know why I just said that." He looked mortified.

George was staring open-mouthed. "Josh. I can't believe you told. Uh, vampires?" He glanced nervously at the Prince. "Er, don't mind him. He watches too many movies."

"It's all right," said the Prince. "I know about Mara's secret ninja life, as you put it. She tells me you have come up with some interesting new weapon designs."

After that ensued an animated discussion of weapons, Josh's favorite topic. Then they slid naturally into the subject George loved most, software. And there was no more talk of vampires being real except as it applied to games.

Mara munched deep-fried calamari and observed the Prince, starry-eyed. Happily, it appeared that he had won the boys over after all, despite his initial faux pas.

"He's gorgeous," sighed Sabrina, interrupting her daydreams. "Where did you say you found him?"

"Actually, you might say I met him in church," Mara said. "Close enough."

"Well, of course! Where else?" Maggie exclaimed. "He looks like an absolute angel."

"More than a vampire," said Sabrina in a low voice. "Why would you say such a thing?"

Mara sighed. Would they ever understand? The Prince glanced over at her. Their gazes locked, and at just that moment, the band drifted into one of her favorite songs. The words caught her up. So romantic, it described her own situation perfectly. If only she could make her friends see. They would always be her friends, with a special place in her heart, besides that of her parents. The Prince was different. His was a space she had not known was there. The words of the song were so, so real, they might have been written for them.

The night passed too quickly. Before they parted, they made

plans to get together again.

"My house?" Sabrina volunteered. "Next Friday, my mom and dad are going out. Timmy's staying over at a friend's for a video-game all-nighter. We'll have the house to ourselves all evening. Not tomorrow, next week."

Mara nodded. "Sounds good." At least Sabrina did not have any inconvenient mirrors, obliging her to explain if she didn't yet feel the time was right.

"We'll see how well your Prince plays cards against the experts," chuckled George.

"And maybe Trivial Pursuit, or one of those murder mystery games," suggested Maggie.

They left the Cup o' Java, and after seeing her friends safely home, she and the Prince patrolled the town hand in hand. The night had gone rather well, after all, she decided.

The Prince met Mara at her home on subsequent evenings for their nightly patrol. Some nights he took time for a game of chess with her father and the occasional glass of wine. Mara was pleased that her parents had begun to accept him as they did her original group of friends, almost as part of the family.

The week went by quickly. Friday evening Mara met the Prince, and they walked to Sabrina's parents' home. Music was playing when they arrived. Sabrina invited them in and offered them snacks and drinks. Mara was relieved when the Prince accepted a plate of chips and a glass of punch. No one seemed to notice that he ate nothing.

They talked and played board games for a while. Eventually, someone suggested cards. The Prince admitted that he had not played cards in a long time.

"We'll fix that." Josh cleared the table. "Hey, come on. We'll show you a real game of Solitaire."

"Yeah, dude, this ain't just Solitaire," George enthused. "We call it Turbo-Solitaire. It's a lot of fun. You'll see."

"You've never played it before?" asked Maggie.

"Not that I recall," the Prince said, "but I'll give it a try."

They were soon seated around the table, each with a deck of cards. George laid out the general rules.

"And at the word go," Josh added, "We just play like hell."

"Sounds like my kind of game," the Prince murmured.

And from the word go, it was a headlong rush to the finish. Sabrina, always the good-hearted one, pointed out to the Prince where to place his cards, thinking to help because he was new at the game. He cooperated to please her, but was already under constraints to move slowly in order to not blow his cover. Mara wasn't quite ready for it yet, he knew. He had remedied his gaffe at the coffee shop by his reversion to his usual self, and mesmerization. He was not about to make that mistake again. He tried not to win too often.

They were shuffling their decks of cards for yet another game when Mara glanced at her watch. "Oh dear, we've got to run, Prince," she said above the clatter of cards and chatter. "It's almost ten."

"What? Where are you going? You're taking off already?" cried Maggie. "Hey, there's no school tomorrow."

"I guess I forgot to mention we have an appointment with Father Mike," said Mara. "We're already going to be late."

"Tonight, of all nights?" frowned Josh. "Why so late?"

"Well, it just worked out that way. We had it set for last night, but Father was called out, so… "

"You're meeting with the priest?" exclaimed George. "Are you getting married or something?" He was half-joking.

Mara and the Prince looked at each other.

"George," Sabrina said in a tone of reproof, then glanced at Mara. "Not that we aren't curious."

Mara blushed. "Um, we'll let you know, okay?" She opened the door.

"Shouldn't you warn them?" said the Prince.

"Right." She turned to her friends, whose eyes were full of questions. "Guys, there's a—never mind, I'll explain later; we've got to run now. Just don't go outside tonight."

"Huh? Like, we have to stay here overnight?" Josh didn't look pleased.

"No, we'll be back. "Don't worry, we'll walk you home, if necessary," Mara said. "Just don't invite any vampires in."
They heard puzzled laughter as they closed the door.

A Serpent Enters Eden

Mara looked up at the sky. A gibbous moon glowed wan behind a skein of black gauze. The points of light she had seen earlier were already devoured by the eerie shadow slowly spreading across the sky. She shivered.

She sensed the Prince's reluctance as they drew near the rectory. That perplexed and worried her; he did not even manage a smile when they passed St. Michael's, and she reminded him of the night they had first met. A narrow strip of light escaped the edge of the curtain in the tall window of the rectory, casting a line of yellow across the graceful weeping willow, the wrought iron fence and the sidewalk. To her, a welcome sight. Not so the Prince. In fact, she got the impression he might have flown away had she not been holding his hand.

Then they were standing on the porch. Mara knocked, and Father Mike opened the door at once. Despite his friendly greeting, the Prince seemed to draw back, his whole body tensed.

"Come in, come in, I've got the teakettle on," Father Mike said warmly. He led the way into the parlor. Mara guessed that his cordial manner hid a certain disquiet. He, of all people, knew the folly of inviting a vampire into one's home; he had only done so for her sake. He turned to them with a smile. "So this is your friend, Mara?" As she nodded, a piercing whistle came from the kitchen. "Would you see to that kettle while we get acquainted? I'll call you when we're ready for the tea."

Mara caught his meaning at once. She gave the Prince a reassuring glance and a squeeze of the hand and left them.

The Prince stood in the parlor, trying to collect himself as the priest closed the door after Mara. A floor lamp stood in one corner, its soft glow illuminating a wall of books. He scanned their titles in an instant, though at the moment, he was too distracted to take any enjoyment in them. And that crucifix on the wall was rather disturbing.

"So, you like books, do you?" said the priest, noticing the Prince's swift appraisal of the small library. "You're welcome to borrow some of them if you wish."

The Prince nodded, murmuring some politeness to hide his increasing dread at venturing into enemy territory.

"I'm Father Mike. You must be the Prince." He extended a hand.

Panic seizes the Prince as he took Father Mike's hand. In an automatic reaction of self-defense—or a need to control the situation—he leveled his eyes upon the priest's to mesmerize him as he had Mara's parents and her young friends. He meant no harm.

Father Mike was not caught napping; he knew more than enough about vampires. That quick, he whipped out his crucifix and held it before him, between the Prince's eyes and his own. The Prince recoiled with a hiss, vanquished in an instant. He cowered against the wall, shielding his eyes with an arm as though from an unbearably bright light.

"Don't give me that look!" Father Mike thundered. "When you come into this house, leave your evil powers outside that door!"

The Prince crouched, trembling, subdued by the crushing power of the crucifix in the hand of God's consecrated. At this horrendous blow to his pride and to his very nature as a vampire, fury sprang up in him, and a desire to kill. But he could not. He would have fled, had the thought of Mara not held him. Only that gave him the strength to do what he must. He fought to master his pride, and his very self, while the priest stood waiting.

"Sorry," the Prince said at last, with downcast eyes.

Father Mike tucked the crucifix back into his belt and reached out a hand. "Come," he said quietly.

The Prince allowed himself to be helped up, though he eyed the crucifix warily. The priest motioned him toward a worn red velvet chair with arms of ornately carved, dark polished wood. He sat, grateful for the prop, but hating his fear and weakness; not something to which he was accustomed. He felt severely chastised, and kept his eyes averted to avoid confrontation. *Mara. Think only of Mara.*

Father Mike took a high-backed armchair facing him, his gray eyes calm once more. A coffee table stood between them. "May I ask," he began in a serious, but not unkind, tone, "what your intentions are, toward Mara?"

"My intentions?" the Prince repeated, his thinking process fogged by the effort to keep his powers under control with those watchful eyes skewering him.

"That's right. She says you claim to love her. Is that correct?"

"It is, yes," the Prince managed, still fighting to regain his composure.

"What exactly do you intend to do about it?"

Taken off guard by this immediate interrogation, the Prince felt at a distinct disadvantage, after the shock of having his powers so swiftly negated. He had thought to gain control of the situation as he usually did, with power and charm; he was not pleased to find the tables turned. A battle raged within him, for despite his resolve, his pride rebelled against the outrage. *Who the hell does this priest think he is, a mere mortal, to speak thus to me!*

But no, that was the old Prince. How could he have forgotten so soon? He remembered Mara and why he had come here. *I said I would do anything for her, and I will. I must.* He calmed himself finally and thought for a while, not quite certain how best to answer the question.

***

Father Mike waited patiently, mindful of the war being waged within the creature sitting before him. Praying, too, for the final outcome. Pride has ever been man's downfall, even in one no longer human.

***

Finally the Prince raised his eyes. "I want to be with her always."

"Not by turning her into a vampire too?"

"Never. I can no longer inflict that curse on anyone."

"What did you have in mind, then?"

The Prince looked up, his eyes deeply shadowed. Stark in the subdued light cast by the lamp across his pale brow and cheeks was the proud aristocratic nose, but the mouth that had been set in a grim line softened as he thought of Mara. "I want her for my own. Perhaps it is wrong, maybe not even possible, but… I want to marry her."

"What? How can you suggest such a thing? You, a demon, say that to me, her confessor? How could I condone this monstrous act?" In his agitation, the priest leaped up and began pacing back and forth. He put his hand to his forehead in consternation. "You, sir, overstep your bounds here! How do you dare to—to— Anyway, I have no authority to allow it, much less to assist in such a thing!" He ran his fingers through his hair anxiously.

The Prince closed his eyes and gripped the arms of his chair fiercely as he tried to control the rising fury and keep his powers in check. *Mara is all that matters. This is her mentor; she listens to him. I must not antagonize him; must not kill him.*

With a sharp crack, the arm of the chair snapped under his grip. Jolted, he snatched back his hand and looked at the broken chair in dismay. "Sorry, I did not mean to—"

Father Mike had flinched at the sound but recovered at once. "Never mind that. It can be repaired," he said, more quietly. "I must apologize for shouting. My Irish temper—a bloody curse, I tell you." He sat down to face the Prince once more. "You see, I love her too. She's like a daughter to me. I can't stand idly by and see her hurt. So I ask again. How is it that you think of marriage? You're a vampire, she is not. If you're immortal, and she must grow old and die, then how — ?"

The Prince closed his eyes, pained by these words. When he looked upon his interrogator once more, his tone was one of deep sorrow. "I have no answer to that. But I cannot let her go. I wish to protect her, always."

Father Mike shook his head. "And yet you torment her like this? She's impressionable, young, and mortal. It isn't natural. Whatever possessed you, a vampire, to — And you call it love? Isn't this about you, your feelings, selfishness, pure and simple? Assuming you don't have other, more reprehensible, motives." He narrowed his eyes.

The Prince felt anger rising again, but despair quickly overtook it. These were fair questions; in his heart, he knew that he deserved nothing. He dropped his gaze and was silent for a long moment. Finally, he looked up at the priest. "Perhaps I should never have spoken to her at all. But I could not help myself. For so long, I have not loved anyone. Could not, even. What have I done? What have I done?" He spoke slowly, shaking his head, as though dazed. "I did not mean to hurt her. I would never, ever, hurt her. Maybe I should leave her now; let her get on with her life." *Why did she not let the dawn take me?*

"So," said Father Mike, after a pause in which he appeared to converse privately with a third person. "You'd let her go?"

"If I must," said the Prince faintly; the very thought tore his heart in two.

"Indeed, you are a beast!" For an instant, the priest seemed surprised that he had spoken the words aloud. He hastened on. "How could you break her heart, after captivating her by your infernal charm? No, you can't just leave her like that."

"What?!" The Prince felt fury explode inside him. *Play with me, will you, priest? I could burn you to a cinder in a heartbeat!* His eyes began to glow.

"Calm down, calm down." Father Mike raised one hand in a gesture of conciliation; the other went instantly to the crucifix at his belt. At that the Prince quickly subsided, though rage seethed just below the surface. Father Mike knew and hurried on. "Consider for a moment. The deed is done. Mara is bound to be hurt now, whatever you do. There are too many unanswered questions. You don't trust me; you fear the crucifix the same as any other vampire. Yet, as I understand it, we both wish to attain the same goal. That is, whatever's best for Mara, right?" The Prince felt Father Mike's steady gaze leveled upon him once more. "Or is this a plot hatched by the master vampire to neutralize the Huntress?"

"The master? No, no, it is not." This took the Prince by surprise, but it too was a fair question.

"Fine. Now, what if you told me your side of the story? Of what happened in the church that night," Father Mike said in a gentler tone. "We may yet find a solution."

The Prince didn't relish the thought of confiding in Father Mike. But Mara was certain that he could help them find a way out of their dilemma. He had to try. For Mara.

He began, hesitantly at first, to relate the events leading up to and including that night at the church. "She was much better than I expected, and nearly killed me twice, but it was as though each time some unseen hand prevented her. Finally I prevailed; I was about to kill her when I was struck by a light from above. I heard the voice of one who identified himself as Michael, her protector." The Prince related the details of the encounter; every word of the conversation between them. "It was as though a veil was lifted, and for the first time, I saw myself as I truly am," he concluded slowly. "He then commanded that I choose which master I would serve."

He raised his eyes to meet those of the priest. "Yes, I too questioned this. He assured me that I was being given a second chance; why, I do not know. I chose Our Lord Jesus Christ. The light disappeared, and I found I was transformed." In a tone of awe, he added, "When I looked upon Mara again, I knew that I would love her forever." The priest flinched, and the Prince realized that his eyes were aglow. He cast them down at once.

Father Mike recovered. "Please continue."

"I was afraid of myself, then. I am, after all, still a vampire. I left her there. Guilt crashed down upon me, and no matter where I looked, I could not escape the accusing eyes of my victims or the ugliness of all the evil I have done. Overcome by remorse, I crept away to at last find refuge in the chapel of Our Blessed Mother. To my amazement, Our Lady took me under her mantle of mercy. I am not fit to stand in the presence of the living God, but she accepted me. She, a mother, took pity on the little child that had fallen in the mire.

"She bestowed upon me a gift from Jesus to mark me as His own. The golden arrow of His love pierced me with such sweetness that I fell on my face in an ecstasy of wonder and gratitude. That is when Mara found me. For the third time that night, she could have killed me, but did not. I do not know why I told her I loved her. My heart was so full that it just spilled out. It was the truth, and is so now. I cannot understand or explain it. She did not want to accept it, and who can blame her? She knew what I was. She ran away. I followed and stood guard while she slept, not knowing what else the master might have sent against her." He fell silent, aware of Father Mike's steady gray gaze. Then he added sincerely, "That is how it was."

"One more question," said the priest quietly. "What exactly did you mean when you said, 'Come be my bride'?"

The Prince lowered his eyes in shame. "Those words haunt me even now. I wish I could deny them, or say I only meant to strike fear into her heart, but that would be a lie. I intended to violate her before taking her head, to please the vampire Nyx, who demanded it of me. I could deny Nyx nothing. Even so, my true interest lay in the drinking of blood," he finished lamely, but knew even as he said it, that that did not excuse him.

"So now you want to marry her," said the priest. "I think you can see where I have a problem with that."

"Yes, I understand what you are saying. Still, it is different now."

"In precisely what way, may I ask?"

"Love. Before, she meant nothing to me. I would have killed her to please the master and thought no more of it, except to exult in the power I gained from drinking her blood. Now I serve a different master. I am able to love, and I love her with all my heart. Also, I feel deep remorse for all the evil I have done."

The priest looked grave. "Yes. Well. What effect do you suppose this will have on her life as Huntress?"

"She needs a protector. The master has decreed her death, and his power is growing. You may have noticed."

"Yes, but she already has protectors, doesn't she? Of greater power than yours, I daresay."

"Ah, you have me there. I did not ask for this; I only accepted what was offered. And I will do my best to stand by her side against all, all of her enemies."

"You can destroy your own kind?"

"I can."

Father Mike sat deep in thought for a while, absently tapping his fingers on the arms of his chair. Finally, he stood. "Perhaps you're right, if Our Lady truly prevented Mara from killing you, unlikely as that seems. But marriage? I don't know....Anyway, I must talk to Mara again. She doesn't seem to want to listen to reason in this matter. She can be headstrong at times, but...she's a good girl. It's only fair that I warn you. If you hurt her, or endanger her immortal soul, you'll have me to contend with." It took an effort for the Prince to meet that hard gaze. Then, apparently satisfied at what he saw in the Prince's face, Father Mike spoke in a gentler tone. "We should have her bring the tea in now, don't you think?"

***

Mara felt the tension in the atmosphere of the parlor as she entered. She set the tray on the coffee table and glanced anxiously at the Prince. Saw the strain in his face, and one of his hands clenched on the arm of his chair. The other chair

181

arm was broken; this told her all she needed to know. Her blue eyes were accusing as she looked at Father Mike. The priest gave her a grin that was meant to be reassuring, but she knew him too well.

"Yes, Mara, I will have tea," he enunciated carefully, then glanced at the Prince. "And you?"

The Prince, somewhat subdued after his harrowing interrogation, shook his head. "No, thank you."

Her lips set in a firm line, Mara poured tea for herself and Father Mike. "Cookies, Father?" she said with chilly politeness.

He helped himself to a cookie. "Your friend and I have come to an understanding."

Mara sat down next to the Prince, put her hand on his and faced Father Mike. "So, you've decided my fate?" She turned to the Prince and softened her tone. "Are you okay?" He managed a faint smile and a short nod. He responded to the squeeze of her hand with a slight pressure of his own, but was unable to hide his discomfort. Not from her. "We love each other, Father, and that's how it is."

"Okay, Mara," the priest said in a soothing tone. "We've sorted that out. However—"

"But Our Lady did this!" she burst out, near tears, and rushed on before he could continue. "She wouldn't let me kill him. This has to be right!"

The Prince spoke up quietly. "It is well, Mara."

She looked into his eyes and let herself be lost in them. Father Mike cleared his throat, and she tore her gaze from the Prince's with an effort. "Okay, I'm listening."

"Remember, with love comes sacrifice. Are you ready for this?"

"Of course, I am." She caught his somber look and added, "Er, what do you mean, exactly?"

"Think. Is it worth the price? What of your parents? Your children?"

"Children? Er, I—I don't think we um—" she stammered,

flushing. "Hey, it'll work out. Love conquers all, right?" She glanced at the Prince for confirmation. He squeezed her hand, but did not comment.

"It's a bittersweet draught, this cup of which you ask to drink," Father said, uncharacteristically grave.

His tone frightened her. "What does that mean?"

"Sometimes we bring suffering on ourselves by praying 'my will' instead of 'Thy will be done.'" He turned to the Prince. "Are you prepared to sacrifice yourself for her, as Christ has for His Church?"

"Have I not given proof of that?" said the Prince.

Father Mike's voice grew stern. "There will be more to come, and it won't be easy. Can you do this? If not, then for Mara's sake, leave her now."

Mara got an uneasy feeling. Father Mike was so blunt, and the Prince seemed to become increasingly restless.

And yet his eyes were steady as they met those of the priest. "There is nothing I would not do for her sake."

Father Mike made no reply, but in his face was a mix of understanding, compassion, and concern.

The Prince's eyes swept the parlor in some disquietude; abruptly he stood, turned to Mara, raised her hand to his lips and kissed it. "I will leave you to it. Excuse me, please."

With a kind of lost look, he turned and glided to the door. Mara opened her mouth to call after him, but Father Mike lifted his hand and shook his head slightly; the words died on her lips. The door closed softly behind the Prince, and he was gone.

The Shadow Reaches Out

Sabrina rose from her seat in front of the television, where the four friends had settled to watch a *Twilight Zone* rerun after Mara, and the Prince left; they had lost interest in card games. Sabrina was still dwelling on the issue of the Prince. "I wonder why they're meeting with Father Mike?"

"Niki seems nice," Maggie remarked. "What was he talking to you guys about at the café? I couldn't hear a thing."

George shrugged. "Knives, games — stuff like that."

"Yeah, he said my knife was excellent work," said Josh proudly. "Like he knew something about blades. He —"

"And guess what?" George interrupted in sudden excitement, "I told him about the game I'm working on. You know, the one I invented. The one about vampires…"

"Breathe, George," laughed Sabrina.

"Go ahead, mock me. He was interested."

"Yeah, sure he was," Maggie said dryly.

"Hey," Josh put in, "Just listen."

"Thanks, Josh. As I was saying, he said he'd help me with it. I thought, *What? Help me how?* I mean, he's no techie. But it was the part about vampires that got his attention and, I don't remember exactly, but something he said gave me an idea. Instead of a game, I could create a program to track vampires. That would be so cool! Imagine what Mara could do with that!"

The others gave him blank looks. "You mean like in real life?" Maggie finally ventured. "Real vampires?"

"Well, yeah." George stopped. "Hey. He said it. And didn't Mara say vampires are real?"

"You're right," said Sabrina slowly. She shivered. "That's what she was warning us about."

"Who is the Prince, anyway?" said Josh. "I never did find out where he comes from. Might have, if he'd taken his eyes off Mara for one minute."

"That's so romantic," Sabrina sighed. "And I swear, he's the handsomest guy ever."

"He does look kind of cool," Josh said. "Kind of like a vampire. Like those on—"

"Yeah, exactly!" said George. "He dresses all in black; all that's missing is the cloak. And, well, there's just something about the look of him."

"You mean like his dated fashion statement?" Maggie cut in. "Think he's one of those Goths? They wear black and, you know, the makeup. Not that he wears makeup. Though he is pretty white-looking, and—"

"Hey," said Josh indignantly. "They're wannabes; he's totally real. Maybe he is a real prince." He shrugged as all eyes turned toward him. "You know, like in some fantasy story. Hey, he's gotta be called that for some reason."

"Omigosh, he is a vampire!" Sabrina blurted out. "Mara told me, but I—I didn't see it until just now. I mean, you know, it's not something you can just believe." The others stared. She clapped her hand over her mouth. "Oops, I forgot, she made me promise not to tell."

"You're kidding," said Josh, but Sabrina shook her head, her face reddening.

"He does look like one, doesn't he?" Maggie said slowly, recalling her first impression. "Weird."

"Yowzers," said George. "He even kind of looks like he has fangs. Though he doesn't really."

"Doesn't he?" Maggie said. They all looked at her.

"Hey, what's Mara going to say when she finds out what you're saying about her boyfriend? Fangs!" snorted Josh. "Everybody has pointed eyeteeth. Look at mine. Anyway, vampires aren't real." His eyes darted toward the window. The darkness outside seemed suddenly menacing. "Let's watch a movie, okay? Something different. *Twilight Zone's* too—"

"Spooky, yeah," Maggie finished for him, her glance following his toward the window that darkly reflected the interior of the room. "A comedy, maybe."

"I guess that leaves out *Alien*, or any of those Dracula movies," George teased.

"George!" shrieked Maggie and Sabrina together.

George snickered as Sabrina rushed over to whip the curtains shut. She began flipping through the DVDs on the shelf. "Timmy won't mind if we watch one of his animated movies. *Spider-Man*?" She forced a laugh. "Or what about *Looney Toons*? Hey, at least they're funny, not scary."

"Nah, I've seen them a million times. Though I'm sure we could use a good laugh—" George stopped talking suddenly.

"What is it?" whispered Maggie, her eyes round.

"I thought I heard a noise." His voice was low as he strained to hear.

"George, stop it," Sabrina complained.

"Shh!"

They all went quiet, hoping against hope that he would say "psych" and they would all laugh and assure each other that they hadn't really been scared. Seconds of silence lengthened into a minute and more. Finally, Josh went over and moved the corner of the curtain aside slightly; with forced nonchalance, he peered out.

"Only thing moving out there is a few moths flying around the porch light." He let the curtain fall back.

There were some relieved sighs and a clattering as Sabrina resumed her search through her brother's movies.

George still stood with his ears pricked up. "I did hear something. Really."

Maggie shivered. "I wish Mara would come back."

"George, stop it," said Sabrina. "You're scaring Maggie."

"Okay, okay. Sorry, Mag," said George. "Must be a stray cat. Sounded like wings flapping, though. A bat, maybe. Or not. Probably my imagination."

"I think I'll lock the door," said Sabrina to no one in

particular, and suited the action to her words.

Josh started switching channels. "Hey, *Return of the Pink Panther* is playing. That's a funny one."

There was a clamor of agreement. Maggie helped Sabrina carry the snacks over to the coffee table. Soon the four of them were lounging in front of the television set, eating popcorn and laughing at the movie. By the time a light tap-tap came at the front door, they had all but forgotten their fears.

"Oops, the door's locked. I'll get it," Sabrina set down her bowl of popcorn and jumped up. "Must be them. Thank goodness."

"Look out the window first, Sabrina," cautioned Maggie. "Remember what Mara said."

Sabrina peeked through the curtain. A tall, dark-cloaked figure stood at the railing, looking toward the street, his pale cheek a line of white glinting in the porch light. "Oh, it's the Prince." She ran to open the door. "Hi, back already?" She looked past him, but saw no Mara. Must be coming. Her eyes slid back to him, questioning. Mara's warning completely forgotten, she uttered the fateful words. "Uh, come on in, won't you? We're just watching a rerun." Then he turned to face her. *He's not as tall as I thought. And he's wearing a cape? No, wait a minute. I don't recall his eyes being so close together (gosh, they look so dead!), or his mouth being so sulky.* Then she realized, this wasn't the Prince. "Oh," she said, taking a step back.

The red lips twisted into a semblance of a smile. She looked into those empty black eyes and felt herself sinking into a cloud of sweet fluff. This did not seem right, but that gaze held her fast; she was unable to tear away from those eyes. Nor did she want to, but knew she must. With great effort, she started to back away.

"Come here," he said softly, and stepped through the doorway. His long white hands snaked out. She turned to flee, but his slender fingers latched onto her arms with an impossibly strong grip.

"No," she protested faintly as the vampire drew her into his embrace and out the door.

He murmured in her ear; his face was too close, suffocating. She tried to scream, but could not, as in a nightmare. Her hands feebly pressed against her captor's chest. She seemed to be floating. *Where am I?* Something flashed, traced a bright arc past her face. Claws—she felt them in her hair; her neck arched back. She had not meant to... couldn't think why... Those mesmerizing eyes released her gaze and turned downward. Helplessly she watched, terrified and fascinated, as the red lips writhed back. Those teeth! The vampire bent its head, and she felt a sting at her throat, heard herself cry out. She struggled feebly to escape.

"What the hell?" said Josh from afar, it seemed.

And George: "What's he doing? Sabrina? Hey, Prince, stop that! What the hell are you doing?" His voice squeaked at the end the way it did when he was distressed.

Help me. Sabrina turned pleading eyes toward her friends and opened her mouth, but no sound came out. She fought to resist the euphoria. Knew deep inside that it was wrong. *But it felt so fine. So fine. No, so wrong.* She felt a deep aching within her chest as she fought for her life, for her very soul. *Fight it, fight it, don't give in.*

From somewhere far away, she heard Maggie scream, "Oh, no! He is a vampire! Stop the Prince! He's biting Sabrina!"

***

Mara couldn't believe the Prince left without her. Father Mike must have said something to scare him off. "Oh, Father, what happened?"

"I'm sorry to say it, but this is just the beginning, if you choose this path."

"But I love him. What else is there to do?" she wailed.

"You barely know him. True love is something that grows over time."

"What about love at first sight?"

Father Mike shook his head. "Often infatuation seems like love, and then it vanishes like smoke."

"But it feels so real, Father."

"Feelings are fickle. You can't rely on them alone as the test of true love."

"Okay, I get that. But Father, I didn't ask for this. I didn't even want it. He was the enemy. He nearly killed me. And I would have killed him, if Our Lady hadn't stopped me."

"Try looking at this objectively."

Her face fell. "I know he's a vampire. I didn't mean to fall in love with him. I tried not to. You know I did."

"But don't you see? This can only lead to heartache."

Her eyes filled with tears. "Without him, I feel lost, empty. That's heartache."

"Is it now? Think a minute. What if you get away for a while? Spend some time by the sea, or on a mountaintop, alone with God. Somewhere away from him. You might see this from another perspective. Then return to take up your life again."

"My life, you say. Yes, my life was fine until he came along. But now, without him—no, there's no going back." She shook her head. "There must be a reason for all this. Why else would he change? Why did he weep? Vampires can't do that. So why does he? Tell me that."

"I don't have the answers yet, but I'll find them if I can." Father Mike would not give up without a fight. There was too much Irish in him for that.

"Maybe there is no precedent. Father, he was a monster when first I saw him, but after our battle..." Her voice softened. "It's as though he was someone else, someone that I was seeing for the first time. Like he'd changed inside." She lifted her eyes. In them was a plea for understanding.

"Those glowing eyes. Doesn't that frighten you?"

"It's a little startling, but I'm getting used to it. Father, you know I'm not afraid of vampires."

"Not when they're the enemy. But could you kill him?"

"I don't need to. But I could if I had to. I'm the Huntress."

Father Mike raised an eyebrow.

"Hey, we're meant to be together. It'll work out, you'll see." Her furrowed brow belied her confident tone.

"But only with God's blessing. Don't surrender your virtue, even to this, um, Prince Charming of yours."

"Father, I never!" Mara blushed. "Fine. But what if, I mean, you know, I could marry him?"

"Marry!" It was Father Mike's turn to be taken aback. "Do you hear yourself, child?"

"I'm not a child, Father, and I do hear myself. Anyway, according to Mom, love and marriage kind of go together."

"If the love is between a man and a woman. But he's not even human!"

She dashed away tears. "He was, once."

He gave her a long look. "He no longer has any legal status in society. Technically he's a nonperson."

"He looks real to me. Feels real enough."

"Too real, I'm afraid," Father Mike said under his breath. "Has he asked you to marry him?"

"Not in so many words, but he gave me this ring and pledged himself to me forever. I'm beginning to think that that's what this is about, and, oh dear, I don't know what to do!"

***

The vampire continued to feed uninterrupted, its mouth at Sabrina's throat, even as it regarded the would-be heroes with dead black eyes.

Round-eyed with horror, George picked up a paperweight from the telephone table just inside the door and, with a yell of outrage, flung it with all his might. The solid metal object bounced off the creature's head; it did not even blink. Desperate, George rushed toward it, heedless of danger. And got a reaction at last. With a growl, the vampire raised its head from the tender white throat. Its fangs were red, and blood ran down its chin. Its hand shot out and sent George reeling, glasses knocked askew. He caught at the doorjamb, straightened his glasses and stared aghast at the horrible apparition.

"No," Maggie sobbed, "Sabrina!" She grasped at her friend's clothing. The vampire turned its fierce gaze on her, snarled and sprang into the air, taking Sabrina with it. Maggie caught hold of her friend's foot. "Sabrina, come back!" she wailed, hanging on for dear life.

The vampire pulled its victim from her grasp with unnatural ease and glided up out of the circle of light to vanish in the darkness. Maggie leaned against the railing, holding one shoe, tears running down her cheeks.

"Come on, Maggie," Josh shouted. "Snap out of it. We can't help her. Call Mara, quick. She'll know what to do." He pulled her into the house and slammed the door.

Maggie picked up the telephone. With shaking hands, she pressed the buttons.

***

Father Mike gave Mara a look of deep compassion. "Let's just take this slowly. I tell you what. If worse comes to worst— I mean, if he does ask you, let me know. We'll try to work something out. Come now, don't cry. Finish your tea."

She obediently reached for her cup and began sipping the now-lukewarm drink.

The telephone shrilled. Father Mike hastened to answer it, then turned to Mara. "Here, it's for you."

"For me?" She put the phone to her ear. "Hello?"

"M-Mara!" It was Maggie, sobbing so she could hardly speak. "Mara, come quick! It's the Prince—he's biting Sabrina! He's killing her!"

***

But guys, it's not the Prince. Sabrina thought she had spoken aloud, but no one seemed to hear. It was important that they understand that this was not the Prince.

She resisted the urge to throw her arms around the

vampire's neck and fall into its arms… and the abyss. No, no, no, push it away. But nothing happened, however much she willed it. She couldn't lift her arms; felt herself sinking, sinking, down, down, into bliss. No! Frantically she arched her back, gasping for air as if coming up out of the water. The stinging, sweet fire at her throat rose up to drag her under once more. Drowning, drowning. *Oh, rapture. Oh, sweet ecstasy. No-oo-ooo! Jesus, help me!*

Josh's distraught face appeared at the edge of her vision, eyes and mouth stretched wide, screaming something she could not understand. In the next insta,nt he was slammed back against the doorway, his head meeting the wood with a loud crack. She wanted to cry, *help me*, but could not get the words out. And then she sank into bliss.

***

Timmy, Sabrina's twelve-year-old brother, turned in from the street, whistling the *Mario Bros.* theme song, and started up the sidewalk toward the house. Halfway there, the whistling stopped as he halted, staring in disbelief at the shadowy figure drifting up and over the tall, rangy hedge bordering the backyard. Moonlight shone palely on a familiar shape within that dark shape, which was now high enough to blot out a patch of starlit sky. He strained to see. Sabrina! Horror of horrors, that shadow thing was carrying off his sister! A vampire? But they weren't real. Everyone knew that.

Then the terrible vision melted into the darkness, and Timmy wondered for a moment. No, he had not imagined it! With a hoarse shout, he ran up the sidewalk, past the pool of light and dived through a break in the hedge. Across the back lawn at the far fence was the vampire, a dark-cloaked form bent over the girl lying helpless in its grasp. Moonlight glinted on her red-gold hair and upturned face. The vampire continued feeding as though undisturbed by the interruption.

A sob caught in his throat. "Sabrina!" Timmy cried. Heedless of danger, he charged in. "Sabrina, what's Mom going to say?" He snatched at the creature's cloak, intending to throw it to the ground (it didn't look very heavy or strong). But with surprising ease, the vampire lifted a slender hand and brushed him aside. He hit the ground face first, hard. His Irish up now, he leaped to his feet and grabbed his sister's arm. "Let go of her!" he squeaked and punched her attacker in the jaw.

The vampire whipped around with a snarl, its talons flashing in the moonlight. Timmy saw stars. When his head cleared, he was lying on the grass halfway across the yard. Slowly he lifted his gaze. A pair of malevolent eyes turned toward him, glimmering red points in the blackness, like demon eyes. Too close to her, too close.

"Sabrina," he whispered. A tear slid down his cheek; it stung like fire. He wanted to be the hero, wanted to kill the thing, but he couldn't seem to move. He could only watch in helpless horror as the vampire bent its head once more to his sister's throat.

***

The Rocket dismissed the boy as of no account and resumed feeding. The thunder of the pretty maid's heartbeat set him on fire. In his frenzy, he could barely refrain from tearing her to pieces, but Charon would not be pleased if he forgot his overall purpose. Though the master was himself unable to reach the Huntress, he had decided that the turning of one of her friends would drive her to make the fatal mistake of coming to him.

For the Rocket, it was all about becoming the master's favorite. He had chosen the freckle-faced blonde, the lucky one, to his way of thinking. She would make a pleasurable companion if she showed suitable gratitude to him for transforming her. He smiled self-indulgently at the thought.

Then he realized that she was drooping in his arms; he tore himself away and looked down into her face. Her half-closed eyes were glassy. A faint sigh escaped her parted lips as she tried to cry out; still resisting with every ounce of her waning strength.

"Give it up!" he hissed, savage in his desperation to control himself. He dared not kill her; not now that he was so close. Never before had he turned a mortal; never was he able to stop before it was too late. He tossed his cloak back over his shoulder with an impatient growl, opened his shirt and raked one sharp nail across his pale chest. A line of crimson-black appeared. "Come to me." He pulled her to him; pressed her lips against the bleeding slash. "Taste. Become one of us." He tried to be calm; he stroked her hair a little wildly. "Drink, and live forever. Refuse and die." No response. "Surrender to me now!" he shrieked.

A chill wave was his only warning of danger; then a sledgehammer blow hit him from behind and slammed him against the fence. The victim flew from his grasp and fell to the ground. He whipped to his feet, hissing. The Prince! He whirled, teeth bared, quaking in his boots. How he feared the Prince. Yet he feared the master more.

"She's mine!" he snarled.

"Never," the Prince grated. "Leave, now."

With a shriek, the Rocket flew at the girl in a desperate bid to retrieve his prize. That quick the Prince had him by the throat, pinned to the fence. He struggled; mad with fear and hate, he lashed out with sharp nails. A line of crimson appeared on the Prince's forearm. He opened wide his jaws and roared.

The Rocket fell to cringing. "Just the maid, Prince," he whined, with a longing look toward the pale form lying on the grass. "The master ordered me to turn her. I must not fail. Please. Let me have her, and you'll never see me again."

The Prince's eyes glowed with a fury and sorrow that the Rocket could not possibly understand. "You will not have her!"

"Brother!" gasped the Rocket. "What is she to you?"

The Prince's teeth flashed, and his grip tightened. The

Rocket scrabbled frantically to escape, certain that the Prince would tear his head off. Instead, he felt himself flung to the ground. Stunned for a moment, he stared up into the Prince's face; saw his eyes glow and was struck with fear. He could not resist a final longing glance at his victim but dared not defy the Prince. He shot straight up into the air like his namesake and vanished into the night.

***

The Prince did not try to follow. The Rocket was too fast, even for him. Why had he let him go? How to explain that to Mara?

He bent over the still form lying on the grass. Sabrina's eyes were half-closed; the Rocket's blood smeared her mouth. The Prince knelt beside her, felt a faint heartbeat. He lifted her up; she sagged against him, her breathing ragged. This is Mara's friend. And I…

"Sabrina," he said brokenly. "No, do not taste. You do not want to become one of us." He wiped the blood from her mouth and pressed her close, torn by pity and shame. "Forgive me, Sabrina. I should have been here sooner."

She gave a final sigh, and her heartbeat was no more. Dead! He wailed deep in his soul as he clutched her to his breast. A groan escaped him. *Mea culpa, mea culpa, mea maxima culpa. Why her, Lord? She was innocent. Could you not have taken me instead?* He bowed his head in sorrow.

The Aftermath

The evening breeze sighed through the trees as the Prince lifted Sabrina, light as a moonbeam in his strong arms, and glided toward the house. Moths flitted in the glow of the porch light; nothing else was stirring. The front door was closed. All was quiet. Even the house itself seemed to hold its breath.

He paused near the porch, uncertain. He did not wish to frighten Mara's friends, or grieve them by appearing without preamble with the body of one of their own. He looked down at the face so white and still, into the once-sparkling green eyes, now glazed and lifeless, and his heart wept. Where was Mara?

At that moment, he sensed her approach, and was relieved. She would know what to do. He raised his eyes to the street in anticipation of her arrival. Heard her quick footsteps on the sidewalk before she came into view.

The anxiety in her sweet face dampened the rush of joy he felt at the sight of her. How could he have considered letting the burden fall on her shoulders alone? To flee when the going got tough. No, he would not leave her now when she needed him most.

The moon was hidden, and the night was black, but the Prince saw Mara flinch, and the color drain from her face as she came up the sidewalk and saw him. She stopped short, and her eyes widened.

***

Mara paused to catch her breath after running all the way, and was pierced to the heart by the sight that met her eyes. When Maggie had phoned, hysterical and almost incoherent,

Mara had promptly assumed her "take charge" mode, as always, in a crisis. But this was one of her friends; she was shocked to the core (though she had prepared for this all her life—or thought she had). Time seemed to stop, but she tucked her worry into the "save for later" file and sprang into action.

At first, she dismissed the accusation that it was the Prince attacking Sabrina. Yet Maggie had seemed so certain. A vampire, maybe; but the Prince? Granted, his actions were puzzling when they had parted, but she refused to believe it of him. Her friends had to be mistaken.

But now, seeing him standing at the porch with Sabrina's body in his arms (and oh, what was the meaning of that look on his face?) she was staggered as though by a mortal blow.

"Sabrina!" she cried out in anguish.

She ran to the inert figure and snatched up the pale hand; there was no response. No pulse or breath. She looked into the face; the eyes that had so recently been full of merriment were now dulled by death. The sprinkling of freckles stood out in stark relief against the waxen cheeks. At once, her practiced eye saw the marks of fangs on Sabrina's throat and, horror of horrors, a smear of blackish blood across her cheek! No—No, not that. Anything but that! Not Sabrina! Not the Prince!

Mara's eyes glistened with tears as she lifted them to his face.

***

Is that reproach I see in her eyes?

"What have you done?" she whispered, pain etched on her countenance. Without warning, she drew back her hand and gave him a resounding slap across the face.

He reeled with the unexpected blow; did not resist as she wrenched Sabrina's body from his arms. Uncomprehending, he touched his stinging cheek. *What is the meaning of this anger as she looks at me? Is it because I, too, am a vampire?*

He stood back and watched in wretched silence as Mara sat on the step holding Sabrina's body close. She gently smoothed

197

the red-blond curls back from her friend's face. Her shoulders shook with silent weeping. The Prince was moved to pity despite the tingling reminder of her slap. He reached out to comfort her. Her grief had caused her to lash out; that was understandable.

"Sorry, Mara," he said softly.

She looked up, her eyes flashing angry sparks as tears ran down her cheeks. "Is saying 'sorry' going to bring Sabrina back to life? You monster! You take my heart and play with it, and then you kill my friend? I can't believe I ever thought I loved you!" Tears blurred her vision, so she did not see the shock and pain in his eyes as her meaning dawned on him. She turned her back.

"I did not—" he began in protest, then fell silent; she was not listening. He bowed his head. Nothing could obliterate the shame he felt at being one of them, or the feeling that he was, at least in part, to blame. *I should have known. I should have been here sooner.*

***

Mara's defenses went up to shut out the world. She wanted to cry, but that was a luxury she could not afford right now. There was no time. She was dying inside. No, she groaned, not the Prince!

The door opened. Josh's tense face peered out at them, while George and Maggie looked over his shoulder anxiously.

"Oh, you're here, Mara," said Josh, relief in his tone. "I thought I heard your voice."

Mara composed herself with an effort and spoke calmly. "Let's bring Sabrina into the house." She had to be strong for their sake. Josh cast an apprehensive glance at the Prince; George and Maggie watched wide-eyed from the doorway.

Josh helped Mara carry Sabrina's body inside. Maggie was about to close the door when she heard quick footsteps coming up the sidewalk. It was Father Mike with his black case.

"She's in here," said Maggie. "Be careful," she added, with a fearful glance toward the yard, but the flicker of moths in the porch light and the faint stirring of leaves in the night breeze were the only movements. The Prince was gone. With a sob of relief, she turned to Father Mike. "Thank God, you came, Father. Mara's—" She broke off as a rustling sound came from the direction of the back yard. "Oh!" she gasped. "What is it?" The sound drew nearer. "Quick, Father, into the house!"

"Wait," Father Mike said calmly, though he reached for his crucifix.

They strained to see. A pale blur emerged from the darkness of the hedge, and shortly after, the figure of a boy stumbled into full view in the light of the porch.

"Timmy!" cried Maggie. "What are you doing here?"

"Did you see? It was a—a—" The boy's green eyes were huge; his face was white, except for a diagonal slash from brow to chin oozing bright blood. "But it can't be. Vampires aren't real."

"Oh, Timmy," said Maggie, with a helpless glance at Father Mike. "He wasn't supposed to be here, Father."

"I was staying overnight at Eddy's," Timmy rushed to explain. "We were going to play Nintendo all night. I forgot *Mario Kart,* so he made me come back to get it. I had to; it's his favorite. His mom said—"

"It's okay, Timmy," said Father Mike. "Come into the house. Let's have a look at your war wounds."

"What… no, I can't. Sabrina yells at me if I get in the way when her friends are here. I better go."

A look of concern passed between Maggie and the priest. "Timmy, wait," Maggie said. "You're hurt. Come inside and get patched up first."

"I have to go now," he said tonelessly.

"He must have seen," said the priest to Maggie. He again addressed the boy, "It's not a good idea for you to be wandering outside alone at night. Come into the house, lad."

"But Eddy's waiting. I got to go!"

"Not without the game," Maggie reminded him.

"Come inside, Timmy," Father Mike said kindly. The boy made no more protest as the priest gently guided him up the steps, though he hesitated in the doorway. At Father Mike's urging, he took a deep breath and plunged into the house.

Maggie cast a quick glance around the yard, then followed them inside and closed the door. "I'll call Eddy's mom, okay, Father?" At his quick nod, she headed for the phone.

The boy seemed to be in shock. He sat on a couch as directed, but gazed uncomprehending into space as Mara came with the first aid kit and sat beside him. "Sorry, Timmy, this might hurt a bit. I'll patch you up, and when your Mom and Dad get here, they can drive you to the hospital. You might need a few stitches." She began tending his wound. "Are you okay?"

He turned his head slowly to look at her. "Are you?"

"No, not really," she admitted. He had always admired her. A true comic book fan, he plainly saw her as a superheroine, the persona she had managed to keep hidden from the rest of the world. "Hold still. Just a minute, now. Almost done. No, Tim, I'm very sad. Today I lost one of my dearest friends." A tear slid down her cheek. *And the love of my life.*

"But Mara, th-they're not real, are they?" His lip quivered, but his twelve-year-old dignity would not allow him to cry; not in front of a girl. "Vampires, I mean."

Mara closed her eyes, unable to speak for a moment. She thought of how they were only too real, both as her deadly enemy and as her sweetest love, lost forever. She opened her eyes to see in the boy's face the belief that she could fix anything. "Yeah, Timmy, I'm afraid they are."

Tears welled up in his eyes. "Is she, is she...?" His voice broke; he dashed the tears from his eyes but avoided looking toward the other couch, where Sabrina's body lay so still.

"Yes, Sabrina's gone, um, passed away. It's okay to cry. It's okay," she murmured, putting her arm around him.

"Dead, you mean. I saw, I was—" He was unable to continue, and she realized that he had witnessed the dreadful event. Finally, a torrent of tears poured forth against her shoulder, and they cried together.

Father Mike administered the Last Rites conditionally and recited the prayers of exorcism (his usual procedure in incidents involving vampires). Afterward, he sprinkled the house and yard with holy water.

Timmy finally looked at the body of his sister. "I swear I'll kill the thing that did this!" Then he grated through his tears, "You better run, vampire. I'm coming for you."

"No, Timmy," Mara said. "That's my job."

Maggie brought a sheet to cover the body. Father Mike finished his blessing of the house and spoke in an aside to Mara. "It's time to warn your friends, don't you think? Tell them how they can protect themselves. It appears they're prime targets now. Meanwhile, I'll call the police and Sabrina's parents."

Mara felt properly chastened, but steeled herself not to cry. If only she had warned her friends sooner, maybe Sabrina would still be alive. Well, she had warned them, but it was a difficult thing to believe, and she guessed that they had never really taken it seriously. She should have insisted, of course, but until now, she'd had everything so well in hand that the possibility of them being in serious danger seemed remote. Then she had introduced a vampire into their midst and led them to trust him. Torn to pieces inside by his betrayal, she wondered, *Is this the "bitter draught" Father Mike warned me about?*

After Mara regained her composure, she spoke to her friends. "I'm sorry. It's my fault. I don't know why I didn't see this coming."

"So you really did know all about these things?" cried Maggie. "And, and then—I can't believe it! You fall in love with one and introduce it to us just like it's human? Now look what you've done!" She burst into tears.

Mara blanched and stood as though turned to stone at this barrage from her dear friend. "I—I—" she faltered.

"No! You didn't talk when you should have. So just shut up and listen for once," Maggie raged. "Sabrina's dead! Get that? Dead! And—oh, we'll never see her again!" she wailed. "You did this, Mara! How could you? I thought we were friends."

"I know," said Mara, subdued. "I'm so sorry I—"

Sparks flew from Maggie's eyes, and her voice rose. "Too late! Too late! What good are apologies now, Mara? Will that bring her back?" Maggie flew at her.

Mara did not block the move or attempt to evade the stinging nails that raked her cheek. George and Josh quickly rushed to her defense. With apologetic glances at Mara, they dragged Maggie back, trying to calm her with soothing words.

"Maggie, Maggie," said George. "She did tell us, quite a few times. Not about what he was, though, I guess." His glance at Mara was full of reproach, despite himself.

"But let's be fair. Even if she had, we wouldn't have believed it," Josh defended her. "Sorry, Mara, it's just too far out, I guess."

"No, Maggie's right. I should have made you listen." Mara sighed. "Now, if you'll excuse me, I've got unfinished business to take care of."

"You're going to kill it, right?" Timmy blurted out.

Mara looked at him, stabbed to the heart by his reference to *It*. She steeled herself not to cry. Told herself that that was all the Prince was, after all: It. Just another creature of the night; a blood-sucking monster, not a man. She had been a fool to believe the impossible. What really happened that night in the church?

No, none of that. I am the Huntress. I will do this.

Timmy regarded Mara, oddly expressionless, as she did her weapons check. Maggie was still weeping. George and Josh's eyes were round with apprehension and their faces tight with fear as they watched Mara's preparations.

"Should I help? You maybe could use some backup," ventured Josh, although his white face said that he was sorely afraid.

"No, thanks, Josh. I work alone." She sensed his relief. "But thanks for the offer." Her eyes were hard and resolute as she went out onto the porch.

"Kind of reminds me of *High Noon*," she heard Josh say to no one in particular. Then the door closed, and she was alone.

The trees whispered in the night breeze; all seemed peaceful and undisturbed, as if nothing had happened. As if Sabrina were not gone forever. And the Prince— Stop. No tears now. Mara took a deep breath. *It's execution time.*

She had not gone far (just past the perimeter of the sprinklings of holy water) when she sensed the telltale chill of his presence. "Come out where I can see you, Prince," she commanded. "You must answer to me now."

He materialized in that disconcerting way he had. Her heart caught in her throat at the sight of him, so handsome and dashing in his sweeping black cloak; his face seemed to glow in the light from the porch, like a wonderful carving of alabaster. How can this beauty hide such a monster? A visual ambushed her just then, of him pledging undying love. She shook her head to dispel the image, determined not to let feelings get in the way of duty.

His expression was unreadable.

"How could you?" she burst out.

***

He stood silent, finding himself once more outside the two worlds. Though he knew he deserved nothing more, what then was the purpose of his transformation? To taste the sweetness of love only to have it swiftly snatched away. Nyx warned me; has she been right all along? And Father Mike had said... Is this, then, the cup of bitterness of which he spoke? *Ah, Mara. You have already torn my heart in two; now all you need do is rip it out of my chest. It is better that I die now. I cause you nothing but heartache.*

"Well? Have you nothing to say for yourself?" She searched those deep black eyes but could read nothing in them. *Why doesn't he speak in his own defense?* she mourned, then caught herself. *No. Why do I hesitate? This monster just killed my friend.* The thought of Sabrina lying pale and still, never to laugh again. Never again would those green eyes sparkle with humor; never again would she see the sprinkling of freckles across the pert nose, or the dimples and teasing smile. "Right. I totally get it." Sorrow and rage and frustration vied for ascendance. "There is no defense, is there?"

He said nothing, just stood unmoving before her as though carved of stone, yet somehow at the same time ethereal, and so insubstantial that it seemed quite possible that he might vanish in the next breath of air.

Of course, this is a vampire. Always has been. How could I have thought – ? She blinked away sudden tears. *No, none of that. I have a job to do. This is the enemy. I will kill it.* She narrowed her eyes and sprang to the attack, stake point first.

He did not move; did not try to evade her.

At the last possible moment, stake point inches from his breast, she halted. "I can't," she said brokenly, lifting tear-filled eyes to his face.

His gaze met hers again, black and unreadable. "Why not? An innocent girl is dead. Just finish it! You know what I am!"

Tears ran down her cheeks as she saw in her mind's eye Sabrina lying cold and still. "My dear friend, dead, and I, I've killed vampires all my life. Why can't I kill the one that did this?" She looked down at the stake in her hand accusingly. Her knuckles went white as she clenched her fist around it.

***

The Prince did not flinch; he just waited for her to finish her work. Oblivion would be sweet in comparison to the bitterness of this heartache.

The stake dropped to the ground with a dull clatter. Mara's

shoulders drooped. "What good am I if I can't destroy the vampire that killed my friend? The Huntress," she said with utter self-loathing. "Like hell!"

The Prince saw her desolation, and it struck him that his accepting of sole blame for Sabrina's death was unfair. That he should cause Mara more anguish was a dart more painful than stake, knife or arrow. Was he not meant to be her Protector? How could he so soon forget that this was the reason for his transformation? No, there must be no wallowing in self-pity.

He spoke softly. "No, my love, you have not failed. Whereas I — it is I who should have stopped him."

She looked up, the light reflecting off her tearstained cheeks. "What did you say?" she croaked.

"I did not kill her, Mara, but — if only I'd arrived here sooner. I was too late to save her. Please forgive me."

"What? They said… They saw you. So how — ?"

"It was the Rocket. I think perhaps they — they mistook him for me." He cast down his eyes in shame.

She shook her head, wanting to believe, yet unwilling to let go her rage and despair just yet. She thought about how for so long their circle had continued intact and inseparable, their bonds of friendship strengthened with each passing year. Now the unthinkable had happened. One was gone. Sabrina. And this, this —

Or was he telling the truth? She wanted to believe him, was wavering when her eyes swept over him again, and something struck her as not quite right. She caught at his hand and turned it palm upward. His sleeve fell back, exposing a crimson-black line angled across his forearm.

She felt cold inside, then hot. "What's this? You tried to turn her? You're despicable!" She slapped him across the face.

He lifted a hand to his stinging cheek. "I did not…"

But she had turned and walked away.

***

Inside the house, the three friends sat around white-faced

and on edge, silent as they tried to imagine what was happening outside and fearing the worst. Father Mike had made the telephone calls and was cautioning them on how to answer the questions that would be asked of them when the police came. It would accomplish nothing to tell tales of vampires. Let the police delude themselves as they would, with their forensics and their DNA testing, and such. They would have no patience with smart-mouthed young people, and may even suspect them in a case of probable homicide. It was better filed as an unsolved case, leaving Mara free to deal with it.

Unable to sit still another moment, Josh wandered to the door, opened it a crack and looked out into the night. Just then Mara appeared on the porch, pale and distraught. Maggie hung back, but George rushed over, his eyes round and huge behind his thick glasses. "Mara! What happened? Are you okay?"

She did not reply. Josh quickly closed the door behind her.

Father Mike stood, crucifix in his hand. "Mara?"

She fought for control, blinking back tears, and finally found her voice. "I—I just can't kill him. He—he—" She choked on the words. "I can't believe it. The Prince tried to turn her." A sob escaped her.

Everyone else was shocked into silence.

Then Timmy dropped his bombshell. "No way, Mara. It wasn't him. That one you like, that you call the Prince. You know that, don't you? He tried to save Sabrina."

They all stared and exclaimed in varying degrees of shock and disbelief. "Wha—? How do you know that?" Josh was loudest of all.

Mara gave the boy a sharp look. "What did you say?"

Timmy opened his mouth, but no words came out.

"He saw," said the priest. "He was there, remember?"

"Are you sure, little Timmy?" said Mara, hope and disbelief warring within her.

He nodded. "That vampire was trying to turn her when the

Prince came. He's a vampire himself, I guess, but he fought with it, and it flew away, then he brought Sabrina back to the house. But she—she—" He burst into tears.

"O my goodness, what have I done?" Mara put an arm around him. "Thank you for telling me that, Timmy. Here, Father, Maggie, look after this brave boy, while I—I really do have some unfinished business to attend to now, I guess." She looked stricken as she went out the door.

The night was dark and silent outside, the dazzling circle cast by the porch light. Mara took a deep breath and steeled herself to face the Prince—maybe the hardest thing she'd ever had to do in her life—for he was out there, somewhere, she knew, and she had done him a dreadful wrong. Down the steps she went, her soft boots making no sound, just a slight rustling as she crossed the lawn and passed through the holy water-sprinkled perimeter onto the sidewalk that lined the street.

Crickets began chirping again, as though nothing had disrupted their song. Mosquitoes were whining, just as on any ordinary night. Like that time at the Cup o' Java when she was so rude to him (here she squeezed her eyes tight shut to stop the tears—didn't succeed). Or the night of the battle when he'd saved her life and… and said he loved her. Or that night he'd given her the emerald ring and pledged himself to her forever. And… oh, how could she have believed *this* of him, without even listening to his side of the story, when… Tears welled up again in her eyes. She dashed them away.

Where *was* he? She could sense the chill of his presence, not far, but… she couldn't *see* him. The night was so, *so* black; even the streetlights seemed so inadequate, so swallowed up by this heavy, oppressive darkness. Or maybe it was the tears blurring her vision… oh, dear, what must he think of her? She'd *slapped* him—*twice!* Accused him, so unjustly. Oh, what to do… how to fix this?

They'd had something so beautiful, and she'd ruined it! *Ruined* it, with her quick temper and hurt pride. It wasn't his fault her friends had reproached her for not warning them, or that Sabrina was gone from them—no, it was hers. She was the Huntress; she should have known. Should have expected this and been ready for it. That was her job, and she had failed. Tears flowed down her cheeks again. *Failed!* And she'd let the Prince take the blame for it.

Now all she wanted to do was run away and hide. No, that was the coward's way out. She'd done this; now she must face him. Whatever came of it. She opened her mouth to call out, but her voice wouldn't cooperate.

There! Or no, that was just the shadow of a tall tree, moving in the soft breeze. *Where is he?*

Then the darkness, the mishmash of tangled shadows, morphed into a shape at last, and—she strained to see, as a tall figure seemed to materialize among those trees across the street in the neighbor's yard. He *was* there—that shape became clearer, a substantial form and, before she could blink, was right in front of her.

His face was a pale blur, his eyes deeply shadowed, so she was unable to read his expression. She hesitated, unsure what to expect from him after what she'd done. He had to be hurt— oh, how could she have been so quick to accuse, without giving him a fair hearing? After she'd promised to love him and wear his ring forever. And said she wanted to marry him—told Father Mike, even. Instead, she'd betrayed him.

She looked into the darkness of the angular shadows of his face, into the black points of his eyes and tried to read them. Couldn't. *Oh, dear, what must he think of me?* Devastated, she would have turned away, but then he reached out his hand. In it he held a long slim object that glinted dully in the feeble light.

"Here, you may need this," he said evenly. "Your stake— you dropped it."

She heard that desolate undertone beneath the calm words, a despairing note, as if he wanted nothing more than for her to put that stake through his heart. And her own heart broke.

"Oh, Prince, I'm so sorry!" she wailed. "How could I have... oh, I've *so* wronged you! How can I ever make up for—for what I've done? I—I—oh..." At that, her voice failed her, and tears ran down her cheeks.

He stood facing her, the stake in his hand. He hadn't moved. She still couldn't see his expression, his eyes—oh, what was he thinking? Would he leave her now? *No, no... please, God, help me...*

What would she do without him? Oh, what would become of *him*? Without a thought, before she knew what she was about to do, she threw her arms around him and held him tight. Pressed her tear-streaked face to his chest—so cold and still, and yet so dear. Felt the softness of the fabric of his cloak against her cheek.

For a long moment, he was still, unmoving, as only a vampire can be. Then she felt his arms go around her, and he held her close. The stake clattered to the sidewalk, and she heard him say softly into her hair, "Thank you for that, my dear Mara. But please understand, I will always love you, now and forever, whatever happens—even if you kill me. Just as I promised."

With that, the floodgates opened once more. She couldn't seem to stop the tears, but he just held her until she managed to compose herself, sniffed, and tried to dry her eyes with her sleeve. Felt him pressing a cloth into her hand. A fresh linen handkerchief.

"Oh, how can you be so...?" She dabbed at her eyes with it. "I—I don't deserve it, I know, but—oh, please, forgive me."

"No, it's okay. It is *I* who deserve nothing. And you—you are everything to me. Without you, I would be—" Here he faltered, paused a moment to collect himself, then went on, affecting a lighter tone. "As I told you before, I am a vampire... see, my heart is already on the mend."

***

The Prince had mixed feelings about still being in existence, even when he once more held Mara in his arms and felt the consolation of her apology and assurance of her belief in him. It seemed he had been on an emotional roller coaster ever since his transformation. He saw now that the elation of basking in the sunlight of Mara's love could be gone in an instant, plummeting him into an abyss of despair because his vampire nature had taken over. Or because she believed it had.

He knew he deserved to be under suspicion because of his guilty past, but that did not make it any easier. How wonderful it would be to hold her in his arms like this forever and not have to think about anything else. That would be heaven.

But alas, his encounter with the Rocket and his victim had awakened something within him that he had hoped was buried deep. Now images crowded his mind with wicked clarity. Death, blood, ecstasy. It took all his strength to crush the craving clawing for ascendance within him. He directed his thoughts instead to the anguish he had inflicted upon countless mortals through the centuries for this only. Would he ever be free? Even now, with the recovery of his conscience and his soul, and the ever-present sense of guilt for and horror of what he had done, he felt the temptation with increasing intensity, even as he stood with the antidote held trustingly in his arms.

The pointed stake still lay on the ground at his feet where Mara had dropped it. In his desperation, it seemed to him that only through oblivion could he be free of this terrible curse. It was not possible for him to destroy himself, or in the depths of his despair, he might have done so. Now he saw that even Mara could not, not even when she thought he had killed Sabrina. His heart sank within him as he wondered how long he could go without killing someone.

Unless... could there be redemption somehow, even for him? If so, his only hope was to find the key before it was too late. There was a purpose for which he had been transformed. It was up to him, now, to accomplish whatever was required of him.

Mother of Mercy, enlighten me. In that instant, he was flooded by a light of self-revelation. *Have hope. Do not despair. I am with you, always.*

The police finally arrived, lights flashing, and the Prince melted into the shadows. Mara and her friends endured the interminable questions; Father Mike defended them to the police, who knew and respected him. The coroner was unable or unwilling to see the cause of death for what it was, or to consider the alleged perpetrator as other than human. Mara was not surprised. She had been through this song and dance before.

The funeral was set for two weeks hence, allowing for further investigation. Time passed quickly, and it was soon over. Sabrina's parents resented the fact that officials seemed to have shelved the case (filing it away with all the other vampire killings, Mara suspected). There seemed to be no answers to their many questions, nor solace in their grief.

Timmy wore his innumerable stitches as a badge of honor and vowed that one day he would avenge his sister's death, however long it took. Mara promised that she would handle it. "I know you're brave, but leave it to me. I'm the Huntress."

"But I want to be like you, Mara," he protested.

"That's not possible," she said firmly, putting an end to the argument, if not to his resolve. She sought to minimize the danger by taking him under her wing, and convinced his parents that it would be a good idea to enroll him in martial arts training. There his anger and energy could be channeled toward a practical activity.

Mara found it suddenly easy to impress upon Josh, Maggie, and George the vampire lore she had so often hinted at in vain, and to persuade them to take precautions for their own safety and that of their families. As time went on, Maggie refrained from further exhibitions of rage, but she often gave Mara reproachful looks as though unable to forgive, and would burst into fits of weeping at any reminder of Sabrina. She was unable for the longest time to bear the sight of the Prince and avoided her friends much of the time.

Mara reminded her own parents to beware, now that the master vampire had showed his hand. Their house had always been vampire-proof, but Mara worried about them being accosted elsewhere, or outside after dark.

They took it with surprising calm, but refused to hide. "What kind of a life would that be? Don't worry, we don't go out much in the evenings, anyway." Her mother patted her arm. "We may occasionally go out to dinner, or attend a play or a meeting now and then, but that's it."

She could see their point but was not sure they understood the danger. Did anyone, ever? And she was still unable to tell them that the Prince also was a vampire.

A Tale of Woe

A few nights later, after they had patrolled the town, Mara and the Prince paused in the park near the zoo, their customary refuge. There, under the trees, where they were somewhat out of sight and sound of crowds and prying eyes, they could take a break and more easily delight in one another's company. There they could talk freely without fear of being overheard. Only the sound of leaves fluttering in the breeze, the occasional call of a night bird and the chirping of crickets broke the silence. Traffic noises were only faintly audible, muted by distance and the surrounding shrubbery.

"That ol' master vampire must hate me a lot to waste so much time and energy trying to hurt me," Mara said to the Prince. "Good grief. Am I so significant?"

"More than you know. You have warned your friends?"

"Yes. Father will keep them supplied with holy water and crucifixes, and they all have garlic wreaths in their homes." Her eyes glistened with sudden tears. "If only I'd told them sooner."

"Do not blame yourself. But I think you should know that Charon ordered the Rocket to turn one of your friends."

"Oh, no, Sabrina's not turned, is she?" Could anything be worse than having to stake a vampire with the face of a friend?

"No, I would know had he succeeded." He looked away.

"Thank God," she murmured, relieved, but loved him the more for pity and held him close.

The Prince was intensely aware of her fast-beating heart and the warmth of her precious mortal body. But to his amazement, what awakened within his cold, still heart was not a thirst for blood, but tenderness and love. Leaves stirred in the treetops high above as joy rose from his heart and passed through them toward heaven.

Lost in the delight of one another's presence, they quietly conversed, oblivious to all nature around them. They did not see the moon reappear from behind the dark mist or the stars shifting in the arch of sky above. They were unaware that the breeze had died, that the sounds of traffic and voices and human activity had dwindled. They gave no thought to the world around them until the nearby song of a cricket broke the silence.

The Prince spoke softly in the darkness. "Would you come fly with me?"

"What?" She had not expected that.

"I asked if you would like to fly with me," he said, a little uncertainly this time. "Yet perhaps it would not be proper for us to be alone together."

"Alone. Oh, you mean, er, without a chaperone?" She laughed a little. "Like every other time we've met?"

His brow furrowed. "Things are different now."

She felt ashamed for making light of his serious question. He was right; things would never be the same again. How easy it would be to get caught up in seventh heaven. She blushed and stammered, "Yes—er, okay, I think I see what you mean."

"Sorry. I did not mean to take you by surprise, or storm."

"Er, you said fly, right? Would that be literally, or, um, metaphorically?"

He laughed.

She was astonished. This was the first time she had heard him actually laugh since his transformation. So different from that malevolent laugh that had grated on her nerves and chilled her to the bone, this was a pleasant sound that thrilled her heart. She was glad of the darkness to conceal her blushes (forgetting for the moment that vampire senses were unimpeded by darkness).

"Both," he said finally. At her puzzled look, he added,

"Maybe I need only ask if you trust me. Once in the air we are entirely alone beneath the gaze of God."

"Okay, I get it. I think. I guess, yeah, I do trust you."

"You have shown me the sweetness of your world, now let me show you the wonder of mine. Hold tight to me now."

She reached up and put her arms around his neck. A swirl of his cloak hid them from mortal eyes as they swiftly rose above the trees. Her breath caught, and she gasped with the speed; the air rushed against her face and fluttered through her hair. Her clothing rippled and snapped as they streaked up, up into the night. Tiny pinpoints of light scintillated high above them. The moon glowed bright, its edges soft against the black silken sky.

Soon they leveled out and drifted high above a sparkling pattern of earthbound lights. Though initially dazzled, Mara was gradually able to make sense of it. The dotted lines were streetlights cutting a pattern across the grid, shot through with random gleams from houses and other buildings. Night mist hung like cobwebs from trees, crept along the ground and swirled upward, muting the traffic noises and diffusing the lights into a brilliant haze.

She took a deep breath, felt the cool air against her face and a sense of exhilarating lightness and freedom. The Prince's flight was smooth and swift, and unlike that of any natural creature. She thought how strange he was; this being that held her so effortlessly within the circle of his arm. How unnatural was his coldness, how unearthly his beauty, how entrancing his eyes—without a doubt a creature of the night. A troubling thought. *Lord, tell me what to do.*

Wraithlike, they descended, easing down, down, toward trees and rooftops. From this unaccustomed view of the town, Mara felt a little lost; disoriented, as though she had been spirited away to some strange and magical land. The Prince seemed not in the least confused, as though he knew exactly where they were.

Suddenly they dropped out of the sky, and the ground

rushed up toward them at a dizzying speed. She tensed, anxious, until she remembered her calming exercises, made herself relax, and breathed more deeply. There was nothing to fear, nothing to fear. This was his element. His strong arms held her easily; she would not fall, she told herself. A quick glance upward caught a look of amusement on his face that vanished as his gaze met hers. He was teasing!

Though she resolved to be calm, when a metal cross flashed upward past them, she squeezed her eyes shut tight and braced for the hit. And was surprised when they lightly touched down. She opened her eyes and saw that they had landed; but so high above the street. Ah, St. Michael's bell tower. Its spire cast a moon shadow on them. Mara leaned over the stone parapet to look down at the black ribbon of street far below. The moving lights made her feel suddenly dizzy. After the whirlwind ride, the unaccustomed height…she clutched the Prince's arm.

"I will not let you fall," he said. "Sit beside me."

Is that the answer to my prayer? He won't let me fall?

He eased her onto a ledge at the base of the spire. She sat with her back pressed to the wall, took a deep breath, and looked around. The crisscross design of the town rolled out like a luxurious blanket patterned with glittering jewels. White gleams of headlights and the red of taillights threaded through the yellowish glowing lines of streetlights; brake lights winked sporadically. A glow of neon colors marked the downtown core. She gazed agog at this lovely, unorthodox view of her familiar old town.

The Prince glanced upward a bit anxiously at the moonlit cross high above them. "Pardon my disquietude," he said, when he saw that she had noticed. "I thought you would feel more secure in the shelter of the cross."

More secure? Does he think I should be afraid?

He sat next to her and put his arm and cloak around her. The night was chill, and she gratefully drew his mantle close. Though very light, it was surprisingly warm.

"Why did you bring me here, if the cross bothers you?" she said, after a short silence.

"Fond memories?" he said tentatively, as though not sure himself. "This is where we first met. Down there, that is."

"Um, yeah. But we can sit somewhere else, if you'd prefer."

"No, I just thought—it is a grand view, is it not?"

"Yeah, but that tall building over there—City Hall, I think it is—would do just as well. Or the clock tower at the old First National. There must be a pretty good view from either one of them. And no cross."

Does she not understand that I must be near my Lord God too? The pain of nearness is nothing to the agony of rejection and abandonment. Of separation, of desolation. And how can I make her see that I fear for her safety, that even with me she needs the protection of the cross? Perhaps now more than ever. How can I explain to her that I need this pain to remind me of the lowliness of my status and the loftiness of hers, so great is my fear that I should forget myself and do her harm?

She turned her face toward him, her thoughts troubled. *How can I understand him? This is my enemy, which I'm sworn to kill— but I just couldn't do it.* She reached up to take the hand that was draped over her shoulder. His hand, so cold. Cold as death. *Though he has a soul now, he's still a vampire.*

The answering pressure of his slender fingers melted her misgivings like snow in the sun. She felt awed by this amazing circumstance.

"I love you," she said, without knowing she was going to say it. She pressed her cheek against his cold hand.

He clutched her to himself, and she caught her breath, her heart tripping like a rabbit's. Oh, why had she said that?

He released her at once. "I'm sorry. I meant no disrespect."

"It's okay." Or, maybe not. *He's a vampire! Oh, dear.*

"This is new to me. I want to kiss you, but I am afraid that if I kiss you I—I may be unable to stop myself, and bite you."

This last he mumbled, and cast his eyes down in shame.

She was touched, as she realized how difficult this confession must be for him. Her hand reached out, almost of its own volition, to touch his face. He slowly raised his eyes to meet hers. "You wouldn't," she said. "Your sense of honor won't let you. You're better than you think. Stronger. I'm sure of it."

He looked pained. "You have no idea. You cannot say that until you know."

"I do say it." She leaned over and kissed him on the cheek. "There. Now our love is sealed."

***

He drew her into his embrace, gently. His heart was full to overflowing. Nyx was wrong. Or was she? He spoke softly, his cold lips at her ear. "Love me if you wish. Just do not forget I am a vampire."

***

She looked toward the west, past the jagged skyline of gabled rooftops with air vents and chimneys, the occasional high-rise building, and beyond where the dark of the sky faded toward the horizon. She lifted her eyes heavenward and saw the stars arranged in the same constellations that she had observed as a child lying on a blanket in the backyard, snuggled between her parents. But this time, she was sitting on a stone tower wrapped in a vampire's cloak and his arms. A sobering thought.

A bright light suddenly cut a streak across the sky, dropped to the horizon and vanished. "Look, a shooting star!" Mara pointed. "Make a wish." She closed her eyes.

"A wish?"

She smiled up at him. "You've never wished upon a star? Come on, here's your chance. Everyone has to at least once."

He regarded her in silence. "Your eyes are the stars I would wish upon. So bright and beautiful, the color of the daytime sky lost to me so long ago."

That jolted her; she felt a little silly. He was so serious. What do you say to one whose life came to a tragic end in the flower of his youth—and yet was still here after how many centuries?

"Do you remember things from, you know, that time, um, before?" she ventured, finally.

He looked into the distance as though searching there for a reply. "It was so long ago, you see. But of late, memories have come back to me, with my soul, maybe. Many are good, like those of the sun and the blue sky. Others, not so much."

"Tell me about it. I'd like to get to know you better."

"Ah, you want to hear the tale of the tragic short life of Niki Sperling, who had everything to live for, but threw it all away for the sake of a pair of bewitching eyes." He lifted his gaze to hers with an effort. "If I must. It has been nearly five hundred years since I gave it a thought. Except, you know, to long for daylight, which is the vampire's all-consuming passion, at least for some of us—second only to blood, that is.

"Since my recent transformation, or whatever happened that night at the church, I have begun to remember more of the past, of the mortal I once was, like it or not. Because I am trying to belong to that world again? Or your father's questions; I feared I would say more than I ought. Oh, he is a wily one." He gave her a quick apologetic glance.

"Yeah, I've heard him referred to as a fox a time or two." She laughed. "Meant in a good way, of course. He's pretty smart; you don't put one over on him very easily."

The Prince lifted an eyebrow. "Much like my own father. He too was a man of honor, and protective. Ah, the memories come back to me with a vengeance. But you do not really want the sordid details."

"Of course, details. How else am I to get to know you? It's not like I can visit your family or ask someone who knew you back then. Oh, sorry. I, um—"

"Do not apologize. I understand. You want to know me. Fine, just never forget, I may have my soul once again, but that mortal boy I once was ceased to exist nearly five centuries ago. I am now and forever a vampire."

"I'm not likely to forget that. Still."

"Right. How can you love me if you do not know me? Only if you know the worst and love me despite it, then…"

The worst? Mara shivered. *That's not quite what I meant.* "Er, I guess. But, um, about that boy—"

"Ah, where do I begin?" He turned to face the eastern horizon, ever mindful of the eventual rising sun, whatever his preoccupation.

"Your family," Mara said. "Start with them. What were they like?"

"My family," he began, and paused a moment to ponder. "My father was a prosperous landowner. It was said that many of our holdings the baron had bestowed upon him for overseeing his vineyards and winery as well as our own, and for his steadfast loyalty. The baron lived in an ancient castle on a hill above the village, one of that noble family's many estates since time immemorial. There was talk of a connection between our two families, but what it was I know not.

"The baron, our lord, was fair and generous, his domain an oasis of serenity in those troubled times. You must have read of the wars tearing all of Christendom asunder at that time. Which, of course, has nothing to do with the story of my downfall, or perhaps everything. You may read of these wider events in history books; I need not reiterate them. No, I'm only trying to delay the inevitable. Let me get on with it.

"We were a large family. I and my elder brothers, Werner, Theodor, and Reinhard, grew up working with my father. Each of them took a turn accompanying him to the great cities: Trier, Brussels, Amsterdam, Paris, Vienna; often as far away as Barcelona or Florence. He dealt with merchants and tradesmen, and with noble, and even royal houses. Our fine wines were widely sought after, you see. That summer Werner was to be married to a beautiful Spanish noblewoman, the daughter of a count my father had dealt with in Barcelona, and would be concerned with setting up his own household. Thus it would be my turn, while Reinhard would take care of the business at home. I was nearly twenty-two, and champing at the bit for adventure, as well as the opportunity to learn new things. First, I would find my place in life, then there would be time enough to choose a wife and settle down, or so I thought. I was filled with excitement all spring, anticipating the wondrous sights and new experiences, my imagination piqued by the tales my father and brothers had told of far places each time they returned from their travels.

"I and my brothers worked hard alongside the peasants, picking rocks on the steep hillsides, maintaining fences, and at harvest time carrying heavy baskets of grapes. How tired did I grow of those long hours sweating in the hot sun. Ah, the sun. Now I wish— but no, it is no use dwelling on that; what is done cannot be undone. We helped out in the winery, too. The wine cellars were extensive, vast caves cut into the steep slope and running far back into the mountain. Almost like an underground town, with shelves of bottles and rows of oaken barrels full of aging wine. The fragrance rising from the wooden winepresses, the crushed and fermenting grapes in the huge open vats, was ambrosia. We would often surreptitiously dip into the new wine, bubbly and sweet. We learned to have a care, though. Woe betide us should our father find us tipsy at our work.

"There was a dark forest roundabout, into which we often betook ourselves to hunt deer or to cut wood. In the winter we ventured there with our dogs to track down wolves that ravaged village flocks and herds when game was scarce. I was a hunter then, as now, but to kill the predators, not to be one.

"You spoke of wishing on a star. We made our wishes upon hearing the first cuckoo call of the spring. I remember well that melancholy sound. But now that I am exiled from the Old Country, so many things I will never hear or see again, especially now that I am a vampire and am banned from the daytime world as well. Only creatures that haunt the darkness, and night-blooming flowers, may delight me now." He paused a moment with furrowed brow, then went on. "But

I remember the flowers that grew rampant in meadow and forest, so lovely. And my mother's gardens so beautiful, her flowers at every window, and roses climbing the fences; ah, I can smell their divine fragrance even now. Man, you see, is much like a flower, made to bloom in the sun. But I, alas, have consigned myself to eternal darkness."

He shook his head, then resumed his tale. "I recall one of those last days. I was mending the fence above the vineyard. At midday, my sixteen-year-old sister Kristina came to me with a basket of bread and cheese and spiced meats. I could hear her singing as she drew near; we called her our little nightingale. I mopped the sweat from my brow and flung myself down in the shade of the fence, glad of a chance to get out of the sun, little appreciating that which was soon to be lost to me forever.

"Of course, I had no idea that soon I would never again see daylight. Never again would I see the sun warming the rows of vines on terraced hillsides, green fields, golden orchards, or its glinting off the church steeple high above the cluster of houses and shops of the village. Never again would I see the monastery standing sentinel on the mountaintop, stark against the blue sky.

"Though I was already a man grown in that final year of my mortal life, I was not above tweaking Kristina's braids. The bells rang out from the village church just then, and together we prayed the Angelus. Then I ravenously tore into the food as she regaled me with the latest bit of excitement: a peddler had come to the house, and from him, Mama and the girls had acquired lace and ribbon for their new dresses they were preparing for my sister Gerda's wedding. Months before, Papa had brought bolts of silks and velvet from Paris so they could sew new clothing for us all, for the occasion." He paused, his expression suddenly sorrowful. "None of us knew that it would also be our funeral attire.

"If only the old abbey had guarded us! Or warned us, somehow. No, that is unfair. No one could have prevented what happened, except I, myself. My brother Theodor was there, at the abbey. He had taken his vows the year before; that is what saved him. He was the only one left alive, afterward." The Prince's voice broke. With an effort, he composed himself. "But I am getting ahead of my story. Life then had its sorrows, of course, but was indeed very fine. We had each other, and we had God. Religion permeated all of society in those days, though then, as now, men were flawed and wicked. My mother taught us that if we prayed to Our Heavenly Mother, she would protect us always. Oh, why did she abandon us?"

There was such a note of tragic loss and reproach in his question that Mara took his hand in hers. "Our Lady wouldn't. We just don't always see why certain things are allowed to happen, but there's always a good reason."

He shook his head. "Perhaps you're right, but oh, how can I believe that, after what happened?"

What can I say, dear Jesus? she prayed, and words came to her. "Maybe that's why you're here today, given a second chance. Remember what happened in the church, with your family, and all that. There's a reason for you being here, you'll see. God will bring some kind of good out of the evil that happened back then."

"You are right. It is not Our Lady's fault. I alone am to blame. And yet, I do not get how, or why…"

"Father Mike says we don't have to understand, but only trust in God, always."

"But my family?" He shook his head, his face twisted in anguish. "My father, mother, Kristina and — oh, poor Georg and Karlchen. All the little ones. All of them. You heard Nyx. Mara, they did not deserve that fate."

"They're in heaven now," she said softly. "You saw that in the church. During your five centuries of hell, they were praying for you. They never stopped loving you."

"But for those five hundred years, I raised hell taking the lives of more innocents. What about that?"

"Uh…" Mara was at a loss for a moment. "Maybe that's the time you're serving now?"

He looked at her for so long without saying anything—had she offended him? Just as she opened her mouth to apologize, he spoke. "I had not thought of it like that. Yes, perhaps you are right. I thought this was hell, but could it be my purgatory? Ah, it will be a long and arduous journey. How can I ever atone?"

"You can't. None of us can. Father Mike says only Jesus could, and He did. We need only repent. Look what happened to the Good Thief. They said you're forgiven, don't forget."

He caught up her hand and pressed his cold lips to it. "Thank you. You have no idea how that comforts me. Know this: I will never stop loving you, though you despise me—no, do not say anything. You have not heard it all yet. My mother…" The Prince faltered at that, but with an effort, he pressed on. "She ran the household, directed the servants, and cared for her children. We were always well dressed, though there were many of us, and we never went hungry; fresh-baked bread and spring-chilled butter were on the board—the table, that is—every day. Papa was the love of her life; this, in an era when marriages were often arranged for connections or convenience. I can still see her with the baby on one arm and the little ones clinging to her skirts as she tossed corn to the chickens or tended the garden.

"Summers were delightful, but winters could be harsh; babies and old ones often did not see spring. I remember the year my grandfather Hummel died; I was only a boy. He was a giant of a man from the Black Forest, with hair black as a raven's wing (Mama too, had hair of that color, as do I, and Theo, Katherine, and Georg; the rest were redheads or blondes, taking after Papa). Grandfather came to live with us in his old age; he always had time for us children. In the winter, he sat beside the hearth, in the summer on the front step, carving wonderful things from wood as he regaled us with tales of war and adventure, for he was a soldier at one time. How fascinated I was by those stories, and as I watched thin slices of wood curling before his blade, it seemed like magic the way a delicate figurine would appear as though it had been hidden inside the block of wood. On occasion he would surprise us children with a miniature horse or dog or cow. Once he made a set of toy soldiers complete with weapons and armor for us boys, and a dollhouse with furniture and dolls for the girls.

"But his musical instruments were a wonder! His mark was famed far and wide, his initials HH intertwined with a white stag. One day he made a violin for me. For me! How honored I was! I played for him often. Thank God he never lived to see what became of me. Though I guess he knows now." His voice trembled, and he paused for a moment. Mara felt a rush of sympathy, for the first time beginning to see his family as real people.

He recovered and went on. "My sisters were refined and accomplished, kind and generous, always ready to accompany Mama when she visited the sick or helped the less fortunate. Young men vied to make a match with one of them, you may be sure. Katharine was already married by that fateful spring, with two small daughters. Gerda's wedding was to be a joyous occasion; we had no idea it would be our last. I can still see the longboards set up outside, laden with platters and bowls, and overflowing with a wonderful feast: smoked pork hocks cooked with sour cabbage and loaves of bread stuffed with spiced meats, buttered turnips and squash, fowl roasted with apples and nuts and spices, bread, sweetmeats and cakes. Essentially my last meal of that kind. Alas, they hold no pleasure for me now, cursed as I am with this unholy appetite.

"People came from far and wide to help us celebrate. The whole village attended; the abundance of my father's table was legend, as was his generosity. Wine and ale flowed freely for many days. Dancing and singing continued late into the nights.

"Ah, yes, my father was proud of his family, justifiably so, until I..." He fell silent and gazed into the distance. After a bit he turned to her. "Shall I torment you longer with this sad tale of how I became a monster? Just say the word when you have had enough. In truth, I did not bring you here to trap you. I only meant to show you your town as you have never seen it. I wanted you to share in my one innocent joy, flying. I also wanted to ask you to—no, not yet. It would not be right."

"No, no, it's fine," she murmured, though troubled in her heart. "I love the flying, and seeing my town as you do. And—and—well, I'd love to hear the story of your life, but if you'd rather wait—" She felt suddenly afraid of what she might hear. "Um, I, er, what would you ask me?"

"No, I cannot, in all honor. Not until you know what I am."

"If you say so," Mara said meekly, not sure she was ready for what he must say next, before he asked her whatever it was. Yet his sense of honor melted her heart. She squeezed his hand. "Hey, you're a vampire. I, of all people, have no illusions about what that means. You know that." She hoped she sounded more confident than she felt.

The Prince was silent for so long that Mara wondered if he would change his mind and not continue his tragic tale. Caught herself hoping, she already knew more than enough about vampires. Of course, this was not about vampires so much as about him.

He stood up, then, abruptly, and his cloak slipped from around her. She shivered. At once, his glance became tender and apologetic. He took off the cloak and draped it about her shoulders, then turned and looked out at the lights of town once more. The breeze picked up, riffling his hair and his black silk shirt as he stood silhouetted against the starry sky. A flurry of traffic noises—horns honking and motors revving—drifted upward on a faintly malodorous cloud of exhaust. The Prince sprang onto the parapet and crouched there; he turned to face Mara.

"Forgive me if I hesitate. How does one begin the tragic tale of the death and destruction of all that he loves, and least, perhaps, though not last, of himself? Alas, there is no nice way to tell it. I shall begin with the last night of Gerda's wedding celebration. That was when I first met Nyx.

"I was strong, handsome, and everyone's favorite. Even the dog liked me best," he said with a sad little smile. "I had worked up quite a thirst dancing the night away, with every maid of my acquaintance, I am certain. They loved me; I could have had my pick, but I was not ready yet to choose just one. I thought I had time. Of course I did not know that my time, and that of many of them, was about to run out. As I went to refill my cup—not for the first time—I caught sight of a strange girl across the bonfire, her glittering black eyes hot upon me. I had never seen anyone quite like her, so delicate, her skin so pale and her hair black as night; so fragile-looking, unlike the sturdy, rosy-cheeked, fair-haired maids of our village. Her black dress was of a somewhat unusual style, though that did not detract from her beauty. I was intrigued and could not take my eyes off her. She was like a Dresden figurine, and those eyes—ah, they were my downfall. Of course, she had no doubt mesmerized me from the first.

"When Kristina took up her lute and began to sing, even the loudest and merriest were silent, swept away by that angelic voice so high it seemed to kiss the stars. Ah, the face of innocence, the last I would ever know. I felt an arm around my waist just then. That was the beginning of the end. Just a moment before, I had seen that vision of loveliness across the fire; now she was beside me. Nyx. Her touch was cold, but her face, those eyes, fairly took my breath away. Quite befuddled, I unsteadily made my way to a bench, and before I knew, she was on my lap with her arms around my neck.

"My faithful dog slunk away, but I paid no heed to him, so entranced was I by those mysterious eyes. By their very wickedness, fool that I was. She bit me, then. The sting of that vampire kiss took me to the sky. It was so… Ah, no wine my father made ever hit me like that."

Tears sprang to Mara's eyes. *I'll kill her.* She hated the

thought of a vampire preying on any mortal. But *this*!

"I was hers from that moment; I cared for nothing else. However, she seemed preoccupied by a ring my father wore. A ruby ring, which he only wore on special occasions. She asked me rather abruptly, why was he wearing it? *Why not*, I said to myself, but other things preoccupied me at the moment. I hardly remember what happened after that. I think she tried to lure me outside the ring of firelight. She seemed nervous about the way 'that man'—the baron's brother—was looking at her. The tall, ascetic red-haired monk did have rather disturbing greenish eyes, intense as an Old Testament prophet's.

"I was pretty lightheaded by that time—from loss of blood, never mind the wine and ale. Werner knew something was wrong; to save his foolish brother from this wanton, he detained me and ordered her to leave. I rather ungraciously complied; I dared not defy him. Her eyes glowed in utter hatred as she looked at him. I thought I must have imagined it; to me she was a vision, her eyes promising the fulfillment of a man's every forbidden fantasy. Yes, I was drowning in those eyes, but I wanted to."

Mara recalled with a chill her own experience with vampire eyes (but only his). *Odd, I thought I was immune.*

"Of course, I knew it was wrong; I knew better than to cheapen myself thus, but the euphoria! Alas, how our senses do deceive us. How could my virtue save me when I trampled it into the dust the moment I saw those bewitching eyes and those red lips, as enticing as the sweet grapes in our vineyard? My fine upbringing—the lessons taught me from childhood, my purity of body and soul in which I unbeknownst took pride—all vanished in a heartbeat. She promised to return the following night only if I showed her the ring. How did I not guess that it was all about the ring? But by then, I would have promised her anything.

"I had no energy the next morning, but my father was not sympathetic. There was work to be done. According to him, that was the best cure for overindulging. 'Moderation in all things' was the motto by which he lived. He expected no less of his sons."

Mara shivered at the thought of what was coming. What had Nyx said? "You killed them all."

The Prince lifted his eyes to gaze into the distance again and went on. "Werner and Reinhard laughed at me for making a fool of myself over a woman; I was not man enough even to hold my liquor, they said. I was mortified. This had never happened to me before. I would show them. I would do my chores as usual, never mind how I felt. I noticed a small wound on my throat, but it was only a scratch."

"So said Mercutio," murmured Mara.

"My mother looked upon me with concern that evening at suppertime when I sat listlessly picking at my food. This was not like me. We boys could easily demolish a well-laden board after a day of hard work. I will never forget her hand on my brow as she gently ruffled my hair." He paused, making a concerted effort to master his emotions. "Yes, I stole the ring. A small thing, perhaps, but in doing so I betrayed everyone I loved. I sold my soul and thus sentenced my mind and body to perpetual shame and bondage.

"We were a close-knit family. The small wooden casket containing the family valuables was discreetly tucked away inside my parents' large oak wardrobe, but it was not locked. I was edgy, but our household was a busy place, so I need not have worried. After supper, as I huddled beside the hearth trying in vain to warm myself, my mother asked for someone to fetch her sewing basket. I quickly volunteered. She protested with an anxious glance, but I was already on my way — to my doom, as it turned out, and that of all of us.

"No one saw me snatch the ring and conceal it, but I knew God sees all. I slunk to the kitchen and gave the sewing basket to my mother, unable to arrest my headlong rush to destruction. Night fell as I sat by the hearth in guilty silence, trying to think of a plausible excuse to go outside. I had to see her! Then I would return the ring, and no one need know. I intended to hie myself to the church the next day to confess, but my tomorrow never came." At that, his voice broke, and he was silent.

Mara wanted to comfort him, but how? And to weep for him, yet it was too late for that.

When finally he continued, his voice was low and sad. "After the sun had set, my chance presented itself. The dog jumped up from beside the hearth and ran to the door, barking furiously. I went out, ostensibly to see what the matter was, my faithful dog leaping ahead of me. All was quiet except for the rustling of leaves and the smell of dampness in the evening breeze. Stars shone bright and beautiful in the darkening sky. I went out the gate, up the slate walk to the winery. Was there a prowler or some wild animal wandering near? Or might it be her? My heart beat fast in anticipation. The dog growled, sniffing along the way, but seemed not to find anything out of order. I went to make certain the doors to the cellar were secure.

"The bar set firmly in place, I turned to go back to the house. Slowly, for I was filled with a terrible longing. Where was she? I scanned the darkness anxiously, for that siren held my every sense captive. Just as I was about to despair of ever seeing her again, I felt a chill, and the dog began barking frantically toward the sky. I strained to see in the darkness; a bat or two fluttered past. A shiver went through me. Then, with a yip of terror, my dog tucked his tail and streaked beneath the hedge.

"And she was there. A deeper shadow in the night, her white face a blur to my mortal eyes. 'Have you brought the ring?' were her first words. I was so anxious to please, in clumsy haste, I pulled it from my tunic. Her eyes lit up with a glow that rivaled the ruby in the moonlight as she plucked it from my hand. I recoiled from that sudden flare of unearthly fire in her eyes. But when her gaze met mine, the demonic glow had faded, and I thought I had imagined it. By then the ring had vanished within her cloak. 'The ring,' I protested feebly. 'I must return it, or I will be found out.'

"Her laughter rang out, so delightful. Yet my conscience stung; I could not bear the thought of my parents' reproach. 'Please, the ring,' I begged. 'Later,' she whispered, and put her arms around my neck. Told me I was beautiful. Fool that I was, I kissed her. She bit me on the mouth. I jerked back, saw her lick my blood from her lips. That was when it dawned on me what she really was. We had heard tales of revenants. I should have known, but there was I, fallen into her trap. With all the strength of my will and body, I tried to fight her off. Too late. She just looked into my eyes, and I could not. I tried to pray, but could not even do that. God had abandoned me to my own chosen devices."

Overwhelmed by pity and tenderness, Mara went to put her arms around him. "It's okay. I understand." And silently swore that she would kill every last vampire.

He clung to her for a moment, gratefully, then gently guided her back to the ledge. "You had better sit down. It gets worse."

He returned to his perch to continue his tale. "She would make me immortal, she said, and sank her teeth into my throat. I was floating, helpless in a wonderful, deadly euphoria, drifting up, up above the trees. Yes, really. In her ecstasy, Nyx levitated, taking me up with her. She finally brought me down, still clinging to me like a bat; I sank to my knees, weak as a newborn pup. I knew it was wrong. I tried to push her away, but my arms would not obey. Then, she looked into my eyes, and I seemed to fall into hers, those deep abysses of mystery and wonder promising every sweet thing. Oh, how I longed to drown in them! I tried to draw her to me. I wanted her to bite, wanted her to..." He paused with an abashed glance. "Sorry," he murmured with a slight grimace, and then continued.

"Then I realized what I was doing and was struck with horror and shame. I wanted to flee, but it was too late, I could not. My mother's face suddenly appeared before me. She kissed my forehead tenderly and spoke soft words, but why was there blood on her mouth? Then I saw: this was not my mother, but Nyx! O God, what had I done? I turned my face away. The grass pricked my cheek; I felt cold hard ground beneath me. The sweet, sick smell of blood and death hung in the air. It seemed a very sacrilege to have so besmirched the night with the foulness of my sin. The stars above glittered unfriendly and cold like shards of ice. I was so weak I felt I was melting into the ground.

"Nyx whispered that all would be well if I would but drink her blood. I would become a very god, strong and beautiful, with more power than I could imagine. I could not speak, but my face must have expressed my horror, for even while I was drowning in that sweet fog of her designing, the truth hit me: she meant to turn me into one of those cursed beings that walk the night terrorizing mortals. At that, she grew angry. With a flick of her hand, blood dripped down on me from a slash on her breast. She lifted me up and pressed my lips to her, bidding me drink, as she whispered sweet words in my ear, flattering words of love, of how she did not want me to die. With all the feeble vestiges of my remaining strength, I tried to resist. Alas, though I knew it not, I was already lost.

"Perhaps it was the challenge of my purity and innocence that intrigued her so. Why else would she bother to bargain, or dare to defy her master? Her orders were to annihilate our whole family. Yet she risked all to take me for her own. When I did not answer as she wished, but lay there dull and uncooperative, she grew weary of the sweet talk. Or maybe she feared I would die and be lost to her forever, for she turned to threats. 'Know this,' she said. 'You are but the first. If you deny me, if you choose to die, your whole family awaits my pleasure. I will turn one of your brothers. Werner is as handsome as you, and Reinhard, though I do not fancy blonds or redheads.' I was afraid for them, but this was my immortal soul at stake. And my brothers had not been fooled by her as I had been. I turned my face away.

"But she is the devil, I swear it. She played her trump card then. Kristina. The master would be pleased by the gift of a nightingale in a gilded cage, she said. He loved music; had exotic tastes. Did I know that eating the heart of a nightingale would beautify one's voice? She knew no pity. I would have wept, but had not the strength even for that. I closed my eyes; wanted to die. But that would bring about the very horror I was bound to avert.

"Perhaps she feared I would die and thus escape her, for she shook me awake and held me to her tenderly. She solemnly promised that my family would be safe from her forever, that she would not touch even one of them, if I became hers. She wanted only me.

"And it was done. She held me to her, and I drank her blood. It was not easy; as a mortal, I had no taste for it. But at the thought of saving my sister, I was able to overcome my aversion. Her vampire blood was dark and thick and powerful, cold and bitter. Though I could drink but little, it spread through my body like white-hot fire, even to my fingertips. A great roaring filled my ears. I was burning, burning, engulfed in unbearable pain. Or was it pure ecstasy? I hardly knew.

"Thus, I sealed my doom. Henceforth I would never know peace or love. Only ruin followed in the wake of my sin. No regret or remorse or sorrow; there was nothing in me to stir my loving Creator to pity or give Him reason to show mercy. When He did so, finally, it was entirely gratuitous. I did not merit it or even know I wanted it.

"When I came to myself once more, I was lying in my own bed, so weak I could not move. I heard the murmur of voices, in the hushed tones that mortals tend to affect in the presence of the dead or dying. But to me every word was clear. I did not know it then, but I was beginning to change. My senses were already enhanced. Apparently, my father had wondered at my lengthy absence, and found me lying in the grass outside the winery door. He and one of my brothers carried me into the house.

"I must have had the look of death, for they at once called Mathias Mond, a highly respected physician and my father's friend. He would have bled me, as was usual then, but was aghast to discover that I had already nearly bled out. There was nothing he could do, he said; it was too late. My distraught mother was determined to the last to prove him wrong; how could it be that one so young and full of life could be so suddenly struck down? Of course, she had no idea.

"She covered me with goose-down quilts, stirred the fire in the hearth and boiled water for tea. Kristina sat beside me and held my hand, trying in vain to warm it. Her pulse and the heat of her body stirred something inside me, though I did not yet understand. My mother brought a steaming cup of tea to my bedside and lifted my head to help me drink, but it was no use. I was unable to swallow, thirsty though I was, and most of the tea ran down my chin. Unknown to either of us, my thirst was of a different kind; tea would not suffice. She set the cup on the night table and pressed me close. I felt her heartbeat at my ear, strong and enticing, but had no idea.

"At my lack of outward response, my mother seemed to wilt. She eased me back down and tucked the blanket round me. Long did she sit beside my bed, contemplating me with a look so sorrowful I could not bear it.

"Clearly, my death was imminent. Father Ludger, our priest, soon arrived. As soon as he entered the house, I felt an inexplicable sense of dread. The feeling grew stronger as he drew near to me. My mother stood aside, hopeful now. She had heard of healing brought about by the administration of the Last Rites. Our good pastor bent over me and spoke gently. He had baptized me as an infant and trained me as an altar boy. I am certain he recalled my childhood and my growing into a young man full of promise. Now, too soon, he would bury me.

"He reached out a hand to bless me. As his thumb touched

my forehead, it burned, and my body gave an involuntary shudder. He began the prayers. I was too weak to move, but I cringed inside. When he signed me with the holy chrism, I would have screamed in sheer anguish, but could not. I lay there as though dead, though I was not, yet. The holy oil burned my skin; all I could do was suffer. And the crucifix… I made no outward sign of terror, but the good Father's brow creased with concern and he looked at me with eyes so compassionate. He must have guessed what ailed me, but without further proof would hesitate to risk incurring the wrath of my father. When he later joined the doctor in the kitchen for a glass of wine, I heard whispered words. Vampire, they said. Reluctantly they agreed that they must speak out.

"I was horrified, but in my heart, I think I knew. The good doctor fortified himself with another glass of wine, took my father aside and courageously revealed their suspicions. Though liking not at all to risk his reputation by acknowledging something considered superstition by educated men, I am sure. But he was never one to shy away from his duty, however difficult.

"He suggested that perhaps after my death it would be prudent to stake me so I would remain dead. Father Ludger, for his part, seemed distressed at such an assault upon my dignity as a man created in God's own image, and was more inclined toward performing an exorcism. I clearly heard my father's cry of anguish and denial to both of them. They were bound to respect the wishes of the family, of course.

"I wanted to plead with my father to listen and to save me from this hell, for I was sore afraid. But alas, though I opened my mouth to speak, no sound came forth. Kristina, who was sitting beside my bed with her anxious gaze upon my face, cried out with great hope and joy, 'He wakes!'

"At once, they all surrounded me in the dim light of candle and hearth; my beautiful, loving family. My mother began to lead the Rosary, whilst my father, Werner, Reinhard, and even

Rudi and Willi knelt here and there about the room, Kristina and the little ones by the bed. I can still hear Karlchen, Georg, Ursi and baby Luisa—well, she was nearly four, but so small—responding in sweet cherub voices. But when at last they came to the final Glory Be and I had made no response, they saw they must accept that I was dying. They consoled themselves with the belief that Our Lady was taking me to heaven. Sadly, in that they were mistaken.

"Our little nightingale sang a last song for me, her voice sweet and mournful as that of her namesake. The elder ones tried to hide their tears from one another; I cannot say how successful they were in their deception. All I know is that their grief was not hidden from me. My eyes were half-closed but, to my increasingly heightened senses, every nuance, facial expression, movement and word told me more than even they knew. And the heartbeats! I did not understand why I was so drawn to them. I did not know that while my mortal body was dying, I was gradually transforming into a vampire.

"The children cried and each one came to kiss my cheek, even Rudi and Willi, the 'brat brothers,' before our mother took them away to tuck them into bed for the night. I think she meant to spare them the sight of their brother's final moments, which was a mercy, for it was not a peaceful passing. From deep in my soul, I cried out in fear and anguish as I saw, in my last few moments of terrible clarity, the choice I had made for all eternity. My body writhed in torment as if to resist the inevitable, but in the end, my soul was wrenched from my body, and at last, it was finished. My mother rearranged my twisted blankets, her face composed, but her cheeks wet. As my father gently closed my eyes and kissed my forehead, a tear dropped onto my face, though he discreetly brushed it away so the others would not notice. I looked on in amazement from outside my body, for he was not a demonstrative man.

"I cannot say if my body looked peaceful in death, but I do know that my soul was not at peace. Caught in a morass of anguish and despair, filled with a dreadful sense of loss, I wandered in restless confusion while my family grieved and prayed, unaware of my true plight." He paused to run a hand over his face as though somehow that would erase the painful memory. "I died that night. Often since then, I have wished that I had lived long enough to see one more sunrise. A small thing, perhaps. But we too often do not appreciate the wonder of everyday events."

Mara nodded in agreement, unsure of how to respond to that.

After a moment, he continued. "That, though, is the least of what I wish I could undo. I know now that my father refused to allow me to be staked; I would not be here if he had. My mother became hysterical at the suggestion and refused to allow this desecration of her dear son's body; such a horror was too much for her to fathom. She put a rosary around my neck, thinking it sufficient to protect me from evil. But the damage was already done. They could not have foreseen the tragic consequences." The Prince paused, his death-pale face twisting as though with bitter regret.

Mara looked on that beloved countenance with heartfelt compassion, though it was impossible for her to imagine or relate. The night breeze played with the stray hairs that had escaped her braid, tickling her cheek. She brushed back the offending locks and shivered more from dread of what the Prince was about to say than from the night chill. She gathered his cloak tightly about her and wished herself away from the tower where there was no hiding from those piercing eyes, no escaping his terrible story and what it revealed of him. The further he proceeded with his tale, the more she saw the great divide between them. He had been a man once upon a time, but so long ago. Now he was something else.

I let a vampire bring me to the top of a tower? Dear God, what was I thinking? At that, the pale triangle of his face turned toward her, and he regarded her with furrowed brow. There was no threat, but she felt a little uncomfortable with the idea that he was perhaps aware of what she was thinking and feeling.

After a long moment, he resumed his narrative (to her mingled relief and dread). "Yes. The funeral. Most people do not remember their own funeral, or at least cannot return to tell the tale. But I can. I was there. It was perhaps my poor lost soul that held this memory, for I did not recall any of it, did not think about it at all, or care, until now. My body was inside the coffin, unaware, but I saw it all, all.

"I was surprised at the size of the crowd. Indeed, I had never seen so many people all at once, not even at my sisters' weddings. They came from near and far, many I did not know, acquaintances of my father, I supposed, to support my family in their time of grief. Yet it seemed such a magnificent display, almost as though it was the funeral of a royal heir. People representing every walk of life were in attendance: peasants, merchants, clergy, and nobles. Even the baron, with a grander entourage than usual, which of course included the tall monk with the green eyes who had so disturbed Nyx. The prince-archbishop himself, accompanied by a great number of priests, offered the requiem Mass; our dear humble Father Ludger was allowed the honor of officiating at the gravesite, though he seemed a little overwhelmed by all the pomp. And I, too; perhaps the death of a young man in the prime of life was a shattering reminder of their own eventual demise and how suddenly it may come about. Though I admit, that does not sound a plausible reason for such splendor.

"Be that as it may, a long solemn procession of mourners followed my casket as it was carried from the church, with hearts weighing as heavy as the ponderous tolling of the bell. They walked in dreary cadence toward the top of a windswept hill above the churchyard. Along the winding trail, long yellow grasses and the faded purple of wild asters from last fall lay askew amidst the green of new spring growth. The ancient cemetery was enclosed within a low stone wall, its grass neatly trimmed. Rows of extravagant stone markers and weathered wooden crosses stood stark and lonely against a cerulean sky.

"My family wept silently. My heart was torn as I watched them surround the grave, clinging to one another for support while my coffin was lowered into the ground. Their sorrow was apparent to me, though restrained and dignified to the eyes of mortals. They would not publicly display their grief. But when the first clods thudded against the wood of my casket, the younger children, Ursi and Georg and Karlchen, broke into wails. I tried to comfort them, but they seemed unaware of my efforts, leaving me with a sense of utter futility.

"That was when I cried out in despair. I cursed God for my fate. But I knew, knew, that through my own pride had I fallen. At once I regretted cursing my own Creator—the only regret I felt for five hundred years. Five centuries! But in that instant of remorse, I cried out in such piercing tones that without a doubt, those at the gravesite heard my wail of lamentation. Some of them looked around, startled. Frightened, even. Father Ludger recovered first and hastily proceeded to read the prayers from Holy Scripture, and in his fine singing voice intoned the *Dies Irae*. At first, his voice trembled, but it soon steadied. Old friends and strangers alike stood respectfully by, though many glanced around and shifted uneasily. That unearthly sound had disturbed the complacency of the people there and, I am certain, stirred up some doubts in those who would deny that there was something sinister and unnatural about my death. Though I do not think at that point, anyone was prepared to approach the prince-archbishop on the matter.

"The good doctor was right to question the wisdom of burying me without staking me first; my father argued that my burial in hallowed ground should suffice. He was an intelligent and prayerful man, but in this, his lack of objectivity clouded his vision. They saw no more concrete proof of vampire activity, so the subject was dropped. I was buried intact, without mutilation. And thus was sentenced to this, my fate. Father Ludger did what he could. He blessed the grave, as did the prince-archbishop and the other priests each in turn, sprinkling holy water upon it in great amounts. They laid a crucifix on top of the coffin to be buried with it, and had a makeshift cross mark the grave at once. Yet even then, it was too late. Only the most drastic of measures could have prevented the tragedy that came after.

"Anyway, I fell into darkness, then, as during this time, my body was changing; even now, I have no memory of that. By sundown, my transformation was complete. I slowly became aware of my surroundings. Something soft enclosed me, yet I felt a burning sensation, like a ring of fire around my neck. This increased in intensity with each passing moment, until I felt I was about to be consumed by flames. The overwhelming sense of dread within me swiftly escalated to a frenzied madness.

"I did not know that the cause of my suffering was the rosary my mother had put around my neck after my death. The chain and the beads seemed to bind me, to choke me. I tore at it mindlessly, until finally it broke and fell away. Still, I had no peace. I did not know it was because of the rosary still in the coffin with me, the crucifix on top, and my burial in hallowed ground. Or that I had become a vampire, and vampires have no peace. Innumerable sounds bombarded me, of voices muttering, whispering, groaning, growing ever louder, driving me mad. I covered my ears with my hands, and after a time, the sounds faded. Then the chanting began. I was filled with a nameless terror that grew and grew until I could not bear it. Later I learned that these were prayers of exorcism offered by the ghosts of ancient monks, perhaps, or those living at the monastery. Theo and his brothers, the monks, may have received word of our pastor's concerns about the circumstances of my death and begun praying on my behalf.

"Anyway, it caused me great suffering. I knew something was wrong with me, but had no idea what it was. I did not recall that I had died. Experiencing my vampire body for the first time was painful and overwhelming, even aside from the added complication of an exorcism. I soon became aware of a heavy, rich odor that both attracted and repelled me. I did not know then that it was the smell of my own blood; I had cut myself about the neck and chest with my razor-sharp claws while ripping off the rosary.

"I became increasingly restless, as though some instinct urged me to flee danger. I did not know that I was in a coffin, or what caused my dread; I only knew that I was confined somehow. Though vaguely aware that I had changed, I had no idea of what I had become. I furiously attacked that which constrained me, tearing at it in animal desperation as I sought to escape. A terrible screaming filled my whole universe. Finally, I realized, it was I, myself. Had I gone mad? Where was I? Only with great effort did I manage to compose myself and put my naturally logical mind to work. Clearly, I had to escape.

"At last, with the power of my newly enhanced will, I sprang up out of the grave without disturbing the soil, as only a vampire can, and looked around in bewilderment. Then I saw Nyx. She stood just outside the fence, mist swirling around her as she hovered there in her flowing starry cloak. Awed by her beauty, I gazed at her slack-jawed, like the idiot I was, while she smiled in open admiration of me, her new creation. I could not take my eyes off her. 'Come to me,' she said softly and beckoned.

"I moved to obey her and was astonished by my own swiftness. I would have collided with her had she not deftly avoided me. She laughed indulgently, as at a clumsy child, and I felt foolish, but in the next instant, her look was one of concern. 'Oh, my dear, what has happened to you?' She reached out her beautiful hands, and I nearly swooned with delight at her touch as she straightened the tattered and bloodstained collar of my white linen tunic. 'You have hurt yourself,' she said, taking my hand and smiling. 'Must watch these claws.'

"I gazed at her in dull incomprehension. Slowly it dawned on me that she meant for me to look at my hands. With an effort, I turned my eyes from her face to my fingers. Saw their gleaming tips and was astonished. Slowly I turned my hand and in wonder watched the moonlight play across the brilliance of my nails. She still held my hand, and I was wonderstruck. I adored her. She was everything to me. With my transformation into a vampire, the attraction I had initially felt for her became an obsession. But perhaps that is something a mere mortal cannot understand."

"Mere mortal? Hey, I like that," Mara was quick to protest, only half-joking. At his hastily murmured apology, she added dryly, "Anyway, I wouldn't be so sure of that. Seems like even mortal men can be pretty obsessed at times."

"No, my dear, not even close. For us, every feeling is so intense and immutable as though carved in marble, just as the vampire body appears to you. It is perhaps our heightened senses that transform these attractions into something like pure madness." He shook his head. "You cannot imagine."

"Um, you'd know, I guess." She wasn't sure she wanted to know that much about his feelings for Nyx.

"Nyx did not seem concerned that I was at that time a… well, more like a zombie than a vampire of her class. She knew that it all takes time. Of course, time is one thing a vampire has in abundance. She informed me that I now possessed wonderful new powers and must learn to use them. I stood there in a daze, trying to comprehend. Only she was real to me; nothing else mattered. I was agog at the sight of her; felt faint at the very sound of her voice. I drank in the scent of her and would have tasted her as well, but I dared not. Ecstatic at her touch, by the mere fact that she looked at me, I lost all remnants of human dignity. I quivered with delight, desperate to please. Like a dog, my tongue hung out as I panted for her favor. I would have kissed the hem of her cloak, or even her feet, had she so wished.

"She patiently guided me that night, leading me to discover

the powers that my newly awakened body possessed. A long slow process, it seemed, though to a mortal a mere flash in time. I was clumsy at the beginning, my movements so swift and powerful that it took a conscious act of will to control them. But my new lightness and freedom were exhilarating. Soon I had mastered my wonderful strength and manner of movement to a certain extent.

"I was no stranger to physical exertion. My brothers and I had enjoyed competing against each other in races, wrestling matches and other tests of athletic prowess. We were justifiably proud of our strength and speed and endurance, yet it was nothing compared to that which I experienced after my transformation. My strength and swiftness were beyond imagining. I was giddy with the excitement of this discovery, and keen to test the limits.

"At last, I was able to control my new-found powers well enough, so Nyx decided that I was ready to go on to the next lesson. This was the one she was most eager to teach me. It was time for me to make my first kill."

And Then There Were None

"Like wraiths, we drifted through the night, hunting. We glided over the ground with ease, as all vampires do, but to me, it was new and wonderful. No more stubbing toes or stumbling over rocks, sticks, or other obstacles. I had always excelled at fencing and dancing, but now I was even more graceful than I had been as a mortal. And though it was the dark of night, I could see as if it were broad daylight. I looked around, amazed, for I still remembered the clouded darkness of my mortal vision. I reveled in my enhanced sensitivity to all around me. The sounds that carried across the distance delighted my ears in sweet symphony, such as I had never known as a mortal. Fragrances emanating from flowers, grapevines, and the rich dark soil were borne to me on night breezes. I was filled with wonder at my new state of being. Eagerly I drank in all the marvelous sensations.

"Then I was struck as though by a bolt of lightning. A new scent rolled over me in crashing waves, nearly knocking me to the ground with its power. It was attractive beyond imagining. Besides that, all else was as nothing. Nyx smiled, for she knew what I did not; this was the smell of human beings, their warmth and blood, the source of all bliss for a vampire.

"We found the man walking unsteadily along the road to the village. His was a familiar face, a man who had a smile and a joke for everyone. Sometimes he indulged in one too many at the local establishment of an evening, but he never did anyone harm. In my detached excitement, none of this seemed relevant. Nyx told me to wait. I was hungry, but had no clue how to make a kill. Then, too, I felt a residual horror at the idea of taking a human life.

"Like a shadow, she descended upon the unsuspecting

mortal. I caught the gleam of her teeth as she sank them into his neck. He fell to his knees as she clung to him, feeding. The sight of it, the smell of blood, set me on fire, but Nyx warned me off with a growl. I hungrily watched as she took her fill. Soon it was over; she let the body slip to the ground. I looked at that pathetic mortal lying there and felt nothing for him. I was only angry that Nyx had denied me, for the hunger in me was fierce by then. She flashed a red smile and told me to wait, so I was forced to restrain myself.

"She beckoned, gliding into the night, her cloak fluttering in her wake. I followed, distracted from hunger as I exulted in my newfound speed. She led the way to the top of a hill. We stood there, at the edge of the precipice, enjoying the vista. Vineyards spread downward like a carpet over terraced hillocks, down and down, to the pale smudge of a mist-enshrouded village and the river beyond. Then Nyx took my hand and sprang upward, into the sky. At first, I was a little disoriented. Then I realized, I could fly!

"I was exhilarated. I felt a sensation of lightness unimaginable; I was on top of the world! We drifted easily but with great swiftness over the landscape. With enhanced vision unhindered by the darkness, I took in the scene below. It was familiar, and yet not. Seen from above, a wonderful sight: fences and walls of wood and stone delineated roads and partitioned off fields one from another. Stands of darkling pine on the steep hillsides hissed with each faint gust of wind passing through. Beech and aspen shivered in our wake. We swept over swamps alive with the creaking harmony of frogs, and farmyards where domestic stock stamped restlessly in the wake of our passing.

"Fierce exultation filled my heart as the wind rushed past my face, ruffled my hair and my clothing. The moon and stars were brilliant as diamonds in a black silken sky. I thought my heart would burst with awe (though indeed, it was cold and still).

"Nyx glanced back at me, smiling, and let go my hand. I

careened out of control, at once confused and terrified. Her tinkling laughter brought me to my senses. I spread my arms and soon regained my balance. After some experimentation, I found that I could drift like a dandelion seed on the air currents, roll and dive, or shoot like a rocket into the sky. There seemed no limit to what I could do with my new powers. Nyx watched in delight as I tested them."

The Prince shifted slightly before continuing his tale. "Nyx drifted toward me and there was that irresistible scent again! I could not stop myself; I grasped at her and pulled her to me. The scent had triggered a desperate craving, but I knew not what I wanted or how to get it. It was the blood on her mouth from her kill, but I had no idea. Like a cat discovering catnip for the first time, I would have bitten her or crushed her to me. Small though she was, such was her power that she only smiled and easily extricated herself. 'Follow me now,' she said, 'and that which you desire shall be yours.' With that, she shot up into the sky. I swiftly followed, afire with a savage hunger that demanded satisfaction at all costs. When at last we slowed, I caught sight of a faint light gleaming among the trees far below.

"We whisked past a structure with heavy doors barred, set into the hillside, then traced a slate walkway to a large house where narrow strips of light shone from shutters closed for the night. A wisp of smoke spiraled up toward us from the chimney. The moss-covered slate of the roof seemed so different from above that at first, I did not recognize my erstwhile home. Nor had it quite registered that I had just passed the door to the wine cellar, in front of which I had met my doom.

"A dog barked frantically as we descended—my dog! But when I reached out to him in joyful recognition, he cringed and slunk under the hedge. I was surprised and hurt that my own dog should hate and fear me. With a pang of something akin to grief, I gazed with longing at the house. At each window were flowers carefully tended by my mother, more fragrant now than ever to my heightened senses. The sounds of children's happy piping voices came to my keen ears, drawing me toward the narrow beams of light escaping the shutters, which spoke of warmth and love within. I realized for the first time that I was now shut out from them forever. The feeling of excitement that had flared up at the scent of humans was eclipsed by an overwhelming sense of loss. I was crushed.

"Nyx quickly called my attention to the fact that a mortal approached. I stood dully watching as my father came up the walk toward the house. His pace was slow, his shoulders bowed as though under a great burden. He appeared stunned; no doubt unable to comprehend why his son had been so swiftly taken from him. My strong, invincible father; it did not seem right. I wanted to comfort him.

"Nyx knew me better than I knew myself and was not about to allow me to regress. She kissed me with her bloody mouth and set me on fire once more. A ravenous hunger possessed me; all else scattered to the four winds—every thought, every feeling. I growled and sprang. Saw the shock on my father's face, the horror, the reproach in his eyes. He knew me, and saw what I had become. That image will haunt me forever. May God forgive me, this was my own father." The Prince faltered, but then doggedly continued. "That first taste of mortal blood surpassed my wildest imaginings. It was the most intoxicating thing I had ever known. It made me feel so alive! I could not get enough. Though a strong man, he was no match for a vampire. I had no finesse. Like a wild beast, I tore his throat out."

Finesse?

He looked at Mara as though she had voiced the word aloud. "Yes, you see, it was only with much practice that I learned to feed with a minimum of damage, or without killing, able to stop at will," he hastened to explain, then saw the tears in Mara's eyes, fell silent and looked away.

After a long moment, he continued in a rush of words as

though compelled by something beyond him. "The others must have heard the noise. They came running outside. I dropped my father to the ground and turned to face them, snarling. Kristina screamed at the sight of me. She had seen me dead and buried; now, with blood running down my chin and the front of my white tunic, I must have been a fright. Our little nightingale, so young and tender. I took her next. I could not stop myself. Did not want to. And my mother! What must she have thought, to see the beast who once was her Niki feeding upon his beloved sister? She flew at me, weeping; grabbed hold of my hair and my clothing, trying to pull me away.

"I did not realize my own strength; I meant only to brush her off. She slammed against the wall with considerable force, and fell stunned." He seemed to choke on the words, then went on. "It was a mercy, for in my frenzy, I dropped the dying Kristina and went for my mother. I killed her, yet it touched not my heart in the least. That was when the dog slunk out from under the hedge and bit me. Even he knew what I had become. I felt betrayed—my own dog! He fled, or I would have killed him too. But I was distracted by sweeter enticements and did not pursue him.

"Though by that time I had my fill, I was wild with the taste of blood. I wanted more; was mad to kill. Reinhard appeared in the doorway, brandishing an ax. He was taller than I, well-muscled, never bested in a fight. But I was drunk on my new powers, and on blood. I sent the ax flying across the yard and was at his throat. I finished him off as the children watched from inside the house, wide-eyed and clinging to one another.

"I rushed at them next, but an invisible barrier at the doorway stopped me. Yes, I had heard that a vampire cannot enter a house uninvited; now I knew for certain that that was what I had become. The children were so close; I could see them, hear them, smell them, so sweet I wanted to taste them. But I could not get at them. I stood at the open door, roaring in frustration. Terrified, they scattered like mice. Even so, they tried to protect each other. Rudi pushed Georg behind the wood box and dived in after him, Willi put Karlchen into the pantry and closed the door, then hid himself behind a chair. Ursi crouched in a corner with baby Luisa, the two of them wailing a terrible duet."

He pressed a hand to his chest and, with an effort, lifted his eyes to meet Mara's. "You see how it is. That monster is right here, so close, so close, always. Never, ever, forget it."

She had to make an effort to meet his eyes. "Hey, I know what vampires are like." Her voice would not come outright.

"Sorry. It is a brutal tale, I know. Has to be."

"Must you be so, um, I mean this is a bit much, I'm afraid."

"Right. Like Nyx said, I killed them all. End of story." He gave her a long look. "That is sufficient?"

"Fine. I get it. There was no feeling, no sense of horror. Nothing hit home, or said what it was really about. But…"

"I do not wish to make you sick. Or must I?" A little line of concern creased his brow.

"Or, how can you not?" she said slowly.

He looked away. "Forgive me."

She reached out and touched his hand. So cold. She looked down at those slender fingers, strong as steel, made for killing. *But so gentle when he places them in mine.*

He saw the direction of her gaze, looked down at her warm hand in his and shot her a grateful glance. Collected himself and resumed his tale. "Werner came out of the back room, where he was probably working on the accounts. One look seemed to tell him what all the screaming was about. Papa had long since begun to confer with him on matters of business, so he may have spoken to him of the doctor's fears. At any rate, he kept a cool head, not rushing heedlessly into danger as the others had. He snatched the silver crucifix off the wall and thrust it into my face.

"I saw it coming, that silvery flash, but did not understand what it meant to me as a vampire. One instant I was roaring in the doorway, on top of the world with that rush of power; in the next, I was clinging to the front gate with no idea of how I came to be there, trembling, disoriented, and shocked to the core.

"I glanced toward the house. The door was now closed. Instantly enraged, I bounded up the steps and slammed against it, raking it with my claws. Still it did not open. How dare they defy me! I rampaged around the house, roaring, infuriated further by a growing sense of dread that I was unable to account for. Finally, I saw through a crack in the shutters, and I knew. The children were gathered around Werner in front of the image of Our Lady, heads bowed as they knelt to pray.

"When Nyx tried to lead me away, I snapped at her in my frenzy. She gave me a look that instantly knocked me against the wall. 'Impudent child! Know your place!' she barked. That cooled me down at once. How devastated I was that I had displeased her. But she was more indulgent than angry, and said that I did well; in time, I would learn control."

Mara was suddenly conscious of being alone and vulnerable, so high above the ground with that very monster so eloquently described. Though she told herself that he was no longer that mad, bloodthirsty beast, her heart beat fast. With a quick, perceptive glance, the Prince said in a barely audible voice, "Please, if I may? I would not have you deceived. If you would understand me now, you must know what I was then."

She really wanted to cover her ears, but managed to say instead, "Um, yeah, I guess, if you say so."

He reached out, and she flinched. He withdrew his hand, regarded her a little sadly, and picked up where he had left off. "Within the next two weeks, I became adept in the use of my powers. I came to love what I was and no longer wanted to be saved from my fate. I had only contempt for my former self. Indeed, I hardly remembered and felt no remorse whatsoever for what I had just done. Of course, as a vampire, I had to flee the daylight, but there was no question of returning to my coffin. After our first rampage, the villagers had dug up my grave and found no body; just a broken rosary and the inside of the coffin shredded. Never mind that extravagant funeral with all its pomp and splendor or the grieving crowds as though for royalty. They knew what I had become, and had they found me, they would have staked me in an instant. In any case, I had no desire to set foot on sacred ground again.

"Nyx led me to a cave in the mountainside where we waited for the furor to die down. We slept away the daylight hours; at night, we got acquainted. Nyx told me of how she had named herself for the mythical Greek goddess of darkness, of night, a being lovely and terrible. She was more ancient than the myth, however, and originally was known by a different name, or names. She claimed to be the daughter of a powerful witch, who in ancient times, was condemned by the King of the Morning Star for consorting with unclean spirits. In order to escape justice, she took to the water as half-human, half-fish, the first mermaid of ancient lore. Nyx, in her turn, after failing to seduce that same king, was herself banished from the world of men. She, with her inherited magical powers, took to the air as a bat; ergo, vampire. She was greatly feared back when mortals still believed in vampires.

"I felt honored that a being so exalted should look upon me with favor. Indeed, she seemed unduly excited by my potential and the challenge of training an unruly neophyte. Not a task for the fainthearted or weak. It was her blood, a vast reservoir of ancient power and knowledge, that began my metamorphosis, the process that eventually transformed me into what I am now. That took time, however.

"Meanwhile, each night after sunset, we returned to prowl my old haunts. I meant to ferret out and kill every member of my family, though I did not know why, or even think about it; I just followed my impulses. Nyx encouraged this obsession, or perhaps had instilled it in me. But I only learned this much later.

"My younger brothers and sisters had moved in with

Katherine and her family. We found them easily enough; there were only so many places the children could be, after all. But we were also being hunted. Nyx had to caution me, for I was wild, giddy with power, and mad with the need to feed. She reminded me that we were not invincible. Mortals were capable of destroying us. In fact, the villagers had deduced that we would turn up at my sisters' houses sooner or later, and torch-bearing men ambushed us one night. It was a close call. Alas, it was not fatal. That would have been a mercy, both for me and my victims."

"Maybe not," Mara pointed out. "Not if you really think about where you'd be right now."

He paused with furrowed brow for a moment, then gave her a sharp look. "I... yes, I had not thought of that. I hope that God may yet bring good out of the evil I have done, since it cannot be undone. Anyway, after that scare, we retreated to Nyx's lair in haste and lingered there for many nights, waiting for the heat to die down. We were not idle, except when we slept, nor perhaps even then. Nyx continued my instruction, initiating me into the delights of being a vampire. I was no longer innocent, and was, as I told you, obsessed with her. She knew what she was about. She took me to the stars, introduced me to every forbidden pleasure in that, our cosmic playground, where we drank of the sweet nectar of the gods and danced to the music of the spheres.

"It was ecstasy, and beyond. There are certain pleasures that a vampire can experience only in the company of its own kind. Vampires cannot love, so it is not about giving, it is about devouring. Vampires stop not at the wanting, but drink each other's blood. A perilous undertaking, indeed, for it may drive one mad, or annihilate one or both. This perhaps explains in part why vampires are such solitary creatures. It bears no resemblance to the drinking of mortal blood, which is, of course, the real addiction and fuels this whole endeavor in the first place. Yet it is a strange and magnificent thing, this exchange of vampire blood; at once savage and sublime. It is bitter and cold, yet exhilarates and sets one afire. It is at once resplendent and dreadful, the epitome of—" He met Mara's glance and was ripped in an instant from his reminiscences.

Her face was white. Her expression said it all.

Abashed, he cast his eyes down. "Oh, I am so sorry. Please, can you forgive me?"

"I—I'm not sure," she murmured.

"Cast me away, if you must, and I shall understand." He looked as though he wanted to throw himself at her feet or off the parapet. Or take her in his arms again but dared not.

His look was at once so wretched and so tender that she sighed. "I, uh, well, I knew there must be, you know, all that, but I, I… you sounded so, so nostalgic."

He bowed his head. "I beg your pardon many times, but the recollection came upon me so powerfully and so clearly that I was overcome for a moment by what I felt then. The vampire memory is immortal; I cannot forget. Though I know now that Nyx did not bring me heaven, but ruin. Her promises of delight and pleasure were but smoke, their fruits destruction and death. She made of me a monster, cursed with a beauteous form and face that shall forever beguile mortals for the sole purpose of feeding upon them for my own pleasure and condemnation. Now I must pay, for I am immortal and cannot undo what I am or what I have done."

"I see. That's harsh. Um, if only I could, you know, do something." Mara felt sorry for him, but was a bit unprepared for his confession and somewhat at a loss for words.

The Prince lifted his gaze to meet hers. "You are my one hope in this world of woes to which I have doomed myself forever, unless God should favor me with death one day. I see now that death is a gift from our merciful, loving God. We get our allotted days on this Earth as a time of testing, after which we are meant to enter eternity through the gates of death, when He shall meet and judge us and perhaps take us home to Himself. Alas, some of us in our pride have tampered with His Law and are doomed to wander this needful world until the end of time. Though I did not choose this immortality for its own sake."

"I see that. Maybe that's why this all happened."

Her look of compassion struck him to the heart.

In that instant, his lips were so close to hers. He shook his head and was back on his perch once more, crouching on the parapet. "No, I dare not. Not yet," he said softly, as though to himself and, with what seemed a great effort, resumed his narrative. "One blustery night we ventured out again. Cautiously we drew near Katherine's house. There was no guard posted this time. Perhaps the men did not fancy shivering in the cold again, lying in wait for nothing, as on the previous nights while we remained hidden.

"I could hardly contain myself. I hovered around the house and peered in through the windows. All was dark, but I could sense the heat of human blood inside, drawing me like a magnet, and the pounding of heartbeats; the children were in there, somewhere, and I was frantic to get at them. The casements were fastened, most were shuttered; only one window high up under the eaves showed a soft glow. I drifted upward, drawn as a moth to a flame. Sweet childish cries of delight, quick-thrumming heartbeats, and the warmth of mortal bodies stirred something within me. In an instant, I was at the window, looking in.

"I surveyed the room through one of the many small panes of glass. A fire crackled in the hearth. Its orange flicker sent distorted boy-shaped shadows bouncing across walls and ceiling as Willi and Rudi jumped on their bed, laughing and shrieking in delight. Karlchen was curled up asleep in a chair beside the bed. Georg, whom everyone said resembled me, sat playing with toy soldiers on a rug before the hearth, oblivious to the antics of his elder brothers. At the far side of the room, Ursi sat on another bed, reading by the light of a candle. Baby Luisa was nestled beside her, fast asleep.

"I tapped the window. None of them heard it at first, what with the fire crackling and the boys making all that noise. I tapped a little louder and dragged my nails across the glass. Georg heard the screeching sound and looked up, startled. Then he recognized me. I was his favorite brother. How often had I carried him across a stream, or helped him climb a tree to look into a bird's nest, or stood up for him against Rudi and Willi.

"'Have pity on me, Georg, dear brother,' I moaned (I, who had no pity). He watched me with wide, scared dark eyes. I must have been a ghastly sight; I was not so beautiful then yet. Also, I was levitating three stories above the ground. 'I am so cold,' I pleaded, 'Let me in by the fire to warm myself.' I was heartless. When I so pathetically called his name, how could he refuse? Or maybe I mesmerized him without realizing. He got up and slowly approached the window. Rudi stopped jumping and turned to look. He saw my face at the pane and blanched. 'No! Georg, stop!' Too late. Even as Willi and Ursi turned to look, Georg unfastened the latch. The casement swung open and he, as in a dream, spoke the magic words. 'Come in by the fire, Niki.' And snip snap! As they say in the fairy tales, I was inside the room.

"I had no pity. None. Georg whimpered as I gathered him into my embrace. The two boys on the bed clutched each other in terror. Ursi was too petrified to utter a sound. I sank my teeth into little Georg's throat. At that, the other boys' protective instincts came alive. They flung themselves at me, flailing wildly with their fists, screaming words I never thought they knew. But I, I was caught up in bliss and heeded them not at all. Until Ursi's wailing of the Name of Jesus pierced my rapture like a painful dart. With a snarl, I brushed them aside. They went down in a tangle of skinny arms and legs; I continued feeding. A few brief seconds—an eternity of ecstasy—and it was done. I dropped the little body to the floor and looked around for more.

"Staccato heartbeats drew me; panting and suppressed whimpers. I caught hold of a foot, dragging Rudi out from under the bed where he had crawled when I sent the boys tumbling. He fought at first, but then looked into my eyes and no longer resisted. A sweet thing, I began to see, was this giving of pleasure to the victim. I nearly lost myself in the ecstasy. Too soon it was done; I dropped him and turned toward Willi's frightened panting, coming from behind the chair.

"More, I wanted more. I started toward him, but just then Karlchen awoke and sat up sleepy-eyed, his blond curls all tousled. He howled in terror at the sight of me. I forgot about my discovery, about mesmerization and so forth, about anything like control. All I knew was, here was another victim, and my ravenous hunger. That is all. I snatched him up and tore into him. He died at once, mercifully. The little ones are so tender and sweet; I held his warm body to me for some moments after and reveled in it. A hideous sight, I am sure, for Willi panicked and ran for the door. I dropped the little body and laughed as I sprang. Caught him with his hand on the latch, poor child.

"He was turned away from me, so without a thought, I bit the back of his neck; I did not mesmerize him, just pinned him to the floor until he died. A prolonged and painful death; I will never forget the sounds he made, or that red hair gleaming like flame before my eyes, so soft against my cheek." A look of anguish crossed the Prince's face. "And it was he who brought me word of forgiveness from our Redeemer. He it was who traced the cross on my brow. Even he forgave me!"

Mara was trying not to be sick. Accustomed as she was to the habits of vampires, and the killing of them, it was too much. And yet, she thought she understood: He was trying to express his amazement at this power to forgive.

He saw her look and paused. "Yes. It was as Nyx said. I killed them all, my brothers, sisters, parents. I cannot deny it. I wish I could. I told you when we first met that there was no mercy in me."

"They were only words, then. You were just a vampire; the enemy. Now it's different."

"Yes, I know." He cast his eyes down and sighed (or what passed for a sigh, coming from a vampire). "You did not really want to know how it was. But this is what I am… was. And yet, after all I did, they forgave me! How can I ever make it up to them? How can I ever atone? I think perhaps if you know all, all of it, you can help me. Now, if I may finish this."

Tears sprang to Mara's eyes. She dashed them away; she could not bring herself to look at him. "Finish us, maybe," she murmured.

His voice softened. "I am sorry if I get into it more than I…Ah, temptation, always a snare set for the unwary. This passion for blood, how it does burst into flame in an instant! I dare not forget. Nor must you forget." With an effort, he set his resolve. "I do not want to put you through this again, or myself. Yet I abide by my promise. If you want me to stop, to take you home, you have only to say so."

"Um, no. Please, let's just get it over with."

He turned his gaze toward the horizon once more. "I might have forgotten the girls; Nyx did not. She came to the window, eager to join me, but had not been invited in. Her growl cut into my trance. She had not fed yet and was impatient. She signaled briefly toward the pathetic trembling lump on the bed. I left Willi breathing his last and — " He gave her an apologetic glance. "I need only say that the girls' screams will haunt me forever. Then I hunted down the rest of the household. I surprised Katherine and her husband downstairs in the kitchen; found their two children asleep in bed. Soon I rejoined Nyx and we moved on to finish off Gerda and her new husband. It was not difficult. However hideous I must have looked, they could not get past the idea that I was still her charming brother Niki." He shook his head. "Through it all, Nyx wore a smile of secret satisfaction.

"My brother Werner was last. I quaked at the thought of facing him, after the shocking experience with the crucifix, but Nyx goaded me on. We found him walking to the village with a friend. At the sight of us, he once again whipped out a crucifix, faster than you can say *Til Eulenspiegel*. He held it up like a shield; even Nyx was afraid. If his friend had not panicked—but he ran, and Nyx took him down in a trice. Werner, of course, tried to play the hero. The instant he turned his back, I was on him. The crucifix flew from his hand, and though I knew not why then yet, it infuriated me beyond all reason. I tore him to pieces."

He was silent for a long moment, then went on, "They were all dead, then. Nyx kept her promise; she had touched not a one of them. Yes, I killed them all. All except Theodor, the monk. Not even Nyx dared invade the abbey. After that we ravaged the countryside, not for need, but just for the rush; for the love of blood. People died, and more people, until it was said by some that the plague had come again. Not the villagers; they knew what I had become.

"There came an end to it, finally. It soon got too hot for us. A solemn exorcism must have finally been initiated, Nyx said. And none too soon; as it was, not one family was left without someone to mourn. Ever after, the village was as though accursed; you will not find it on a map, or mention of it in any history book. Perhaps there is something in myth or legend, nothing more. Nyx took me away, then. She had accomplished her purpose, and it was not fun anymore; the risks were too great, she said, now that the Church was in on it."

"So what was the point of it all? I mean, um, you know, getting rid of your family?"

"It is all about Charon's intent to rule the world. He is forever studying old scrolls and star charts, and he takes great stock in portents and omens. There is a prophecy warning of a great Destroyer who was to spring from our line to one day vanquish him. He could not have this, of course, and came up with the idea that by eliminating the entire line, he could take out the Destroyer as well; before the fact, so to speak.

"Only Nyx, with all her ancient power and knowledge, could accomplish this daunting task, the master decided. Even she had had to plot her strategy carefully; she dared not alert the enemy to her presence or her purpose. The fact that Gerda's wedding occurred just then proved fortuitous. A gathering of the entire village all in one place, outside, at night! It was the perfect setup. This of course would include the doomed family. At first Nyx had marked the baron's family, not ours, but when she saw the ring on my father's finger, she realized her mistake. Yet the whole thing nearly unraveled, due to a fatal distraction. Me. At first sight she wanted me, and have me she would. Never mind that I was of that family she must destroy. Dead or undead, what did it matter? So she reasoned. If I became a vampire, I would not generate any future Nemesis. But only she would have dared to so defy Charon."

"Was there no huntress then? The day I'd have let that happen!" said Mara, with furrowed brow.

"Perhaps that was the enemy of which Nyx spoke; at the time I knew nothing of that. It was only later that I learned that such a thing as a huntress existed. I am told that God appoints your kind only when there is dire need, as now; and that only at the behest of those closest to His Heart, such as cloistered nuns.

"Anyway, Nyx had her way with me. Then came the sticky part. She had to take me to Charon. Of course, he was furious that she had not done away with me. She gave me to him as a peace offering. I thought at first she had done it to save her own hide, but later realized it was to save mine. I was sure he would kill me even so, but instead he took me for his own. Of course, he was not pleased that Nyx had let Theodor live, though he knew well the perils of the abbey. I assured them that they need not fear he would break his vows; never would he produce a line from which the Destroyer might spring. Time proved me right.

"So there you have it. All that was centuries ago and only the beginning of the evil I have done, of the havoc I created wherever I went. But it is enough to give you an idea of what I was, and of how I became what I now am. It was Nyx who first gifted and enhanced me by the power of her blood. Then Charon took over and made of me what you saw that night in the church: a creature fashioned in his own image, superior to all others, yet totally twisted by evil. There a miracle happened. You know the rest." He lifted his eyes to meet hers for a moment.

She was silent, so he went on. "There were other Old Ones; immortals, that is. Charon perhaps feared they would contest his right to rule, so he decided to move to the New World, where he could pursue his dream of world domination without interference. Thirteen of us accompanied him across the ocean. Once here, we wandered for many years in search of a more or less permanent safe haven. During that time we gradually increased our numbers. I personally never turned but one—Styx—though countless mortals met their doom in the service of my appetite. I deserve hell for what I have done."

"God will be the judge of that," Mara murmured, relieved that his tale seemed to have come to an end.

"Yes, I fear He will. My only hope is to throw myself upon His infinite mercy. I do not try to escape justice, for He cannot be deceived." The glow of his eyes suddenly pierced the darkness. "Nor will I deceive you. If you have a question, just ask it."

"No, no questions," she said, more abruptly than she intended, resolved as she was to endure no more. But questions there were. He'd said his obsession with Nyx was as though carved in stone. Did that mean he felt something for her, even now? How would that affect them?

To Mara, what Nyx had done to the young Niki Sperling seemed far worse than all he had done in the years since; she was ultimately the cause, after all. Tears of fury sprang to her eyes. What chance had a young man of little more than a score of years, against that ancient, centuries-old lamia with her wiles, her powers of mesmerization, her vast experience? *God, where was Your huntress?* Horrible as the Prince's story was, she could not find it in herself to judge him so harshly as he judged himself.

And there was Styx. She could not get the picture of Styx kissing him out of her mind. Jealousy raised its ugly head. Yet there was no denying that he was responsible for what she had become. Certainly it would be best to get to the bottom of this; but for now, she had heard enough.

With an effort, she softened her tone. "I have no questions," she said again. "Not now. One day soon, I will. Count on it. For now, there's quite enough to think about." *Or forget, if I can.*

"As you wish." There was a long silence, during which they looked at each other. "So now you know," he said finally. "If you wish to change your mind, I understand. I must endure the consequences of my guilt, but there is no need for you to do so."

Mara said nothing, trying to quell the relentless visuals running through her mind. *Well, I asked for it.* Nyx and Charon made of him a monster. Mara closed her eyes. And even if he is so changed, are there ties that still bind him to them?

There was a whisper of movement. Her eyes sprang open. But he had only turned away to gaze out across the gloom descended upon the town. A swirling mist thickened to a fog rolling in from the ocean. The air was damp and depressing, reflecting her mood. Wrapped in his cloak against the night chill, she studied him in silence.

Sounds of squealing tires and revving motors drifted up from the streets below. Hours must have passed since they had flown here just after sunset. A sudden gabble of voices and the twang of bluesy country music blared as the doors of late-night establishments on opposite sides of the street opened to disgorge their patrons at closing time. Like a great dark bird, the Prince looked down at the mortals below. She shivered. Was he thinking of them as lunch? Not anymore, surely, but he was still a vampire and much more powerful than most. After what he had just told her, her own gifts felt a little inadequate. She was used to being in control. This was an uncomfortable switch: she was entirely at his mercy, just after he had told her he had none. Monster. No, that was then, this is now. Still, she shivered; recalled the incident at the zoo. His loving words, his gentle manner, his good intentions. Yet, how swiftly could he revert to that nasty predator? She caught herself looking for a way to return to the ground without having to rely on him. He turned toward her, and she started, with a sharp intake of breath.

"Do not be afraid," he said, with a touch of sadness.

Mara regretted that her feelings had betrayed her. But she had seen him at his worst, a frightful thing. "I'm not. Or, maybe I am. After what you just told me, and I, um, I haven't a rope to rappel down from here. Oh, you know what I mean. Gosh, what a fix this huntress has got herself into, when she can't kill a vampire even to save her life!"

His eyes glowed suddenly, so pleased was he at her admission of love and trust. "Sorry," he murmured, and the glow faded. "But that won't be necessary. I'd never hurt you." Mara went to him, and he gathered her in his arms. "Time to go," he said reluctantly, "or the question may be settled by the dawn."

"Oh, dear, is it so late?" She gave him a troubled glance.

"Do not worry, there is time." His actions belied his words, however, as he donned his cloak rather too quickly, it seemed to her. "I will take you home now."

Picking Up the Pieces

Over the summer, the friends gradually recovered from the shock of Sabrina's death.

The Prince kept a low profile for quite some time after the tragic event, but even so, when he rejoined them once more, all found that the stark horror of that night could not be easily swept from their imaginations. Not now that they knew he was a vampire.

Maggie, especially, had a hard time coming to terms with it. She still eyed him with reproach. "Sabrina said it was you. She looked out the window and said, 'Oh, it's the Prince.' Then she opened the door and—" Maggie burst into tears. "It was horrible!"

"Yes, I know," he said, looking away.

It was the profound sadness in his eyes that convinced Maggie that the Prince was not the one, when she, at last, dared to meet his gaze. Those eyes were dark, too, she recalled, but cold, pitiless, and empty; there was no mistaking the difference. Still, he was one of them. But finally, she saw the injustice of holding him accountable for the actions of another, and overcame her fear and outrage enough to manage an apology. "I'm sorry if I—I didn't mean to say that—"

"It's fine. I understand."

Even so, she continued to have difficulty looking at him, or even being in his presence. The reminder of the tragedy was too much. It took even longer for her to forgive Mara. If only they had known, she accused, Sabrina would still be alive. She would have been more cautious, at least. Mara took it as well deserved. She had failed in her responsibility. All that Maggie said was true; with these same words, she had lashed herself ever since the tragedy had occurred.

It seemed for a while that their close-knit group would be torn apart forever by their loss and grief. But eventually Maggie had to admit that laying blame would not bring Sabrina back, nor would Sabrina want to be the cause of their ruin. Time would heal all, if they stuck together. Finally, she and Mara reconciled.

George was shocked to the core by the confrontation with an actual vampire. He had played around with the concept in his imagination and in games for years, but never thought to encounter them in reality. Now he stared hard at the Prince, trying to get past the thought of how he was one of them. But not *that one*, he kept telling himself. Mara said it, and she would never lie. And Timmy was there, saw it all, and he had said it too. The Prince had not killed Sabrina; he had saved her from a fate worse than death.

It was difficult to deny what he thought he'd seen with his own eyes, but after a long and uncomfortable silence, George too relented. "I guess you're right, Mara. Sorry, Prince," he managed to add, though doubting he would ever feel at ease in his presence again.

Josh studied the Prince with dawning comprehension. "Sorry, man, I could have sworn it was you. It looked a bit like you, but yeah. There was something different. I guess the light isn't that bright out here." His mouth set in a grim line as he remembered Sabrina lying so pale and still.

"You did not know. How could you?" said the Prince. "I should have, though. I should have been here sooner."

"No, really, Maggie's right. I should have made them believe my warnings, long ago," Mara said. "Still, we can't turn back the clock, can't erase what happened. The important thing is, now you know vampires are real and they're out to get you. You've got to take precautions, like not wandering around outside after sunset."

"Are you kidding?" said George, pushing his glasses into place. "I won't be going out in the dark ever again. Not after that." He cast a wary glance at the Prince.

Timmy's wound was healing well, though a fine livid scar would ever mar his face, cutting a line across it diagonally from brow to chin. Even now, his green eyes flashed fire whenever vampires were mentioned. "I hate vampires!" A sob caught in his throat, and he furiously dashed away tears. "I'll kill 'em all, I swear it! Except you, Prince," he added in a subdued tone. He seemed much older than his twelve years. "I'll never stop, ever! Not until they're wiped off the face of the earth, or I'm dead!"

Mara knew now that the time had come to tell her parents that the Prince was a vampire. She wished she had told them long ago. The Prince had by now become a regular visitor at their home, and they had come to accept him as her dear friend, and perhaps more than that. By now, he was almost as much a member of the family as Mara's original group of friends.

Joe Amarantides was a carpenter by trade, but in his spare time he delved into not only languages, but the study of history, literature, and the classics as well. In the Prince, he had discovered a kindred spirit ever willing to discuss in depth the chosen topic of the night. As for Annie, she enjoyed the Prince's music most of all. Ever since the night that Joe had brought out the old violin, saying, "Mara mentioned that you play. Think you can coax a tune out of this? My dad used to entertain us kids with it. I love music, but I'm all thumbs, it seems. Tone deaf, you see. This fiddle's been sitting idle way too long."

The Prince's eyes shone as he took the instrument in his slender hands. "It's been a while," he said modestly, and began to play. Softly, at first, but not at all hesitantly. Not like he had been away from it for centuries. He had often played for Charon in the beginning, but other interests soon distracted him from music. It was upon mortals that he had indulged himself and taken his pleasure for five hundred years. They were the instruments on which he played, or preyed; the drinking of blood was the ecstasy, the music upon which he had soared to the heights. Now he played as though he had never stopped. On his face was an expression that seemed almost happy.

Mara smiled as her parents looked on in amazement. Tears streamed down her mother's cheeks, and what was that shining in her father's eye? Her parents had grown to like him very much, but with this, they fell hopelessly in love with him. Each time he came to visit, they insisted he play, and he seemed to enjoy it as much as they did.

Ah, how I hate to spoil a good thing, Mara sighed. But it would be unfair to leave her parents in the dark. Someone would let it slip, anyway. As it was, her mom and dad might be hurt that she had not confided in them sooner.

That night she laid all her cards on the table. Told them enough so they would know what he was, without the brutal realism with which he had confided his tale to her. Even the censored edition was almost too much for them. They questioned her sanity and suggested ways around this terrible mismatch, though they could not but see that it was nothing more than a desperate grasping at straws.

If she could not have him, she wanted no one. They would have preferred that she never marry, then, if those were the only options. In the end, they had to be resigned to what seemed to them a foolhardy, if not terrifying, decision. All they could do was pray for things to right themselves.

Gradually Mara's friends began to be more at ease around the Prince. George's misgivings faded with time; he became more and more preoccupied with work on his new software program. What had started out as an experiment in fantasy quickly became an exercise in reality, now that he had encountered vampires firsthand and was convinced that they actually existed. For school purposes, he still referred to his project as a game, but now he saw new possibilities. It could be developed into a useful tool for Mara's line of work. The difference between his program and others with similar functions was that this one had as its object not fantasy creations, but real creatures that could be monitored, tracked and eliminated. Already it had proven efficient at cross-referencing, but a few problems needed to be ironed out before going further.

The Prince soon gained his trust by sharing firsthand knowledge of vampire lore without reservation, heedless of his own possible peril, and eventually, George dared to reciprocate: he invited the Prince, a vampire, into his home. On many a night, they spent hours poring over papers, discussing the scribbled notes and rough sketches, or in front of the computer, trying to work out some glitch. The program soon surpassed George's original dream. Its practical application looked to be possible in the very near future.

Mara soon learned that if the Prince did not at once meet her as she went out on patrol, she would find him at George's house. Sometimes she left them to it because they were too engrossed in solving a problem that had them stumped. She would begin her rounds by herself until the Prince found her. This made her uneasy; there was a reason why they were meant to be partners.

One other thing made her uneasy. It seemed that George's work on his project had stirred up something of a furor in the classroom, so upon her advice, he tried to be a bit more low-key about it. Then one day he told her that Trevor, who was also in the class, had recently sidled up to him and stood admiring his work.

"You know, dude, that's going to be one wicked game, I wish I had your smarts. Vampires, man! They're real, you know. Chuck and me, we seen that one at the zoo that time I told you about, right? I swear, it really happened, just like I said!"

"Cool," George said agreeably, and went back to his work; he wasn't about to be drawn into any conversations in class about vampires being real. Never mind that his "game" was all about them.

After a lengthy silence, Trevor blurted out, "And last Saturday night, me and Chuck picked up this hitchhiker on the way to a party over at Red Rock Hills. A cute blond chick." He paused. When George made no comment, he went on. "True story, man. She was something else—beautiful, long blond hair and wasn't afraid of nothing. You know Chuck and his convertible, and how he likes to show off. She loved the speed—wasn't a bit scared. And what a party girl. To hell with the beer, man! She took us higher than—the moon, I swear! And you should have seen everyone when we walked in that door. Man, they were so jealous. I mean, me and Chuck with this gorgeous blond vampire! It was the coolest thing ever."

George glanced up, startled. "What did you say?"

Trevor grinned. "I think you heard me."

George snorted and turned back to his work.

"It's true, man!" Trevor lowered his voice. "She liked us so much she's going to turn us into vampires. Isn't that the wickedest?"

"Literally," said George, then he glanced up. Trevor actually looked serious! "Hey, man, you better lay off the pot. Why would you even think of doing such a thing?"

"Hey, why not, it'd be so rad," protested Trevor. "And I ain't smoked a joint in—I don't know how long."

"Last night, probably."

Trevor laughed sheepishly. "You got me there. But I really mean that. She said all we got to do is some jobs for her, and..."

"Jobs! What kind of jobs?"

Trevor wagged a finger in his face. "Nah-nah-nah, none of that. She said we ain't to tell nobody."

"Something illegal, then?"

"No, nothing like that. What're you saying, we're criminals? Man, I'm hurt. You're just jealous 'cause she didn't make the offer to you. I can see you like vampires as much as I do."

"Jealous? Hah! We'll see about that. You introduce her to me, then, okay? Unless you're chicken. Afraid I'll take her away from you?"

"No way, man. She picked us. Anyway, we don't contact her; she comes to us."

"You guys still at the zoo?"

"Just until summer's over. Then I'm working in my uncle's shop, and Chuck's got a job as security at the hospital. Not for long, I hope. Vampires don't need to work." He smiled to himself and wandered back to his desk.

When George told Mara, she wasn't sure if Trevor was just talking big, or if some of his story was true. She warned George not to get involved and discussed it with the Prince.

"That sounds like Styx," he said. "Looks like she's made them minions. Jobs? I wonder what she's up to now."

"Well, we'll keep our eyes peeled. Also, it won't hurt to check up on those two boys now and then. They might be trouble. Or in trouble themselves. Idiots!"

One night disaster finally happened, something of enough importance that it took Mara's mind off the little problem of Chuck and Trevor. The Prince was at George's again. They were taking too long, but the Prince just couldn't let it go. Mara paced, impatient to begin her nightly tour of the town.

"We're doing this for you," George tossed back at her while staring at the screen.

"Yeah, whatever."

"We are almost there," the Prince assured her. "See this—"

She cut him off. "Games!" Just the one word, but her tone left no doubt of her opinion.

"It's not a game, Mara," George protested. "If we can just work out this glitch, it'll be a totally awesome help in your work, I promise. Give us fifteen minutes."

"Fifteen minutes! Yeah, I know how that goes. Two hours later, you're still at it. No way. I'm outta here. See ya 'round."

"Wait," the Prince called after her. "Don't go alone. I'll be with you in a minute."

"Sure, you will." She went out, slamming the door. A moment later, she opened it again. "You locate the master vampire for me. Then I'll believe you have something more than a game." Deaf to the Prince's apologies and George's protests, she went out into the night. "Fine," she said bitterly. "Who needs you? I can take care of myself. Always have, always will, I guess."

Not one vampire had appeared since Sabrina's death, oddly enough; it was about time something broke. Like the calm before the storm or the eye of the tornado, the silence seemed to presage the approach of chaos. This waiting was the pits, the tension unbearable, but Mara knew better than to relax her guard; it would be only too easy to be lulled into inattention, and that could be fatal.

She wandered down the street, patrolling half-heartedly, under a dark cloud, it seemed. The Prince was preoccupied with George's project now. How she missed him! At first, he'd had nothing and no one in the world of mortals, except her. She, who for so long had no one she could relate to on equal terms, had quickly grown accustomed to having a companion, and to being the center of his world. Now that he had other friends (her friends!), it seemed he no longer had time to walk and talk with her.

A light breeze ruffled her hair and swept through the trees. Autumn leaves drifted downward. Traffic rumbled in the distance. George lived in a quiet cul-de-sac where a cat yowling on the back fence was the noisiest thing that happened; the most exciting was when someone threw a shoe at it.

No vampires tonight, again. She sighed, almost wishing for one to appear, or better yet, a whole slew of them; she needed to thrash something. She growled. Punching the bag at the gym wouldn't cut it this time. She took a deep breath of the autumn air, but it was as yet too mild to be exhilarating. Still, the leaves were lovely, with their changing colors: red, gold, and brown mixed with the green. Halloween was just around the corner. Maybe the real vampires would come out along with the little trick-or-treaters. It was so dead around here she could scream. A little undead would be a breath of fresh air. (At that she chuckled to herself.) They were out there somewhere. She could sense them now. Her hopes rose. Maybe she would see some action yet.

What were they waiting for, Christmas? Ah, what would it be like, her first Christmas with the Prince? That was one thing they hadn't talked about yet. She drifted into happy reflections of Christmases past and speculations of the future.

After a while, she came to the mini-park a block from home. The breeze had picked up; leaves danced in slow pirouettes above the ground. Swings in the playground creaked; she sat on one and, with a rush of nostalgia, recalled the long-ago days when her mom or dad would push her higher and higher while she shrieked with delight. Even then, she had possessed a sense of daring and a flair for adventure.

She and her friends had often played here, carefree children whooping and laughing as they went down the slide. Back then it had seemed so high and grand. She smiled as she looked at it now, an ordinary child-sized slide, worn with use. And the merry-go-round. She remembered her elation as the boys, out of sheer deviltry, tried to spin the girls off. Maggie and Sabrina would stagger dizzily away, but Mara was in her element. Occasionally they had to pause to search for George's lost glasses. That was how Josh discovered the silver arrowhead and an interest in metalwork and the crafting of weapons. He was unaware that the artifact was designed to kill vampires, but Mara knew, even then.

If only the Prince were here. She sighed.

At that moment, a scream pierced the night.

"Joe! Help! Jo-oo-ooo-oe! Mara-a-a-a-a!"

Mara leaped off the swing, adrenaline pumping.

Mom? The scream cut off. Must be serious; her mother never

screamed. Vampires, after Mom and Dad, now? *Heaven help me. Well, I wanted some action!* She ran at top speed toward her home. A waft of chill air and the smell of death hit her all at once. Past the familiar pink azalea hedge—there, in the front yard, several dark moving figures. One was bent over a limp form, in the familiar posture of a vampire feeding. Mara homed in on it, praying she wasn't too late, aware of others lurking nearby.

With a flying kick to the head, she sent the vampire sprawling, whirled and whipped out a stake in each hand, prepared for attack from any direction. She heard a rustling of the grass as the vampire scuttled away, but let it go. She could smell them all around. Now, all was silence.

She glanced down at her mother lying on the ground. "Mom, get up," she urged, helping her mother to a sitting position.

Her mother looked around. "Wha—what happened?"

"You'll be okay, just go into the house." Mara sensed the approach of the enemy creeping in from every side. "Mom!" She took her mother's arm and pulled her to her feet. A dark form rushed in. She staked it; it shrieked and disintegrated. As she brushed the dust from her eyes, something struck her from behind. She rolled and was on her feet again, another stake in hand, but her assailant was gone. "Mom, go to the house, now!"

Her mother turned toward the porch, unsteady. Black shadows came out of the darkness, flitting like bats, rushing past in a chill wind of death. Mara whipped out her crossbow and sent arrows with lethal precision into the swarm, one-two-three. Shrieks and puffs of dust issued from the cluster. A vampire loomed in front of her. She staked it. Others melted into shadow.

The front door opened. "Is someone out here?" Mara's father called from the doorway. "Annie? Is that you? Oh, Mara. I didn't know you were here. What's going on?"

"Dad, get Mom into the house." She propelled her mother

toward the porch. Her father hurried to assist her.

"Come into the house, quick!" Joe said to Annie. "I knew I shouldn't have let you go to that meeting alone."

Shadowy forms surged out of the dark. Stakes appeared in Mara's hands like magic, and two vampires were annihilated. Another knocked her father off balance and grabbed hold of her mother's hair. Mara whipped out her bow and sent a quarrel into its heart. It fell to the porch shrieking and thrashing. The blade of her knife glinted as she sprang, and with one deft movement, cut off its head. Its struggles ceased.

Joe had managed to retrieve Annie and was helping her toward the door. So near and yet so far. A rush of lethal shadows kept Mara busy with her flashing knife and flying stake; one was after her mother again. Her father seemed to be losing the battle. She turned from her attackers to help him. That tall vampire seemed to be trying to make off with her mother. They meant to turn her?

"No! No! You! Let go of her!"

She felt their claws in her hair, at her back, but had no thought for anything except to free her mother from that tall one's clutches before he bit her again. She flung herself after him with a great curving arc of her blade; he darted out of reach. Hands clutched at her. She hacked about her and they were gone. She leaped at the one making off with her mother, but her slashing blade missed as claws caught at her elbow. *Jesus, help me.* She turned and pulled the trigger of her crossbow. The one at her elbow shrieked and disintegrated.

No! One had her mother in its clutches again. Her father caught hold of its cloak and threw it to the ground at Mara's feet. Black empty eyes stared up at her, its mouth opened wide in a hiss.

"Die, then!" Mara slashed downward with her razor-sharp blade. At the last possible moment, the vampire moved; she just missed decapitating it, instead cutting a deep diagonal slash through its face, cleaving its skull. It scuttled into the shadows shrieking and streaming black blood.

Mara glanced up to see her father again helping her mother

toward the door. Just then, a rush of figures came at her, in another concerted attack, like the one in the alley, she realized. She narrowed her eyes. *Come and get it, suckers, I'm wearing my crucifix this time!* She charged to meet them head-on, a whirlwind of blades, stakes and arrows.

Her parents were almost to the door and safety, leaving her free to battle with a will. With stakes and blade, she made short work of anything that dared to come near. Then she shot all that were still visible with her remaining arrows. They exploded into dust and the rest of them scattered. She had just breathed a sigh of relief when a blur of black streaked in, plucked Annie from Joe's arms, and melted into the night.

As her father bellowed with rage and sadness, Mara sprang once more into full battle mode, all senses alert. "Wait, Dad. I'll handle this." She paused as bell-like laughter rang out in the night. "Who are you?" she called out. "What do you want?"

Nyx materialized at the far end of the lawn with Mara's mother in hand. "You know who I am and what I want."

"Nyx," Mara acknowledged, easing toward her. "Love your outfit. Wish I had pants like those."

"Shut up," Nyx said with a dark look. "I want you, now! Or your mother dies."

Mara had no fear of the power of those eyes. She gave her look for look. "No, really. Where'd you get the pants? And those boots? Cool." At Nyx's hiss of fury, Mara's blue eyes hardened. "Sure, you can have me. When she's safe inside the house; not before."

"Do not toy with me, Huntress. I could kill her right now," Nyx snarled. "Lose the weapons, now."

"Let her go, first," Mara said, her voice tight.

Nyx's shriek of rage died to a deep demonic growl. She glided toward the porch, her eyes fixed on Mara. "Weapons! Now!"

The Trap

Mara began to divest herself of her weapons, slowly dropping them one by one to the ground, to buy time. "If you hurt her, I'll —"

"You know I keep my word. My Prince can vouch for that," Nyx sneered as she flowed up the steps and onto the porch. "The weapons, Will!" she barked.

There was a rustling in the shrubbery as the one Nyx called emerged; one side of his face was destroyed. He hesitated, his good eye fearful.

"Get those weapons, you useless piece of —!" Nyx let loose a string of obscenities.

He shrieked and rushed toward Mara. She stood her ground, and he came to an abrupt halt, quivering.

"Are you going to take that from her, tough guy?" Mara jeered. "Come on, dude, get a spine."

He eyed her warily as he began snatching up the weapons and tossing them across the yard.

"Is that it?" shrieked Nyx. "Is that all? I want them all!"

Mara showed her empty hands; Will jerked back at the abrupt movement. "Now let her go," she said evenly.

In one swift move, Nyx flung her captive at Joe and sprang toward Mara. Her roundhouse kick sent Nyx flying, but she was up in an instant and at Mara again, her eyes burning. Dark figures rushed in from all sides, and down Mara went, sinking, whirling into a vortex of suffocating blackness.

Crucifix. She whipped her tiny crucifix out of the front of her shirt and thrust it into the nearest face. The mouth opened wide, shrieking, and the face vanished into the night. Another instantly took its place, and another; she repelled them, but others came, and they were too many. Oh, to have her weapons. Just when she thought all was lost, she heard whooshing sounds in the distance and a chorus of screams. The noise grew louder, as though coming nearer. Her assailants fell away.

Free, at last. She gasped, dragging air into her lungs. Rejuvenated, she leaped up. They were gone from her now. All of them. But what was that noise? Fierce bellowing echoed through the quiet neighborhood. Finally, she saw it, a whirling flame roaring through the yard, setting shrieking vampires afire and spinning them away. Dad? It was her father, holding aloft a burning brand, swinging it this way and that, sweeping the yard clean of the foe. Eventually, the rain of sparks vanished, and darkness ruled once more.

"Dad!" She ran to him. "Are you okay? Is Mom?"

"She's inside," he panted. "One bit her. I got it but good, though. Set it afire."

"You saved my life, Dad. Got rid of the lot of them too. By yourself. Wow, that's great. How, er, where did you find your weapon? I mean, a burning brand?"

Her dad looked down a little ruefully at the smoldering ruin in his hands, which looked somewhat like a stick with charred tufts along its length. "My poor old scarecrow's done for, I'm afraid. After I doused him with kerosene and lit him on fire, the old fellow made a pretty good weapon, I must say. Sure scared those vampires." He sighed. "I don't think he'll be fit to return to duty after this. Ah, well, I can always make another."

"Okay, Dad, but maybe you better go now and check on Mom while I find my weapons. The vampires will be back, sooner or later. You and Mom be careful."

"Sure you're okay out here, Mara?" He paused at the steps.

"Yeah, Dad." She laughed a little. "They'll think twice before they tangle with you again. I'll get my weapons – just be a minute. You go see to Mom. She didn't look so good." Mara watched as her father went back inside and closed the door.

She began to gather up her weapons. The night seemed

friendlier now that the vampires had fled. Their stink was fading, though a scorched smell lingered. She laughed to herself as she searched the yard, gathering her weapons. She had just tucked the knife in her belt when she caught a sudden whiff of death. Her only warning.

Like a bolt of lightning, they struck, coming at her from all sides in a rush of wind. They had her arms pinned before she could draw a weapon, and her legs, so she had no leverage for kicking. She went down, her face in the grass, the stench of scorched hair and cloaks all around, suddenly overpowering. *What the – ? I swear they weren't here a minute ago.* She heard Nyx laugh.

"So. I have you now." Nyx leaned down, her face inches from Mara's. "Take my Prince, will you? Well, if I take your head, that's only fair, I think." With one swift move, she whipped Mara's knife from its sheath. She held out the blade so that it glinted in the moonlight and tested its edge. "Yes, this will do." Her eyes narrowed as she turned and bent down again.

Mara gasped as she felt the cold edge of the knife against her throat. She spoke quickly, "You can take my head, but you'll never get the Prince back, ever."

"Thus is his death already written," Nyx said coldly.

"Man, you guys are such sore losers!" Mara shot back, heedless of the knife at her throat, though she fought tears at the thought of Nyx carrying out her threat. Of course, she was no fool; divide and conquer. Oh, if only they'd faced this fiend together.

"Watch your tongue!" Nyx let loose a stream of foul epithets. "You need to learn your place, Huntress." She straightened up; her gaze swept across the vampire faces. "Sweet William, you may do the honor, or rather, the dishonor. After what she did to your face." Her lip curled in an unpleasant smile of triumph. He backed away. "Will!" Nyx barked, giving him a black look as she grabbed a handful of his cloak and flung him to the ground next to Mara.

Mara looked into the ruined face inches from her own and shrank back in revulsion. Her gaze snapped to Nyx in fierce defiance as she struggled to free herself. The imprisoning claws gripped her hands and feet tighter. Nyx stepped on her braid.

"Bite her, Will. That will tame her down; maybe give you some fire too." She gave a scornful laugh.

He crouched over Mara, quaking visibly. His gaze zeroed in on the flicker of a pulse, and he went for it. The silver crucifix nestled in the hollow of her throat threw him back. Shocked and wailing, he scuttled into the bushes. Nyx reached down and slid the blade beneath the fine silver chain, gave a jerk, and the chain snapped. The crucifix flew off, tracing a bright arc before it vanished in the darkness. All vampires shrank back, hissing.

Mara struggled, feeling a little desperate now that her crucifix was gone, but all efforts availed her nothing. She sank back, panting, while her mind sought some means of escape. *Prince, where are you when I need you?*

Nyx shrieked invective toward all and sundry, but mainly her curses rained down upon the head of the hapless Sweet William. At last, he came skulking out of the bushes, head hanging. Nyx's look softened; he was her child too. She caressed his good cheek. "The trinket's gone now. Drink her blood; its power will heal you." He hesitated, his eye flicking to Nyx and back to Mara. "Here, my shy one," Nyx said, "Maybe this will help,"

Mara felt only a light touch against her throat, but the instant reaction of the vampires told the tale; the quick swipe of the blade had drawn blood. All eyes were suddenly ravenous. Sweet William's ruined face turned toward her; his tongue whipped out, his eye fixed on her throat. Slowly, slowly he bent down. Mara tried to free herself; almost had one arm free, but many hands held her fast. Her captors were themselves captivated.

She shrank away from Sweet William, away from that

dreadful gaping wound where his forehead and eye and cheek should have been (a vampire's face was repulsive to her at the best of times). Black blood oozed from it. The smoke-stench of his singed hair and cloak nearly choked her. She pressed flat against the grass to avoid the teeth gleaming inches from her face. He bit. She flinched at the first sting, in vain trying to slip free from his jaws. Cold spread through her and then the burning.

Nyx stood over her, smiling. Mara shut her out, determined not to scream or panic, pinned to the ground as she was and unable to move. She tried to retain her calm, to distance herself, but Sweet William was like a nightmare, pressing her down. She couldn't catch her breath. Burning, burning inside. She felt herself sinking down, and down, melting into the ground.

Suddenly screaming came from afar. "Hold her!" Nyx shrieked, cursing. "Or I will have all your heads!" There was a sound like that of a great rush of wind, and Mara vaguely sensed that Nyx was no longer beside her. She heard a familiar voice.

"Mara, Mara! Where are you?" Her dad sounded frantic.

No, please don't let them kill Dad, too. She opened her mouth but was unable to sound a warning. There was more shrieking in the distance and sounds of violent action, fading.

Nearby Nyx snarled suddenly. "Get off, you dunce! I don't want her dead yet!"

Air! Mara gulped in deep breaths, felt herself free of that dead weight. She opened her eyes. There stood her father, Nyx's talons at his throat. Mara moved to rise, but had no strength.

"Mara! Thank God you're alive," said her father. "I thought for a minute that—" he stopped, unable to continue.

Mara felt herself slammed to the ground as Nyx planted a foot firmly on her midsection. "You stay there. I'm not finished with you yet."

Mara looked up at her father, tears blurring her vision. Now they would kill him. *Oh, why hadn't he stayed in the house?*

Nyx turned toward Sweet William. He crouched nearby with blood running down his chin, avid for more. "Get over here, Will. She should be docile now." She laughed unpleasantly. "We can't have her dying innocent, now, can we?"

Sweet William's tongue whipped out. He fixed a single glassy eye on Mara.

Heedless of his own peril, her father shouted and would have flung himself at Sweet William, but with terrible ease, Nyx restrained him. She tightened her grip on his throat and forced him to kneel.

"Watch this, Dad," Nyx sneered, with unholy glee. "Now the fun begins." She nodded at those holding Mara's feet and hands. "Take her weapons and release her. She won't get far."

They snatched the stakes from her belt and tossed them across the yard, then cautiously let go of her and backed away. With her powers of resilience, Mara gathered her wits about her and her strength of will. She managed a half-sitting position as Sweet William prepared to spring.

Her father's protest was cut short as Nyx's fingers closed on his throat like a steel trap. His muscular workman's arms were of no avail against her, slender though she was.

Mara saw the glint of a tear on his cheek. She tried to reassure him with her eyes. *I'm not dead yet, Dad.*

Sweet William leered now, with a boldness in his eye that had not been there before. Drunk on her blood and filled with courage at the sight of her so pale and helpless, he sprang.

Mara stuck out her foot and caught him in the groin. With a squeal, he sailed over her head and tumbled into the shrubbery. Nyx shrieked an order; the others overwhelmed Mara at once. Weakened from loss of blood, she managed only a feeble resistance. A growl from Nyx brought Sweet William to his feet. He fixed his black gaze on Mara. She stared back, steeling herself not to look afraid, though inside she felt faint and a little terrified. Again he sprang.

And in the same instant, he was gone. Mara stared in surprise as he flipped like a rag doll into the flowerbed amongst his namesake. The other vampires scattered to the four winds, heedless of Nyx's shrieking to regroup. They well knew the cause and were more in dread of it than they were of her. Nyx turned in a fury, hell blazing in her eyes. Mara looked up to see other eyes glowing, two red points of fire in the night.

The Prince, sublime and terrible as an avenging angel, materialized out of the darkness, his face pale and dazzling. As he levitated above them, his eyes flashed flame. A loud report echoed in the night, and sparks flew as his fiery glare clashed with Nyx's. A firm, decisive gesture of his hand tore her grip from Mara's father and threw her back. With one last piercing shriek, she fled into the night.

Mara heard her father call her name. Then she fainted.

She opened her eyes and looked around in confusion. Light, warmth, the familiar old couch. She sat up in alarm, too quickly. A veil of blackness closed over her. Strong arms caught her. She pressed her face into the soft fabric of the Prince's cloak.

"Oh, thank God! You're still alive," Mara exclaimed. They talked over one another with a flurry of apologies, protestations of love, and a storm of self-recriminations. She held him tight. He pressed her close.

"I should have gone with you," he said, overcome by emotion. "They hurt you. He bit you. Please forgive me."

"It's not your fault," she protested. "I could have waited. I'm sorry."

"No, no. You saved your parents. I should have been here to protect you, as I promised."

"Mom? Dad?" Mara looked around, worried, and was suddenly aware that she and the Prince were not alone.

"We're fine," said her father from his chair across the room. "Mom's sleeping. I told her you'd blame yourself if she didn't rest, or she'd be in the kitchen right now making tea."

"Thank God. Oh, Dad, I'm so sorry. I never expected—well, yes, I did, but it doesn't seem real until it happens."

"We're fine, thanks to your Prince Charming. You look like you could use a little pick-me-up. Wine? Or, here, have a drink of water." He brought her a glass filled to the brim.

The Prince sorrowfully regarded Mara's pasty face and the twin puncture wounds at her throat. "If only I could heal as easily as harm. I did not think Sweet William had it in him."

His comment struck Mara with a new thought: her enemies, those soulless creatures, were no strangers to him. He knew them well, both their strengths and weaknesses, their personalities and their quirks. "He didn't, really. Not of his own accord," she said slowly. "Nyx made him. She pulls the strings and they jump. Gosh, I thought that was it for me."

"Ah, yes," the Prince said. "It need not have happened." He gave Mara's father a nod of approval. "Smart move with the fire. They all looked a bit singed when I got here."

"They ambushed me," Mara said. "I can't believe I didn't see that coming."

"Nyx is something else. Ancient as sin and possessed of all its dark power. Better not to underestimate her."

"But I'm the Huntress! What was I thinking?"

"You were thinking you could take care of yourself," said the Prince. "While I, your protector, was playing games with George."

"I'm sorry I nattered at you for working on George's program. I just hate it for taking you away from me."

"George is right about this program having great promise, though. He is a genius, that boy. Once it is up and running, you will know just where the vampires are. You can hunt them down like rabbits and stake them to your heart's content."

She sighed. "If you say so. I shouldn't have let myself get distracted. That can be fatal in my line of work." She paused for a long moment, then added, "I miss our walks."

"I, also. But I think now you need a few days' rest." His forehead creased with concern. "You are nearly as pale as I am."

She managed a wan smile. "I'll be fine, don't worry."

"She's always been able to bounce right back, no matter what," interjected her father. "A blessing, seeing what she gets herself into sometimes."

"Imagine. In all my years of killing vampires, I've never been bitten, until now." She winced as her fingers sought out the wounds at her throat. "Ow. I guess I'm not used to getting the worst of it."

The Prince frowned. "If Sweet William crosses my path, I—"

"Oh yeah. We'll kill them all. Together, from now on."

***

He crushed her to him, suddenly overcome by the thought that he could have lost her. "Yes, never leave me. Not ever."

"Ow! I won't, but you have to let me breathe."

He released her. "Sorry, I forgot myself there for a bit."

A little line of concern appeared on her brow. "You be careful too. Remember the tiger cage. I'm surprised I don't have gray hairs from that experience. You don't want me getting old any sooner than I have to."

"Must you remind me of your mortality? To think of losing you, even a hundred years from now—"

"I'm so sorry. I didn't mean—" She pressed close.

He held her to him with a sort of desperation.

"Not to interrupt your, er, tête-à-tête," said Mara's father, dryly, "but I think my little girl needs her rest."

The Prince released Mara in some confusion. She sank into the cushions of the couch and closed her eyes. Exhausted by the effects of the night's ordeal, she fell asleep.

A Courteous Request

"I thank you for your help out there," Joe said to the Prince. He looked down at the sleeping Mara with tender affection. "I don't know what we'd do if we lost her. My Annie and I could have been killed tonight too. A sobering thought. I don't know how I can repay you."

"No payment is necessary," murmured the Prince, as he too looked at Mara. "She is all the world to me." He fell into a troubled silence as he saw how her head drooped against the high arm of the couch. Purple smudges beneath her eyes accentuated the pallor of her cheeks, usually so rosy and healthy-looking.

"Yes, I can see that," Joe managed after a bit of thought, his voice tight. *That this unnatural thing should presume!*

At that, the Prince felt a sharp sword of anxiety pierce him to the core. So, she had finally told them. There was nothing for it except to get the difficult part over with, quickly. "Maybe this is not a good time, sir, but if I may—" he began, then faltered at the look that met his.

"Just say it!" the man rasped out.

A glance at Mara strengthened the Prince's resolve. "I wish to ask you formally for Mara's hand in marriage."

"So, ask!" Joe barked.

"Pardon my presumption, sir. You know what I am. I confess that which I have no doubt you are already thinking. That is, I am not worthy. Neither of us asked for this, nor wanted it initially, but it happened. I have not yet proposed, but she has indicated her consent. I preferred to wait until you give your blessing. Thus I beg your kindly forbearance, that you hear me out: may I have your daughter's hand in marriage?"

***

The words seemed to hang in the air. Joe felt stunned, as though he had just taken one on the jaw, even though he had been certain what was coming. His worst fears were realized, though delivered in a courtly manner. *It's only a formality; he means to do this with or without my consent.* He glanced up at the clock on the mantel, one of those heavy wood-cased clocks with a chime that sounded the hour. And looked away. Quickly, before he made any rash moves. Like killing the rogue. Or making the attempt, that is. After what he had seen, maybe it was not even possible. But at the moment, he felt capable of anything to protect his family. To prevent this, this abomination. He leveled his gaze at the Prince.

"Now you've asked. This is my little girl we're talking about. Just don't expect me to say 'fine' and throw her to the, er, wolf. Pardon the expression, but you must have some idea."

"Yes, I too know what I am. I don't plan to eat her," the Prince could not help saying.

Joe grunted and let that pass, for the moment. Though in all honesty, it was not far off the mark. This was a vampire, after all. "What is your plan, then?"

"I shall cherish her always."

"Sure, you will. And when she grows old, as we all must, and you stay young forever? Will you tire of her then?"

***

"How so? Have you tired of your wife?" the Prince rapped out. At the flare of anger in the man's eyes, his tone softened. "I love Mara for who she is. Time will not change that. I am far older than she. I have no reflection; I cannot see myself. If I appear younger than she someday, others may notice, but it will make no difference to me. My feelings for her will not change."

"Yes. Well." The man was suddenly at a loss for words, not having thought of it in quite that way.

"The only thing that grieves me about her mortality is the fact that I cannot share it with her, and one day death will take her from me."

"You wouldn't, er, make her one of—of your kind?" Joe could not say the word; nor was he able to conceal his repugnance.

The Prince bowed his head. "No. I would not. That would damn us both to hell forever."

Joe narrowed his eyes. *He has an answer for everything. I need to quit thinking of him as young.* "And your means of support?"

"I have sufficient."

"You have something concrete to show me? Not that I doubt your word."

"You have seen the ring I gave her. There is plenty more where that came from. The treasure I can claim for my own would rival that of Smaug. Upon my honor. I will bring you a bride price, if you like."

"Heck, no, how old do you think I am? And money's not everything. Have you thought about er, what happens in the event of—" He groped for words. "What of children? What kind of curse would you be handing on to them?"

The Prince looked startled for a moment. "That is not possible. Vampires cannot have children."

"Okay, er, yeah. Undead. I guess that makes sense. But there you have it. How can you marry Mara, knowing that she'll never have children? Is that fair? Does she know?"

"I assume so. She knows much about vampires."

"Yeah. Well. I think you should know. She might say it doesn't matter, but don't believe that for a second. Most women need to have children. She may think otherwise at the moment. But the ultimate expression of love is a child. Consider that, sir, and tell me honestly you can love her as you ought."

The Prince blinked. "Perhaps you are right. Still, she has pledged her love to me and refused my offer to release her from it. She has said that if it were not for me, she would marry no one. So regardless, there will be no grandchildren for you."

Joe ignored the gibe and set his jaw. "She thinks she wouldn't marry anyone but you. Girls her age don't always realize, but the fact of the matter is this: if she's with you, what are her chances? Mr. Right would probably keep his distance. So, if you love her as you say—well, let's face facts."

"The facts are these: I have vowed to love her forever. I am immortal; so is my love. If, for any reason whatsoever, she wishes that I leave her, I will do so."

"But oh, dear God, you're not even human!" Joe's voice broke.

Struck to the heart by that undeniable fact, the Prince's eyes flared up with a terrible light, then gradually faded to black. "You are right, of course," he admitted calmly, as though he hadn't just warred and won against the demon within. In his heart, he knew: even if he fell to his knees at this man's feet and begged for his blessing, it would be to no avail. And who could blame him for not wanting to wed his daughter to a monster? "But I cannot deprive her of my love and companionship," he went on, a little desperately. "As you saw tonight, she needs me."

"Maybe. But we don't marry everyone we love or need."

"I realize that. But if she consents, I in all honor—"

"What's the point? You admit you can have no children. Which, I must say, is probably a mercy."

The Prince's look darkened, but he managed a calm reply, "Companionship is a perfectly legitimate reason."

"Honor, you said. I suggest you suffer unrequited love as did the knights of old, rather than dishonor a lady."

The man had a point. But Mara lost to him forever would be hell. "All that I am and have I give to her," the Prince went on doggedly. "Must she be denied a treasure because the vessel containing it is imperfect?"

***

Joe shook his head. "If only you weren't a vampire. I like

you. You're intelligent, you value honor, and you appear to know the meaning of love. As a man, you'd be perfect for her. But you're not."

"Touché," said the Prince with a troubled brow. "Yet Mara and I do have a common interest. Her life's work is very difficult for her alone. I give you my promise: never will I abandon her to the wolves."

But are you not a wolf, yourself? The man thought, with sinking heart.

After the Prince had left to once again flee the coming dawn, Mara's father, feeling tired and beaten, covered her with a blanket and went into the bedroom to check on his Annie. She too was asleep, breathing easily, and peaceful. With feelings of both relief and deep sadness, he drew out his rosary and, with bowed head, knelt to pray.

***

Mara recovered promptly from the ordeal of her battle with Nyx; her father did not. She could tell by the set look on his face that something was on his mind, but knew well enough that he would not be drawn out on the subject until he was ready. She did not guess what he and the Prince had discussed after she had fallen asleep.

She was still amazed at the ease with which the Prince had scattered Nyx and her crew. Clearly, she need fear nothing the Underworld sent against her, not with him around. All her life, she had been sufficient to the task on her own, but now something had changed. It was as though they had united against her. United: that was so totally against vampire nature. Someone had gathered them together. How? Why? She turned it over in her mind until her head hurt. One thing she did know. A big battle was coming. Thank God the Prince was on her side.

The pangs of jealousy that stabbed her to the heart at his telling of the tale of his original fall were now laid to rest where Nyx was concerned. But the thought plagued her: how dearly had it cost him? And the other question: What hold might Styx have on him? These issues needed to be brought into the open, talked out, and laid to rest, but she wasn't quite ready for that.

One thing, however, she had decided: in the future, whenever she found the Prince at George's house, she would sit down to wait without complaint. George had the tech smarts; the Prince had firsthand knowledge of vampires. They made a good team. If they believed this program would help in her work, she would accept it, even though she didn't understand.

***

Likewise, the Prince vowed to himself that he would never fail to accompany her on night patrol.

Light of the World

December 1998

Christmas crèches sprang up around town in houses, churches, and in yards or on roofs beside lit-up snowmen and Santa with his reindeer. Strings of colored lights festooned trees, houses, and fences. Every lamppost glittered with snowflakes and stars. Salvation Army Santas stood on street corners with round pots in hand, ringing sleigh bells to attract donations. Malls and shops shimmered with tinsel and sparkled with the glow of many lights, while Christmas music proclaimed holiday cheer and the holy season.

Mara looked out her window. A few spots of light appeared, and then more lights, as daylight faded. So many colored lights. Christmas! This one would be special, her first with the Prince. It seemed like forever before the sun finally set. As the last rays faded, Mara was out the door and on her way. She met him at the park. He seemed more tense than usual.

"Are you okay?" When he didn't reply, she took his hand. "Hey, it's Christmas Eve. No need to patrol tonight."

"I know that. Just as every other vampire knows it, and flees in dread to the depths and darkness."

It was so easy to forget that he, too, was part of that darkness. "But not you," escaped her before she thought.

His arms went around her, and he pressed her close. "My place is with you."

"Then maybe you, um—what if you came to Midnight Mass with me?" He was suddenly still, as only a vampire can be. An alarming thing, to be embraced by the chill arms of Death, unmoving and hard as stone. She fought down panic. "Or not," she managed.

Then he spoke, and moved, and she breathed again. But it wasn't what she expected. "Dare I?" he sounded anxious. "Yet I would go anywhere with you, even if I die for it."

"You won't die. Er, you won't, will you? I thought maybe—"

"It has been a long time."

"We can sit at the back. I'd love to share the experience with you. But if you'd rather not..."

He met her gaze with one so deep and tender that she felt a little flustered, suddenly. She took his hand, and they walked on. Without any more perilous stops, just a pause now and then to exclaim over some especially pretty or excessive decoration in a window, yard, or on a roof.

When finally they reached her home, they stood for a few moments admiring the Christmas lights twinkling along the eaves and around the windows. A holly wreath hung on the front door.

"What, no garlic?" the Prince joked.

"No need, tonight. But watch out for the mistletoe."

"I will. And then you watch out."

She laughed, surprised and pleased that he would join in the fun. He was so often serious, even when she teased him.

Once inside the house, he looked around in delight at the decorations of red, green, white and gold. Ropes of tinsel scalloped the walls. Lights and ornaments sparkled on the Christmas tree, a pine just tall enough for the star at its top to touch the ceiling. Its fragrance vied with those of cinnamon, almond, chocolate and peppermint wafting from the trays of cookies and candy, and the two half-empty mugs on the coffee table. Mara's parents were putting presents under the tree.

They looked around with glad smiles and exuberant Christmas greetings. Mara wondered a little at the measuring look her father gave the Prince. Though it was gone so fast she couldn't be sure she hadn't imagined it.

"Have a snack," her mother said, rushing over to offer a tray of goodies.

"How about a little Christmas cheer?" her father suggested.

He tweaked Annie's apron string, his eyes twinkling. "Mom, why don't you go pour some of that eggnog?"

"Joe, we've got company!" Annie scolded under her breath as she retied her apron.

He chuckled a little maliciously, then winked at Mara, "No, it's not spiked. We're saving the good stuff for after church."

"I'll get it," Mara volunteered, grinning as she headed for the kitchen.

"Shucks," Joe said in a low tone to Annie. "I meant to catch you under the mistletoe. Foiled again!"

Mara blushed at her dad calling attention to the mistletoe, but the Prince didn't appear to notice. Even when she walked through the doorway a few minutes later with a tray holding two mugs topped by nutmeg-sprinkled white froth, the Prince only said politely, "Here, let me get that," and took the tray from her.

Pleased by his consideration, she went to sit on the couch while he placed the tray on the coffee table. He handed a cup to her and then sat beside her.

"A toast, Dad," Mara said. "Merry Christmas, everyone!"

They lifted their cups with words of cheer. After the drinking of the toast, they fell to discussing their plans for the next day, which included the exchange of presents and a turkey dinner. Father Mike and Mara's group of friends were invited.

"The Prince is going to Midnight Mass with us, Mom. Cool, huh?" Mara just kind of tossed that out there.

There was an abrupt silence. Her mother recovered first.

"Oh. That's wonderful," she said in a dubious tone, with a hesitant glance at the Prince.

"Midnight Mass, eh?" rasped her father, his eyes darting toward the Prince. "She talked you into it, did she? How's that going to pan out, do you think?"

"Dad," said Mara in a warning tone. Not sure why her dad was so short with the Prince lately. Ever since Nyx —

"I'm willing," the Prince said. "It did not take much

persuasion, if you want to know. Not when something is this important to Mara. However it turns out." Then he added, "Just so we are clear on that."

"Uh-huh." Mara's father gave him a long look and drained his mug. He got up from his chair. "I think I'll get ready." He vanished into the other room.

"Is it that time already?" said Mara's mother anxiously, looking at her watch. "Oh, my goodness. We don't want to miss the Christmas carols. You'd better get dressed, too, Mara. You'll excuse us, please, Niki?"

"Certainly. And there is no reason why I cannot make myself useful. If it pleases you, I'll play some music."

She brightened. "That would be wonderful. Mara?"

"Sure, Mom, I've got it." Mara took down the worn black case from where it reposed among some books. "Here you go. Serenade away." She handed the violin to the Prince. His fingers brushed hers. "Later," she whispered.

He watched with his heart in his eyes as she turned away and started up the stairs. Once out of sight, Mara paused to listen as the sweet, clear tones of the violin began. She resumed her climb; she felt as though she was floating upward on the magic of his music.

When she came downstairs sometime later dressed in her holly-patterned blouse and long green skirt, she stood watching the Prince from the doorway, entranced by his music and his hands. How she admired the ease and grace with which those long, tapered fingers drew forth from the old violin such heavenly sounds. With his eyes cast down and that rapt expression on his face, he looked like a very angel, even if he was dressed all in black. And her heart beat fast.

The song ended. He looked up and smiled. Then he was across the room, taking her in his arms. "Beautiful," he murmured, his eyes burning. He kissed her.

Her first real kiss. *Uh-oh, Mom, Dad – ?* She tried to push him away, but he was like a rock. Not still and unmoving and dead, like before, but there was nothing she could do. Or wanted to do. She melted into bliss.

And then he was kneeling at her feet, his arms about her waist. "Forgive me. I just—well, there was that mistletoe, and I couldn't resist. I didn't mean to mesmerize you. You may behead me now if you wish. It is no more than I deserve, I know."

She caught her breath and somewhat came to her senses. Behead! He looked so solemn when he said it, she laughed. Laughed! He looked up at her quizzically, the glow of his eyes fading. She clapped her hand over her mouth.

"Oh! I'm so sorry! I didn't mean to laugh. Behead you! No, no." She stroked his hair and pressed him close. "You're so sweet I couldn't help myself. Better get up. If my dad sees, he may want to behead you."

"No, can't have that. Only you are allowed," he said, flowing to his feet in an instant. "The mistletoe made me do it."

"Good grief, I was the one who told you about it; it's on me. I can't say I regret it, though." She felt a bit giddy, and also relieved that the Prince wasn't insulted.

"It was worth the risk of losing my head," the Prince said, still uncharacteristically cheerful. "Or, maybe I should play another tune. You know, to soothe the savage—er, I mean your dad." Quick as a wink, he was back by the couch, violin in hand, playing a soulful song.

Shaking her head, and still with a smile on her face, Mara got her coat and put it on. It was a long cranberry red wool coat, one of the few cheery colors brightening her wardrobe. Dreamily she stood watching as the Prince coaxed celestial sounds from the mediocre instrument.

Her parents reappeared, and they too seemed enraptured by the music as they donned their coats. When the song was finished, the Prince returned the violin to its case, caught up his cloak and tucked it into a pocket as he joined them at the front door.

Annie was dabbing at her eyes with a handkerchief. "That

music always makes me cry. I don't understand it."

"None of that, now," said Joe gruffly as they left the house and he locked the door. "Your eyes are red."

Mara thought it looked like he too was blinking away a tear. *Can't be. Not Dad!*

"It's such a nice night for a walk," she said, as she took the Prince's arm. "The stars are so bright and clear, even with all those Christmas lights. Isn't it pretty!"

The Prince smiled down at her. "Yes, it is, and so are you. Are you warm enough?"

"Of course. It's not that cold. Mom, Dad, see you at church."

Her parents waved and drove away in the car, leaving Mara and the Prince to themselves.

The air was brisk, but not very cold for a winter's night. It made the distance to the church a refreshing and invigorating walk. As the familiar façade came into view, Mara looked up and recalled the night she and the Prince had met, of their fight on the sidewalk in front of St. Michael's, their unintended but fateful entry through those great double doors and into the church.

She glanced up at the bell tower and smiled at the memory of her first flying experience with the Prince. The time she was first allowed a glimpse into his past, and his soul. It had been a rough initiation, and she was not at all sure she would want to go through it again, but she wouldn't trade it for anything now that it was over. But was it over? Reminded of the hard questions she must ask, her heart sank; she tucked them away in the back of her mind once more and clutched his arm tighter as they approached the great oaken doors. Was he trembling?

"Remembering the night we first met?" She smiled at the thought.

"How could I forget?" he said with a somewhat tight smile in return. "I feel the same dread, but without the overpowering need to take your head, which was all that sustained me then."

She gave him a quick glance. "Funny, at the time, you didn't look very intimidated. It was pretty scary; you dared to enter a church! Gosh, any ordinary vampire trapped like that would have been cringing at the doorway in a panic, and I'd have staked it without a second thought." She caught his pained glance and hastened to add, "It's different now. I'm here by your side, not to challenge you to the death."

"Yes, your love sustains me this time."

She squeezed his hand and led him through the great doors into the vestibule. The woman handing out thin candles gave the Prince a startled look. Thoughts buzzed in Mara's head. Is she the one? Does she remember him and how close she came to death? The Prince thanked the woman for the candle and quelled her perplexity with a glance, gently, Mara noticed. Did he remember her? Of course, how could he not? His memory was immortal.

The church was rapidly filling with people pouring in through all the doors. A large crowd attended Midnight Mass, even many who otherwise did not.

Tall candles burned, as did the red sanctuary lamp. Soft lighting was diffused throughout the nave. The sanctuary was lavishly decorated with Christmas trees and lights as well as an abundance of flowers: lilies, poinsettias and holly. The altar was covered with a white lace-edged cloth, the tabernacle cloaked in shimmering white satin and lace threaded through with gold. A nearly life-sized nativity scene took pride of place at a side altar, though the Baby Jesus statue was absent from the manger.

Mara disentangled her hand from the Prince's to dip her fingers into the holy water font. He gave it a wide berth and a wary look. She recalled how the holy water had affected him during their fight, and was careful not to sprinkle any on him when she crossed herself. Then she led him to an empty place in a pew near the back, where they knelt down and tucked their candles in the rack with the hymnals. Mara could see her parents up front in their usual pew.

The Prince appeared calm, outwardly. He kept his eyes cast down because he dared not look directly at the crucifix or the tabernacle. Only Mara knew how he longed for that which many humans seemed to take for granted with little awareness of the treasure available to them. She squeezed his cold hand, so stiff with tension; he gave her a grateful glance. She bowed her head to pray for him and to prepare her heart for Mass.

Soon the choir began singing. Mara and the Prince opened the Christmas songbooks and joined in the carols and hymns. The Prince was familiar with some of them and had little trouble following along with the rest. As soon as he burst into song, heads turned, and people smiled in admiration and awe at his amazing vampire voice. There was nothing quite like it for beauty and splendor, magnificence of tone and timbre and resonance. Sweet and captivating as the voice of Orpheus, a wonder that caused members of the congregation to sigh with longing for their heavenly home, as though the sound was not of this earth but the singing of an angel.

And then it was over. Too soon, judging by the sighs of regret and longing. But this was not about glorifying the Prince, so recently the emissary of darkness, but about the celebration of the birth of Jesus, the Light of the World. Of God becoming flesh for the salvation of men.

The lights went out and in came the procession, beginning with an acolyte holding aloft the crucifix (at which the Prince was obliged to turn away his eyes and clutch Mara's hand to steady himself). Two servers followed bearing large candles to place at the altar, then the lectors and someone chosen to carry the statue of the Holy Babe. Finally came Father Mike, arrayed in snowy vestments embroidered with silver and gold.

After the statue of the Child Jesus was laid in the manger, all returned to their places while Father proceeded to the altar to begin Holy Mass. After the introductory prayers, he lit the servers' candles, and they passed the flame to the many thin candles held by the congregation. The light spread until a brilliant glow illumined the entire church, and the paintings on the high vaulted ceilings were visible even to mortal eyes.

Then came time for the blessing with holy water. Mara leaned toward the Prince to whisper a word of warning. "Father likes to really douse us. You might want to get out of the line of fire. Come back after." And he was gone, out into the dim vestibule (she assumed), sheltered from the burning drops. After sprinkling holy water on the congregation, Father blessed the altar and the crèche. Then the Prince was in his place beside Mara once more. She felt his hand trembling, and with a pang of sympathy, pressed it to her cheek. "If you can't stay—" she began, sorry she had made him feel obliged to return for her sake.

"No, please. Let me attend to our Lord with you. Do not banish me to the outer darkness."

Oh. She gave him a startled glance. She hadn't known he felt like that. Would she ever understand him? She prayed she would be a help and not a hindrance to him on his road to redemption. With a sigh, she considered that maybe it was time for another heart-to-heart talk and those hard questions. She felt anxious, afraid of what she might hear. Would it ruin everything? No, better to clear the air, whatever the cost. If she couldn't give him up, she had better grit her teeth and take the bumps.

After the readings, Gospel, and an inspiring homily, Father Mike announced that they would now have the veneration of the image of the Child Jesus. He went to the crèche and knelt to kiss the Holy Face. Then he picked up the statue, returned to the center and stood on the top step facing the congregation. The people began filing up the aisle to kiss the blessed statue of Jesus.

Mara squeezed the Prince's hand. "It's okay, you don't have to." She knew how he dreaded approaching the sanctuary wherein resided the tabernacle. He would find it difficult, if not impossible.

"But I wish to do so," he whispered back, his eyes burning.

"Be my strength."

She gave him a worried look. What did he think he was doing? He was a vampire! She breathed a prayer as she went up the aisle, her stomach tied in knots. Her turn. She genuflected, kissed the Face of the Infant Jesus and turned away to return to the pew. She glanced back to see the Prince bending to kiss, not the face, but the foot, of the Holy Child. As his lips made contact, there was a flash of light, a hiss, and he was down on his knees, bowed to the floor.

Father Mike looked startled for an instant, but quickly recovered. He gave Mara a glance of understanding (which she desperately needed at the moment). Confusion reigned momentarily as a knot of people milled about at this disruption in the proceedings. Father signaled sharply to them to continue on.

"Forgive me, Lord," Mara heard the Prince say as she rushed over to help him to his feet. His face was pale and ghastly. Not beautiful, but like death, with gray smudges beneath his eyes, his lips blackened and blistered. His eyes were aglow with an eerie flame.

"Your eyes," she whispered, and he quickly veiled them with his lids. He didn't know? True, he did not seem quite himself. A little unsteady, she noticed, so she tucked her hand in the crook of his elbow to support him as they returned to the back of the church. Heads turned and people stared. Not with admiration this time, but with curiosity and—fear, maybe?

He was trembling visibly now. She thought of leaving the church before he fainted. But he halted at their pew, and there was nothing for it but that she led him back to their place. He knelt and bowed his head, though to her mind, he ought to sit down for a minute to recover. She kept her eye on him as Mass continued. He looked sick. Certainly unlike his usual self. She grew anxious, her eyes darting toward him every few seconds. His face had not recovered its usual glimmering white, but seemed to grow more gray and haggard. She was reminded of how he had looked in the tiger's cage when the dawn had almost caught him. Ah, yes, that time it was the sun. This time it's Jesus, the Son.

The Offertory. The Preface. Now everyone was singing Holy, Holy, Holy. They fell to their knees. Terror clutched at her heart. She couldn't breathe. The consecration was next. How could he withstand the Lord God appearing physically before his eyes if the mere image of Jesus devastated him so?

"Prince!" she whispered sharply into his ear. He had knelt with the rest, his head bowed, his eyes closed. His arm was rigid under her desperate fingers. "Think of the sun, the coming dawn. You must leave now. Please, for my sake!" Her voice cracked. Only seconds now. Father was halfway through the Eucharistic Prayer. He took the large host in his hands and began to offer it up. "Prince, please." Her eyes brimmed. She shook him.

He lifted his head slowly, opened heavy lids and with an effort focused on her. Lethargic, just as in the advent of that dawn that nearly killed him. "Mara," he croaked, and tried to smile, but only looked more ghastly.

She feared that if he fainted, she would not be able to save him this time. "Come, we must go now."

He gave her a long, uncomprehending look, but did not resist when she took his hand and pulled him to a shaky standing position. Quietly urging, she guided him out into the night.

The heavy oaken doors closed softly behind them. All was now silent under the stars and streetlights, aside from the usual traffic noises and raucous music and crowd chatter from the tavern down the street. She felt the weight of the Prince lift from her shoulder as he swiftly recovered. She frowned, anxiously inspecting him for damage. But he stood straight and strong again, his face once more exhibiting the pale translucence of alabaster, accented by obsidian eyes. Only his lips retained evidence of his misadventure, looking as though badly burned.

"Ah, my dear, your poor mouth," she lamented.

"I'll be okay. You just go back so you do not miss Mass. I will wait for you out here and see you home afterward."

"Sure, if you don't mind," she said dubiously. "I'm so very sorry. I didn't—"

"Go now," he urged. "Our Lord awaits. You have the privilege. Do not squander it."

"Yes, of course," she said, ashamed that he, a vampire, must remind her of what she was missing.

She gave his hand a quick squeeze and hastened back into the church. Breathlessly she took her place, knelt and bowed her head. Father Mike was praying the words of consecration over the Host. Shocked, she stared. Hadn't he already begun them while she hurried the Prince out the door? How, then, could he still be saying them? Or had the Prince meant exactly that, when he said Our Lord awaits?

He really was waiting for me! So now who's the one with the faith? Tears filled her eyes as she adored, and as in a dream, she went through the prayers and joined the line to receive Communion. She returned to her pew so filled with joy thinking of this privilege she possessed (of which the Prince had reminded her and no doubt envied), that for quite some time, she was unaware of her surroundings. She knelt, enraptured, until someone tapped her on the shoulder and glad voices wished her Merry Christmas. She glanced up, only then realizing that Mass was over and people were crowding toward the doors. She saw her mother and father approaching amidst cheery greetings exchanged with other people along the way. She went to meet her parents and walked with them toward the back of the church.

"Where's Niki?" asked her mother.

"So he couldn't hack it, eh?" said her father at the same time. "I don't wonder."

Mara blinked back tears as she thought of the Prince in dire straits. "Dad." The word came out as a mere squeak.

"What happened there at the veneration?" asked her mother.

"Did he trip? I couldn't see very well."

Mara took a deep breath. "Mom, I don't know why he did it. Maybe he wanted to kiss Our Lord too." She burst into tears.

Her father cleared his throat. "He, er, he should have known better." He clumsily patted her shoulder and turned to greet someone he knew.

"Here's a tissue," her mother whispered. "Do you need a ride home?"

Mara dabbed at her tears. "No, the Prince is waiting. He'll see me home. You go on and enjoy yourself. Looks like they're having coffee and goodies downstairs. Look at all those people trying to wish you Merry Christmas."

"If you're sure," her mother said.

"Yeah, I'm okay, Mom. I'll be home later."

Beyond the Pale

The great oaken doors closed with a sigh behind Mara. She exchanged cheery greetings with several people exiting the church at the same time and watched as they hurried to their cars and drove away. Then she took a deep breath and looked around.

She glanced up and down the street and scanned the star-speckled sky. This automatic precaution was from force of habit and not really necessary on this most holy night. No shadows dropped out of the sky or crept from behind buildings. The tavern down the street was turning off its lights now, its inebriated patrons rapidly dispersing. Otherwise, the night was quiet.

Mara sighed without realizing and started down the deserted sidewalk. She hardly dared contemplate what had happened back there in the church. Like her mother, she asked herself the question: Why had he done it? And her father was right: He should have known better. She sighed again. And caught her breath as the Prince appeared beside her. He had donned his cloak again and was nearly invisible in the night, even to her.

He pressed her close. "Come to me, sweet beloved of our Lord, who may carry Him within your heart while I cannot."

She was speechless for a moment at his unexpected remark, then put her arms around him and buried her face against his chest. "Oh, Prince, why? You might have been killed!"

"You can think of me at such a moment? Yet how grateful I am that you should draw near to me while He resides in your heart. You are my shield. See what happened to me there?"

"I—of course. Oh, but what would I do if I lost you now?"

"I'll never leave you. What then would become of me?"

His gaze was so intense she nearly fell into that bliss again. Just in time, he broke it off, whipped his cloak about her, and then they were up, up, high above the town, flying with great speed. The wind rushed past her ears, whipping her hair about. With a little cry, she clutched at him in panic for a moment.

"Sorry." The Prince spoke softly in her ear as they now coasted downward toward the pattern of lights below. "I thought you would find it interesting to view the Christmas lights from this perspective, too."

"Yeah, well—" she managed, her heart still pounding. She took a deep breath. "Oh, aren't they pretty? Look, over there, at that nativity scene! It must have hundreds of colored lights! And the big white star is shining right on baby Jesus. Cool."

They drifted for a while, enjoying the sight of the town lit up with Christmas lights, of decorated trees in windows of houses and outside in the yards. Then they were descending again, dropping down, and down. The cross shot upward past them just before they touched down on the bell tower of Saint Michael's. Still a bit shaky after the wild flight, Mara clung to the Prince for a moment as his cloak settled around them. She looked around and was reminded of those hard questions she kept putting off. Of course, they weren't just going to go away.

"Here, have a seat," he said, guiding her to the little ledge that ran around the spire. He sat beside her and put his arm and cloak around her, as before. "Are you cold? I am sorry, sometimes I forget that you—or, you want to talk, I see. Would you prefer I take the parapet again, and face you?"

"Hmm, which question should I answer first?" she said in a vain attempt at humor, and to delay the inevitable. Not working; she scrapped the light mood. "Okay. With this wool coat, I'm not going to get cold. And as much as I enjoy being close to you—"

"Ah. You have questions, then?" He moved away, and they

faced each other in silence for a long moment, he in his cloak, crouched on the parapet, and she in her red wool coat seated primly on the ledge with the wall at her back.

"Oh, why did you do it? You might have died!" A sob caught at the words.

He cast his eyes down. "I am sorry if I caused you pain. But alas, my body instinctively preserves itself from danger. At worst, I may shame you, I think, and myself. Proclaim to the world what I really am. But everyone else went up, and for a moment I thought I could be one of them—of you. It was hard, but I so wished to kiss my Lord Jesus too. I dared not kiss His face, but I thought if I only kissed His foot…"

"But your mouth," Mara protested, reaching out to touch his face, avoiding the painful-looking blisters on his lips.

"Do not weep for me on that account." He pressed her hand to his cheek. "I brought this on myself. Though I regret that because my lips are burned, I cannot kiss you just now. Yes, it is painful, but well worth it. I kissed the foot of the statue of our Lord, though He repulsed me. I would do it again, if only to feel that fire of Divine Love once more, though It consume me." He paused, his eyes alight. "If I go to confession one night soon, maybe I will have the courage to receive Holy Communion—His Precious Blood, of course—though I be annihilated in the attempt. I know I am not worthy to receive the kiss of God as you mortals do, but to feel Divine Love once more would be ecstasy."

Kiss of God? She stared at him in wonder and felt humbled by such words coming out of the mouth of a vampire – ordinarily, a soulless creature, proud, vain and damned, as the Prince too had once been. But now, who could countenance this? He made her think, with his total awareness of the majesty of God and of himself as nothing and his humble acceptance of his position as one far below that of puffed up, arrogant Man, who held the place of honor as God's adopted child in the grand scheme of things. Suddenly she saw herself as the proud, ungrateful creature in this story. Now, as she contemplated this mystery, and him, in an effort to understand, to sort through all that he'd just said, a thought struck her, and horror clutched at her heart. To approach the Real Presence was nearly impossible for him; to touch it would be the death of him. She was sure of it.

"No!" she cried. "You can't do that. You'd die, and—no, stop. Don't say it doesn't matter. That just won't cut it. You would choose to die, just for the sake of one last ecstasy? Isn't this less about love—for God, or me, or anything but yourself—and more about grasping for a new high, just as you've done for the past five hundred years? Never mind that this may be the real thing. That's not love, it's gluttony!" He flinched as though she had slapped him, looked at her with an expression she could not fathom and said nothing. Tears of frustration welled up in her eyes. "Hey, it's nothing but a cop-out," she said hotly. "We both know a big battle is coming. And you'd leave me alone to deal with it? No, oh no, you don't." She dashed the tears away with her sleeve and fixed fierce eyes upon him. "You said you'd be my partner, my support. You promised. What of that?"

Her voice cracked at the end. She buried her face in her hands and wept. No matter that he meant well; he hadn't thought it through. She felt betrayed.

He was silent for so long that she began to think he had left. She felt lost and alone, at once regretting her flare of temper. What if she had gone and done it now? Laid one more guilt trip on his already overburdened shoulders. Maybe the virtue that had so suddenly bloomed in this newly restored soul was crushed now because of her quick, sharp tongue and hurt feelings. Or, what if the purpose of his transformation was something between God and him that had nothing to do with her, ultimately?

Selfish is what I am. She was afraid to look, to see the parapet empty (a vampire could vanish without a sound so that even she may not hear). Slowly she lowered her hands to her lap, but kept her eyes cast down, ashamed to face him if he was still there. Then she felt something soft pressed into her hand. He was offering her a handkerchief.

"Dry your tears and weep no more, my darling," the Prince said. "I apologize for my ill-conceived desire. You are entirely right about my motives, I see that now. I did not realize. I thank you for pointing it out to me." Suddenly ashamed for doubting him, she blushed. His response was instantaneous, a sudden glow of the eyes and a hiss. It was his turn to be ashamed and to drop his gaze. "Sorry. Even now, I cannot seem to entirely quell my vampire nature. A timely reminder. Forgive me, please."

"Uh, it's okay. I mean, of course, I forgive you. How could I not? Good grief. You take your punishment and loss so meekly. Gosh, I'm sure I'd make all sorts of excuses. How precious you must be in His sight."

At that, he was so moved that he fell to his knees at her feet and took her hands in his. "How you do overpraise me, my love. You saw the Lord God repudiate my kiss. When the angel touched Isaiah's lips with a burning coal, they were purified, so I thought perhaps—but I know not for certain, as you point out; this may be a warning. I dare not presume and risk disrespect to Him and injustice to you."

At that, he kissed her hand. She felt him wince. With a cry of protest, she pulled her hand away. He looked crushed.

"I'm sorry," she wailed. "I don't like to see you hurting." She kissed his cheek. "Oh, dear, what have I done? What if I'm wrong, and God meant for you to be only His, and not mine?"

He gave her a long look. "Where did that come from? No, no, I think that it is only through you that I may go to Him." His arms went around her; he pressed his cheek to hers. "I will love you always," he said into her ear. "I want you for mine only, forever. Will you marry me?"

She was stunned. *Marry. He asked me to marry him.*

"Take your time," he said finally after the silence grew long. "Sorry, I did not mean to spring it on you like this. You said you love me, and....You do not have to give me your answer now. Only when you are ready."

He's a vampire; I'm a mortal. How could he think such a thing? Or, did You seriously intend him for me, like this? Oh, dear God, tell me what to do!

"I am sorry, it is a little unorthodox, I realize," he resumed, after another lengthy pause. "What will people say? And of course, you have to think of your parents."

Parents. Oh, dear. And how am I going to tell Father Mike? What was that he said? Somehow everything they had discussed about marriage or the Prince had scattered to the four winds. The Prince. Wasn't this what she wanted? *But he's a vampire. I'm the Huntress. Um, yeah, those hard questions. That's right. Nyx. Styx. I need answers first.*

"Uh, yeah, of course," she said finally, somewhat at a loss for words. "But what about—I mean, a vampire and a mortal? It didn't turn out so well for Romeo and Juliet, did it? I mean, well, you see—" She paused for a deep breath and went on, "I'm a huntress. I kill vampires." (At this he winced.) "And then there's my mom and dad, but we'll talk about them later. I have to think about this. I have my answer, right here." She pressed her hand to her heart with a pained expression. "But first, I have questions." She stopped talking, a little out of breath, and lifted her eyes to his, shyly.

His look softened. "I am ready."

She cast her eyes down in self-defense, away from his tender, heart-melting glance. "Maybe sit over there," she said, lifting her eyes to his again. "I can't, er, I can't think when you're so close."

He touched her hair with a gentle hand, and was on the parapet again, that disturbing gaze fixed on her. "Please continue."

"The way you sent Nyx and her goons packing when they attacked me—" She sighed. "Well, I have to admit, it looks like I need a protector, a partner. But something you said about your obsession with her—um, how the feelings of a vampire are as carved in stone, and immortal—got me wondering. Is that feeling still there, carved into your deepest self? If even just a bit, like the Snow Queen's splinter of ice in Kay's heart, it's kind of an obstacle. Hey, it's only fair for me to ask you to be mine only. You want me to be yours only." She took a deep breath and rushed on. "You've known Nyx like forever, were very close, I get that. So. When you—um, rejected her, did it leave a scar? And, how will it affect us?"

"So very direct," he murmured, looking away. "You would listen to more confessions of a miserable wretch on a beautiful night like this? On Christmas?"

"It wasn't my idea. You're the one who chose tonight to propose. We can wait, if you prefer."

"Let us not. Now is a good time."

"Start with the last question, then."

"First of all, vampires have no scars. Nyx cannot come between us; it was our love that broke the chain with which she bound me to her. Yes, once upon a time, she took me and I did choose her, as she said. But not for love, you may be sure. One's heart cannot be taken; it can only be given, for that is the essence of love. After she turned me, I was unable to give it, for a vampire cannot love." He paused, as though nearly overcome for a moment, then collected himself and went on, "After the light blinded me that night in the church and I chose Jesus as my master, I was given the freedom to love. The broken heart I suffered was of stone. In place of it, I was given a heart of flesh, cold and still though it may be. I looked upon you and, as for the first time ever, loved. My heart belongs to you, and you only. Total, immortal, as if carved in stone. Forever."

She exhaled in relief. *Thank you, God.* "Thank you, Prince," she said aloud. "Now, one more question. Um—"

"Yes?"

With an effort, she blurted out, "I don't know if I want to know, but what about—what's between you and Styx?"

He dropped his gaze. When he lifted it to meet hers once more, it was so sorrowful that she was afraid.

"Ah, do you really want to hear this tonight? You must be quite numb from the horrors of my past, after the last time we were here. Might this not wait for another time?"

"No. Let's get it over with. Your answer to the first question totally wasn't as bad as I was afraid it would be. I wouldn't get any rest, now, wondering."

"I never loved Styx. A vampire, as I said, cannot love. As when Nyx bound me to herself, just so did I enmesh Styx in those infernal chains. Now I have repudiated them all. All, all. I have cut all ties to the Brotherhood, to Styx. You saw; you were there. If I grieve, it is not for loss of her, but for the wrong I have done her. I sinned against heaven and against her, stole the Lord's own bride." He lifted his eyes to hers. "I warn you; it is a long and vile tale of a wretch wallowing in his sin as though it were a triumph."

"Don't spare my feelings," said Mara. "Or yours. Let's get everything cleared away so we can maybe start afresh."

He blinked at the 'maybe' and said softly, "This may be the hardest of all, and yet, you have a right to know." He reflected a moment and began. "Styx—"

Mara felt as though a dagger pierced her heart at the catch in his voice when he said that name. She feared the worst; couldn't repress the image of Styx clinging to him, kissing him as though she had a claim on him, like a jilted lover. Mara dashed away the tears that sprang suddenly to her eyes.

He reached out as though to comfort her, but she shook her head, and he withdrew his hand. Resolutely he gripped the edge of the parapet. His voice was low and sad as he began again. "Styx is perhaps the most wronged of all. She was innocent. I corrupted her. I made her into the thing she now is. The others I have wronged might be in heaven now, but she— she is damned forever. I must answer for that, I know.

"The powers I had accumulated over the centuries—the initial dose forced on me by Nyx, those bestowed upon me by Charon, and those I soon learned to take for myself—were not enough. I wanted more. Always. Power is addicting as well as corruptive. Nyx was always there, driving me on to achieve excellence, to enhance my gifts, and to turn them to evil purpose. I would have done anything to please her.

"One night she said I could not turn an innocent. Taunted me with it, as though it were an imperfection. I took this as a challenge, as she knew I would. She was very adept at manipulating. Nyx would eat her words, I vowed. To turn the innocent was impossible, it was said, unless one could first lead it into sin. Well. I was very good at that game. Nyx had taught me that insidious little pleasure long before; I had come to enjoy it (though sinners were easier prey, of course). This time, I vowed, my chosen victim would end not in death, but ruin.

"I had never been interested in creating new vampires, though I dabbled in it half-heartedly upon occasion, on a dare or for fun. Never was successful or concerned with my failure. I was not interested in complicating my life (existence, rather). I was sufficient unto myself. And after observing the experiments of others, it seemed to me the results were always in some way wanting. The drinking of the blood of mortals was what really mattered to me; not whether they lived, died, or turned. Mortals were food and fun, and that was all.

"Once I had set myself upon that course, I soon chose for this new experiment a sweet-faced maid with big blue eyes and long, fair hair. It was her resemblance to Kristina, I think, that fascinated me. The twisted remains of my mortal affections had often filled me with longing for what I once had, and like all vampires, I was desperate for something to fill the godforsaken emptiness inside. I sometimes thought if only I had not killed Kristina, if I had instead turned her, I could have had that delight forever, but alas, what was done was done. I could not bring her back from the dead. That, too, galled me. With all my powers, I could not alter that fact. How often did I curse in impotent fury at this proof that I was not a god. All I had ever created was havoc. This, I decided, would be different. I would create from this maiden another Kristina.

I would repair the bond I had severed long ago. I would be not just a god, or play God, I would be God. Yes, I told myself that.

"When Nyx heard that I had found the maiden at a convent, she jeered, 'Fool! Even I dare not enter an abbey, have you forgotten? This one you will never turn. She will be the death of you. Choose another. There are many just as sweet, but not so protected.' 'I do not want them. Only that one,' I replied, furious at the suggestion that I was incapable of carrying out my designs. 'Impossible,' she told me, 'I have seen this before. She will die rather than sin, if the priests do not kill you first.' I laughed. 'You underestimate my powers of persuasion, Nyx. As for priests, hah! None can touch me.'

"I wonder that God did not strike me dead then and there to prevent me from corrupting His bride. I swore that nothing would stop me. By then, I was well aware of the effect of my appearance on mortals. Any vampire could frighten them into submission; most had the power to mesmerize. But I had the unique power to entrance them, unconsciously. One look upon my face, and they were mine. It was quite the rush.

"So when I confronted her alone on the convent grounds, I assumed I would return to Nyx that very night assured of victory, and laugh in her face. However, the laugh was on me. My chosen victim foiled my scheme by modestly casting her eyes down. I was astounded and annoyed by this resistance to my charm, of which I was so vain. Still, I had other tricks up my sleeve.

"I had assumed clerical garb for the purpose, and soon persuaded her that I was a visiting priest sent by God to be her spiritual director. That part was not difficult. She was but a naïve girl. The sound of my voice alone had the power to mesmerize as well, though her innocence did protect her somewhat. She seemed a bit troubled when she found that no one else knew of me, and was puzzled by my actions at times, like when I had to fade into the shadows to avoid sisters emerging from the chapel or walking in the garden. Still, I had a few centuries of experience in the art of seduction and easily diverted her.

"One night she innocently remarked that their regular confessor knew nothing about me. I quickly assured her that I meant to consult him later that evening. It was a lie, of course. I dared not go near him, or I surely would have lost my head. I was not pleased that the foolish maid had discussed me with others. How soon before they guessed what I was? But this proof of her innocence fired my obsession the more. Then one night, she said that her superior forbade her to see me again. She truly meant to obey, to my chagrin, and for a while, I haunted the convent grounds in vain. On some nights, I persisted almost to the point of discovery, only to slink home just ahead of the dawn, vilely cursing those who protected her.

"Meanwhile, Nyx hounded me, always, warning me to give it up now, before it was too late. She would say, 'Remember, they belong to the church of our adversary. Persist in this folly, and you shall awaken that monster. You will be unmasked and slain.' Of course, I had no death wish, but neither would I be deterred. I became increasingly edgy and impatient to have this done with.

"In the end I cheated. I obtained a philter from Letha the Witch. How could that innocent suspect me, whom she thought was a priest? Shamelessly I clouded her mind with my erudition, and my beauty as well, though she never looked directly at my face. She could see my hands, and otherwise get an overall impression of my physical attributes (even as she tried to convince herself that that was not the cause of her attraction). I could sense the war within her, yet for some reason, she never once tested me with crucifix or prayer, which would have settled the matter, of course. Finally, overcome by guilt for her disobedience, she begged me not to see her again. That was when I knew she was mine.

"On a stormy night soon afterward, I braved the hallowed grounds once more to fly into the inner courtyard. The wind was wild, lashing the rain furiously against the lighted windows of the convent kitchen. As I approached the door, I heard domestic sounds inside: a lone mortal singing softly amidst the clatter of dishes. With growing excitement, I sensed that it was she. The doleful ticking of the clock and the cheerful crackling of the fire in the stove were her only company. The coast was clear. I reached inside my cloak and touched the glass vial to reassure myself that the philter was there. Time was running out, I feared. I meant to have her that night.

"I tapped lightly on the door. The humming ceased, and I heard the approach of footsteps. The door opened. I stood in the rain with rivulets of water streaming from the brim of my hat and winds whipping at my cloak. At the sight of me, her long lashes veiled her eyes at once. But I, I was captivated, by her sweet face and her long, beautiful hair (uncut, as she had not yet taken her vows), their brightness and innocence impossible to be concealed, even by the plain homespun habit. The crucifix she always wore was at the moment tucked beneath her apron, to my relief.

"Of course, in all Christian charity ,she could not but invite me in to warm myself by the fire. As I entered, I had to avert my eyes from the crucifix hanging on the far wall. It caused me great suffering, but I managed to fix a benign smile on my face as I took off my hat and shook the raindrops from it. She offered me a chair by the fire and would have gone to fetch someone, but I begged her not to disturb the household. I could not stay long, I explained; this very night I was leaving for missionary work in a land across the sea. As I would be gone for a long time, I had come to bid her farewell; then I would be on my way. Also, a cup of hot tea I would not take amiss. She seemed to take heart at this assurance that I would be gone far from here, never more to play havoc with her vocation.

"If she hesitated, my deathly pallor and my cold and trembling hands convinced her that I did indeed need something to warm me. I was soaked to the skin, as far as she could tell, and maybe catching a chill. I presented a pathetic sight, I am sure, and it was not all playacting. Though I tried to make small talk, it was a strain with the crucifix on the wall numbing my ordinarily keen senses. I steeled myself to endure as she hastened to stoke the fire and make tea. When at last, she poured the hot brew, I suggested that it would be a corporal work of mercy for her to join me. She was touched, poor innocent maid, and poured a second cup for herself. I asked her for sugar, and while she went to the pantry to fetch it, I slipped the potion into her drink.

"I exulted in the depths of my cold, black heart. She would be mine at last! I could hardly contain myself as she sat on a chair across from me and lifted her teacup. I wonder she did not notice my agitation, but still she did not look into my face. I sensed that she was anxious; then she explained that her partner in chores had taken a basket of towels to the laundry and would soon return. No doubt she hoped I would leave before that happened, though, of course, she had not the heart to banish me to the stormy darkness outside. I set about allaying her fears with practiced charm, though more than a little anxious myself. Not because of that other sister; I was this close to being crushed by the holiness that surrounded me.

"I sipped the tea, becoming more frantic beneath my external composure with every passing second. Would she never drink? Then, just when I was on the verge of despair, she took a sip and drained the cup. She looked down into the dregs as though wondering at the taste. Too late. The potion had begun its work.

"She lifted her eyes slowly to look me full in the face for the first time. I captured her gaze at once; felt no pity for her distress at what she knew to be a sin. She could not help herself, of course, and I, I was blasted into ecstasy by her longing. The glowing of my eyes gave me away, then. A little cry of horror escaped her as for the first time she saw me for what I was. In that instant, I feared that she would flee from me. Like a cat, I sprang. She feebly resisted, despite the potion. How, I do not know, unless it was her innocence. I bit her and was as though engulfed in flame. Caught by the enchantment of untarnished purity, I was elevated to the sky. Her arms went around my neck; her fingers tangled in my hair. It must have been the potion. Never before had I tasted such—oh, sorry." He quickly subdued the glow of his eyes and gave Mara a quick, apologetic glance.

Her look was pained, but she managed a slight nod.

"Er, yes," he continued. "The other sister came back just then. I heard the sound of approaching footsteps from the corridor, but could not tear myself away. I was caught up in ecstasy. She appeared in the doorway and started to say something cheery, then halted, her smile fading, to stare; scandalized, I am sure. I raised my head, blood running from my mouth and down my chin. I should have fled, of course, but instead pressed my victim to my heart, electrified by the mortal warmth, as passion, and pride, ruled. I bent again to my bliss, lifted my gaze and watched the young sister impudently as I fed.

"With a little whimper of fright, she stood undecided for a moment. Would she run toward us, or away? Either would have spelt her doom. She innocently did the one thing that could save her; she made the Sign of the Cross, which slammed me to the floor, as though by some invisible force. I was paralyzed, shocked out of all sense, all power, and deprived of my swooning prey. A moment later, my instinct for survival kicked in. I sprang up with a shriek of frustration and pain and fury. In complete disarray, I scrambled out the door and fled into the night.

"At first, Nyx laughed when I came slinking back. But when she heard that I had gone into a convent, fed in front of a witness and left marks on the victim, she flew into a rage. 'You are not going back, ever! The priests know what you are now. They will kill you!' she shouted, 'You fool! You may have endangered all of us!' 'She is hooked,' I argued, 'She will come when I call, if she can.' Still, I knew I would have to be discreet if I wanted to keep my head. And Nyx was right about the danger to us all, if mortals should gather to hunt us down.

"Of course, in those 'enlightened' days, most educated people no longer believed in vampires. They often managed to explain away scientifically even such blatant evidence. Witnesses were often dismissed as afflicted with hysteria, a common malady among females, apparently. Even when the victim died, the 'wasting sickness' was often thought to be the cause. Yes, I could do this! If I could get her to drink my blood first, she would rise from her grave of her own accord, and be mine forever. More determined than ever, I set about my task.

"I lurked in the shadows night after night, but no longer could I penetrate the boundaries of the convent grounds. I finally concluded that the priests must have performed an exorcism and, no doubt, blessed the entire perimeter by sprinkling it with holy water and salt. My prey was, of course, forbidden to cross that magic line, and the nuns were vigilant, foiling my every attempt to get near her.

"I decided to lie low for a while. It was not easy, but I managed to stay away. We had other enticements, Nyx and I. But I had not forgotten my chosen victim, and after quite a long time, I finally chanced it once again. Sure enough, they had relaxed their guard, perhaps thinking I was gone for good. One night I espied her returning to the convent from a retreat house across the drive, though, of course, amidst a flock of nuns. But she had dared cross their magic line! That was her downfall.

"I silently called to her. She stopped, sang out that she had forgotten something, and spun around to retrace her steps up the path to the door. The nuns belatedly protested, but she heeded them not. They were only a few steps away and the moon was full; it must have seemed okay. Still, they urged her to hurry, shivering at more than just the chill of evening, I daresay. They did not see me concealed in the shadows, or notice when I took her in my arms. A feeble protest died on her lips as I wrapped her in my cloak and spirited her away.

"I set her down gently on a windswept hilltop far from them. The night was cold, so her heavy woolen cloak hid her crucifix, and I exulted in my good fortune; it could so easily have been the ruin of my plan. All I had to do now was to persuade her to drink my blood. Then she would be mine forever. But she kept her eyes averted, much to my chagrin, and seemed so unaccountably distressed, I was a little at a loss. Usually, my victims succumbed to my charm with little or no resistance. It must be her innocence, I thought to myself, fired up the more. I assured her that she had no need to be affrighted. But it was not that, or anything I would have imagined, as it turned out.

"She fell to her knees at my feet and asked me to hear her confession. I nearly panicked, quickly taking her hands in mine to prevent her from making that fatal Sign of the Cross. It was a close call. She kissed my hands then (thinking they were the anointed hands of a priest) and confessed to me that she had desired a man consecrated to God. Monster that I was, I smiled cynically above her bowed head as she wept inconsolably, certain that she would be damned for all eternity. She was right. I would see to it. I said to her, as I did to you, that I would take her to heaven. Unlike you, she fell for my line. I drew her into my embrace and—took her to heaven, all right. Hell, more like. How can I ever atone for corrupting the Lord's own bride?" He bowed his head.

This Mara knew to be a rhetorical question, so she made no reply. There was nothing to be said. For the first time, she could sympathize with Styx. Of course, she already knew the little beast had been mortal once upon a time. There was no denying the perniciousness of what he'd done, and this time she felt the heartbreak. This time the Prince was the vampire turning a mortal.

"So," he said, finally. "You are waiting for me to get on with it. Pardon me for wallowing in my grief. That is, I know, pointless and tiresome. What you really want to know is how it all turned out afterward."

"Yes, I guess that's the only thing left to be said." She took a deep breath. "Was she the companion you'd hoped for? What is she to you now? That's what I need to know. The rest, foul though it is, is in the past. Has to be; we can't change it. We both know what she has become. Only this one thing affects us." *Keep telling yourself that, Mara.* She could feel his eyes on her, as though he guessed her thoughts.

"I understand. Sorry, but you asked. My offer still stands. Anytime you feel the need to exterminate me, I will not lift a hand against you. Fine. I get it. You cannot." He grimaced, then composed himself and continued. "No, it did not turn out as I had hoped. I was selfish; disappointed that she was not Kristina. I doubt Kristina herself would have measured up had I turned her. Anyway, Styx.

"After that first flash of wild and glorious ecstasy, the novelty wore off soon enough. She turned out to have feelings, needs and wants, and looked to me to satisfy them. But that would have been too much. The universe revolved around me, after all. No, what I felt for her was not love. I was incapable of that. I was arrogant, insufferable, cold-hearted, selfish; I see that so clearly now. I made her what she is, then like a spoiled child who has grown tired of its new toy, I tossed her aside.

"Perhaps, as she accused me so recently, because she was no longer innocent, no longer a challenge? No, I do not mean to excuse myself. There is no justification for what I did. I shall regret it forever. I took her and made her into an image of myself, a monster of uncleanness, a pathetic distorted shadow of what she once was, what she was meant to be — and then I rejected her. Now, when I would make amends, I find it is not possible. It is only what I deserve, of course, but that will not save her, or change what I did, to my eternal shame."

He paused, and when Mara remained silent, he lifted his

eyes to hers. "There you have it. Does that answer your question?"

Mara shifted her gaze, unable to think of any words to either console or condemn. By that river of words he had managed once more to bring every reeking detail of his foul deeds into the present. She was sickened. Of course, he had done it deliberately, as though he felt compelled to pound home the brutal reality so that she could not just gloss it over, or brush it aside as just one more list of the misdeeds of a vampire (yawn). He meant that she should understand how deplorable it was; how it had marked him. These were real people whose lives he had destroyed, mourned by real families, if he had not laid them waste as well. What he had done was not romantic or cool; it was despicable, deserving of shame only.

She had asked for it; she had stepped into the ring with him a second time, knowing from before that he pulled no punches. Did he think because she loved him, because she was attracted to him, that she would excuse him if he softened the story in the telling? As Huntress, she knew what vampires were about and in general how they had become so. Still, the graphic images he painted struck her to the heart. He made certain that she would not forget that he was not as angelic as he looked. Now every time she looked at that face, into those eyes, she would be reminded of what damage they had done. Of how they had brought about the violation and untimely demise of innocents.

They sat in silence for a while, looking at each other.

"Well," she said, finally. "Sad and terrible as your tale is, it does ease my mind about you and her. There is one more thing I must say. This might seem callous, but I am the Huntress. What you did was evil. She was innocent and you guilty, but in the end, she made her choice. And there's no turning back the clock to undo what's been done." Mara took a deep breath and looked him in the eyes. "Now it's my duty to put Styx to rest if the opportunity presents itself. She'll be in God's hands then, where she belongs."

He gave a shudder. "Spoken like a true huntress," he said with a bitter laugh. "Forgive me if I react like a true vampire. Your statement conjures up unpleasant images I prefer not to dwell upon."

She softened. "I'm sorry; I meant no offense. It's how things are. I just thought I'd better make that clear."

"I know you have a job to do," he said slowly. "But what if—what if a huntress had staked me? Mercy as that would have been, now see me as I am. Is there a chance for the others, too?"

"Ouch! Where would I be, then?" Mara said with an anxious frown. "My life's work, totally out the window. And me, guilty. Still, in the light of all that's happened, I think yours is a special case. My cause is just. I can't let vampires ravage the world of men unchecked. It wouldn't be right. Regardless, we'd all be safer in our Maker's hands. I'm not insensitive. I take no joy in my work. I believe it's necessary, an act of mercy."

"I agree. It is difficult for me to believe that I can never right the wrongs I have done. I cannot give back the lives I took, nor restore Styx to her former innocence. Alas, that is my pride speaking again. I am not the god I thought I was. I must bow my head before the one true God. Only He can remedy the wrongs I've done, or avenge them."

She reached out and took his cold hand in hers. "I guess we're really all in the same boat. And look at the blessings He showers on us every day, though we don't deserve them. None of us. Now we have each other, you and I. Who would have thought?"

Before she even knew he had moved, he was on one knee in front of her. "Maybe this is not the time, but may I have your answer now? I beg of you, keep me in suspense no longer. If only I had brought you a diamond, a real engagement ring. I have the means and will remedy that as soon as possible."

"No, no, please don't. You've already given me this awesome emerald ring. And, well, you know I'm not one for a lot of bling."

"If you wish. Then accept with it my heart, my whole self. All that I am, and have, forever. This is my promise."

Tears welled up in her eyes as she lifted them to meet his, a bit overwhelmed, even frightened, after all he'd just told her, and she wondered: what would such a promise mean to her future? Still, in her heart was written the answer she must give him.

"Yes. My answer is yes."

He kissed her hand and the emerald ring. When he raised his eyes to meet hers, they had a golden glow of which he seemed unaware. He gathered her into his arms and her heart thudded against his cold chest. He pressed his cheek to hers. "If only I could kiss you now."

Song of Songs

The following week, Father Mike answered a knock at his door to find the Prince standing on his doorstep with a startling request. He wished to go to confession. The priest blinked and stood for a moment with a finger marking the place in the book he was reading. The Prince saw his hesitation and hastened to assure him that he had been baptized as a mortal.

Father Mike quickly recovered. "I never doubted it," he murmured. "Just one moment. I'll get the church key."

The Prince apologized for having disturbed his quiet evening. "But there is no need to unlock the church. I can confess here more easily. The Real Presence is a difficulty for me, I am sorry to say."

Father Mike understood. The rectory parlor it would be.

The Prince had long ago taken Mara's suggestion to heart, but it was a while before he could gather the courage and the humility. His body could never again be mortal as he so dearly wished, but he resolved to restore his soul, for Mara's sake as well as his own. A daunting task, after nearly five centuries of wreaking havoc on the world of men.

"What hope is there for me when I cannot even look upon the image of Our Lord?" he groaned.

Father Mike donned his stole, praying silently for the grace to deal with this. Had there ever been a precedent? He looked at the Prince humbly kneeling, waiting patiently with bowed head. Finally, he spoke. "If mortal men, who have been elevated to the status of children of God, are unable to gaze upon the Beatific Vision and live," he said slowly, "it stands to reason that beings of a lower state (begging your pardon) dare not even look upon His image."

Though kindly put, the barb was sharp and thrust deep into the Prince's proud heart, but his soul had come a long way from what it was at their first meeting. This time there was no rise of murderous rage. He now realized that he had, by his own fault, brought himself to this miserable state, so he crushed his pride, took the hit with humble acceptance, and confessed his sins. Sometime later he came to the end of it, at last.

Father Mike prayed for illumination. He had never heard the like in variety or number; not at one time. The sin of becoming a vampire was one he was certain he had not heard before.

The Prince knelt and waited in silence, head bowed. His remorse and desire to sin no more were sincere, yet doubts assailed Father Mike. Would absolution (or matrimony, when it came to that) be valid? Good heavens, this was a vampire, not a man! And yet, how could he in all justice spurn this soul to whom God had seen fit to show mercy? This creature that He had drawn back from the pit to bestow upon it an unheard-of privilege: the return of its soul and a second chance! If he refused, might it not be lost forever? And thus would he be called to account when it came time to face his Maker, his Judge? He felt the burden of great responsibility suddenly shift onto his shoulders, and cried out in his heart, *Why me, Lord?*

The Lord answered, *Good and faithful servant, I have chosen you to bring this lost sheep, a beloved child of mine, back to the fold. Because of his instant of regret so long ago, his sincere sorrow, though it was swept away at once by her, that bane of my people, I show him mercy. I abandoned his body to five hundred years of his chosen iniquity while his soul wandered lost and forlorn; now I grant him this reprieve, due to the unending petitions of those who love him, though he had killed them. From this day forward shall he taste the consequences of his fall. From now on shall he suffer and atone, in both body and soul, until the day that I call him to Myself.*

And so, Father Mike absolved him and gave him penance as well as a few words of advice.

The Prince listened, thanked him when he had finished, then stood up and prepared to leave. "One more thing." He reached inside his cloak, drew out a leather pouch and handed it to Father Mike. "Please accept this for the damage done to your church that night."

Father frowned down at the mysterious gift. "Ah, the battle. But—no, no, that's not necessary."

"Yes, it is. I must begin somehow to compensate for all the evil I have done. Go ahead, have a look. It is little enough, I realize, but it is a start."

Father Mike opened the pouch. A glitter of many colors tumbled out onto the coffee table with a clatter. He stared, astonished. Reflections leaped from emeralds, rubies, amber, diamonds and more, to dance across the ceiling and walls, brightening the room as though with a light supernatural. "Jewels! My dear boy, where did you get these?" *Boy? What am I saying? He was born hundreds of years ago!*

"That doesn't matter, does it?" the Prince said a little sharply, then quickly added in a softer tone, "I'm sorry, Father. I did not steal them. They are mine to give."

"Of course. I never thought otherwise. It, er, just took me by surprise, that's all. I didn't expect—you don't need to do this. Er, what am I going to do with them?"

"Make something beautiful for your church. Sell them. Feed the poor. Whatever you want. They are yours."

Father recovered. "I see. As you wish. Thank you."

"No. It is I who must thank you. What you have given me is worth more than a few gems. I will never forget."

"Of course not," murmured Father as the Prince went out the door and vanished into the night. *You're a vampire.*

***

The Prince left the rectory that night with a great burden lifted.

***

A few days after the Prince's confession, Mara and the Prince visited Father Mike together with the dreaded request.

They wanted to be married. Somewhat sadly, he consented; but only on one condition: the way must first be made clear in the eyes of the Church.

He wished with all his heart that it had not come to this. To him as a man, union between woman and vampire was a horror; as a priest, an impossible joining of light to dark. But as mentor, confessor, and spiritual director, he could vouch for the purity of Mara's heart and soul, as well as for the renewal of the Prince's. And of course, where light is, darkness is vanquished.

"It's a hard road you've chosen," he warned Mara. "The Prince has told you of his fall from grace, and you have no illusions about vampires, I know." Father Mike paused with brow furrowed and eyes sad.

"Yes, Father," Mara said, with a glance at the Prince. "I know enough." More than enough.

He took a deep breath and forged ahead. "Mara, you've been a good girl all your life, never meriting serious censure or punishment. Whereas, your, er, your fiancé here has, well — Do you realize that by binding yourself to him and sharing your life with him, you share everything? Everything. Including the effects of the damage he's done for five centuries and the atonement he's bound to suffer. Do you have any inkling of what that means? If you choose this road, you must prepare for heartache."

"Heartache. What road in this world doesn't promise that?" she murmured. After a moment of reflection, she lifted big eyes. "Father, the Prince is the one I love. Should I turn my back on him for fear of hardship? When have you ever advised me to take the easy way out?" She turned back to the Prince, and her tone softened. "I'll gladly share with him every good thing and his every burden too. Justice must be served, of course, but God will be with us in our trials."

"One more thing." Father Mike glanced at the Prince, then back to her. "What about children? If you go through with this, my dear Mara, you may never have any of your own."

She reached for the Prince's hand. "We've talked about that, but I'm sure that we're meant for each other, whatever else we must do without. Of course, I'd love to have kids of my own, but I leave it all in God's Hands. He knows if it's possible for me to be both Huntress and a mother. I put my trust in Him."

Father Mike gave a little nod, his look sorrowful but resigned. "You understand, of course, that we may proceed no further with this without the approval of the bishop."

"Yes, Father," Mara said, a bit anxiously. "I suppose there's not much hope there."

"I'm afraid you're probably right about that," he said in a tone of compassion.

"Hey, I'll be praying night and day. He'll come around, you'll see," she said, feigning a confidence she didn't feel.

"You know, of course, that if the bishop does forbid this, you must resign yourself to it humbly as the will of God."

Mara sighed deeply. "I, yes, of course. But you know me, Father. I'll totally fight to the end for this."

And she did. Somehow, she hadn't expected it to be such a big deal. Then again, it wasn't as if they were an ordinary couple seeking to tie the knot, with some minor hang-up to untangle. When Father Mike left to meet with the bishop, it hit her; this was coming down to the point. There was a very real possibility that it might not go down quite as she hoped. Really, what would this situation look like from the perspective of an outsider, an eminent prince of the Church and shepherd of souls, no less? Maybe a whole tribunal would be involved (she wasn't sure) with canon lawyers and the whole nine yards.

She went down on her knees before the Blessed Sacrament and stormed heaven while Father Mike was gone, keeping vigil three nights, in prayer and meditation until dawn. Just as Christians of old traditionally prepared for knighthood or battle, she, too, was a warrior on the brink of a life-changing event. What would she do if Holy Mother Church pronounced this step unworthy of her calling or a sin? But no, surely not.

God had directed her toward this path. She was sure of it.

When the lightning bolt had struck so suddenly that night in the church, she was horrified; devastated. She hadn't asked for it; didn't want it, this impossible thing. She had tried to flee and prayed to be released from those terrible golden chains that bound her heart to that of the enemy, a vampire. But now, if God had arranged it, He wouldn't abandon her. But what if it was only a test? What if this was but one more false promise of the prince of darkness? She knew of only one sure way to be certain: obedience. She bowed her head, resigned, and continued to pray.

Father Mike found her asleep before the tabernacle when he came in to offer Mass on that third morning. He awakened her gently. "We'll talk after Mass," he said, as she scrambled to her feet, rubbing the sleep from her eyes.

All through Mass, she was in an agony of suspense. It was difficult to attend as she ought. She offered this up, crushing her pride, praying that she could abide by the decision made by her betters, however it turned out. She feared the worst; she knew what Father Mike thought. He was too honest to give her false hope. And now—well, he'd given her no sign one way or the other. Or maybe he looked a little sad. What could it mean?

Her eyes were dry, all tears spent after hours of weeping, and she was filled with dread as all the worst possible scenarios went through her mind. Was the Prince like a light bulb, bright and beautiful and mesmerizing, and she the moth mistaking him for the moon, only to singe her wings and fall maimed to the ground? Better to be dead. No, death was not the answer. She had a mission, with the Prince or without him. She lifted her eyes to the crucifix above the altar and resigned herself. Tried to turn her attention to the responses, but all seemed to pass as in a dream. Not until Father Mike laid a hand on her shoulder did she realize that Mass was over, and they were alone in the church. She smelled quenched candles. The dreaded moment had arrived.

"Sit," he said, the word softly echoing through the empty nave. Should she run away? *No. Been there, done that.* She took a deep breath and steeled herself for the worst. "You spent the nights in prayer, too, I see," he began.

She nodded, unable to trust her voice. There was a lump in her throat and tears just below the surface, ready to spring forth at the slightest provocation. She forced herself to concentrate on the kind face in front of her.

"Just so you know, I did my best. I went on retreat for two days and spent the nights in the presence of the Blessed Sacrament before meeting with the bishop. I know how important this is. For you, for him—" That last word seemed to catch in his throat. She suspected that as much as she wanted this, he did not want it, and she dreaded what was coming. After a slight hesitation, he went on, "—and for all of us. My dear, no sacrifice is too great for the sake of your soul and the ongoing battle with the powers of darkness. Whatever happens next may determine many souls won or lost."

Her soul cried within her at the realization that he meant her response. She still had her free will. The burden of this decision rested entirely on her shoulders. What she did with it would have repercussions of cosmic proportions. Like a solar flare, it could light up the sky with a magnificent display of aurora borealis, or burn the Earth and everything on it to a crisp. Or, like a meteor shower, it could present a fantastic light show, or it could destroy life on Earth as we know it. One wrong move on her part could mean the rise of vampires and the annihilation of the human race. *I must not fail.*

Suddenly she felt small and unworthy of the task. The temptation was presented: why not throw it all to the winds and indulge her own desires for a change? Hadn't she given her life to preserve an ungrateful, unknowing populace? Why shouldn't she have this one thing? Was companionship too much to ask? *You deserve it*, said an insidious voice. She felt herself weakening and scrambled for prayer, her lifeline. *But what of the Prince?* sprang from the depths of her heart (or was it that voice again?). With an effort, she crushed the willful complaint and admonished herself. *Jesus, I trust in You. I know You love him more than I do. You died for him, too.* And with renewed resignation and resolve: *Here I am, Lord, come to do Your Will.*

"The decision has been made to sanction this marriage in the eyes of the Church," Father Mike said with a sigh (of which he seemed unaware). "The bishop wasn't keen on the idea and resisted from the start. Without the intervention of the Holy Spirit, I'd never have managed it." He took a deep breath. "You know my personal opinion on the matter."

At first, Mara could not quite grasp what he was saying. The words were shocking, unexpected. Were they real? Had she heard right, or was that wishful thinking? His voice droned on like the low humming of bees; there was an odd buzzing in her head.

"Mara. Mara, did you hear me?"

"I, er, what was that you said?" She hardly dared hope, but it sounded like—had he said… ?

"Yes, the answer is yes. You may go unto the altar of God and pledge your life and your whole self to this, this—" He seemed to stifle a sob (but this was Father Mike—a priest doesn't cry, does he?) "—to your Prince. Talk to him, and we'll set a date to begin preparation. We must follow the proper steps. Mara, did you hear what I said?"

From somewhere came a flourish of trumpets and a drum roll, then harps and a whole orchestra. In her wildest dreams, she hadn't dared imagine—

"Are you okay? Mara? Mara, here, drink this."

Something cold touched her lips, and a fiery liquid burned her throat. She sputtered and sat up.

"Wha—" Bewildered, she pushed the object away from her mouth. A silver flask? "What happened?"

"Sorry, dear child. You fainted. I'm afraid I've shocked you with my unhappy choice of words." The good Father waxed apologetic. "Hope you don't mind my clumsy attempt to revive you with this flask of Irish whiskey. My grandmother swore by it, as a cure-all, that is. I try to avoid it myself, but in a pinch—"

Mara straightened, embarrassed with the return of full consciousness, and brushed him off without thinking. "Gosh! I'm okay! Just a minor glitch. Father, I don't faint. Good grief! I'm not such a wimp as all that!"

"Of course you're not," he protested earnestly, but with a twinkle in his eye.

She flushed. Okay, maybe she had fainted. Weird. "Sorry."

"Never mind. I'm glad to see you're back on track. So I won't need to call a doc after all?" He chuckled.

A doctor? When had she ever needed a doctor? She shook her head and managed a smile. Anyway, the news was good, wasn't it? Even now, she hardly dared hope. "Did you say— did you say what I thought you said?"

He nodded, steadying her with a hand on her elbow as she shakily got to her feet. "I can see you haven't had your Wheaties yet this morning. Let's talk over breakfast. Mrs. O'Hara is already cooking up a storm. You'd think I was inviting the whole congregation. Help me out here."

"Sure, if you put it that way." Mara managed a grin. "Yeah, like you just happened to have that flask handy. Grandmother, my eye."

He returned the grin, relieved that she was herself again. "She carried it in her purse. Honestly, she did. In times of emergency, she just whipped out the old flask and played Good Samaritan. Fits nicely in a pocket, too."

Mara was still in shock as Father Mike walked with her to the rectory. Once in the dining room, he drew out a chair for her at the table. She seemed to be way off somewhere in la-la land, but she smelled bacon frying and fresh coffee brewing. The table was set for two with orange juice and coffee already poured, as though a guest was expected. Mara noted the cheery green-and-white checkered tablecloth and the cluster of items at the center—butter and jam, cream and sugar, salt and pepper. Just as they sat down, the door from the kitchen swung open and Mrs. O'Hara entered carrying a serving dish in each hand, waffles on one and bacon and sausages on the other. Red-faced and beaming, she placed the steaming platters on the table.

"Eat hearty, my dear, never mind Father Michael," she greeted Mara kindly. She leaned nearer and lowered her voice. "If it wasn't for me, he'd be eating one boiled potato for a week, like St. John Vianney." She shook her head as though in exasperation, but the affectionate glance she gave the good father ruined her attempt at severity. Mara warmed to the pleasant, smiling woman.

"If it was good enough for him," interjected Father Mike, unruffled, "it's good enough for me. We're far too soft nowadays, indulging ourselves at every turn."

It looked to Mara as though his dear housekeeper didn't often let leftovers go to waste. With difficulty, she suppressed a giggle as she bowed her head to join Father Mike in the grace before meals. She must have been hungrier than she realized. She soon finished a plate of picture-perfect waffles, crisp bacon, and sunrise sausages. Mrs. O'Hara appeared at her elbow like magic, and without waiting for assent, loaded Mara's plate with seconds.

"Don't be shy, young lady. It takes energy to do the work you do. For that, you need a good, healthy appetite."

After Mrs. O'Hara retreated to the kitchen once more, Father took a bite of waffle sparsely drizzled with syrup in an effort to hide his smile. Mara glanced ruefully down at her own waffles swimming in buttery syrup. Their eyes met and they laughed.

He encouraged her to enjoy her seconds, allowing that Mrs. O'Hara would be grateful for the appreciation of her toiling in the hot kitchen. Mara protested that she had already eaten more than usual, but he reminded her that she didn't usually fast for three days straight.

"Ah, the joys and sorrows of young love," he added, to her

surprise. What did Father know about that sort of thing? He passed a hand over his eyes, and the thought came to her that he was dashing away tears. He rushed on. "Keep God as the center of your life and your marriage. Remember the Old Testament and how turning from His precepts brought ruin upon individuals, houses, and nations. There's a lot at stake here."

"Stake—yeah, I get a lot of that," she snickered, but for once, a play on words did not elicit a laugh. She quickly went on, "Um, always. Good grief, where would I be without prayer in my line of work?"

"Six feet under, if you're lucky." He sighed and looked at her. "I wonder if His Eminence didn't believe vampires existed, whatever I said, and maybe gave the go-ahead just to get this well-meaning crackpot out of his hair."

Mara laughed, then realized that maybe he was serious. What trials he endured for her sake! She hastened to apologize for all the trouble she had caused him. He assured her that he felt privileged to be her mentor, whatever the cost. Life and love were about sacrifice.

That warmed her heart, but she saw that he meant that as a lesson for her too. Ah, the Prince. "So," she said, after a short silence, "what method of persuasion did you—and, um, the Holy Spirit—use on the bishop, if you don't mind my asking?" He gave her a long look, and she quickly added, "Or, unless it's confidential. I wouldn't want to—"

"No, you deserve to know. It wasn't what I meant to say at all. You see, they weren't even my words, and least of all, my opinion." He took a deep breath. "I explained the situation to His Eminence to the best of my ability, not sure he wouldn't send me to the loony bin. I mean, vampires. Seriously, who believes in them nowadays? Yes, we—you and I—know what they really are, whatever popular opinion makes of them. They've been romanticized to death in books and movies; society goes crazy over any drivel that comes out of Hollywood. In reality, vampirism is a sick and twisted thing, a perversion of nature. It has nothing to do with love, whatever silly young girls might fantasize. And those poor benighted lads in Hollywood have no idea—nor do they care—they're just scrambling after the almighty buck.

"So I had no idea what reaction I'd get from His Eminence. He didn't bat an eye, consummate diplomat that he is; unlike his secretary, who was recording our meeting." Father Mike chuckled. "A young seminarian, obviously shocked and disbelieving. At first, he turned pale and stared, then looked as though he might burst into laughter until the bishop gestured to him rather sharply, and he went back to his recording. Then His Eminence spoke. 'Married love,' he said in ponderous tones, 'is about mutual complementarity. Nothing of the sort can exist between a human and a vampire. At least, not without completely rewriting vampire nature somehow. The vampire has nothing to give and everything to take; the human has everything to lose and nothing to gain. A human may complete a vampire, but a vampire doesn't complete a human any more than a lion completes an impala.'

"I was amazed. Mainly, of course, that he didn't dismiss my question out of hand as some insane delusion, or even as a waste of his time and toss me out on my ear. But he'd hit the nail on the head, of course. I'd have said the same myself. But to my surprise, and maybe his, too, I respectfully suggested that the finger of God has rewritten this particular vampire's nature. He allowed it to regain its soul. We know not why or how. But God's ways are not the ways of man. I explained that I've come to believe that this isn't a temptation to turn the Huntress from her God-given path, as I'd first feared, but is part of His purpose. His way of giving her a partner suited to aid her in her life's work. Or maybe more than that; something we cannot yet perceive that will be revealed in the future. I have a feeling that there's more to this than meets the eye." Father Mike looked thoughtful for a moment, then went on, "There was more discussion, of course, but that, my dear, is what I believe turned the tide in your favor."

Mara was speechless, afraid that if she opened her mouth, she would cry. At long last, he had said the words aloud that validated her decision to marry the Prince. Not only had he convinced the bishop of the rightness of her cause, but he also set her own mind at ease, somewhat.

"One more thing," Father Mike went on, "An account of the marriage will be written in the books of the Church, but just so you know, there can be no status according to the law. Because, legally, the Prince no longer exists."

"I see." Mara shrugged. To her, what was right in the eyes of the Church was all that really mattered.

"If that's settled," said Father Mike with a sigh. "Bring in your, er, intended, and we'll begin the process."

Night Wedding

February 13, 1999

They chose the day before St. Valentine's Day (patron of love and marriage) for their wedding, the Saturday before the beginning of Lent. Mara felt that this was the time; she wasn't sure why, but it just seemed right somehow.

It was a small ceremony, attended only by a few friends and family, after sunset at St. Michael's in the chapel of the Mother of Mercy. The Prince felt less ill at ease there than he would at the main altar. After his experience at the Christmas Mass, he dared not chance ruining this night of nights, his dream come true.

He looked at Mara, radiant in her long white dress with her golden braid coiled on top of her head and intertwined with flowers. He was pleased to see that she carried a bouquet of his favorite moonflowers and sweet-scented jasmine. Her usual night-warrior image was not in evidence; she seemed to him a very angel.

***

Even in her high-heeled shoes, Mara had to tilt her head back to meet the Prince's eyes. He looked so elegant in his black, if somewhat antiquated, style. For the occasion, he'd worn his cloak; by now everyone present knew who, and what, he was. His pale countenance was less somber than usual, happy almost, though maybe a little anxious. Mara thought he had never looked more handsome.

***

The Prince's heart swelled at the sight of her. He felt faint at the realization that she would soon be his wife (or was it because he was in the House of God?). With an anxious glance toward the high altar and the tabernacle, he wondered if he would make it through the night without disgracing himself. He sent up a heartfelt prayer in the old familiar words from his long-ago childhood: *Ave Maria, rose without thorns, you were born to comfort me. A queen of high birth, help me that I shall not be lost.*

Father Mike, vested in alb and stole, brought the book to the side chapel where the small crowd watched with mixed emotions as Mara and the Prince stood before him, holding hands. He began the opening prayers of the ceremony.

The reading was taken from the Book of Tobit. Mara saw that Father was looking at her when he spoke of Sarah, whose seven husbands were killed by a demon on their wedding night. Young Tobias was much afraid, but the angel told him not to fear, but to trust in God, for Sarah was destined for him from all eternity. Tobias and Sarah were then united in matrimony and left alone in their chamber, where they prayed that the Lord might have mercy on them. The next day Sarah's father, who had already dug a grave, went to see if Tobias had survived the night. Happily, he was still alive; the grave was filled in and all celebrated. For the angel Raphael had bound the demon in the desert.

Mara knew that Father Mike meant this as a very thinly veiled reference to their own total commitment to each other for the sake of the purest love, but maybe more to the demon on the wedding night, for the Prince's vampire nature was said to be demonic.

This too weighed heavily in her own mind, for she had no illusions about the nature of vampires. Yet as she now held the Prince's hands and gazed into his eyes, everything around them faded into the background, and she saw only her sweet beloved. All else was forgotten as they spoke their vows and exchanged rings. As though from afar, she heard Father Mike pronounce them husband and wife. At these words binding them together for life, tears sprang to Mara's eyes, enough for them both. They were one at last, forever.

Tears flowed from other eyes in the chapel that night, not all of happiness. Who would wish a vampire on one whom they loved?

Mara set her bouquet at the foot of the picture of the Blessed Mother, symbolizing the placing of their future in Our Lady's care.

The dance and midnight supper were held afterward in the church basement. When Maggie sat down with her cello and began playing, the Prince took Mara's hand and led her out onto the dance floor. He was a good dancer, she found—another surprise, though she should have known—he was a vampire, after all. She forgot that all eyes were on them, and he must have too, so lost did they become in that world of their own.

For as the sweetly melodious cello tones floated around them, the Prince all at once burst into song with the full power of his vampire voice. He had no need for a microphone, so great was his command of volume and range. All were amazed by the clear perfection of his voice, and stared in wonder, moved to tears as he sang.

So great was the power of his voice to stir the emotions that Maggie ceased playing to dash away her tears and was unable to continue. When the song ended, the whole world seemed to hold its breath, and everyone stood in awed silence for what seemed an eternity. At last, a single clap was heard and then everyone was applauding, a tear in every eye. Mara and the Prince parted, glancing around, and for a moment, Mara was surprised to see they had an audience. Then she realized where she was and smiled as she turned back to the Prince.

Timmy put a CD into the player and started another song. Other couples drifted out onto the dance floor.

A month-and-a-half later, Mara and the Prince held hands

and looked up at the night sky. The air was chill, and the great pale disc of the moon high above them glowed brightly, its halo washing out the nearby stars.

"Look at that moon. Did you know that that's the second full moon this month?" said Mara. "It's called a blue moon—or maybe you knew that. We have two this year, George says. First in January, now March. Isn't that cool?"

"Somewhat uncommon, I believe," the Prince said. "Charon was forever studying the skies—in books and the like, of course, since he cannot abide the light even of stars—and he often discussed his findings with me. He would say this is an omen, I am certain. I wonder, what does it mean?"

"George didn't say anything about that." Mara got a sudden chill at the mention of her foe and of omens. "Anyway, I'm not superstitious," she added bravely, though she pressed closer to the Prince and looked up at the moon a little anxiously. "It's not red, at least."

"I did not mean to cast a shadow on our happiness," said the Prince apologetically. He took her in his arms. "I say it marks a new beginning of our life together. Certainly an event of cosmic importance, deserving of a sign in the heavens. More rare an occurrence than two blue moons in one year, I'll warrant."

She exhaled slowly. "You're right, of course." She snuggled close, leaned her head against his chest, feeling happy and safe in his arms.

"Yet it is amazing that this should occur during the month before our wedding and the month after," mused the Prince. "Almost as wonderful as the mercy God has shown me after all I have done, and that he should give you to me forever."

"And what of me? He's given me a Prince Charming all my own." She sighed, content. "I feel so safe with you. Funny, I never thought I needed that before. Just didn't know what I was missing, I guess."

For a while, only crickets and the usual traffic sounds broke the night silence.

Both were remembering their wedding night as they stood on her parents' balcony, looking at the stars, when he said to her, "I fear I must warn you. When this Prince kisses Sleeping Beauty, she may not awaken to live happily ever after." And she had replied, "But if he doesn't kiss her, she'll surely die." They'd held each other a while, then he said, "We must pray as Tobias did, so that God's mercy will preserve us from the demon on this our wedding night."

With the full moon shining down on them, Mara basked in emotions she had never hoped to feel. She looked up at her Prince, wondering what more she could ever ask from life.

A few months later, she felt a flutter. Startled, she pressed a hand to her belly. No, that was said to be impossible. But she knew. And wondered: What would this child be?

The End

About the Author

Mina Ambrose was born in Oregon, a cradle Catholic, and grew up on a farm. Along with taking care of animals, she enjoyed reading, drawing and painting, playing music (mainly accordion, but a smidgen of piano, organ and guitar), and of course, writing. She began with stories and poems, as well as jotting down pages of notes—ideas for novels that never went anywhere due to the distractions of her many other interests. But she kept them on file and took them out occasionally to dream.

At age 21 she moved to British Columbia with her family. There she married, and for a number of years was raising children and running a busy household, her other interests relegated to the back burner (though she took them out and dusted them off occasionally). During this time she found new interest in sewing, gardening, and baking dozens of cookies and muffins for her growing family.

After her five sons and three daughters were grown, she returned to college, determined to at least get her Bachelor of Arts degree. (And did.) Meanwhile, she had a short story and poems published, and reawakened that life-long dream of writing a novel. As she wrote, it grew and grew, until the novel became a series: *Shadows of the Sun. Moonchild Rising* is Mina's first novel, Book One of the series.

Mina is a member of the local art society, Catholic Writers Guild and the American Chesterton Society (as well as volunteer typist for their online project) and has also been involved in the pro-life movement for many years. Mina has recently begun playing violin, and, since her retirement, once more finds herself baking cookies, in order to have some on hand for when her grandchildren come to visit. She lives surrounded by her eight adult children, eighteen grandchildren and one great granddaughter.

Published by Full Quiver Publishing
Pakenham, ON Canada
www.fullquiverpublishing.com